The Spirit of Fear
A Spiritual Warfare Novel

Demon Strongholds Series
Book One

Eric M. Hill

Published by SunHill Publishers
P.O. Box 17730
Atlanta, Georgia 30316

The Spirit of Fear: A Spiritual Warfare Novel
(The Demon Strongholds Series)
Copyright 2016 by Eric M. Hill
www.ericmhill.com

This book is a work of fiction. Names, characters, places, incidents, and plot are pure imagination. Any resemblance to any person, living or dead, events, or locales is incidental. The passing reference to the first president of Johns Hopkins University was meant solely to show the emotional and spiritual state of the main character.

Unless otherwise noted, Scripture is from the *King James Version,* public domain; or **NKJV**: Scripture taken from the New King James Version®. Copyright © 1982 by Thomas Nelson, Inc. Used by permission. All rights reserved.

ISBN-13: 978-1519606358
ISBN-10 1519606354

A Note from the Author

Hello! If this is your first time reading one of my stories, I welcome you and thank you for choosing my book to read among the millions that are available. If you have read at least one of my stories and have returned for more, that says it all! I can't think of a greater compliment and vote of confidence than for someone to read one of my books and ask for more. ☺

May I ask you a favor?

Once you read the book, if you find that you enjoyed the story, would you mind going online to Amazon.com, iTunes, Kobo, Barnes and Noble, or wherever you purchased the book and writing a review? Many people determine from book reviews whether or not a story is worth their time. Your review (even a short one!) can help convince others to join the fun!

Let's Stay In Touch!

Readers who sign up for my mailing list receive and/or do the following:

- Receive advance news of stories I'm working on.
- Receive *free* portions of stories before they are published.
- Receive whatever wonderful written *freebie* I can come up with.
- Provide me with feedback on what they liked or disliked about a story.
- Share their ideas about what they'd like to see in future stories. (*Trial By Fire* was written in part because a fan of *Bones of Fire* strongly encouraged me to turn the book into a series!)

Join my newsletter at www.ericmhill.com/newsletter. Here's my contact info: ericmhillauthor@yahoo.com or Twitter.com/ericmhillatl. God bless you!

Other Books by the Author

Spiritual Warfare Fiction

The Fire Series
Book 1: Bones of Fire
Book 2: Trial by Fire
Book 3: Saints on Fire

The Demon Strongholds Series
Book 1: The Spirit of Fear
Book 2: The Spirit of Rejection (March/April 2016)

Other Fiction

The Journey Series
Book 1: The Runaway's Journey

Non-fiction

Deliverance from Demons and Diseases
What Preachers Never Tell You About Tithes & Offerings

Chapter 1

He peered suspiciously from behind her eyes at the old woman sitting across from his human home. There were a number of things about the old woman that unnerved him. Foremost was she was at peace. He had never seen her before, but he instinctively knew that her peace was deep. It was no shallow stream coursing through the self-delusion of knowing and serving a Christ of her own imagination.

No, this old woman was an old warrior who had suffered much and whose peace was yet as deep as the ocean. It filled the immense valleys and covered the highest mountain peaks of harsh life, persecutions, and disappointments beneath its rolling waves. He knew that kind of peace only came from a deep trust in the enemy's words. And that kind of trust only came from experiencing His faithfulness. This old woman and her Christ-centered peace was everything he despised. His eyes narrowed at the threat.

The old woman's eyes moistened with joy and gratitude. She looked up from reading Oswald Chambers' classic devotional, *My Utmost for His Highest*. Her tired, kind eyes landed on a beautiful, little blond-haired girl with a delightful smile. The little girl's entire face brightened into a smile that rivalled the sun.

He looked at this trading of smiles and knew what would come next. His vile body was always in a slight tremor, something that came with his nature. But his permanent slight tremor heightened into an involuntary shaking that he strained to control. Too much or too little, depending on the situation and company, could be the difference in victory and defeat. Perhaps even the difference in staying put or being cast out.

The old woman looked across the café at the little doll's mother who was smiling adoringly into her daughter's little face. "She's absolutely beautiful," said the old woman. "What is her name?"

The mother's beautiful face immediately changed into a portrait of terror, as though she were frozen on a train track watching the train's menacing approach. Then just as suddenly as the terror had replaced the smile, a smile replaced the terror. But the old woman had lived long enough and had seen enough pain to know the terror was real and the smile was forced.

Get out of here! Take Amanda and get out of here! Now! She's going to hurt you and your baby! Pangs of fear followed the foolish, but powerful thoughts that were trying to compel the mother to inexplicably run away. Only with the greatest of camouflaged effort was she able to not literally run out of the café with her child and get lost in the crowds of walkers, joggers, and bike riders who were enjoying the concrete trails of the Atlanta beltline on a sunny Saturday morning. But the strength of the thoughts were crushing her will. She knew that she was maintaining control only from one excruciating moment to the next.

Elsie certainly knew she had problems with fear—big ones—but she had no idea she had problems with *spirits* of fear. Therefore, she could not have known that the general sense of fear she carried at all times, or that her periodic eruptions of tormenting fear, were actually manifestations of something far more sinister and destructive.

Demons.

They had been in her family for four generations. The door of fear opened on a Tuesday morning in January, 1917 at 10:53 a.m. Elsie's great grandmother, Lucille, was all of six years old when it happened.

Hal, I don't want you to go. I don't want you to die," she had heard her mom protest to her father through tears. Why should he have to go to Europe to fight someone else's war?

"I'm not going to die. I promise you, Edna Mae," he answered.

"How can you promise me you won't be killed? The whole world is at war. What will happen to our little girl if you die, Hal? We don't have nobody but you."

Hal's and Edna Mae's little six-year-old daughter had overheard the conversation from another room in the tiny farm house. Her hand shook as she rolled a white lily back and forth between her trembling fingers. She was no match for the swarm of fear spirits that roamed the nation in those days energized by talks of America entering the Great War.

Fear of Death, Fear of War, Fear of Loss, Fear of Losing Parents, Fear of Abandonment, Fear of Starving, and others rushed through the open door of the child's magnified fears like the mad waters of a hurricane rushing through the open doors and broken windows of an unprepared beach home. Once in, they buried themselves deep in her mind and personality. She carried these spirits the rest of her life. They were there when her own child was born in 1930 during the Great Depression.

The Great Depression had begun as a stock market crash in 1929 and had developed into the most devastating economic downturn the nation had ever suffered. Chronic unemployment, widespread homelessness, painful hunger, and debilitating hopelessness all contributed to the party atmosphere within the kingdom of darkness. Open doors were everywhere during those days. Any demon who couldn't find a person to invade was beyond incompetent and deserved to walk through dry places.

Mary Beth was not born in nor raised in a Christian family. Her parents considered themselves Christians—they were born in America, weren't they?—but that's as far as it went. There was always so much to do around the house.

So Mary Beth was born with two strikes against her. First, she was born with the spirits of fear that had inhabited her mother. Second, since she had no proper Christian spiritual covering from her parents, she was susceptible to further attack and infestation from the seemingly unlimited waves of Great Depression demons that fed upon the unprotected and unwary like hungry locusts descending upon inviting crops.

Mary Beth gave birth to Judith, who inherited the spirits of her mother and grandmother, and who later married and had three lovely daughters of her own—two of which were fraternal twins—before she developed phobias that made it all but impossible for her to go outside.

Elsie, the most strong-willed of the three girls, was one of those beautiful twin daughters. She pressed her head upward against the fear that was trying to keep her from looking into the old woman's face.

"She wants to kill your baby!" shouted Fear of Failure. He was the lead demon inside of her. What he said didn't make sense, but then much of what spirits of fear said didn't make sense. The object was not to make sense, but to control.

Elsie lifted her face with the slightest grimace of a smile forced by social custom. What was happening to her? Why did she feel like her body, no, her body and mind were trying to separate and float off into space in a hundred different directions?

"Her name is Amanda." Elsie felt as though she had just wrestled with a crocodile to get those four simple words out of her mouth. *What's happening to me?* Her panic was rising.

"Amanda," the old woman smiled, nodding her head, her heart flooding with love for this tormented mother. She put her book down and walked towards the woman to join her at her table.

"What now? What now?" came a panicky voice from the horde of fear demons inside of Elsie.

"Shut up! I'm trying to think." Fear of Failure clenched his teeth. His quick calculations were fueled by his own panic. Fortunately, he wasn't a stranger to this kind of trouble. But he had never been in this kind of trouble with Elsie. She was one of the better victims he had dominated. No Christian friends. No Christian neighbors. No Christian acquaintances. And best of all, she had no interest in God. Any god. God didn't exist. She just wanted to live her life and be left alone. "Hide!" shouted Fear of Failure to his comrades.

"That's it? Hide?" answered one.

SMACK! The blow was heavy across his head. "Now shut up!"

The old woman had come upon the lead demon before he could get Elsie out of there. So he resorted to a tried and true tactic of spiritual warfare.

Silence.

Christians couldn't cast out demons they didn't know were there. Of course, there was always the probability that this old intruder was like most Christians—ignorant of spiritual warfare, and a believer in only parts of the wretched book they called the Bible.

Yet, the peace that seemed to ooze out of the pores of her deeply wrinkled skin made him wary. She had obviously believed enough of God's word to produce peace. Perhaps she was one of those rare saints who believed what the wretched book said about casting out demons. The thought of being discovered and cast out made the decision for him—*SILENCE!*

Elsie knew the fear she felt of the approaching old woman was ridiculous. She looked at her face. It had been around a long, long time. In fact, the face seemed to have come as an afterthought to the wrinkles that owned the fleshly terrain.

Oddly, however, the woman's face emitted an endearing and comforting softness that was at odds with the fear Elsie felt draped over herself. Actually, the woman was covered in peace. Elsie could feel it coming from her. *And for some reason, this peace terrified her.*

"Children are a gift from God," said the smiling old woman as she pulled a chair and sat next to Elsie.

Elsie smiled politely, but not without effort. She hoped her face didn't disclose her unease. But she didn't believe in God, and had a rather strong resistance to the idea of God. She had an even stronger resistance to Christians pushing their religion on others. But it wasn't the woman's presumptuous statement about God, or her forwardness in inviting herself to sit at her table, that disturbed her. Under other circumstances, minus the talk about God, she would have welcomed the old woman's company.

Rather, it was the conflicting emotions she felt right now of tormenting fear and soothing peace. Fear was all over her; peace was all over this woman. And most baffling was that her fear feared this woman.

Elsie's eyes squinted thoughtfully as the old woman looked down at her daughter. *The fear in me is afraid of the peace in her.* She didn't shake her head, but she did wonder at this nonsensical conclusion. "Amanda's three," she offered, fighting through her feelings.

The old woman gleefully slapped her own thigh. "Three years old. Of course, you are."

"I can ride a tricycle," said the little girl.

Elsie saw the old woman's eyes light up. An involuntary smile appeared on her face in response to the woman's interest in her daughter.

"The bike with three wheels?" asked the old woman, as though this was the greatest accomplishment she'd ever heard of.

Amanda's blue eyes went as wide as the sky. "It has two little wheels in the back," Amanda's speech turned excited and her little voice skipped, "but, but, but, the wheel in the front is bigger."

The old woman threw her head back. "Oh, that's just marvelous! An angel as little as you, and you can ride a tricycle— three wheels." She clapped her hands lightly.

"Can you ride a tricycle?" Amanda asked the old woman.

"No. I don't think so," the old woman answered with a chuckle.

"If you don't think you can, you can't," said the three-year-old.

The old woman looked at Elsie and gave a smile that said she was going to try to get more from her toddler. "I'm too big to ride a tricycle."

"If the tricycle is too little, get a bigger one. You can ride a big one," she said.

"If I ride a big tricycle, I may fall off and hurt myself," the old woman answered.

"Riding tricycles are fun. If you're too scared to ride, you won't have fun." The toddler turned to her mom. "Right, Mommy?"

Her daughter's words touched something in her heart that made her eyes glisten with moisture. "That's right, Amanda." She rubbed the little girl's long, blonde hair and moved as though she was preparing to leave.

"I'm not scared. I can do anything!" the little girl proclaimed, remembering what her auntie Anna had told her.

"Isn't it amazing?" said the old woman. "Out of the mouths of babes Thou hast perfected praise."

Elsie's mouth tightened in an attractive half-smile that said she wasn't familiar with what the woman was saying.

"Sometimes God speaks through the little ones, the most unlikely people. If you're too scared to ride, you won't have fun," she repeated. The old woman's face grew sad, her eyes moist. "Amanda's words can apply to so much of life, can't they? How often do we let fear keep us off the tricycle? Relationships, businesses, occupations, we settle for something far less than what we really want because we're afraid. Afraid of failure. Afraid of rejection. Afraid of ridicule. Afraid of this. Afraid of that."

Elsie's smile as she looked into the face of the old woman wasn't really a smile. It was the frozen leftover of the smile that was there a few moments ago. What she really was feeling were competing waves of fear and peace, depression and hope, a sense of opportunities forever lost and opportunities waiting to be found.

She didn't know the connection between this old woman and what she was feeling, but she knew they were connected, entwined. She could leave this old woman's presence and escape the unexplainable discomfort she felt. But not without also leaving the peace and hope that emanated from this woman and that somehow had found their way into her soul.

The old woman sensed the thoughts going on inside Elsie. She put her other hand atop the hand that was already resting on the young woman's hand. "What about you?"

"What do you mean?"

The old woman looked into Elsie's eyes. "I'm very, very old." She chuckled. "Even older than I look. I've seen a lot. I've talked to a lot of people. Some have listened. Sadly, most have not. There was a woman," the old woman's face brightened, "God smiled when He created her. He had such an exciting and fulfilling life planned for her. He put gifts within her, music and singing and lifesaving gifts." The smile faded until it was no more. "The thief stole them all through fear. Now she's only a shell of what God created her to be, and it's sucking the life out of her."

Elsie was unnerved at the old woman's speech. She could've labeled it odd. She could've labeled it religious gibberish. Her soul exhaled the breath her mouth was afraid to release. She could've labeled it an x-ray of her life.

She had always loved music. She could sit and listen to it for hours. All kinds. It didn't make any difference what style. It was all beautiful, euphoric, mesmerizing. As a child, Elsie didn't understand the nuances of timbre and pitch and melody and rhythm and tempo. But when she closed her eyes and listened to songs or instrumentals, her spirit drank in and celebrated what her mind didn't understand. Music and song were like powerful drugs that entered through her ears and took her to a world of rapturous bliss.

From what she had heard from her father and grandfather and others, and from some tidbits of conversations she had overheard, her mother and grandmother had the same love of music. They had once had beautiful voices and each had achieved above average skill on the piano and guitar, even Granny. Elsie had taken this musical penchant a step farther and had become quite good on the xylophone.

The irony was that with all of this love of music and skillful ability in the family lineage, Elsie's grandmother and mother had both abruptly stopped playing and singing. One could never get a straight answer from either of them as to why they stopped. But others in the family said it was because of fear. Both of them somehow developed an irrational fear that if they didn't abandon music and singing, something tragic would happen.

They had no idea what that tragedy was; just that it was bad. Even odder was the fact that Granny and Elsie's mom were both thirty-six when they gave up music. Elsie's thirty-sixth birthday was coming up shortly.

The old woman's troubling speech had pushed away the large stone of a secret family tomb, allowing embarrassing light to shine on corpses that hadn't died of natural causes. Songs and musical ability weren't the only corpses strewn about on the cave's dirt floor. Now the light shone brightly on another body.

Elsie had always wanted to be a neurosurgeon. Of course, as a child it was "brain doctor." She had everything she needed to achieve this goal. She was a whiz in math, science, chemistry, and biology. Great study habits and a wonderful memory gave her a head start.

Everything was going as planned. Great grades. Great MCAT scores. Acceptance into a great medical school. Graduating from medical school at the top of her class. Acceptance into a great neurosurgery residency program.

Then the unexplainable fear.

Then the heartbreak of dropping out of her residency when she was close to completion.

Then the humiliation of retraining to become a registered nurse.

Almost a neurosurgeon. Now a nurse.

"Me and Amanda have somewhere to be shortly," said Elsie. This time she made definite moves to leave.

"Where, Mommy?" asked Amanda.

"Nice meeting you," said Elsie as she wiped off the table.

"Nice meeting you, too, Elsie."

Elsie put Amanda in her stroller and looked at the old woman for a final polite farewell. "Have a nice day?" she said graciously.

The old woman smiled at God's creation. "Elsie," she called.

Elsie looked back at the old woman.

The old woman's voice was weak from advanced age. "Fear has determined to destroy you. Don't let him steal who God created you to be. Don't let him destroy you the way he's destroying your mother and grandmother. God can help you."

Elsie stood there chilled in her bones. *I didn't tell you my name.* She was frozen in place in surprise and dread. How did she know she had a problem with fear? How did she know Mother and Granny had a problem with fear? And why did she talk about fear as though it were a person? She called it *him* and *he*.

Elsie answered her own questions by quickly pushing her daughter out of the café and onto the sidewalk. The old woman's words echoed hauntingly in her mind as she tried futilely to shake off the encounter.

Fear has determined to destroy you.
Don't let him destroy you.

*****

The spirit entered the room and stood before Terror. He trembled, but not because his nature as a fear spirit demanded it. No, his shaking came from his fear of being summoned to the office of Terror. He had done nothing lately worthy of commendation. So he must've done something wrong. What had he done wrong? It had to have something to do with that old woman.

Terror sat behind a large, dark desk that had nothing on it but his two large hands, which were balled into fists, and a globe of the world on a stand. Behind him on the wall was a map of the world. Different colored pins were stuck in various places. The high-ranking demon's face resembled a human man's face. But a human could only get such a face if he lived through a bad fire.

Fear of Failure looked Terror in the eyes and dropped his own in shame. He didn't know what he was ashamed of, but he was certain that he had done something worthy of shame.

Terror spoke with accusation in his low, clenched-teeth voice. "I am told that the woman, Elsie, met someone interesting." The demon's thick fingers rolled heavily on the desk.

"She met an old woman."

The agitation on Terror's face was proof that he wasn't impressed with Failure's abbreviated response.

"The old woman is a Christian."

Terror looked at Fear of Failure with utter contempt. First, a five-word answer. Now a six-word answer. "What you lack in competence, you excel in brevity. Are we at the place where you actually tell me something I don't know?"

"The old woman was full of peace. Like she really believed the cursed book." Terror was still not impressed. "She knew things about Elsie. She told her that we were trying to destroy her." Terror's eyes narrowed in growing anger. Fear of Failure was running out of things to say. "She told her that we had destroyed her grandmother, and that we were working on her worthless mother."

Terror stood and looked down menacingly at the demon he towered over. Fear of Failure was no weakling demon. He was large and powerful. He had long claws and long teeth. But standing before Terror, he was the jackal. Terror was the lion. King of the jungle.

Fear of Failure's words rolled rapidly out of his mouth. "I don't care who this woman is or what she says or does. We will destroy Elsie."

"How?" Terror demanded.

"The usual—lies," he answered. "Lies, lies, and more lies."

Terror wanted more. It showed in his eyes and in his icy silence.

"We'll try to increase—"

"You'll *try*?" Terror challenged.

"We'll increase her bondage," Fear of Failure corrected himself.

"How?" pressed Terror.

Fear of Failure didn't dare follow his feeling and roll his eyes. He'd wake up blind and with his eyeballs rolling around on the floor if he did. "We'll speak directly to her mind. Sometimes we'll whisper. Sometimes we'll shout. We'll deceive her with logic and illogic, facts and fantasy. We'll go rational and irrational. Our irrational lies have worked really well in her mother and grandmother. They're working well in her, too. We'll keep going with the irrational lies.

"We'll talk to her through people. We can count on her family to support us. They all belong to us, and they've got big mouths. Always in her business. Always got something to say. None of it from the enemy."

"How do you know?" Terror was leaving nothing to chance.

Fear of Failure had recovered some of his confidence. He almost smirked as he answered. "Always negative. Always looking for the bad. They're full of death. No light in them." Fear of Failure saw that Terror liked this. Nothing like a good family.

"And the husband?" asked Terror.

"He's fed up with her and her family," said Fear of Failure.

"He's lasted longer than you led me to believe he would. He should be gone by now."

"He's showing signs—" began Fear of Failure.

"Get rid of him," ordered Terror.

"He'll be gone soon," promised Fear of Failure.

"How soon?"

"We have a plan in place," he lied, hoping that Terror didn't ask for details.

Terror wanted that vacant director's position at Fear Academy. He couldn't afford to get a blemish on his record, especially not when he was being considered to take over the academy. "Is there anyone around Elsie who could cause complications? Any Christians anywhere. *Any—where?*"

"Not a one, my lord. Not—a—one."

"What about that wretched sister of hers—Anna?" asked Terror.

"They don't talk to one another," said Fear of Failure. "And whenever they do, it turns into a knock-down, drag out fight. That Anna's something else. Too angry with sinners to help any of them. She complains about Elsie, but she doesn't pray for her. We don't have to worry about her."

"Make sure you keep her complaining instead of praying."

"Of course. Of course," said Fear of Failure. He let himself smile. "And I respectfully remind you that our girl is an atheist. She doesn't believe in God."

Now Terror smiled. It had been the goal from day one of the Garden of Eden to deceive the human idiots into not believing in God's character. One of his eyes arched in satisfaction. But who could've anticipated the ease in which they had been able to convince the enemy's creation that He didn't exist. The fools believed they popped out of nowhere.

Terror sat down. His anger temporarily satisfied. But they did need to be careful. "That old woman…" Terror's eyes peered into the vast expanse of his experience. "Be on the lookout for her. She was not a coincidence. She knew too much." He thought some more. Words from the cursed book came to mind. *Great peace have those who love Your law.* "I don't like her peace," he said with a gravelly voice. "Hard to control people like that. Now go make a trophy of this Elsie."

Chapter 2

The mood between them this fine Saturday afternoon wasn't cold enough to be classified as icy, but there was definitely a chill in the air. Daniel loved his wife. He loved her desperately. Always had. She was his air, his blood, his water—his *life*—since the moment he had met her.

There had been literally no elapse of time from the moment his roommate, Tommy, introduced them to one another on the campus of the University of Georgia in Athens and him hearing himself think, *This beautiful woman is my wife, and she's going to have my babies.* Elsie had smiled widely, and probably quite deliberately, crushed his hand with an *I'm a woman, but I'm not weak* handshake that would've made the most militant feminist giddy.

Though they were strangers to one another, the fairy tale love officially began that moment. Daniel knew that was the moment of its official birth because though he had a full life up to this point, it was at this point, the point where he conversed with Elsie, that he began to live. There was something magical about her...*everything* that made him feel more alive than he had ever thought possible.

And although their first meeting was anything but private and romantic, Daniel's imagination managed to see it that way. The presence of Tommy and three other people couldn't hide or lessen the instant connection he and Elsie had. Plus, he was sure—well, maybe not one hundred percent sure—that she had winked at him. Whether the wink was real or imaginary was still a point of debate between Daniel and Elsie.

But there was another undebatable reason that this day was the official start of their love story. One that caused him a lot of grief with the guys: He started suffocating the moment he left her presence. It was obvious to everyone who knew him. He couldn't hide it. *He was hooked. Incurably and eternally hooked on a girl he had just met.*

The fairy tale's carriage swooped him up and galloped away at the speed of love. But apparently he wasn't the only one suffocating. There was a certain beautiful, ambitious, and immensely intelligent girl with a lumberjack's handshake who was also gasping for air. She, too, was tossed into the runaway carriage.

In the days that followed, Daniel and Elsie delightfully learned that their tentative life's journeys could have been written by the other. They both wanted to be neurosurgeons. They both wanted to get married and have two children. Of course, each wanted at least one of those children to be of their own sex. They both loved the outdoors. They both loved to travel and wanted to visit every state in the country, every country in Europe, and every continent on the planet. They both loved dogs. They both believed in and practiced helping those less fortunate than themselves. They both were demoralized liberal Democrats—the Republicans were wrecking the country! And as a cherry on top, they both were atheists, although she was more passionate and vocal about her atheistic beliefs than was he.

The merging of the two journeys into one was only natural. What wasn't natural was how perfectly the particulars of their journeys synced. They both graduated from the University of Georgia with double majors in biology; and biochemistry and molecular biology.

The stars were perfectly aligned when they both were accepted into medical school at Johns Hopkins University. *Are you kidding me? Who would've thought?* That was all the sign they needed to get married, and get married they did! But, of course, there would be no, no, no children until they both finished their residencies.

Daniel and Elsie soon proved that they couldn't stop winning the lottery. This time they were both accepted into the same residencies, their general surgery and neurosurgery residencies. Daniel's father, who himself was a neurosurgeon, and who was close friends with the man who was the director of both the Department of Neurosurgery, and the Hunterian Neurosurgical Laboratory at Johns Hopkins University, assured his son with a sly grin that he had nothing to do with his and Elsie's acceptance.

Daniel and Elsie were elated. They were meant to be together. Nothing could separate them.

Nothing except fear.

The fairy tale's carriage that had carried them from the University of Georgia in Athens, Georgia to Johns Hopkins University in Baltimore, Maryland hit a fear ditch, lost a wheel, and careened over a cliff and tumbled violently before crashing against the reality of rocks that cared nothing for fairy tales or happily ever after endings.

Daniel had known that Elsie's mother and grandmother had problems with fear. Elsie had shared this with him. Plus, he had witnessed some of their eccentricities himself. They had even shared good-natured chuckles about some of her family's oddities. But there was nothing in her behavior that would have revealed similar problems with fear. And Elsie had never told him that she was having problems with fear.

Until she dropped out of the clinical research portion of the residency program in the sixth year of a seven-year program. Only one and a half years before completion and she quit.

Daniel tried to suppress the anger that was now boiling in his belly and chest. His neck and face felt on fire. Surely his complexion was red, and she could see through the shaving cream and his façade of calm. It wasn't so much so that she dropped out of her residency. It wasn't that something they had planned so long for and worked so hard for was obliterated in a day.

Couldn't a disease or accident do the same thing? What would he have done had Elsie had to drop from the program because of something like that? Get angry? Be resentful? Feel betrayed? Absolutely not! He'd be crushed, devastated. But he'd stand by his beloved—it was getting harder to think of her as his beloved—and spend every moment possible by her side, assuring and reassuring her of his love.

But Elsie had not been surprised with a crippling or mortal disease out of the blue. She had not had a horrible car accident and come out of it so wrecked in body that finishing her residency was an impossibility. No, his beloved had abruptly dropped out of one of the most coveted neurosurgery residency seats in the nation because of a sudden fear that she couldn't do it.

Daniel was now a neurosurgeon. He had spent years studying the brain under the most grueling of esteemed academic and clinical environments. He understood that fear could develop to such a degree that it could become a phobia. A phobia that could simply irritate or cause embarrassment—something that could be managed. Or a phobia that could cripple and destroy—something that managed you.

What he didn't understand was how his wife with whom he had withheld no secrets could have a growing fear that finally erupted into her dropping out of her residency. He had rehearsed her explanation in his mind a thousand times.

Yes, I've always struggled with fear, but I told myself it was nothing. That I could, I would beat it. I was determined to not become like my mother and grandmother. I didn't think it would ever become an issue. So I just ignored it when I could, and gritted my teeth and pushed forward when I couldn't. But this time I fought it for a year before the fear became consuming...tormenting. I couldn't shake it. The only way to get rid of it was to give in.

She had fought it a year before giving in. This recollection helped him not one bit to get rid of the anger that was like lava inside of him. *A year and she didn't tell me. She didn't think it would become an issue. An issue. Dropping out of her residency.*

An issue. She waits until she drops out to tell me she's had a lifelong problem with fear. What else is she not telling me?

Daniel wanted to scold himself for questioning his wife's integrity. He wanted to reach inside and pull out the ability to see past his pain, disappointment, and confusion, and perhaps feel as much compassion for his wife as he felt anger toward her. It wasn't there.

Elsie stood at the mirror of their large bathroom and applied her makeup. Daniel stood at his mirror and shaved. The silence was excruciating and the room seemed to be as large as a football stadium. Finally, she couldn't take it any longer. She turned. "I'm sorry," she said, adding another apology to the hundreds she had already offered over the past four years.

Daniel kept shaving. He knew what she was talking about. "I know you are," he said, trying his best to speak evenly. Trying his best to not let the anger come out.

Elsie leaned her tall frame down on the marble counter, supporting herself on her left hand. Daniel didn't look at her. He bent down and splashed water onto his face, taking the last of the shaving cream away. It was painful for her to watch him dry his face with a towel.

The pain was because prior to her meltdown, she had sometimes shaved his face. She hadn't done this since the dropout—that's what the default name for the calamity had become. Oh, she was sure that had she attempted to do it again, he'd let her. Since the dropout, he had *let* her do a lot of things.

Things that used to be normal, things that used to happen without any thought and conscious effort whatsoever, things that once flowed naturally down their stream of love had now been diverted by a dam of indifference. Things like holding her hand. Things like looking into her eyes with soft affection. Things like kissing her with no aim in mind other than to remind her of his love. Things like phone calls just to see how she was doing. Things like gushing ad nauseam over how well she cooked. Things like being so extraordinarily patient with her intimate needs.

Now these things no longer happened without some kind of prompting or manipulation on her part. And when they did, it was like something vital was missing. Like a lukewarm can of flat Coca-Cola. Same packaging and wet as ever, but tasteless. Not even worth opening the can.

But Elsie loved her husband. Now more than ever. A lesser man would've left her and her problems long ago. A lesser man would've had an affair by now, and somehow she knew in her heart that Daniel hadn't done this. That he was incapable of it. He was cold, but not by his own choosing. She loved him, and she knew that he loved her. That's why she kept trying.

Yet, despite this, each time she made an overture to him, she felt like she was a door-to-door salesperson walking past a big *No Trespassing!* sign with a skull and crossbones on it. He wasn't deliberately mean or consciously cold, but he was angry. And it was this anger, this simmering undercurrent of anger that was beneath all of their conversations and interactions that made her feel isolated and so alone.

Even worse, it was the reasons for his anger that weighed so heavily on her. She had disappointed him by dropping out. But she had broken his heart by not sharing her struggles with him until it was too late.

Maybe it's too late for us.

Elsie struggled hard to not think this thought. And when it thrust her hopes aside and fought its way into the foyer of her mind, she refused even then to accept the reality of its presence.

"Daniel," she said. He rubbed his hands in the towel as he answered by looking into her eyes. "I know I'm sorry doesn't fix this, but I am."

Daniel's eyes were an unremarkable brown, but the whites were bright and their eyelids were slightly squinted, giving the appearance of thoughtfulness. Something remarkable flashed in his eyes. It was only a flash, but Elsie saw it. Warmth. It looked like warmth.

Elsie was three inches south of six feet. Daniel was two inches north of it. He placed his large hands on both of her shoulders and squeezed lightly. She gasped and looked at his eyes. There *was* something there.

Then it was gone.

"We have to go, Elsie. We don't want to be late for your mother's birthday party." He dropped his hands and walked out of the bathroom.

Her eyes didn't follow him as he walked away. Instead, she looked emptily, mournfully at where he once stood. In a few moments, she thought with panic, *Oh, no!*

The *Oh, no!* was because of Fear of Abandonment, a demon who preferred to go by the moniker, Gone. Elsie had felt his presence enter the room.

The spirit was definitely in the bathroom with her. He had an outline, a shape. But he wasn't like the other demons of fear that inhabited Elsie and came and went as they pleased. This one didn't appear to be all there. He was like a hologram. There, but not there. Nonetheless, when he wrapped his long trembling arms around the heartbroken and terrified woman, she felt him just as surely as if she had just put on an invisible straightjacket.

"He's going to leave you, you know," he whispered.

"No, he's not," she said, responding to the voice in her mind that was so strong it could've been in her ear. This was the first time the thoughts had been this real. It was terrifying.

Gone's vacant pale face smiled, revealing sharp teeth. "Ohh, yeeesssss, he is most certainly going to leave you. The only reason he hasn't left already is because of Amanda."

Another demon, Fear of Loss, spoke up from within her. He came across as a strong thought, not a voice. "He's going to take Amanda and leave you by your crazy lonesome. Look at Nicole your sister. Rick's trying to take the boys from her. That's what's going to happen to you, Elsie."

Elsie's eyes were wide with fright. She had to get out of the bathroom. But first she made her eyes go to their normal size. She didn't want Daniel to see her like this. It would just be one more thing to lie about. She walked quickly out of the bathroom.

Daniel looked directly at her. "What did you say?"

Elsie's eyes went wide before she fixed them. Daniel noted this. "What? Oh, nothing."

Now his eyes looked slightly suspicious. "Nothing?"

Tell him. Just tell him, she thought. *Isn't this what got you into this mess to begin with? Keeping it to yourself? You can't handle this alone. You have to tell him.*

Gone sensed what was going on. "And what do you think he'll do when you tell him you're now hearing voices and talking to them? The first thing he's going to do is think about your crazy mother and sister. He's going to think about that nutty grandmother you girls have holed up in the cottage. He's going to think he's stuck with a basket case. He'll get rid of you, Elsie."

Yeah, thought Elsie. *He'll think I've gone crazy, too.*

Amidst the chatter, something bubbled up from deep within Elsie's spirit. *Remember the old woman. Remember what she said. God can help you.* Elsie was desperate for help, but she shut that option down immediately. There—was—no—God.

She smiled to keep from crying. "Just talking to myself. Inexpensive therapy."

Daniel sort of smiled. "No such thing." The sort-of smile vanished as a thought entered his mind. He told himself that there must have been something about the word *therapy* that made him want to ask this question. "Is the fear getting any worse?"

The question caught Elsie by surprise. She felt like a building with glaring code violations about to be inspected. "No," she said, hoping that somehow the crooked stairs, slumping floors, and dangerous and exposed wiring hadn't caught the inspector's attention.

His thoughtful eyes burned holes in her.

"Why do you ask?" she said, hoping to lessen her discomfort by talking.

Daniel's response was direct. "Because from what I'm told, your mother and grandmother started going downhill really fast as they approached their thirty-sixth birthday. Your sister is thirty-seven." He let that linger. No need for further narration about Nicole.

Elsie's face didn't reflect her horror. This was the first time he had brought up the fearful obvious.

"And you're almost thirty-six," he said.

There. The gorilla was out of the cage.

Elsie felt an eruption of nervous prickling, like tiny seeds sprouting all over her body and pushing up through her skin. She swallowed and shifted positions, taking her weight off one foot and putting it on the other. The gorilla was too big to ignore, and he'd only go back in the cage if he wanted to go back in the cage. And he'd only *want* to go back in the cage if he got the right answer.

"Daniel, I don't know why some of the women in my family have problems with fear." She was mentally noting the exception to the family fear rule, her estranged—actually ostracized—sister, Anna. But there was no way she would mention her. Elsie's voice was strong. She hoped her feigned confidence would convince him. "I don't know why thirty-six seems to be the magic number. But it is not inevitable that I go down that road. I am *not* going down that road."

Daniel continued looking at her, saying nothing. His intentions weren't to grill her, but since the dropout, trust was no longer his default with Elsie.

Elsie took his silence and expression as him being unconvinced. "Daniel," her voice raised in exasperation, "they all have *phobias*. Mom and Granny can't even go outside."

Daniel's face went soft, more out of kindness than of being convinced. She may not have been as far gone as her family, but dropping out certainly had to count as a triple scoop of something. He had worn his brilliant brain out researching and trying to figure out what was wrong with his wife.

He had considered Didaskaleleinophobia, fear of schools, but she wasn't afraid of schools. She was afraid of finishing her residency. Besides, if she were afraid of schools, she wouldn't have gone back to get training as a nurse. With all of his learning and contacts, he was as baffled now as he was when she had first dropped out. *Why, Elsie? Why?*

"You're right, Elsie." His voice was low. His heart conflicted. Conflicted because he had seen growing peculiarities in her that he had first ignored, hoping that the odd behaviors would die of neglect. Then when ignoring them became impossible, he had tried rationalizing them into a less troubling context. But creativity and dishonesty had run their course. He was nearly too emotionally tired to not admit that Elsie would end up like the other women in her family, and that he would end up like the men who had married into this—

He ashamedly let the curse word drop. He didn't want to attach that word to his wife. "We better get going," he said, and went into the closet for a shirt.

"I'm not my mother," Elsie said softly to herself once Daniel left the bathroom. "Fear won't have me." She squinted her eyes and looked to the left and right. She was unsure, but it was almost as if she could hear muffled laughter in the back of her mind.

That was exactly what she heard. The laughing demons couldn't wait for her to get to her mother's party.

Chapter 3

Daniel drove the black Range Rover down the slight decline of Elsie's parents' four-acre property and passed through the densely shaded canopy of trees. He landed on a side driveway large enough to serve a fast food restaurant.

He and the family had visited this beautiful North Fulton county home many times. For it to be in the city, it was magnificently peaceful. Large trees everywhere. Squirrels darting here and there across the gravel path, and others sailing from one tree limb to the next. Deer munching on foliage as though their names were on the property's deed. A pond on the west side of the large home. A man-made lake in the back. A gentle touch of paradise.

Inside the lovely home was dramatically different. If outside was a gentle touch of paradise, inside was a bar room slap of hell. This visit's slap stung even more than the last visit. Daniel felt it the moment he stepped inside. The place was lit up and bright, but it felt dark. Like a well-furnished late 19th century insane asylum with every light on.

Actually, now that he thought about it, each visit seemed progressively worse than the previous one. This probably was due to him expecting the worse. But doggonit if the prophecy didn't come true every time. And here was Elsie's sister, Nicole, proving his point.

"Okay," she said once the greetings were over, "off with your shoes and out with your hands."

"Make sure you get everyone," Elsie's mother, Judith, said from what Daniel guessed was the living room.

"Got it covered, Mom," said Nicole as she smiled at everyone.

Daniel and Elsie removed their shoes.

"Amanda, too," said Nicole, looking at her niece with a big smile. "We don't want those bad germs following you around the house, now do we?"

"No!" Amanda said playfully.

Daniel tensed as Elsie removed Amanda's shoes. He didn't mind respecting house rules, but he did not want them putting their irrational fear of germs on his daughter.

Amanda's shoes off, Nicole now squirted hand sanitizer in their outstretched hands. "Oop! Oop! Oop!" she said, and put her palm up.

They stopped rubbing their hands together.

"I should've given you your footies—"

"Make sure they put on their footies before sanitizing their hands." This was Judith again with more cleansing instructions.

"Got it covered," Nicole answered, as she went to a small table a couple of yards away. She came back with footies for all of them.

Daniel and Elsie put on their footies. Daniel smiled tightly at Nicole. He did not like the idea of Amanda having to wear footies. "Oh, look Elsie, they even have footies for Amanda."

Elsie smiled at Daniel, but she thought she saw anger behind his. *If your mother is this afraid of her granddaughter's three-year-old feet, maybe we shouldn't bring them over here that often,* he seemed to be thinking. No, that wasn't like him. She was reading too much into this.

Amanda ran past Nicole and into the next room to get to Grandma. Daniel and Elsie took a couple of steps to follow before Nicole stopped them. "Do you have any music?"

Daniel glanced at Elsie and looked at Nicole with a question mark on his face. "Music?"

Elsie knew what this was about. She felt like a witness in court being compelled to testify and afraid to do so because the truth of her own guilt may come out.

Nicole's eyes slowly went from Daniel to Elsie. She looked at her sister with a *So he doesn't know* expression. She looked back at Daniel. "It gives Mom fits. She had a terrible panic attack a week ago from looking at a car commercial on television."

Daniel's face was neutral while he waited for her to explain the connection in a car commercial, him having or not having music, and her mother's panic attack.

"The commercial," she said as though he should have gotten it by now. "It had music in it."

"Music triggers panic attacks in your mother?" he asked.

"Yes. I'm surprised you didn't know," she said.

"And how would I have known this?" he asked, looking at Nicole, but knowing that this was a question he should be asking his wife with his nose pressed against hers.

Nicole arched an eyebrow and asked, "Does either of your phones have a musical dial tone?"

Daniel pulled out his phone and turned it off. "Phone's off. Can I go into the living room now?"

She smiled. "Of course. Thank you, Daniel. Mom appreciates it."

When Daniel turned the corner, Elsie looked sternly into her sister's eyes. "That was inappropriate, Nicole."

Nicole pulled her sister by the arm into another room. She said in a whisper, "No, Elsie, what's inappropriate is you living a lie. You know our family's problems. You know we have this…this…this *curse*. That's what it is, a curse. And you want to go on pretending like you don't have it. You have it, Elsie. You've got the curse, and it's going to get worse. The best thing you can do is to be honest with yourself and Daniel and learn to live with it." Her words came out as though she had been wanting to say this a long time.

Elsie's mind wasn't empty. It just wouldn't slow down enough so she could respond. When it did finally allow her to clearly see from Point A to Point B, she said, "I am *not* cursed, and I will *not* make plans for a cursed life." With that she walked past Nicole and into the living room. *Cursed,* she thought angrily. *I could've been talking to Anna.*

*****

Daniel was a neurosurgeon and obviously smart. But had his eyes been opened to the spiritual dimension, he would have been shocked at how perceptive he had been in diagnosing the darkness of his in-laws' home.

Including Amanda and Nicole's two boys, and excluding Granny (she was in her cottage behind her daughter's house), there were eleven people gathered for her birthday party. But the number of demons that were there solely on account of Granny Mary Beth, Grandma Judith, Nicole, and Elsie outnumbered the people by at least twenty to one. The actual number constantly changed because there were so many coming and going all the time.

Adding to the mystery number of the demons among the women were flocks of vulture-like demons that came from under the floor and through walls and the roof in a noisy swirl. They moved in a blackness that covered their separateness until a graveyard calm replaced their noise. Then they could all be seen perched in their respective places. Hundreds of them. Some content to sit on one of the women. Some sitting on one before deciding to enter. And others wasting no time, diving in immediately.

Considering the high volume of unimpeded demonic traffic among the women, there was a peculiar oddness in what was occurring around Amanda. The larger demons ignored her. They'd go by her as though she weren't in the room, and if she got within a yard or so of one, it was moved away from her. Not moved away, but *was* moved away. Like one magnet getting too close to an opposing magnet and being naturally pushed away by its force.

The vulture demons, however, didn't ignore her. They'd swarm around her aggressively looking for a place to land and finding none, they'd go away only to repeatedly and with the same results try another landing.

The entirety of the property was draped in a dusk-like spiritual darkness that was uniform with the darkness that covered the adjacent properties on both sides and the one directly across the street. But the main house and the cottage was enveloped in a more dense darkness. It was dusk over the property, but midnight over the homes.

And the demons were ready to play.

*****

Elsie entered the living room. "Hello everyone."

Heartfelt smiles everywhere.

"El-seeeee," said Judith with gladness, her arms open wide while she sat.

"Mom," Elsie hugged her, squeezing with closed eyes. It felt so good to hug her mom. Squeezing over, she pulled back and kissed her on the forehead. "Love you, Mom."

Judith looked up from the chair with slight alarm on her face. "That's not perfume I smell, is it? There's all kinds of chemicals and foul things in perfume. A lot of it's not on the label. You know they get some of that stuff from beaver's and cat's anus's." She looked toward Nicole. "Nicky, what's that cat they use to get perfume from its butt?"

Gary, Judith's husband and Elsie and Nicole's grandfather, looked at Daniel and winked. Daniel absorbed the wink, now super conscious of the smell of his aftershave. When had Judith added perfume and cologne to her long list of banned products?

Daniel looked at Jack. Jack was Granny's husband. His ex-wife was a prisoner of the cottage in back of the house. He wore a smirk. He could. He had escaped. He didn't live with her. He looked at Rick, standing and brooding darkly in a corner, but forcing an approachable expression onto his face. He was Nicole's husband and was, judging on his recent filing for divorce, presumably just as or more angry at his wife than Daniel was at Elsie.

"It's a civet cat, Mom," Nicole answered readily.

Judith looked at Elsie with intensely sincere eyes. "It's a civet cat."

"Mom, it's a shower that you smell."

"What about the soap? Did you shampoo your hair?" Judith looked at Elsie's head. "Your hair looks clean. What did you use?"

Elsie's father came to the rescue. "Judith, I'm sure Elsie's taken the necessary precautions. She loves you and knows your concerns." He extended both arms for an embrace.

Elsie could've leapt into his arms. They hugged. "Thank you, Dad," she whispered. "I owe you one."

"No problem. What about Daniel?" he whispered. "Is he wearing any cat butt?"

"Yeah. He's got aftershave."

"We better cover for him," whispered Dad. Gary pulled away from Elsie. "Okay, everybody, that's enough of all this gushy family love business. I need all the gentlemen to follow me out onto the deck. Finally enlarged it."

Daniel, Rick, and Jack were like bullets shot out of a gun's barrel. They couldn't wait to get out of that living room.

Gary showed them the deck and looked over his shoulder through the large windows at the women. He motioned the men to the farthest corner of the huge deck. He sat at a rectangular table under a large umbrella. The men joined him on the cushy seats.

"Daniel, Elsie told me you got cat butt all over you. Had to get you out of there," Gary said with light laughter.

"I appreciate that."

Jack was eighty. His voice wasn't weak, but it wasn't strong, either. It seemed to not be able to make up its mind what it was. Sometimes it would start out strong and suddenly go weak, or vice versa. It started out strong. "Me, too. Would rather be out here with you fellas," his voice ran out of steam, "than, than…"

Gary tapped the old man on his forearm. "We understand."

Jack finished in a soft voice. "Than...to...sit through that." His voice went strong. "It's crazy, you know."

Gary looked at Daniel's face and read him like a book. "Nothing wrong with addressing the obvious. You're a neurosurgeon. You operate on people's brains. You're brilliant, for crying out loud! Jack, he's a retired, successful businessman. He's got four patents."

"Five. Five patents," said the old man.

"Five patents," continued Gary. "Has traveled around the world more times than I've gone to the bathroom. Me. A turnaround specialist. I fix businesses that have no hope. And make a ton of money doing it. Rick here's got probably the most successful real estate agency in metro Atlanta. If he can't sell it—" He looked at Rick. "What's that saying you say?"

"If we can't sell it, it's crap. Put a match to it."

Jack, the old man, looked at Rick with surprise. "And *why* aren't you in prison?" he asked softly.

Some of the anger left Rick's face. "Well, 'cause we don't put that on billboards and business cards. Just something we say among ourselves."

"But it's the truth," Gary continued. "Winsome Realty. Everyone knows, you want to sell it, go to Winsome. What's the point?"

Rick's anger surfaced. "The point is that we all went wife shopping at the same crazy house. The point is that my boys can't play sports because their mother is afraid they may get hurt. The point is that we can't leave our windows or doors open because a ladybug may get inside." Rick's eyes glared. "Did you hear me? I didn't say a rat. I didn't say a spider. I said a lady bug. You *have* heard about the epidemic of lady bug related deaths, haven't you? Can't use the microwave because the microwaves will kill us. I could go on an hour talking about Nicole's growing list of rules. Oh, and did I mention that she no longer drives?"

Daniel took special interest in this. "Nicole has stopped driving?"

"Why else would I be here?" His answer was angry.

Jack and Gary took long breaths and looked knowingly at one another.

Rick rested his elbow on the table and put his head in his hand. He rubbed his forehead and eyes and looked up. "I'm sorry, Daniel. I don't mean to take this out on you. It's just that I feel like I'm in a prison. Like my life is in a vice. Nicky's fears are squeezing the life out of me. I gotta get out before she drives *me* crazy. And I am *not* going to let her put that crap on my boys!"

Daniel thought about Amanda. "Don't worry about it, Rick."

"Rick, Daniel, the point I'm trying to make is that yes we all married into a family of women ruled by fear, but we're successful. We have our own lives."

Rick had no idea what Gary was trying to say. He opened his hands and gave a *What's the point?* look.

"Live around it," said Gary. "Live your own lives. We all have enough going on outside of the house that we can put up with some foolishness for the sake of peace."

If Rick thought he was the only one who thought Gary had gone as crazy as his wife, he was wrong. Gary had just touched an exposed nerve in Daniel. That nerve was his fear that he would end up like Jack and Gary. That he would spend the rest of his life getting used to Elsie's irrational, life-changing and life-sucking fears.

Jack joined in strong. "Gary's right. Just live your own life. I got my own place," his voice went weak, "been…living…by myself…last fifteen years. No reason…why you can't…live around it." His voice went strong. "You have to manage what you can't fix."

"I love Elsie, but I have no intention of my little girl living in a prison. Even if it's Elsie's prison. I want Amanda to have a full life." Daniel was surprised at the words that had come from his mouth. He understood what he was implying. But something had happened. A line had been crossed. Perhaps it was when Nicole put the booties on his little girl. Maybe it was the perfume and the cat's butt. Maybe it was seeing Rick in the process of making a break for it. Whatever it was, it had happened. He felt it in his heart. He was not going to become Gary or Jack, and his little girl was not going to become like her mother, grandmother, great grandmother, or her aunt. She was going to live free of fear.

When the men could duck out no longer, they made their way back into the house. Daniel entered the living room a different man.

*****

Fear of Failure stuck his long hand in the air and walked down the line of fear demons in Elsie. His hands met theirs in high-fives as he said with a sly smile and a bobbing head, "We got 'em. We got 'em. I told you we'd get him. He's outta there. Almost time to call in the band. It's a birthday party, right? What's a party without music?"

Chapter 4

A long neck attached to an ugly face made more ugly by an exaggerated look of fear penetrated one of the cottage walls from the inside and hung over the grass outside. The frightened creature's yellow eyes fixed on the approaching intruders and their vermin child. One by one, sometimes by twos and threes, other startled demons looked outside the cottage walls.

They all searched for the same thing. Signs of trouble. Light. Peace. And darkness forbid, angels. One by one, each demon's external fear was calmed. The man was full of anger. The woman was full of fear. They both were full of sin. And as if it couldn't get any better, they both were fools. Atheists.

"Hey, it's Elsie," said one of the demons to the rest of them.

There was an even greater sense of calm among the spiritual creatures.

"I wonder how come we couldn't see them until they got so close?" said the same demon as he looked questioningly at Amanda.

"Who knows?" said another spirit of fear. "Whatever it is, it's nothing to be concerned about. We're talking about Elsie and the Smith sisters." Confidence filled his face. "We own them. We have a ninety-eight-year-old contract on these women."

The spirit knew all of this, but it was darkly comforting to hear it spoken. He eyed the little girl. Still, there was something about this cursed child that wasn't right.

*****

Daniel caught up with Elsie and Amanda halfway before they got to Granny's cottage in the back of the house. Amanda reached for his hand and he instead scooped her up protectively. Granny was worse than Judith.

"You boys solve the world's problems out there on the deck?" Elsie asked with a smile.

"Some," he answered.

Still smiling, she asked, "Some? Not all?"

A smile was trying to show itself. That was the right thing to do, right? Answer a smile with a smile? She'd have to settle for a twenty-five percent smile. That's all he could muster. "Some problems are complicated."

She looked at him with her own twenty-five percenter, sensing all was not well. Elsie put her hand on the door handle and pushed down with her thumb. The door didn't budge. She rang the doorbell.

Daniel watched this and felt his anger level rise a notch. Elsie knew good and well that Granny was barricaded in there like she was defending the Alamo. She was living in denial about her family, and she was living in denial about herself.

They waited for several minutes before the solid wood door. Daniel imagined the old woman studying them through the peephole and mentally checking items off of her foolproof plan of not opening the door to danger.

Call Judith to find out who was at her door.

Look through the curtains behind the blinds to see who was at the door.

Study the subjects one last time through the peephole—to make sure a switch hadn't occurred in the five seconds it took her to travel from the window to the door.

The whole thing reminded Daniel of Will Smith in *Enemy of the State.*

Retinal scans, CIA, NSA, and Interpol background checks completed, Granny opened the door, but just a crack. She peered out at them with squinty eyes.

"Granny, is that you?" asked Amanda, eager to see her great grandmother.

"It's your granny, sweetheart," Daniel answered softly, his anger softened somewhat from the old woman's pitiful condition. "She just needs a little time."

"Time for what, Daddy? She knows who we are," said the three-year-old. "We're the same people we were the last time we visited her."

"Hi, Granny," said Elsie. "It's me and Daniel and Amanda."

Granny closed the door and took the chain off. The door reopened quickly. "Come in. Come in. Hurry." Granny pulled Elsie's arm, then Daniel's arm. She hurriedly closed the door behind them and made sure the door knob lock was locked, the two deadbolt locks were locked, and the chain was back on the door.

"It's dark," said Amanda.

It was dark. All the lights were off. All the shades were closed, as were the heavy dark curtains that covered the shades.

"It's okay, sweetheart, we can still see," said Elsie.

Elsie's response ticked Daniel off. He knew he had now crossed the line into being insensitive. What was Elsie supposed to do? Flip on Granny's lights knowing she (he guessed) now had a problem with light? But as insensitive as he knew he was being, he couldn't help the resentment he felt. He held Amanda tighter.

"Come have a seat," said Granny. She walked quickly to a deep, cushy chair and sat down.

Granny was old, but she was quite energetic. Up until now, she had bypassed the usual elderly problems of bad knees and broken hips. But she hadn't escaped cancer, arthritis, diabetes, multiple sclerosis, polio, lupus, epilepsy, and half a dozen other self-diagnosed diseases.

A small demon that resembled an eel, and who specialized in fear of getting a disease, lay across her lap like a kitten.

"My brain tumor's not getting any better you know," said Granny to Elsie. "Malignant. My days are numbered. It won't be long now."

An hour ago Daniel would've never asked the question that came uncharacteristically out of his mouth. "How long have you had a malignant brain tumor?"

"Excellent question!" said the spirit of anger that had been periodically hanging around Daniel since the dropout.

Elsie winced inside at her husband's question. It wasn't like him to behave this way. "Oh, you'll be with us a long time," she said, trying to cut short this conversation. "Is that a new vase?"

"Sixteen years," answered Granny.

"Sixteen years is a long time to have a malignant brain tumor." Daniel's voice was soft. "If you beat it this long, I'd say the odds are in your favor that you don't have anything to worry about."

A slow smile came to Granny's face. "You think so?"

Daniel smiled. "I'm a neurosurgeon, Granny. I know so. In fact, I'd be willing to examine you myself. Just so you'll know for yourself that you're okay."

Elsie felt a weight roll off her. *Maybe Daniel wasn't being mean,* she thought.

A loud voice boomed in Granny's mind. The smile left her face. "I *know* I have a malignant brain tumor. No x-ray can change that." Her statement had that *I don't want to talk about this again!* edge to it.

Incredible! thought a shocked Daniel. *No x-ray can change that,* he repeated in his mind. *You'd rather believe a lie than the truth.* He shuddered at his contemplations of the power of fear. "Okay, Granny," he said, a tinge of disappointment in his voice. He took Amanda off his lap and pointed her in Granny's direction.

Amanda ran the short distance to Granny and buried her face into the old woman's belly. Granny laughed and wrapped her arms around Amanda's waist and pulled her back into the chair before bringing her back to a standing position.

"I'm big," said Amanda.

"Yes, you are. You're all grown up."

"Do you have a snack?" she asked.

"A-man-daaaa, you're going to eat birthday cake in just a little while," Elsie scolded lightly.

"Granny always gives me a snack," said Amanda.

"It's tradition, Elsie. Can't break tradition," said Granny.

Elsie looked at Amanda with a playful, frowny face. "You little stinker," she said, standing up.

"Two," said Amanda.

"One," both parents said.

"Okay, one." Amanda smiled in triumph.

Elsie walked into the kitchen. She looked into the jar and into every food cabinet. "Wow, that's a lot of food, Granny," she said to herself. "When are you going to eat all of this?" She closed the last cabinet. "Jar's empty," she called out.

"There's more in the pantry," said Granny.

Elsie opened the large pantry. It was filled. She stepped inside, closed the door, and turned on the light. It was incredible. There were hundreds of cans of food, several fifty-pound sacks of rice and beans and other stuff, maybe a hundred bags of various pastas. Granny could not shop for another year and have food left over.

Elsie turned off the light and closed the door. She hadn't found the snack, but she had found another evidence of her family's fears. She rubbed her face and let out a sigh of discouragement. "Nothing doing, Granny. Unless we want to start a new tradition of giving Amanda a snack of stewed tomatoes."

"Eeeww, no!" said Amanda.

"I'm sorry. Look in the other pantry. That's where the sweets are," said Granny.

"Yeah!" said Amanda. "Sweets!"

The other pantry? What other pantry? There's no— A thought came to mind. Elsie's face tightened. Her eyes watering immediately at the possibility. She walked down the short hall, hoping that it wasn't so. It was. One of Granny's bedrooms had been converted to…a food warehouse.

It was too much. Elsie fell to her knees and buried her face in her hands and cried. Try as she may to minimize or ignore her heritage of fear, it was everywhere. Even in the pantry. The Great Depression had ended nearly eighty years ago, and to Granny it may as well have ended last week. Her fear of going hungry had finally graduated to the food warehouse phase.

Elsie reentered the living room carrying a cookie and new fears.

"Was just telling Daniel about an aggravating pain I get sometimes," said Granny. "I get it all over. It comes and goes. Sometimes I can feel it moving around inside of me."

Daniel looked at Elsie with a straight face. "Doctors haven't been able to diagnose it."

She decoded his statement and gave the cookie to Amanda. Her eyes went watery again. She pinched the inside corners of her eyes, cutting off the would-be tears, and sat down to visit in the dark with her grandmother.

This time Daniel and Elsie had made a mistake. Granny's mysterious, undiagnosed physical pain wasn't all in her mind.

The spirit causing the pain wasn't a spirit of pain, although the dark kingdom was filled with demons that specialized in causing pains that baffled sufferers and their doctors. No, this spirit was actually a fear demon.

The fear he caused was not a trophy of his existence, but rather an irritant of it. He didn't like the pain. It drew attention to him. It took him out of the safety of darkness where he could manipulate, oppress, and torment, and put him into the danger of light where unpredictable things happened. Yet, he was powerless to stop it. At times he felt like a pile of human excrement dropped in the middle of a small room full of people and trying not to stink. Fortunately for him, no one in this cursed family was in a position to sniff him out.

Nonetheless, this didn't stop his dark mind from wandering back to a nearly two-thousand-year-old incident that still made him frown. He had been sitting in the synagogue inside of a man he had inhabited since a child. There they were enjoying the message. The speaker was saying something about what the God of Moses used to do, or maybe it was something about what He was going to do one day in the future. Anyway, it included nothing about Him helping anyone that day, and *that* made it a good message.

Then this new guy stood up and started talking about God like he was moving in the present. That's when the fear spirit knew something was wrong. Then no sooner had he perked up to study this vagabond further, he found himself involuntarily and definitely uncharacteristically stepping out of the safety of darkness and challenging him.

"Let us alone! What have we to do with you? Jesus of Nazareth? Did You come to destroy us? I know who You are—the Holy One of God!"

"Be quiet, and come out of him!" the Lord had ordered.

With his expulsion, the fear spirit had walked through dry places, seeking rest, for six years before finding another host. And to add permanency to his humiliation, the enemy had ordered His servant, Mark, to record the event in that cursed book—the very first chapter!

Apparently a side effect of that horrible encounter with the Lord was that he couldn't hide in the darkness as perfectly as he once was able. Now he had this annoying pain accompanying his movements. But Granny was scared to leave the cottage, and none of her family believed the Bible or understood spiritual warfare... Sooooo, he could have some fun if he wanted to.

"Ouu!" said Granny, putting her hand on her side. "I feel it right here. The pain; it's right here on my side. It's moving around in a circle."

Daniel put his head down and rubbed his forehead.

Elsie looked tenderly and politely at her grandmother. She got on an arm of the chair that Granny sat on and reached across her. "Here?"

"Oh, it's moved over here." Granny moved Elsie's hand to the other side of her belly. "Now it's going down my leg. It's moving in a circle. Here. You feel that, Elsie? There it is."

Elsie pressed gently on Granny's thigh. "Here?"

"Wait. Wait. It ran back up my leg and across my belly. Felt like something with little feet running. It's in the other leg now."

Amanda laughed. "Daddy, it's like a squirrel. Remember the squirrel in the attic? He had little feet. Does Granny have a squirrel?"

Daniel's anger had turned into nothing but deep pity for Granny and Elsie. *Does Granny have a squirrel?* Yes, Granny had several squirrels in her attic. He answered Amanda by picking her up and saying, "Granny just has pains in different parts of her body. That's all."

"Granny said her pains have feet. Pains don't have feet, Daddy, but squirrels do," she said.

"It was just a figure of speech, sweetheart. She was trying to give us an idea of what the pain feels like."

"But she said the pain moves around. That sounds like a squirrel," said Amanda.

"People don't have squirrels, Amanda. Okay?" said Daniel, trying to add another fact to his persistent daughter's three-year-old mind.

Her lips drooped in a pout. "Okay."

Daniel bounced her in his arms, smiled, and kissed her.

"Granny's got a squirrel inside of her," said Amanda.

Daniel watched Elsie kiss her grandmother and say something softly to her. "Ohhh-kay, me and Amanda are going to wait outside." He carried Amanda toward the door, stealing kisses from her each time she dropped her hands from her hiding face. "Take your time, Elsie. Granny, I'll stand right outside the door. So you don't have to get up to lock the door until Elsie leaves. Tell Granny you love her, Baby."

"I love you, Granny," she said. She wiggled to get free of her father.

He put her down, embarrassed with himself that he was about to whisk Amanda away without a final hug and kiss.

Amanda ran to Granny.

Granny wrapped her arms around her and squeezed her precious great granddaughter. "Granny loves you. Now you go eat a great big piece of cake for me."

Amanda beamed a brilliant smile. "Okay." She turned away, ran a few steps, and turned and ran back. "Granny."

"Yes, Amanda."

"God can get rid of your squirrels," she said, and ran back to her astonished father.

Granny felt a sharp pain in her abdomen. She smiled through it and said, "Go have fun."

Once the visit to Granny was over, Daniel and Elsie left the cottage wondering, but not asking, where Amanda had gotten a hold of the God talk. Television? They'd have to provide better supervision of her.

As they got closer to the stairs of the deck, Fear of Failure was also wondering where that troubling statement had come from. Where had that little cesspool heard someone talk about God? And in such a disgusting way?

It's okay, he told himself. *The little kid's not a threat.* But he did decide to amp this party up just to make sure it was fresh in the sisters' minds who was in charge of this family.

Chapter 5

"Well, come on in," said Gary with a wide smile. "We've been waiting on you. How's Granny?" he said to Elsie.

"Daddy, look!" said Amanda pointing at the big birthday cake. "Look at the candles!"

Daniel put her down. She dropped the cookie she had gotten from Granny's and ran toward the cake.

"Granny's having some aches and pains, but she's doing fine." Elsie looked at Gary. "She's got a lot of food over there. When she'd get the new pantry? What brought that on?"

"Great Depression's what brought that on?" Jack's voice was strong. "Afraid she's going to starve to death."

Judith thought she may have heard a hint of humor at her mother's expense in Jack's voice. "She did have it hard, Daddy. Those were hard times. Granny's family had to live in one of those Hoovervilles. They had to stand in line for soup, too."

"I *do* know a little something about the Great Depression," Jack paused to let his strength catch up with his thoughts. "Unlike a certain historian daughter who shall remain unnamed." He paused again. No one interrupted. They were used to Jack's speech patterns. "Me and my parents lived in a Hooverville. Hundreds of us. Maybe a thousand. Lived down by the river. That's where the soup kitchen was, so that's where the Hooverville was. Hoovervilles followed the soup."

"What's a Hooverville?" one of Nicole's son's, Chad, asked her.

Jack answered. "Eighty years ago. Hoovervilles were…well, it's where you lived if you didn't have a house." His voice was slow and deliberate, but not from age or weak lungs. It was from the freshness of the harsh memories. "You got together whatever scrap material you…you, could find…and made yourself a house. It was hard, really hard."

"That's why Granny has so much food?" asked Chad. His expression showed that this didn't make sense. "But that was so long ago?"

"Different rules for fear, Chad." Jack's voice was robust. "Something bad can happen eighty years ago, and fear can control you today just as if the thing happened yesterday. Fear's like that. You don't get over it, it'll control you."

"Why aren't you scared?" asked Chad. "The same thing happened to you and Granny."

Jack opened both hands. "Who knows? People are different."

"That's enough about Granny," said Judith, giving Jack an evil eye, only half playing.

"Mary Beth," Jack gathered his breath, "was my wife long before she was your mother."

"You're in trouble, Gramps," said nine-year-old Robbie, Nicole's and Rick's other son.

Jack put his coffee cup to his lips and grinned over it. The grin could've been in response to his daughter's scolding face. Or it could've been that his coffee included a shot of Irish whiskey, two teaspoons of brown sugar, and fresh, cold whipping cream. He sipped it and looked at Judith with a Clint Eastwood squint. "Gramps is not in trouble. I'm old, but she's old, too. I think I can still lick her."

"I'm not scared," said Amanda loudly.

Gramps put down the cup. "Well, that one's not scared."

Amanda heard her great grandfather and took that as a que. She began marching around the room stomping her feet and swinging her arms and elbows to her new song. "I'm not scared. I'm not scared. I'm not scared. I'm not scared…"

The toddler's march stilled every conversation and movement. Everyone watched Amanda with the utmost attention.

"I'm not scared. I'm not scared. I'm not scared."

Daniel felt something in his heart like a midnight sunrise interrupting the darkness of his family's predicament, and of their future. Maybe the Smith sisters' curse had skipped his daughter. Maybe Amanda was like Anna.

He cut that thought off at the root. What was he thinking? That was his desperation getting the better of him. Life was not a choice between fear and idiocy. His little girl wasn't going to be a slave of fear. But she wasn't going the idiot track of religion either.

Elsie's eyes couldn't seem to stay dry. First, Granny and the hopelessness she felt sitting in that dark house fighting the thought that she would inevitably end up like her grandmother. Now, Amanda marching around the room singing a song of victory at three years old that she probably wouldn't be able to sing ten years from now.

Probably.

There just had to be a way her daughter could lead a normal life. Elsie watched Amanda march toward them with her swinging elbows. *I have to find a way...for me and my daughter,* she thought.

Judith and Nicole had perplexed looks on their faces. Their looks bordered on alarm. The spirits inside of both women rumbled.

"Is that singing?" This was the Melophobia spirit in Judith talking to the spirit in Nicole.

The spirit of Melophobia in Nicole didn't have as strong a hold on her as the one who dominated Judith, but it was strong enough. He thrashed about like a wild animal that was just captured and put in a small cage.

Fear of Music stopped thrashing and hunched down on all fours as though it was preparing to pounce. "No, but it's close enough!"

Both women's alarm shot up to the near panic level.

"Amanda," Nicole and Judith called simultaneously, both trying to hide their fear behind plastered smiles. "Amanda."

"Come here, darling," said Judith, opening her arms.

Amanda marched to her grandmother, and her grandmother held both of her arms. "I want you to do me a favor. Will you do me a favor?"

"Yeah," she answered.

"Yes," Elsie corrected.

"Yes," said Amanda.

"Singing and music make your grandmother sick. Will you stop singing?" asked Judith.

Elsie looked instinctively at Daniel. Her instincts were spot on. She could almost see fire coming out of his eyes and ears.

"Okay," said Amanda. "I won't sing."

I won't sing.

It wasn't enough that fear was systematically destroying his wife and marriage. Now the Smith sisters' family sinkhole was swallowing his little girl's song. Daniel had *never* felt the rage that now surged through his entire being. He felt totally out of control of himself and what he would do or say if he did or said anything. So he planted his feet, pressed his lips tightly together, and tried not to let this hurricane of anger move him out of control.

I won't sing.

The strong winds blew hard against him. He sturdied his stance.

I won't sing.

His foot slipped.

I won't sing. I won't sing. I won't sing.

The winds of rage were too strong. All control was lost. He'd go wherever the winds drove him. He looked at Judith with eyes that may as well have been pure black.

"Daniel." Elsie's voice reached into the winds' swirl and grabbed his arm, stopping his tumble.

He looked at her and saw the pleading on her face. There was something about her expression that told him she knew what he was feeling. She knew his feelings *exactly.* This had the effect of him hearing the hypnotist snap his fingers. The rage was still there, but he no longer felt out of control.

Elsie saw the spell break. She smiled in pain and relief. "Amanda," she called. She walked to her mom with the look little children have when they've just been scolded. Elsie got down on one knee and hugged her, twisting from side to side. She said this as much for Daniel's benefit as for Amanda's. "Your song and your voice are beautiful. You can't sing at Grandma's house, okay? Songs and music make her sick. But Daddy and I want you to sing to us on the way home." Elsie said this for Daniel. "You're going to sing for me and Daddy forever, okay? You're *never* going to stop singing."

Rick looked at Daniel and pushed himself back in his chair. He had been one second away from whisking Daniel out of that loony tune house to go get some smokes he didn't need.

Daniel must have sensed the support coming from his brother-in-law. He took Amanda by the hand and went and took a seat by Rick.

Rick slapped him on the leg and bent over and whispered in his ear. "You're a better man than me. I'm tempted to turn on my iPod and get some music in here so I can shut this thing down and get my boys out of this haunted house."

Nicole saw Rick whispering into Daniel's ear. She knew he was trashing them. What ever happened to 'For better or for worse'? Why had he suddenly gotten so tired of her fears that he wanted a divorce? She was sure that he had met someone. Probably even having an affair. "Amanda, Mommy's right. It's a lovely song. I didn't mean to scare you," said Nicole.

Amanda sat with her back to Daddy, straddling his lap as his leg bounced her up and down. "I'm not scared. God hasn't given me a spirit of fear. I have power. I have love. I have a sound mind."

Daddy's leg stopped bouncing. He looked at Amanda.

Elsie looked at Amanda.

Judith and Nicole looked at Amanda.

Gary looked at Jack. Jack looked at Gary. They smiled and looked at Amanda.

Rick pulled his head back and looked at Amanda. He thought, *So little Amanda's not going to join Team Crazy. Hhmmp.*

Nicole looked at Elsie and shook her head in slight disgust. What Amanda said about God didn't register on her, but she did hear the part about fear. When was Elsie going to stop living in denial? And now she was feeding this stuff to her daughter. It would be better for her to train her daughter to manage her fears than to give her false hope.

"Amanda, who told you that? Where did you hear it?" Elsie asked this from the large granite island where she was pouring punch into little paper cups. Amanda looked at the pitcher of punch in her mother's hand. "Amanda?"

"Auntie Anna told me," she answered.

There was a collective nodding of heads in the room, and a *That explains it* look on faces that found other agreeing faces.

Rick's face wasn't in that group. He had a wicked grin on his face that he would not have tried to hide had he known it was showing. Anna was the youngest of the three sisters. She was a nut in her own way; a religious nut. But he liked her. She could always be counted on to boldly lay it on the table that her family was nuts. That's why she had stopped being invited to family gatherings. Not that she would come if they did invite her. She had gotten more hardcore about Jesus. Boy, he sure did miss Anna. There was nothing like watching the preacher and the atheist get into it over God.

"Auntie Anna?" said Elsie. Now she felt her own wave of anger.

"Why would Anna tell Amanda something like that?" Judith put it out there.

Nicole huffed and rolled her eyes. "Where does she get that stuff? And why can't she keep that religious stuff to herself? It's bad enough she's brainwashing her own child. Now she's trying to brainwash someone else's child."

Nicole's words heightened Elsie's anger. "When did Auntie Anna tell you this, Amanda?"

"At Chrissie's birthday party?" said Amanda.

"See!" said Nicole, "Chrissie's birthday party. Elsie can't even let Amanda attend her own cousin's birthday party without something like this happening. She has no right to tell Amanda that God hasn't given her a spirit of fear. Who is *she* to talk for God? And she knows the problems we have with fear."

Nicole's words triggered a memory in Amanda. "Auntie Anna said this family fears everything except God."

"She—said—what?" Elsie was livid.

Amanda looked around. Grandma was mad. Aunt Nicole was mad. Mommy was mad. Daddy was mad. She had gotten Auntie Anna in trouble. She'd get her out of trouble. "Auntie Anna made the devil leave me."

"She did what?" demanded Daniel.

Amanda's eyes widened.

"I'm sorry, baby. I'm sorry, Amanda. I wasn't yelling at you. I was just—Amanda, what do you mean she made the devil leave you?" Daniel tried to mask his frown with a smile, which only made him look scarier to Amanda. "You can tell me. Daddy's not mad at you."

"I declare. What is that child of mine going to do next?" said Judith.

"She's in a cult," added Nicole.

Amanda looked around the room and back at Daddy. Everyone still looked mad. Daddy still looked mad. They were still mad at Auntie Anna. She had to help Auntie some more. "She said our family had demons. She said she could make my nightmares go away by making the demons leave me alone. She cast the devil out of me."

Rick covered his mouth with a hand. Anna wasn't here, but Amanda was, and that was good enough for him. He didn't believe in demons, but if there were such a thing, this family was full of them.

Daniel looked at Elsie. His index finger bounced in the air while he tried to find a way to say what he was thinking without cursing— Amanda was here. "Your...sister...cast the *devil* out of my little girl."

Amanda smiled. "I saw him leave. He was ugly and scared," she said, but no one heard her. "Auntie told me that if he tried to come back, say"—she pointed her finger and made a mean face—

"in the name of Jesus, you can't come back." No one heard this either. Then she said, "And that's why I don't have fear."

Elsie raced for her purse. She was going to tell that sister of hers exactly how she felt about this transgression. She went outside. Her hand trembled with anger as she worked to punch the numbers on the phone's screen.

Chapter 6

Anna clutched her Bible over her chest and looked at her big, beautiful kitchen and let the tears roll profusely from her eyes. She looked at the lovely cabinets; so many of them. She looked at the granite counters. The backsplash. The stainless steel appliances. She looked at the little picture of a coffee cup with its visible aroma rising. She smiled.

She looked at a different space on the wall. There was another picture—a sign really. Coffee was good, but this was better. It read, *Taste and see that the Lord is good.* It was too much. Anna couldn't contain what was in her heart any longer. Her emotions broke. Tears rushed out. She put her Bible on the island and bent over, resting her head on the blessed book while her body shook with grateful sobs.

"You rescued me, Lord. You rescued me. Why? Why did you rescue me? I didn't do anything to deserve this." Anna's forehead pressed into the Bible. Her tears fell on its leather cover. "I was so prideful and rebellious." Anna picked the Bible up with both hands, hugging it to her chest while she leaned backwards against the island. She looked up with shame. "I spoke evil of You. I made fun of You and everyone who believed in You."

This admission dropped her to her knees.

"I don't deserve this. I don't deserve Your kindness. I should be like my family." She fought her cries to get her thoughts out. "Like Nicole and Elsie and...and..." a surge of tears pushed through when she thought of her mother and grandmother, "Mom and Granny. I was so afraid I was going crazy. Everything was closing in on me. Everything! Everything! Everything!"

Anna was too lost in prayer and worship to hear the sound of little feet running toward her, stopping, then running away.

"Daddy," said their three-year-old Chrissie as she ran to the back yard, "Mommy's crying again."

Anna finally heard something other than her own voice and crying and the sweet thoughts sent her way by the precious Holy Spirit. It was her phone. Elsie? She shook her head in wonderment.

"Elsie?"

"Anna, we are here at Mother's for her birthday party." Elsie slammed her words like a butcher slamming a knife against a stubborn piece of meat. "Amanda says you said some horrible things about the family."

The surge of anger in Anna's chest was immediate. She knew what she should do. Her family were lost sinners. They were spiritually blind. She couldn't expect them to understand the things of the Lord. She should patiently listen to Elsie and pray. She should love those who said all manner of evil against her. She should turn the other cheek. She should *not* render evil for evil. God would fight her battles.

Anna walked angrily to her iPod station and pushed the pause button, turning off the worship music. "Horrible things like *what*?" Anna was pretty good with a butcher's knife, too.

"She said you said we fear everything except God."

Calm down, Anna. Anna stiffened instead. "Are you and Daniel still atheists?"

"Of course, we are. What does—?"

"Nicole still part-time atheist, part-time agnostic, so-called?"

Elsie fumed. "What, Anna? Is there something wrong with her saying she doesn't know whether or not there's a god?"

"Mother's still sitting in her chair paying more attention to germs than the coming of the Lord?" asked Anna.

Elsie's mouth dropped open. "Oh, my God! How dare you speak about our mother like this! You're impossible, Anna. It's the reason no one wants to be around you. It's why you're not welcome in your own mother's home."

"And what god would that be?" answered a feisty Anna.

"What?" asked Elsie.

"You said, 'Oh, my god.' Last I checked, you didn't have a god. Who were you talking about?"

Elsie's jaw tightened. It would be impossible to explain to such a bigoted person that her choice of words was a figure of speech. "You said we have demons."

"And what if I did?" snapped Anna. "You don't believe in anything but yourself anyway. God's not real. Angels and demons aren't real. All that's real is your silly big bang and human ingenuity." She paused, and ignoring the Holy Spirit, said, "How's that working for you?"

Elsie wasn't one to curse, but she heard the foulest language volunteering for service. "Why you little—"

"What?" Anna demanded. "You little *what*? I'll tell you what I am, Elsie. I'm a child of God, and you can't curse what God has blessed."

Curse.

That word jumped in front of Elsie like a sudden red traffic light. Nicole had said that she and the family of girls were cursed, and that she needed to passively accept her fate. She had rejected her sister's dismal diagnosis and prescription. Now her other sister, the other cursed sister, was declaring boldly that she was blessed and couldn't be cursed.

Elsie simmered at her sister's arrogance. She told herself that one of them had to behave like an adult. It certainly wasn't going to be Anna. She was a Christian. A Christian who had deceived herself into thinking that she was free. Or worse, was deliberately putting on a front to make her mythical god look good.

Elsie moderated her voice. "You said we have demons." Good. The words came out evenly and without the anger that bubbled inside.

"And?" answered Anna.

Elsie inhaled deeply and exhaled slowly. "And why would you say we have demons?"

Anna inhaled deeply and exhaled slowly. "Okay, Elsie. You really want to hear this?"

Elsie controlled herself. "Yes."

Her answer was genuine. She was her fraternal twin, and they'd been practically inseparable until Anna surprised everyone and turned a sudden corner and became a Christian. And not just a Christian, but the worst kind. Intolerable of others. Hellfire and brimstone. Creationist. Miracles. And now demons. So, yes. She wanted to know how an otherwise intelligent person could lay her brain aside to believe in fables and superstitions.

Chrissie came into the living room pulling her father by his index finger. She gave a pull in the direction of Anna and dropped her hand and watched Daddy go fix Mommy. He didn't move fast enough, so she got behind him and pushed.

Ben looked at Anna with a smile and walked toward her. She was beautiful and getting more beautiful by the day. "You okay?" he whispered. "Inspector Chrissie said Mommy was crying."

Anna smiled and put her hand over the phone. "Just witnessing to my sister."

"Really? Which one?" he asked, thinking Elsie.

"Elsie," she answered.

"Yep," he said. "Knew it. You get desperate enough, you'll listen to truth. Come on, baby," he said to Chrissie. "Let's let Mommy talk to Auntie Elsie. We can pray for her while Daddy fill up the pool."

Chrissie heard pool and ran outside.

Anna braced for the argument. "I said our family has demons because demons are real, and because they can cause problems like this."

Elsie had her own ideas about the inevitable argument. "Where did you get the idea that demons are real, and that they could possibly be the reason for our family's fears?"

"What? No condescending statements?" Anna asked suspiciously.

"No condescending statements."

Now Anna felt ashamed that Elsie had beat her to the high ground. The confrontational edge in her voice went down a notch. "I got it from the Bible, Elsie."

"The Bible talks about demons?" asked Elsie.

"Yes." Anna braced herself, anger at her side, ready to fight.

"How did you go from seeing demons in the Bible to demons in our family?" Elsie had asked with a calm that defied hot feelings in her chest, neck, and face.

"Elsie, I don't know about this sudden willingness of yours to talk about the Bible, but—"

"Honestly, Anna, I don't want to talk about the Bible. But if this is the only way I can find out why you told Amanda that we all have demons, then, well, I guess we're talking about the Bible."

Anna went through the books of Matthew, Mark, Luke, and Acts. She referred to several examples of stories of either Jesus or His followers driving demons out of people. As a person with a medical degree, she was naturally intrigued at the encounters of people who had supposedly been healed of physical infirmities simply by having a so-called demon cast out. A mute man in Matthew. An epileptic boy in Mark. A crippled woman in Luke.

Anna finished with Mark 5. "In case you're ever so inclined to read it," the edge had crept back into her voice, "this guy was totally gone. You can't get more mentally ill than he was. Jesus healed him by casting demons out of him."

Elsie's patience had run its course. Anna had a degree in accounting, and here she was diagnosing a two-thousand-year-old fictional character. Imagine that. There was no need for medical science. No need for doctors. No need for surgeons and psychiatrists. No need for MRIs and CAT scans and drugs. Just cast out the demon and *Presto!* All is well.

"Amanda said you cast the devil out of her," said Elsie.

Anna knew the sucker punch was coming. She'd beat her to it. "You outta try it some time."

"What did you do to her? She's three years old, for God's sake! If you want to cast demons out of children, cast them out of your own and leave mine alone!"

"I did," said Anna.

Elsie was stunned and silenced. "You did *what*? Cast the devil out of Chrissie?"

"Yes. I cast the devil out of Chrissie," said Anna.

"My God, Anna! What is wrong with you?" Elsie shook her head in exasperation. *Poor Chrissie. Who knows what they're doing to her. At least Amanda's with me.* "You can't do this to little children!"

"Do what, Elsie?" Anna snapped. "Set them free? Let them live a life free of fear? God have *mercy* on me for doing something so cruel!"

Elsie's head shook. She looked into the trees that surrounded her parents' home. "Just…tell me, Anna. What exactly did you do to Amanda?" It would help to know this in case she needed to take Amanda to therapy to get over whatever they had done to her.

"Okay, Elsie, get a pen and paper. You may want to write this down. I wouldn't want you to give Amanda's therapist the wrong information."

Elsie pulled the phone from her ear and looked into it. How'd she know that?

"First, I gave her an Oreo cookie and sat her on my lap. Second, I said, Amanda, Jesus can make your nightmares stop."

"Oh, my God," said Elsie.

"Third, I asked Amanda if she knew who Jesus is."

Elsie put her hand on her forehead and shook it. "An…na, tell me you didn't."

"Fourth, I told Anna that since she is so little, Jesus would make the nightmares stop even though she doesn't know Him. But I told her that if she wants to make sure that the nightmares never return, she needed to know Jesus, and she needed to become God's little girl."

Elsie's heart was breaking piece by piece. Oh, why didn't these religious nuts mind their own business? "Anna, did you try to turn my little girl into a Christian? She's three and a half years old. She doesn't even know what she's doing."

"Fifth, I explained the gospel of Jesus Christ to Amanda and asked her if she wanted to live for God. She said she did, and we prayed."

Elsie almost dropped her phone.

"Sixth, once I was sure that she understood salvation and wanted to live for God—"

Understood salvation? thought Elsie. She's three!

"—I took authority over Satan in Jesus's name and told him that he wouldn't hurt Amanda while I was praying for her, or after I was through praying for her."

He wouldn't hurt Amanda? Oh, no. Now something else to make my baby afraid. "Did you pray out loud? Did Amanda hear you say this?" asked Elsie.

"Of course, she did." Anna wondered where she was in her count. "Seventh, I told Amanda to not be afraid. That I was going to tell the demons to leave. I asked her to tell me if she saw or felt anything when I prayed."

The more Elsie heard, the harder her heart became against her sister, and the more determined she was that Amanda would never be in her aunt's presence without either her or Daniel being present.

"Last, Amanda gave a little cough and said she felt lighter. She said she saw Jesus pull monsters out of her. Did you get all of that, Elsie?"

Monsters. It wasn't enough that her precious daughter had been tormented every night for the past year with nightmares. Now her nut sister had added more monsters. It was a harsh way to refer to her, but it unfortunately described her perfectly. Plus, she had done something to make her child think she had seen Jesus.

"Anna."

"Yes, Elsie?"

"It's bad enough that Chrissie has to grow up in that kind of household. But what gives you the right to cast demons out of my daughter?" Elsie yelled. If they were face to face, she'd be nose to nose in her sister's face, and she wasn't even this kind of person.

Anna's answer shot out of her mouth like a bullet. "What gives me the right is Anna is three years old and she doesn't have to end up like you, Nicole, Mother, or Granny. She doesn't have to live with your curse. She doesn't have to let fear ruin her life."

"Anna!"

"What!"

"You can't get rid of fear by casting out a demon! It's a psychological problem! It's not a demon!" Elsie yelled.

Anna's voice dropped to calm. "When was the last time Amanda had a nightmare?"

"What?"

"The last time Amanda had a nightmare. When was it?" asked Anna.

"What? Huh? The last time…last—" Last night, she was going to say. She thought back a couple of nights. Then a few. Then a week. She went back two weeks. Chrissie's birthday party was exactly two Saturdays ago. Now that she thought about it, that was the last time Amanda had had a nightmare."

"Are those crickets I hear?" asked Anna. "Don't worry about your atheism, Elsie. It's probably just a coincidence that my niece has been free of nightmares since the imaginary Jesus made the imaginary demons leave your daughter. I'm *sure* you and Daniel will find a scientific reason for this event." Anna cut the conversation short.

Click.

Ben and Chrissie walked into the living room. "How'd it go with Elsie?" asked Ben.

Anna blew out a heavy breath. Her expression said it all. "I blew it again. I told her the truth, but I wasn't very loving doing it." She huffed in dejection. "I just get so angry when I talk to my family."

Ben squeezed her shoulder. "They've beat you up pretty good. It's understandable." He smiled. "God will help you minister to them in kindness."

"It's just so hard talking to them," she said. "I try to keep my temper, but then I just..." She looked at her husband with a sad smile.

"Jesus had a rough time with His family, too," said Ben. "Hey, if you can't talk *to* them, let's talk *about* them."

She looked at him quizzically.

"To God," he said. "Come on girls." He took Anna and Chrissie by the hand. "Let's talk to God about Auntie Elsie and Auntie Nicole and Grandma and Granny. Let's ask God to do something big today to open their eyes so they'll see that they need Him."

*****

Elsie heard the phone go dead. Her hand dropped to her side. *There must be another reason for this. There is no way Anna can be right.* She went back inside to talk to Daniel.

Fear of Failure's eyes were narrow with troubled thoughts and scenarios. He could hardly believe his ears. A lot of conversation had been garbled, but he had caught enough to know that things had changed.

Oh, how the band was about to play!

Chapter 7

"She's not even here and she's ruining Mom's party," said Nicole of Anna.

Judith went to where the cake was. "Well, that's not going to happen. We've talked enough about Anna. It's time to talk about me."

Nicole rubbed her mom's back. "That's right, Mom. This is your day." She turned to everyone and motioned, trying to hurry them. "Well, come on. Come on everybody." Her face lost some of its shine when she looked at her slow-moving husband. She asked him with her eyes to join them. He did. She breathed a sigh of relief.

A peculiar tradition had developed in regards to Judith Smith Mills' birthday parties. It was on account of her phobia of music. The medical term was melophobia. It had begun as it had begun in her mother. First, a discomfort of music and singing. Then a greater discomfort. Then a moderate fear. Then a phobic fear—a belief that something terrible would happen in the presence of music or singing.

One difference in Judith's melophobia and her mother's was that unlike Granny, her phobia had not progressed to including a hatred of music. Yet another difference was that unlike Granny, Judith's melophobia now included instruments. So no music, no singing, no instruments.

The family stood around the table.

"Make a wish, Mom," said Elsie.

Judith closed her eyes and made a wish. She opened them and took a deep breath and blew out all of the candles, which wasn't hard to do since there were only three. Candle smoke caused cancer. Judith wasn't having any of that. And there would not have been any candles at all had Elsie not prevailed upon her mother to allow them to use all-natural vegetable wax candles. What Elsie had not succeeded in doing, and what she had stopped trying to do, was to modify the upcoming birthday tradition.

Judith looked around the room in silence with a wide, closed-mouth smile. Everyone looked at her with smiles and bobbing and swaying heads. Daniel and Rick wore what were obviously smiles of politeness—Rick's measurably less so than Daniel's. The sisters, Elsie and Nicole, shared warm looks with their mother and with one another as they bobbed and swayed.

Every head stopped at exactly the same time.

"Happy birthday!" everyone said.

Amanda's bottom lip poked out from her saddened face. "Daddy, I don't like how we do birthday here. They do it different."

Daniel took a quick glance around to see if anyone besides Rick had heard Amanda. Good. No one but Rick.

Rick bent down. He and Daniel were at Amanda's face. "They do everything differently over here, Amanda," whispered Rick with a cynical smile and looking at Daniel. He stood up and looked at his watch. *And why shouldn't they?* he thought. *It's a mad house.*

"Sweetie," Daniel rolled her bottom lip with his finger, "Grandma has her own way of celebrating her birthday."

"You're supposed to sing at birthday parties," she said.

"That's what we were doing when we were shaking our head," he said.

"That's not singing, Daddy. You have to open your mouth to sing." She paused, then asked, "Can we open our mouths and sing at Mommy's birthday party?"

Daniel thought about Amanda's question. She had no way of knowing the significance of what she had asked. *Would they sing at Mommy's birthday party?* She'd be thirty-six. Would she go the way of Judith and Nicole? Would she suddenly get a music phobia on her thirty-sixth birthday? Dread filled his heart. The Smith sisters' curse. "We'll see."

Amanda's little face frowned.

"I mean of course we're going to sing, Amanda," he corrected. "Birthdays are happy days, right?"

"Right!"

He picked her up and bounced her. She was lighter in his arms than his heart was in his chest. "Let's have some fun," he said.

Phobia was the lead demon in Judith. This was her house, which meant this was his party. Not hers. Not Fear of Failure's. His. "Have *fun?*" A crooked smile came to his large, scaly face. "That is exactly what we're going to do."

*****

Fear of Failure couldn't get any angrier than he was. Sure, it was true that Phobia was stronger than him. And the fiend was within his rights to claim authority over the party since he had authority over the owner of the house. But that didn't change the fact that the band was his idea.

Phobia couldn't care less that Fear of Failure felt slighted. His long tongue danced in and out of his mouth between commands as he directed the demons with their instruments to their appointed places. "You, put those drums right there. No, closer. You with the cymbals, get behind her. Yeah, yeah, there. Right behind her. We're going to get her real good. You, put the speakers right there. Turn them around to face her. Oh, yeah, we ought to have great reverb." Phobia looked toward Elsie and saw Fear of Failure still sulking. "Fear of Failure, this was your idea. Would you like to tell the others where you'd like them to go?"

Why, this was quite unexpected. Phobia publicly giving him credit for the band idea? Most of the sour look left his face, at least that which wasn't permanent. "I want guitars to the left and right. One by Judith. One by Nicole," a rejuvenated Fear of Failure barked. His menacing eyes squinted. "Lead guitar, Judith. Bass guitar, Nicole."

Phobia watched Fear of Failure direct the rest of the demonic band. He had a surprise for him and the others.

Fear of Failure watched a procession of demons whom he hadn't invited. He looked at Phobia.

Phobia looked snugly at Fear of Failure and sneered. "What's a band without singers? We've got rock, pop, R & B." A fat spirit came in. Phobia put out his hand. "Opera."

The fat, costumed opera demon fired off a loud and long piece that was unbelievably agile. His voice rose effortlessly to the third F above middle C. Then after a pause and a sneer, it went higher.

"Coloratura soprano," said Phobia. "Nicole used to like opera. Let's see if she still likes it."

Demonic laughter and hisses.

"What about rap?" a demon yelled out. "I like rap."

Two ferocious demons entered, cursing, and looking angry at everyone.

"And rap," said Phobia. He looked at Fear of Failure. "The honor is all yours." He knew this would go a long way. He needed Fear of Failure to help him keep his bondage as strong as possible.

Fear of Failure was too dark a creature to glow, but if it were possible, it would've happened that moment. He looked intently at the band as he approached them. Their intense gaze of him matched his own gaze of them. His long arms shot above his head. His fingers stiff and wide and unnatural, as though petrified by arthritis. He put his head back for a moment and breathed deeply. He opened his eyes and looked wildly at the band. His hands whisked down.

"Play!" he yelled.

*****

Amanda felt a chill. "Daddy, I'm cold."

"Really? I was just thinking it's a little warm in here," he said, as he tried to warm her by rubbing her bare arms.

Rick froze. He had seen that weird look on Nicole's face before, all too often. *Nicole, do tell me that you are not about to freak out here in front of everyone.* "No, Nicole," he murmured, pleading actually.

Daniel noticed something, too, about Elsie. She looked up and around as though she was looking in the distance for someone who had called her name. Then she placed the fingers of her right hand over her right eye. He could see her squinting. Two screams snatched his attention.

"Judith!" Gary gripped both of her shoulders and shook, trying to shake her out of the world of terror she was lost in. "What's wrong? What's wrong, Judith? Come out of it. It's going to be okay."

Her continued screams told him otherwise. She bolted from him and ran from one room to the next with her ears covered. He ran behind her calling her name.

Daniel turned with wide eyes from where the fleeing woman disappeared and looked at the other screaming woman. Nicole had both hands pressed to her ears like someone was drilling into them.

"Stop the music! Stop the music!" she screamed. It almost defied description. A combination of opera and rap music filled her head. A fluttering sound of a soprano's voice doing acoustic gymnastics in the background and rappers yelling, *Freak me, girl. Freak me, girl. Yeah, like that. Yeah, like that. Freak me, girl. Freak me, girl. Yeah, like that. Yeah, like that.*

Rick's anger and hardness remained for a couple of seconds. He had been through so much pain, disappointment, humiliation, and lies that all he wanted was to escape with his boys before Nicole and her family drove them all crazy. Besides, if he got all flustered every time Nicole did something strange, he would've had a stroke a long time ago. Yet, her screams broke his heart and his hard shell collapsed and fell away. He darted to her side and hugged her. "Nicole, calm down. Calm down, baby. The music's going away."

She looked at him, wanting desperately to grab him, to hold him and feel his body next to hers, giving her strength, helping her to outlast this attack. She couldn't. She had to keep her hands to her ears. She had to at least try to muffle the music.

"It's not going away," she said frantically.

"It's going to go away. I promise you, Nicole," said Rick.

The demon with the cymbal stood behind her. *CLANGGGGGGG!*

"Aaaaaah!" screamed Nicole. She jumped up and ran out of the room.

Her sons had seen her frightful episodes before and weren't shocked, but they were traumatized. They stood frozen, looking at their father.

"You boys stay here." Rick hurried after his wife.

Gary and Rick passed one another in pursuit of their wives.

"Nicole!" Rick called after his runaway.

"Judith!" Gary called after his sprinting wife, who was proving surprisingly quick and agile for an older woman with bad knees. "Judith, now you stop running like this before you hurt yourself."

Each time the faint thought came to her mind that she could stop, the demon running behind her with the saxophone blew his horn. Judith turned and slid around the corner by the staircase. A demon with a guitar was waiting on her. He smiled evilly and lifted his hand and came down hard on the guitar. His wicked fingers danced with dark energy on the strings from hell.

"Aaahhhhh!" she screamed. "It's a lead *guitaaaarr*." Judith bolted for the front door.

Gary finally caught up and grabbed her from the back around her waist. She wiggled and squirmed. "Judith, doggonit woman, you're gonna make my back go out. Now stop it!"

"Lord, have mercy!" Judith groaned in agony. Her rescue call was more the product of spontaneous social custom, what you say when you're in trouble, than it was a conscious call for help from God.

Nonetheless, it was enough.

The demon's guitar dropped out of his hands when he saw him. He had seen one before, but not this close up. He was large, very large, taller and wider even than Phobia. The demon looked at his large jaws. They were known to use those large jaws to rip demons apart. They had to be the most inappropriately named beings ever created by God.

The mercy angel looked down at the befuddled demon. "Take your instrument of torment."

The demon was still as possible as he tried to process this. Mercy angels were ruthless and lacked any tolerance for provocation. "Take it...and *go*?" *Please say yes.*

"Take it and go."

The demon knew there would be no other words spoken by the angel. God's uppity servants rarely spoke to them. It was beneath their so-called dignity. He cautiously touched the tip of the guitar's neck and pulled it backwards a few steps. He didn't rise until he felt he was far enough away that it wouldn't be seen as a provocation. He took off in a flash. The band was down its lead guitar player.

The mercy angel put his hands on the sides of Judith's head, covering her ears.

Judith's eyes looked like a dark room that had just had the light turned on.

Gary saw the relief in her eyes. He wiped her wet face with the fronts and backs of his hands. "It's gone, isn't it?"

She fell into his chest and cried. "It's gone, Gary. The horrible music is gone."

In the birthday room, Daniel looked at his own wife as though she and he were alone in a tunnel. Her actions drowned out the commotion caused by Judith and Nicole screaming and running wildly through the house with their husbands hot on their tracks.

Really, it was Elsie's lack of action that baffled him. She hadn't rallied to her mom or sister. Instead, she sat on a chair with her elbows on the table and her head resting in her hands. Apparently, she hadn't even noticed the cups of overturned punch caused by her elbows.

Daniel clutched his crying child protectively, gently pushing her head onto his shoulder. He looked at Nicole. She was having an absolute fit. And for all Rick's tough talk and crass jokes, he was down there on his knees apparently trying to hug the terror out of his panicked wife.

Daniel didn't hear any more commotion coming from the foyer area. Maybe Judith had made it out the door and Gary was out there chasing her in the woods. He turned with Amanda and looked at Jack. He was like an expressionless mannequin. Just sitting there. Like nothing was going on. Finally, the mannequin's eyes looked at Daniel.

Jack's voice was strong. "Too old to get riled every time there's a problem with one of the Smith girls." The burst had run its course. His voice was now tired. Strong enough to only carry a word or two at a time. "Have to...learn...to live...with...the fear. It's a...mess. But...it's here...to stay."

Daniel's neurosurgeon brain wondered at the spectacular scene. A delusional fear could certainly cause a person to hear things that weren't there. To hear things that would cause debilitating fear. But two delusional people going into an episode like this at exactly the same time? And what about Elsie? She didn't run around screaming like her sister and mother. But *something* strange had happened. And whatever it was, it happened at exactly the same time as her sister's and mother's episode. So now that would make three spontaneous episodes at exactly the same time. Fascinating.

That was Daniel the doctor. Daniel the husband and father wasn't fascinated at all. He was horrified at his future. At his daughter's future. Jack. Sitting there at a table. Wife in the back cottage sitting in the dark, eaten up with fear. Daughter and granddaughter running through the house screaming in delusional fits. Husbands chasing them like cops trying to catch a purse snatcher. And his advice was, 'Learn to live with the fear.'

And then there was Elsie. His lovely, lovely Elsie. What was going to become of her? Five women. Three of them definitely mentally ill. One of them, his Elsie, probably mentally ill and simply covering her growing tracks of oddities. Although dropping out of residency was too big to cover. And then there was the final Smith sister. Anna.

Of all the people for the mental illness gene to skip over, why her? His thoughts were harsh, he knew. But he had to ask. Why had the gene skipped over the least intelligent person in the family? How could someone reject science as truth, accept God and the Bible as true, with all of its errors and nonsensical horse manure, and be the one spared this illness? It didn't make sense. It wasn't fair.

Incredible. Absolutely incredible, Daniel thought angrily. The only person spared is the one who believes in God and demons of fear. The one who believes a person can get rid of chronic fear by casting out a demon.

Daniel cursed under his breath, taking the Lord's name in vain. His and Elsie's eyes finally met. He knew she knew he had taken note of her behavior during the commotion. What she didn't know was that he had made up his mind to bypass the matador and bull routine. He wasn't going to ask her about her behavior. He knew there were no truthful answers behind that red cape.

Her birthday was only two weeks away.

Chapter 8

The weeks passed with cruel rapidness.

It was ten minutes to midnight.

Daniel lay on his side, awake, facing away from Elsie. There was no way he could sleep. There was no way he could face her. He had seen enough. Or had he? Nearly every odd thing she had done the past two weeks could have been attributed to something else. Even normalcy. Like someone failing a lie detector test not because of dishonesty, but nervousness.

Elsie had become much more protective of Amanda. She seemed anxious when she wasn't in her sight. She didn't know that he had awakened the several times a night she checked on Amanda. Was this the fear curse? Or was it something else? Like a loving mom simply being overprotective of her child.

She had become much more concerned about germs and chemicals and cell phone radiation and the purity of their food and drinking water. Was this the fear curse? Or was he being unfair? Was this guilt by association? Was he judging her actions through the actions of her family? Maybe she simply wanted to take more control over her health.

Where were the lines that separated responsible concern, rational fear, and mental illness? Daniel knew that the separation wasn't always as simplistic as mentally healthy versus mentally ill. An otherwise mentally healthy person could be eccentric.

Whereas a mentally ill person could exhibit no eccentricities whatsoever.

Besides, there were levels of mental illness. And to further complicate things, there was the multilayered category of people near to or on the borderline of medical diagnosable mental illness who were fully functional.

And besides the obvious that he wasn't a psychologist or psychiatrist, there was another factor that complicated the situation more. Despite all of his medical training, when all was said and done, this fear thing in Elsie's family had reduced him to nothing more than a desperate, scared husband who didn't know how to interpret what he was seeing. He didn't even know if he was seeing what he was seeing.

A hot tear of fear and desperation rolled down Daniel's face. The hopelessness he felt was like a smothering pillow pressed hard against his face, cutting off his air. But this pillow wasn't on his face. It was on his soul. He felt the essence of whatever he was at his basic core being buried under the weight of a fairy tale gone bad.

Elsie's birthday was officially in ten minutes. She'd be thirty-six.

Daniel was like a death row inmate strapped down and waiting for the deadly moment when the needle with its lethal poison would enter his system and extinguish his life. The only power left to him by the executioner was to select which arm the needle would enter.

Another hot tear coursed from his eye and across his nose, settling onto the other cheek.

*****

The dark, slow swirling cloud resembled a tornado. Its origin wasn't heaven, but it descended from the dark sky. It hovered over, then lowered itself onto the home. From a distance, a company of evil spirits saw the sign and walked toward the marked home like a pack of wolves closing in on wounded prey. Their eyes focused hungrily on the exterior of Elsie's home.

At the front of the pack was an extraordinary demon. He was a foot taller than the next tallest demon and wider than any other. His physical size was imposing, his appearance fearsome. His eyes weren't the common red or yellow. They were the less common black. But there was a frightful quality of his eyes that encompassed much more than color. The blackness of his eyes were alive with the essence of his nature. And his nature was revealed in his name.

The spirit's name was Unreal.

Unreal was a type of fear spirit, but of the highest sort. That kind of demon whose powers and features were comprised of the qualities of several other fear spirits. He was a spirit of psychosis. He specialized in causing or aggravating conditions within people that were diagnosed as serious mental illness. His specialty was unreality.

There was absolutely nothing as satisfying as manipulating a person to the point where they lived in a world of unreality. Unreal had many notable accomplishments recorded in the *History of Exploits and Defeats*. He even had one that was recorded in the cursed book.

Israel's first king, Saul, had come under his power. He had expertly used the king's pride and insecurity to produce such fear in him that his fear created a world of unreality. A world where Saul saw his most loyal friend as his worst enemy. A world of orchestrated fear built on lies and insecurity that ended in attempted murder of his friend, loss of his kingdom, and loss of his life.

Aahhh, those were good days.

He stopped and rested his hands on his waist. The other demons stopped behind him. He looked stonily at the house. The hard, and now angry, stare came from the fact that according to one of the enemy's many unjust rules of engagement, he couldn't get immediate access to Elsie. He'd have to wait for other fear spirits to prepare her before he could take control and sit on the throne of her mind.

Unreal sneered. His upper lip raised, revealing sharp, discolored teeth. He'd have to wait. "Go!" he ordered his contingent of fear demons. "Prepare her for me."

It was midnight. Elsie's thirty-sixth birthday.

*****

Elsie lay with her back to Daniel. She looked at the iPod player. In five minutes she'd be thirty-six years old. She delicately got out of bed and walked downstairs to the kitchen, got a drink of water, and went to the basement.

Except for the dropout, the past two weeks had been the most bizarre two weeks of her life. Her general sense of fear had grown into several baffling specific fears. It had taken so much energy to maintain a sense of normalcy during the past two weeks that often she had to stop herself from screaming. She was sure Daniel was aware of her odd behavior, but he had said nothing.

It's the birthday, she thought to herself. *He's waiting for the birthday.* Elsie looked at the acoustic guitar on the stand. Granny stopped playing and singing at thirty-six. Mother stopped playing and singing at thirty-six. Nicole stopped playing and singing at thirty-six. In a few minutes, she'd be thirty-six.

Elsie's eyes narrowed in defiance. She walked with determined steps to the guitar. She picked it and sat down on the carpeted floor and crossed her legs. The guitar rested on her right thigh.

She played.

She sang.

She'd greet the so-called curse on her terms. Fear had stolen her career. It would not steal her music.

The second hand approached the eleven, crossed it, then crossed the number twelve. It was midnight.

Elsie was thirty-six.

Elsie looked at the wall clock. Thirty-six and singing. Thirty-six and playing. Tears of joy joined the eruption of air that came from deep within her chest. She played and sang and played and sang. Ten minutes. Twenty minutes. Thirty minutes.

Elsie's song was indistinguishable from her crying. Her song had turned into a song of crying. Each passing moment was a light year away from the so-called curse. She didn't understand her family's fears. She didn't understand her dropout or her own fears. She couldn't explain either. Nor could she explain why her grandmother, mother, and sister had lost their music at thirty-six and she had not. But she had *not*! And that's all that mattered.

Elsie looked up with a wet face and saw Daniel standing there with his own wet face. Her face fought to speak. She caught her breath. "I'm playing, Daniel. I'm singing."

Now he fought his own face to speak. He smiled. "You're playing, Elsie."

Elsie's voice bounced with trembling as she said, "Anna was wrong. It's not God and demons and superstitions. We don't need God. We need to believe in ourselves."

Daniel sat beside her and watched as she played and sang. He closed his eyes and got lost in the beauty of her voice. But when he opened his eyes...

*****

The pack of fear demons stood there frozen. Two mercy angels. Where in the world had they come from? And why were they here? Elsie was theirs. She was an atheist. Her husband was an atheist. The kid was three. There was no justifiable reason for mercy angels to interfere with their mission.

Yet none of the several demons volunteered this information to the angels. The angels who were staring intensely at them.

Then they all heard the words that ended the standoff.

"We don't need God."

The demons saw the angels break. The big monsters looked as though they were going to start crying. In a flash, they were gone.

The demons hurried down the basement stairs and turned the corner.

*****

The music abruptly stopped. Daniel opened his eyes. Elsie's face was filled with terror. She tossed the guitar on the floor as though it were a snake and jumped up and scurried several feet to her left. Her eyes wide. Her posture rigid with defense against the evil that had been attracted to her on account of the music.

"What?" Daniel didn't ask. He lamented.

Elsie didn't answer. Her bulged eyes peered at the guitar. They darted toward the staircase and back to the guitar. She ran the few steps to the guitar and kicked it toward the stairs. "Take it!" she said to the evil presence.

Daniel knew he should rush to his wife's side and hold her tightly. He needed to assure her that everything would be okay. For better or worse. His brain and knees couldn't cooperate. He slumped to the floor and doubled over and moaned. But not for himself. He was the husband and father. He should've figured out some way to save his family. "Oh, El...sie. Oh, Amanda. I'm so sorry. I've failed you both," he cried.

Elsie was backed against a wall. She didn't hear her husband's gulping sobs. She didn't see him on the floor. She couldn't see through the blanket of terror that had fallen over her. She couldn't see through the curse of fear.

Hours later a thoroughly traumatized and humiliated, yet surprisingly resilient, Elsie fell asleep with this determined thought on her mind, *I am not cursed. There is no such thing. I am strong. I will find a way to beat this.*

Beside her bed stood Unreal. "It makes no difference what you believe, my dear and brilliant Elsie. Reality is reality. And the reality is you've rejected God. And he's the only person who can stop me." He bent over her and breathed heavily on her face and head. "I will have you."

Chapter 9

Daniel kissed her tenderly on her eye and forehead before he left for work. Elsie had pretended to be still sleeping. She wasn't ready to talk about what had happened, and she was sure he wasn't either. Where could such a conversation begin? Where would it end? With her cursed? With her sitting in a dark room surrounded by hundreds of pounds of rice and beans and beef jerky, waiting for the apocalypse?

She rolled over onto her side and blinked hard. It was silly to even use such a word as curse. Whatever she and her family had, it wasn't a curse. It could be explained medically...eventually. Psychology and psychotherapy were her answers, not religious superstition.

Elsie deliberately excluded psychiatry from being a first choice. She knew that psychiatry most likely meant medication. She naturally had no philosophical biases against medicine. But she didn't want to go down the path of trying to *manage* her fears by covering their effects with anti-anxiety drugs. She didn't want to cover the problem. She wanted to get rid of it.

But Elsie was as practical as she could be stubborn. Truth was, her dropout had killed her career of being a neurosurgeon, but not her desire to become a neurosurgeon. She believed passionately in medicine and all branches of orthodox medical science and practice.

Her real underlying reluctance to psychiatry lay in the dismal fact that Granny, her mother, and Nicole—Anna never came to mind—had run the gamut of everything available. Psychiatry, psychology, psychotherapy, counseling. Nothing worked, and medical tests showed there was nothing wrong with their brains.

So what made her think she'd be the exception to the family rule? Besides, her family didn't know it, but she'd hiked those same arduous mountain trails of false hope. All she got from her efforts was mental exhaustion and a broken heart.

Her phone rang. She didn't have to look at the number to know who it was. As a defensive measure, Elsie had given Anna a distinct ring. Curiosity replaced the low-level revulsion the ring caused. How had her fraternal twin sister done with her birthday? She'd never come right out and ask such a thing. Anna's mind was almost as sharp as her tongue. She'd take a question like that as her giving credence to her ridiculous superstitions.

Besides, thought Elsie, *you're a Smith girl. I know how your birthday's going no matter what lies you tell me.* "Hello, Anna. Happy birthday." Elsie's voice sounded as perfunctory and shallow to her as she knew it must sound to her sister.

Ben had joked with Anna that unkindness and insults probably wouldn't help her win her sister to the Lord. Anna reminded herself of this and answered, "Happy birthday, Elsie! We're getting closer and closer to the big 3-0."

Elsie paused. She had to reorient herself. "Two years to go," she cautiously went with the joke.

"Two? Maybe we aren't fraternal twins. I have three years to go. Look, we're having a little get together at the house this Friday for my birthday, and I thought...*well,* why not invite my sister." Anna was pleased at her own behavior and surprised at the warmth she felt. This was so unlike their usual conversations which normally began bad and ended worse. But she added to herself, *Please don't say anything stupid, Elsie.*

"A birthday party?" asked Elsie, trying to figure out Anna's angle.

Anna heard the unspoken question loud and clear. She took a deep breath. *Love is not easily provoked,* she quoted the Scripture to herself. "No, it's not Amway, Mary Kay, Primerica, or a Bible study. Just a birthday party with your family and mine."

Elsie was impressed at Anna's smoothness. She had just maneuvered around a perfect opportunity for them to get into it. Her sister *really* wanted her to go to her house for some reason. The birthday party, of course, was the given reason, but there had to be another. "Can I get back with you on this?"

"Sure," said Anna. "But we'd really like to see you." A moment of silence. "I'd like to see you."

Elsie tilted her face toward the high, exposed beam ceilings of her bedroom and let out a short breath. She walked to the full wall window and looked out over the golf course. She thought about their last conversation. Her anger was still fresh, and so was Daniel's. He had brought up Anna's name several times since she had disclosed that she had cast a so-called demon out of Amanda.

A new flash of anger struck.

No, Anna, we won't be there, were to be Elsie's next words.

"Ben seems to think my mouth gets in the way of my heart," said Anna.

Elsie said nothing. Ben was a Christian, too, but he wasn't as offensive as her sister. In fact, she liked him. He wasn't in the least way quiet about his faith. Yet he and Anna could say the same thing to her, and she could listen to him, but no matter what Anna said about Christianity, it just grated on her nerves. She knew Anna loved her. But she just couldn't stand her arrogance. The way she pushed religion down her throat. The way she insulted her intelligence. *A person who believed in demons and the Bible attacking her intelligence!* It just got under her skin.

Anna knew Elsie was still angry over their last conversation. She broke the silence. "Imagine that. Ben saying my mouth is a problem."

Elsie knew her sister. This was as close as she would ever get to receiving an apology. Perfect people had no need to apologize.

Elsie shook her head in mild disgust. *I'm not going over there.* "Look, Anna, I don't—"

"How's Amanda sleeping?" Anna asked humbly.

Elsie's words got caught in her throat. She closed her mouth, then answered, "She's…she's…"

Anna smiled. "I know. I know. Amanda's such a sweet girl. I'm happy for her. Chrissie's sleep has been sweet, too." Anna's heart became too full to not praise God. "Thank You, precious Lord Jesus for helping our little girls."

Elsie found herself surprisingly not revolted by her sister's religious outburst. How could she be mad at someone, anyone, even if it was Anna, for caring about her child? And maybe this was just an overflow of tolerance she felt for Anna on account that Amanda had mysteriously and coincidentally stop having nightmares around the same time Anna did her…her demon thing.

Demons.

There it was again. Anna's uncharacteristic niceness had been convincing, but Daniel was right. A person who would try to cast a demon out of a child was beyond superstitious. They were dangerous. "Look at how many cases there are of parents killing their kids while casting so-called demons out of them," he had said as he showed her articles on the Internet.

"Anna, I'll have to say no to your invitation."

"Oh, you're not coming," said Anna weakly.

Elsie heard the apparent hurt in her voice and felt badly for her sister—in all of her ignorance, she knew that she really meant well—but she wasn't going.

"Elsie, I was going to keep it a surprise, but there's another reason I wanted you to come over."

I knew it! You probably had lined up a professional exorcist to cast the devil out of me, she thought. "And what is that, Anna?" Her voice had a trace of accusation.

"I really wanted it to be a surprise." She paused. Elsie heard crying. "I passed the fourth part of the CPA exam. I passed the exam, Elsie. I'm a certified public accountant."

Elsie was stunned. Then she went numb. She turned in a stagger from the window overlooking the golf course and turned her attention to a chair. She stretched out her hand for it several feet before reaching it. She fell into the chair.

Congratulations! Oh, Anna, I'm so happy for you! This is what you always wanted! This is what Elsie would have said under normal circumstances. But there was one thing absent from the lives of every generation of Smith females. Normal circumstances.

Anna heard Elsie grunt into the phone. Anna understood. It's why she wanted to tell her in person.

"How...I don't...when did...Anna...I..." It was a miracle Elsie had gotten this much out of her dumbfounded mind.

Anna's face was wet. She let out a breath. "I took the test, Elsie." She wanted to say more, but her emotions were getting the best of her. Anna heard the words she wanted to say, but somewhere from the path of her mind to her mouth, they detoured and came out of her eyes as tears.

Elsie was finally able to communicate past her shock. "But you dropped out. Like me. The fear, Anna. The fear made you drop out after you took the first exam. You couldn't take it. You were like me. I...I don't understand."

Anna wiped her eyes and left a streak of mascara on her face that looked like a single, dark railroad track. "Elsie, please come to my party. Please...will you?"

*****

Daniel's curiosity overruled his anger, but not the demands of his work schedule. On Friday Elsie arrived at her sister's home alone, without Amanda. Irrespective of Anna's CPA news, a babysitter seemed the most responsible choice.

Anna's home wasn't as large as hers or as opulent as Nicole's or as peacefully picturesque as Mom's, but it was nice. The sprawling ranch-style home would have been beautiful had she not unconsciously compared it the way the Smith girls did. And perhaps it would not have been compared so critically had Anna not declared war on the family when she flipped out and became a Bible-thumping Christian who never passed on an opportunity to slam her family.

Elsie drove into the long driveway and parked. She noticed approvingly and with relief that there were no other cars in the driveway or parked on the street directly in front of the house. Of course, this didn't mean there wouldn't be a coincidental drop-in visit from some wacky church friend who'd innocently bring up the subject of casting the devil out of her.

"Avocado dip. Oh, how delightful. I just love avocado dip. I used to be afraid to eat it because it's so high in calories. But I've overcome my fear because they're so good for you. Hey, while we're on the subject of fear…"

"I swear," Elsie said to herself as she approached the door, "one I-just-happened-to-be-in-the-neighborhood visitor and I'm out of here."

The door opened and Ben and Chrissie greeted her.

She was relieved to see Ben. And Chrissie adorned in a yellow ruffled dress with yellow ribbons tied at the ends of her long hair was as precious as ever. Elsie's smile was genuine.

"Auntie Elsie!"

Little arms and big eyes all reached for her. "And yellow socks and shoes," said Elsie, as she picked her up.

Ben looked at Elsie's car. "Darn it. Daniel had to work, didn't he?"

"Yes. He wanted to come, but…well, you know how it is," she said.

"I'll tell Mommy you're here," said Chrissie.

Elsie put Chrissie down.

Ben was as tall as her husband. He stepped to her side and hugged her around the shoulders as he rested his cheek lightly on her head. "It's not easy being Superman. Everyone wants a piece of you. I'm just glad there are people out there like Daniel with capes and big S's on their chests." He stepped away and looked at her. "Thank you for coming."

Elsie was no one's fool. She knew the good cop-bad cop routine. Ben wasn't obnoxious Anna. But they were both on the same Christian team. They believed the same myths. They had the same narrow worldview. But Ben's demeanor and kindness were so disarming that she didn't feel threatened around him the way she did with Anna. To her, Anna was like someone in a judo match, always looking for a way to flip her opponent. And her opponent was anyone who didn't believe in Adam and Eve and talking snakes, virgin births, and roasting in everlasting hellfire.

Elsie looked at Ben's eyes. Was Good Cop sending a subliminal message with his soft, tender, gray eyes? Was he saying, I'm so sorry that my wife did something so idiotic as to traumatize a little girl by telling her she had demons inside of her? No, probably not. He just had soft, tender, gray eyes. For all she knew, he could have participated. She hoped not. She needed to believe that someone in this home wasn't insane.

Elsie returned Ben's smile. "How could I not? Anna says she passed the last CPA exam?"

"That's right," said Anna, stretching out the word *right* for around three seconds as she walked toward the open door. She took Elsie's hand and pulled her toward the living room with the giddiness of a little girl pulling her best friend toward the playground. "I wanted to tell you in person."

When they got near the sofa, Elsie abruptly stopped, causing Anna's hand to slip from hers. Anna looked at her stiffened sister with a question in her eyes.

"Anna, you said there would be no one here this evening but your family and my family."

"Yes. Where's Daniel and Amanda? Are they coming later?" asked Anna.

"No. Daniel had to work. Amanda's at a babysitter."

Anna looked at Elsie's face. It was like an exquisite marble sculpture. Beautiful, cold, and hard. She filled in the blanks. Daniel? He probably really had to work. Amanda? She wasn't here because of their fight.

Anna felt the pilot light in her belly ignite. A slow burning fire of anger tried to melt the smile from her face. The whole reason there had been a fight at all was because Elsie was too stubborn and pigheaded to listen. She knew everything, and she was willing to bet her daughter's future on her stupid belief that there was no God and that humans evolved from monkeys.

The heat reached Anna's chest, but the smile was still there. "Oh, Chrissie was looking forward to seeing Amanda."

Anna's words bounced off the marble. "Is *anyone* else coming?" Elsie asked. An undercurrent of an ultimatum in her starched words told Anna that should the answer be yes, Elsie was leaving.

The flame in Anna erupted.

Ben sensed it and made his move. "Elsie," his voice was soothing, "no one else is coming. I promise you. And if by chance that doorbell rings, whoever it is stays out there." Now he was smiling. "Even if they're wearing a FedEx or UPS uniform."

Good Cop was masterful.

Elsie sat down.

Ben placed a knowing hand on his wife's tense back and stiffened body and gently nudged her to the sofa. "Uninterrupted girl time. You got it, Elsie. Honey, I'm sure she's dying to hear about your blessing."

Yep, thought Elsie, *Good Cop wasn't Anna, but they were still a team.* Elsie sat on the edge of the sofa, her small purse in her hand.

Anna sat and looked at Ben. Her eyes blinked with energy she was trying to calm. She turned to her sister and placed her hand on Elsie's knee. "Sit back and relax, Elsie." She hoped her smile didn't look phony.

Elsie wasn't relaxed, but she sat back into the sofa. "Please, tell me about this development with your exam."

"All business," said Anna, offering the supposed playful rebuke with a smile.

Elsie suffered this theater with a non-expression. Yes, it was all business.

Ben looked at Chrissie and balled his fists and started pumping them up and down. "Sto—ry. Sto—ry. Sto—ry. Sto—ry."

Chrissie smiled brightly at Daddy and started pumping her hands looking at him. He gave a little point in Mommy's direction. Chrissie now looked at Mommy while she pumped. "Sto—ry. Sto—ry. Sto—ry. Sto—ry."

Elsie's non-expression turned into a smile.

Good Cop's intervention gave Anna enough time to quote a couple of Scriptures to herself. *Love is not easily offended.* And, *the wrath of man does not work the righteousness of God.* "Okay. Okay. I got the message." She moistened her lips by licking and smiled more genuinely.

Elsie saw the excitement in every feature of Anna's face.

"I did it, Elsie. I passed the exam," Anna gushed.

"Tell her how, honey," Ben said. "I'm sure Elsie wants to know *how.*"

Elsie cast a quick glance at Ben. Yes. She wanted to know how. What treatment had the family overlooked?

Tears rolled out of Anna's eyes. "Elsie, I hope you don't get offended."

Okay, thought Ben, so now you've prepared her to be offended.

"Why would I be offended?" The light bulb clicked on the moment she asked. Her disappointment came out as a breath.

"Well, I know how you hate God," said Anna.

Good Cop grimaced.

Chrissie frowned. "You hate God, Auntie Elsie?"

"Al—righty then. On that note," Ben picked up Chrissie under her arms and held her high above his head. "Time for you and Daddy to go to the birthday room and make sure everything's ready." He lowered her onto his side. "We'll be in the birthday room when you girls are finished talking," he said, as he carried Chrissie off.

Elsie looked at Anna as she watched Ben and Chrissie disappear. Anna braced for the fight and turned to her sister.

Elsie's voice was soft and controlled. "How did you do it?"

Anna was puzzled that there was apparently not going to be a fight. *Oh. Okay,* she thought. "Well, you know how devastated I was when the fear came on me. Elsie, it was so bad. When the fear came on me, I couldn't think straight. It paralyzed me." Anna looked at Elsie with a vulnerable softness. She shook her head with a grimace. "The fear, Elsie. It was like…like it was a person. I can't explain it. I mean…at the time I couldn't explain it."

Like it was a person. Like the fear was a person.

Elsie remembered the mysterious old woman she had met at the coffee shop. What was it she had said? *Fear has determined to destroy you. Don't let him steal who God created you to be.* She had also talked about fear like it was an entity and not just an emotion.

Anna looked at Elsie. "I know you know what I mean." This was meant as an apology for her telling her sister something they both knew Elsie understood by experience.

"And now you *can* explain it?" Again, Elsie's words were without provocation.

Anna made her way out of the trouble of her memories, and for a few seconds stumbled around mentally, wondering at her sister's apparent willingness to go down a path she knew would lead to her talking about Jesus and prayer and demons and stuff that would just tick her off. But she had asked. So…

In a flash too quick for Anna to mentally process the decision, she made it—and did it. "Someone cast spirits of fear out of me, Elsie."

Chapter 10

If there were going to be a fight, it was going to be now. Anna waited for it.

"And by spirits, you mean *demons*?" said Elsie.

One of Anna's eyes narrowed as she tried to unearth any hidden insult. "Yes."

"Go on. I'm listening."

It was amazing. Anna had wrestled and fought her sister because she wouldn't seriously listen to what she had to say about God. And she had wrestled and fought her when she had listened to her. But now that Elsie listened without attacking her position or defending her own, she found that talking to her sister was more difficult than arguing with her.

Anna tried to adjust to the unfamiliar setting. "I was at the end of myself. I didn't know what to do. I had tried everything. You know we've tried it all, Elsie."

"So you went to an exorcist," Elsie stated.

Anna winced. Then acknowledged that her reaction was due to previous encounters with her sister, not this one. For there was nothing in Elsie's tone to get upset over. Oh, how this version of Elsie was throwing her for a loop. "No, not an exorcist. That's Hollywood...and the Catholic Church. It was more like me freaking out at a women's Bible study, and one of them ordering the fear in me to come out."

Elsie's expression and posture revealed nothing.

"What do you think about that, Elsie?" Anna heard a challenge in her own voice that was like a dog bolting out of a crack in the door for lush green grass. But *what—ever.* She was ready for whatever smart answer her atheist sister had.

"What else happened?" Elsie asked, not a trace of anything amiss in her voice.

"What do you mean, what happened?"

"What happened when the lady ordered the fear to come out?" asked Elsie.

"Elsie?" said Anna, scrunching her eyebrows. "What are you doing?"

"I'm listening. I'm trying to understand."

"You're trying to understand," said Anna. This whole thing was suspicious. "Okay," she said. *You'll show yourself soon enough.* "I was telling these women about my fears, and about how the fear made me stop my studies. They started asking me a bunch of questions."

"Like what?"

"Like how long I had the fears. What did I fear? Was there anyone else in the family with irrational fears?" said Anna. "I told them yes."

Elsie interrupted Anna's long pause. "Then what?"

"Then one of them said it sounded like a generational curse of fear. That's when it happened."

"That's when what happened?" asked Elsie.

"That's when I fell out."

Elsie's face was still expressionless. "You...fell out. On the floor?"

Anna looked at Elsie's face and saw no scorn, no ridicule, no atheist smirk. She examined her words and tone. Nothing. This enraged her. "Yes! On the floor! Where else would I fall onto? The ceiling? What is the *correct* way to fall out, Elsie?"

"Are you okay, Anna?" Elsie's inquiry was even.

Anna jumped up and marched off to the birthday room.

"What's wrong?" asked Ben.

"It's Elsie! She's impossible!" she shouted in a whisper.

"What did she do?" he asked.

"Nothing!" said Anna.

Ben looked at the anger in her face. "Tell me about her doing nothing that's got you this upset."

"Chrissie, I need to talk to Daddy for a moment." She pulled him into a corner. "I told her that someone cast those spirits of fear out of me."

"Oh, goodness, what did she say to that?" he asked.

"She asked me if I went to an exorcist."

Ben laughed several seconds with a closed mouth.

"What's funny?" asked Anna.

Ben answered through the last of his laughter. "Sounds like a reasonable question to me. I'm sure in her circles they don't talk a lot about deliverance ministry. All she knows is what's at the movies. What else did she do?"

"That's what I told her. That that's movie stuff. I told her what happened at Sheila's. How the ladies ordered the demons to come out."

"Ooohh-kay. Here we go. What she say to that?"

"She asked me what else happened." Anna looked at Ben for agreement.

"That's it?"

"Yes," Anna answered in a hiss. "You see?"

"I'm beginning to," said Ben. "Then what happened?"

"I asked her what she thought about this. She—didn't—answer. All she said was, 'What else happened?' I asked her what she meant by this?" Anna twisted her mouth in a mock replay of her sister's offense. "She said, 'What happened when the lady ordered the fear to come out?'"

"She didn't," said Ben.

"Yes, she did," answered Anna, too caught up in her version of things to see that Ben was making fun of her.

"What else did she do?" Ben asked with feigned seriousness.

"She said, 'I'm trying to understand.'"

"Yep," said Ben, nodding his head.

"I told her that I fell out when they said my problem sounded like a generational curse of fear. Do you know what she said to me?"

"What did she say?" Ben asked.

"She said, 'On the floor?'"

"She actually said that?" said Ben, trying to hold a straight face.

"That's when I lost it. I had to get away from her before I said something I'd regret." Anna looked at Ben for comfort. "Do you see the problem? You see what I have to go through with her?"

Ben squeezed both of her shoulders and pulled her into his chest. He hugged her. "I do, honey. I see the problem." He pulled back and looked at Chrissie. "Chrissie, come here, baby. I need you to help me pray for Mommy." Chrissie took her thumb out of her mouth and ran to Daddy. He picked her up and positioned her on the side of his hip. "Lay your hand on Mommy's head." She did.

Anna smiled and closed her eyes and raised both hands to the Lord.

"Repeat after me, Chrissie," said Ben."

"Okay."

"Say, in Jesus name."

"Say in Jesus name," she repeated.

"No, I want you to say in Jesus name. Just say in Jesus name. Don't say say. Okay?"

"Okay."

"In Jesus name," said Ben.

"In Jesus name," said Chrissie.

"You foul demon of pride," said Ben.

"You foul demon of pride," said Chrissie.

"You foul demon of deception," said Ben.

"You foul demon of deception," repeated Chrissie.

Ben tried to think of something else. "You foul demon of impatience."

"You foul demon of impatience," said Chrissie.

"Come out of Mommy!" said Ben.

"Come out of Mommy! said Chrissie, pushing Mommy's head emphatically.

It was a few moments before Anna realized what had happened. She snatched her arms from over her head.

Ben put Chrissie down. "Run, Chrissie, run!"

Chrissie ran out of the dining room.

Ben made like he was going to make a run for it. She grabbed his arm. "Just what was that all about?"

When Ben stopped laughing, he said, "I should've pushed Chrissie down. I could've saved myself." He started laughing again.

"What do you mean a spirit of pride?" she demanded.

His gray eyes twinkled. "I left out the spirit of offense."

"Ben," she pushed.

"Baby, they got the fear demons out of you, but they left some others. Did you keep the receipt on this deliverance?"

Anna folded her arms and leaned heavily on one leg. "Will you please be serious? My sister is sitting in there. I need to say something to her."

"Okay, you want serious?" he said, his face carrying the memories of a smile.

"Yes."

"Okay, Anna, you need to *seriously* check yourself. I know that your family have said terrible things about you. I know they think you're crazy and that you're in a cult. They probably think you're a blood-drinking, flesh-eating cannibal, for all I know. So they're going to say some things. They don't know any better. *They're blind, Anna.*"

"That doesn't mean we have to be doormats, Ben." Anna looked away from him a little, knowing deep in her heart that her position was indefensible. "You know how my family treats me."

Ben looked at her sympathetically. "Yes, I know how they treat you." He gave her a few seconds. He didn't want to lecture her; he wanted to help her. "Was Jesus a doormat?"

"He's the Son of God," she offered in a whimper.

Ben smiled supportively. "And? You're a daughter of God."

Anna's expression showed her surrender.

"You can do it, Anna. You have to. Elsie doesn't know any better. She doesn't have the Holy Spirit; you do. She doesn't understand the Bible; you do. She asked you those questions because she really doesn't know. You can't expect her to know what you know. Or to believe what you believe just because it's the truth. Anna," Ben pleaded, "she doesn't know it's the truth. You have to be patient with her. You have to treat her the way God treats you."

Anna's eyes moistened.

"You're the closest Christ she sees," Ben continued. "If you get offended at her and rough her up, she's not going to see the true Christ. I know you love your sister, Anna. You just have to love her, pray for her, and let God work on her heart."

Anna's moist eyes released shame-filled tears. "I did it again, didn't I?" She shook her head in dejection.

"You're human, Anna. You're just responding to your family out of your pain of being rejected by them. And maybe…"

"And maybe what?" Anna asked.

"Well," he bobbed his head a few times, searching for the right words.

"Just say it, Ben. I won't get angry."

"Well, I think you're being a bit prideful and insensitive." He saw her question. "I'm not saying you stop telling them the truth. I'm just saying that you have to remember where you came from. Sometimes when you talk to your family, it's hard to hear the love that I know is there."

Anna lowered her head. "I guess I just can't do it. I can't minister to my family."

"Now you're being foolish," said Ben softly. "Are you fishing for a hug?"

"Maybe."

He pulled her to his chest, squeezed the back of her neck, took advantage of the moment and got a nice kiss. "Now go love your sister. Love her enough and she'll let you talk to her about anything."

Anna spun around toward the door with her chin pointed to the ceiling like a high-schooler who had just received a pep talk from the coach. She wiped her eyes and reentered the living room.

Elsie wore the same expression. "Is there more?" Elsie behaved as though she had never left the room.

Anna marveled. "I should not have left the room like that."

Elsie smiled cynically inside. *I guess that's an apology.* "I find this story of demons intriguing."

"I can imagine it would be," said Anna. "It's quite a wild story."

Elsie knew that Good Cop had reined in Bad Cop. That much was obvious. Besides, since Ben and Anna got "saved" a couple of years ago, Ben had played the part of moderator well. But what was new was Anna, even if it was only a shadow of sensitivity, admitting that the concept of demons would be seen as wild by an intelligent, rational person. She wouldn't put too much stock into this slip-up on Anna's part. The real Anna would snatch the steering wheel back any moment and aim the bumper at her.

"You left off the story with you on the floor," said Elsie.

"That's right. That's where I left off. Thanks." Anna's tone matched the politeness of her words.

One of Elsie's eyebrows lifted.

"After I fell to the floor," Anna curled her lips, then continued, "let me say this, Elsie. What I'm going to tell you goes way beyond wild. It's...well...I wouldn't believe it had it not happened to me. So I don't blame you if you don't believe me. I won't be offended."

Now Elsie was more intrigued than her cool appearance showed.

"When I fell to the floor, voices started coming out of me."

Elsie lowered her eyes and head and pondered this for several seconds before looking at her sister. "Were the voices internal or external? Were they in your mind, or could the others in the room hear them?"

"Everyone heard them. They said they didn't have to leave because I belonged to them and because they had a legal claim on our family." Anna felt good. She felt calm. She was simply telling her sister what happened. If she accepted it, she accepted it. If she didn't, she didn't. She wasn't God, and she wasn't going to try to be God to her family any longer. She'd do less arguing and more praying.

Elsie had never heard anything as fantastical as this in all her life. Internal voices could be symptomatic of any number of medical or psychological possibilities. But voices that others could hear? That was something altogether different. Then the oddness of what these voices supposedly said came to mind. *A legal claim on the family?*

"Did these voices clarify what they meant by having a legal claim on the family?" Again, Elsie's inquiry was without any apparent scorn or condescension.

"Oh, they had a lot to say. Sheila and the others had to make them shut up. They were all over the place," said Anna. "They said they were given the family."

"Given the family? What do you mean *given?* Like a gift from one demon to another?" asked Elsie.

A gift from a demon? Wow, Ben is right. She doesn't have a clue, thought Anna. "No, not a gift like that. He meant access. They were given access at 10:53 a.m. on a Tuesday morning in 1917. And there was another one who said he stole my music on June 25th, 1966."

The creases that formed at the corners of Elsie's mouth were the only outward evidence of how she felt about this dubious bit of information. They were born in 1979. How could a so-called demon steal Anna's music from her thirteen years before she was born?

Anna added, "Demons lie. So you can't believe everything they say."

So you can believe some of what a demon says? Elsie reminded herself that a cyclone of fear had shipwrecked both of their career dreams and had cast them on a desolate island of humiliation, hopelessness, and growing bondage. But as silly as this sounded, Anna had somehow found a way off the island. She had to sort through her sister's story to figure out how.

The brain was an immensely fascinating organ. It was often compared to a computer, but certainly not among those who understood it. Or at least not by those who understood about it what they understood about it. It would be more accurate to compare a teaspoon of water to the Pacific Ocean than to compare the human brain to a man-made computer. For every computer had fixed, limited powers. But growing research showed that science only understood a thimble of the brain's possibilities, which were enormous.

Elsie looked at Anna and wondered. What if there is something in Anna's superstitions that affects the brain in such a way that it causes a self-correcting service that changes perception? Or maybe this service changes not the perception, but the response to the perception? What might that do to irrational fear? This isn't farfetched. What about the effects of stress and meditation on the brain? Those changes can be seen in brain scans.

"The demon gave the exact day and time," said Elsie. "What significance do you think this has?"

"The best everyone could come up with is that something happened at that time on that day that somehow opened a door for the demons to enter." Anna couldn't believe the conversation had gone on as long as it had. Was Elsie really interested in what happened to her? A darker possibility arose. Or maybe she was listening just to have more to criticize her. That was it! That was exactly what her conniving sister—*Shut up, Anna. Just shut yourself up and trust God,* she ordered herself.

"How did they make the demons—there were more than one, right?" asked Elsie.

"Yes. One of the ladies read a book that said there's usually more than one."

"If the demons had a right to be there, inside of you, how were they able to make them leave?" asked Elsie.

"The name of Jesus," Anna said simply. Elsie's expression showed this wasn't enough. Anna elaborated. "There's power in the name of Jesus. All power is in the name of Jesus. Demons have to obey you when you use the name of Jesus."

"I don't mean any offense by this question, Anna."

"Okay," said Anna.

"Several petulant demons living inside of a person seems to me to be a worst case scenario."

"No," said Anna, "a worst case scenario is to die in your sins and rebellion, and to open your eyes knowing that you now have to suffer eternal punishment for rejecting God's mercy which He offered you through Jesus Christ." Anna was surprised. The words had bypassed her mind and had effortlessly and spontaneously come out of her mouth. She knew these were fighting words, but she didn't feel bad about them. How could she feel bad? Sure, she had been the mouthpiece, but this was the Holy Spirit's doing.

A faint shade of scorn and derision was definitely on Elsie's face now. She pushed it back, but not before Anna noted it. "Hellfire and brimstone," said Elsie.

Anna was surprised that she felt no urge to give a slashing reply. "Some things just are, Elsie. Nothing we can do about them one way or the other."

Elsie nodded. "I suppose so. Anna," Elsie was ready to end this conversation, eat an obligatory piece of cake, and get out of there, "after they used the name of Jesus to drive out the demons, what made you attempt to do something that you previously couldn't do?"

"You mean, take the exam?"

"Yes," said Elsie. "What dots did you connect to get from demons being cast out of you in someone's living room to you taking the CPA exams?"

Anna looked at her sister's expressionless face. She knew this was deliberate. She disregarded all the wild accusatory possibilities that ran through her mind and reached over and picked up Elsie's hand. She squeezed it tenderly.

Then she did something that didn't change her sister's expression, but it did touch her heart. She lifted Elsie's hand and lowered her face to it and kissed it. Then she turned her face and pressed the hand to it, and with closed eyes, said, "I love you, big sister." Then she did something that caused a sunburst in her own heart. "I'm sorry," she said. "I'm sorry for treating you so badly, for talking to you so meanly." Emotion welled up in her face. She took a deep breath. "Ben shared something with me that helped me to see myself as I really am. I'm prideful. I'm arrogant." Now she was crying. "I'm mean. I've said things to all of you in a wrong spirit." She wiped an eye. "I hope that you can forgive me."

Elsie was somewhere between stunned at this in-depth, uncharacteristic apology and wondering cynically how long Ben's intervention would last this time. "And Amanda and her demons?" asked Elsie.

Uh oh.

Anna's first panicked thought was, *What do I say?* She decided to simply tell the truth. "Elsie, I'm sorry for being a poor Christian witness to you and the family. Chrissie and Amanda were both tormented by nightmares most of their short lives. Chrissie was set free by the power that's in the name of Jesus. There was no way I could see my child rest peacefully night after night knowing that little Amanda was still being tormented by demons of fear. If I could do it all over again," she looked Elsie dead in her eyes, "I would. And, Elsie, you should ask yourself who benefits by Amanda being hurt."

Elsie's Mr. Spock expression evaporated. Her eyes widened. Her nostrils flared.

Anna continued calmly. "And you must ask yourself honestly, why are you so afraid of the possibility that Jesus Christ is who the Bible says He is that you are willing to sacrifice your daughter's well-being to keep believing the lie that there is no God?"

Sacrifice my daughter? The thought burned in Elsie's belly.

The small anger spirit wasn't assigned to anyone in the home. But as his good fortune would have it, he was in the area—next door, to be exact—drawn there by the hot anger of an arguing couple who were fighting about money. When the husband got angry and stormed out of the home and drove off, the demon of anger followed him out. That's when he felt the dark energy coming from the home next door. Naturally, he followed the invitation.

The demon of anger looked at his nature simmering in the woman. She had no protection. A slow smile came to his face. Was it Christmas? He attached himself to the woman's anger and screamed until his vile body shook.

It happened so fast that neither sister saw it coming. Elsie's hand slammed across Anna's face with two years of anger, causing a loud *SMACK!*

Anna grabbed her stinging face and said, "Oh...oh...oh..." Part of Elsie's palm had caught enough of Anna's nose to start a flow of blood from a nostril. Anna lifted her face. Her fingers covered the bottom of her face. A short laugh that resembled a cry pressed past her palms. "Thank you, Jesus," she said. "This is nothing in comparison with how You suffered for me, but thank you for letting me suffer for Your name's sake." Then she took her hands down from her face, her fingers reddened with blood. "I love you, Elsie."

Elsie jumped up and took two steps backward. She was angry. But she didn't know she was so angry that she'd hit her sister. She had never hit anyone before in her life. She took another step backward and shook her head no and ran out the door.

"Lord, she can run from me, but she can't run from You. Chase her down, Lord. Don't let my sister go to hell."

Chapter 11

The newly promoted angel's widened eyes carried his surprise at its arrival. When he had first heard that Anna had replaced her criticism of Elsie with prayer, he was momentarily stunned. This could change everything. For God's anointing wasn't upon the complaints of the saints, but upon their prayers. What had caused Anna to start praying for her sister?

The angel shook the thought. It didn't matter what caused the change. All that mattered was change had come. He cupped both his hands and stretched them out to receive the sacred bowl. The heavenly attendant of *The Altar of the Prayers of the Saints* smiled triumphantly as he lowered the small bowl into the angel's hands.

"It has been mixed with the blood of the Lamb," said the attendant. "It is now acceptable and ready for presentation to the Lord God Most High."

The angel looked in awe at the bowl's contents. "There's so little," he said.

"Yes," said the attendant, "but it is one hundred percent pure, full of love and humility. Sometimes the quality of the prayer can overcome its small amount. It is enough to provide a little help."

"Enough for her salvation?" the angel asked.

"The quality and quantity of prayer doesn't decide this. Elsie will decide this. This is always decided by the person being prayed for. The prayers only help the process."

"How will this be done?" asked the angel.

The attendant of the prayer altar wasn't surprised at such a question. He himself had ministered at the altar for thousands of years and he still had questions. "How it *will* be done is a mystery. But the Lord most often uses His kindness to appeal to the conscience of the person being prayer for."

"Elsie is an atheist. She doesn't believe in God. What if God's kindness doesn't open her eyes?" The angel sounded as though this was a foregone conclusion.

"Then the Lord will use His severity," said the attendant. He saw alarm in the angel's eyes. "There is nothing else. Kindness. Severity. That's all there is."

The angel knew little about the nuances of prayer, but his previous assignments had taught him a lot about the sons and daughters of Adam. They were corrupt, depraved, and blind beyond his capacity to understand. He had personally witnessed Adam's offspring respond to God's kindness and severity in baffling, and ultimately, tragic ways. To most, His kindness only convinced them that sin had no consequence of retribution. To others, his severity only hardened them in their sins.

The angel thought of Elsie and shuddered. How would she respond to God?

*****

This was the first time Elsie was grateful that Daniel had been called in to work extra hours. The surgery he was to perform would take at least four hours. She needed this time alone to think. To figure out what in the world had happened at Anna's. Did she really hit her sister tonight?

She pulled the cover up to Amanda's neck and gave her a peck on the cheek. She went to her bedroom, disrobed, and showered and brushed her teeth. Going to sleep was out of the question. Her mind was racing. And the anger that had caused her to hit Anna was still simmering in her chest.

"I've got to talk to somebody," she said. She looked at the time and ruled out Nicole. She sighed and punched in her mother's number. *This may be no better than calling Nicole.*

"You did what?" Judith asked in shock. "Why would you go over there to that crazy woman's house? You know we cut her off, Elsie. You're just making things worse."

"Yeah, they're worse," Elsie said. *If you only knew how worse.*

"What would make you go over there?" Judith asked.

"She invited me to celebrate our birthday together."

Judith was on the other end shaking her head in disbelief. "It's bad enough we have one nut in the family, Elsie. We don't need two. You could've said no, you know."

"I said no initially."

"Have you forgotten all the mean things she has said and done? What mother besides me do you know of who had to have her own daughter arrested for marching around the house with those crazy people shouting Bible scriptures? You remember the You Tube videos she put out saying all those mean things about us?"

Elsie heard her mother crying.

"She made us sound like the Manson family. I will never forgive her, and I will never let her in my home again. And if she even farts in my direction, I'll get another restraining order."

"I had to go," said Elsie.

"Why?" demanded Judith. "Why did you have to go? Especially after what she did to Amanda."

"She took the CPA exams. Mother, she's a CPA."

It took Judith several moments to recover from those shocking words. "That's...not possible."

"It is possible, Mother. I saw the test results."

"But it's *not* possible, Elsie. We all have the same condition. Granny. Me. You. Nicole. Her. We all are the same. We are knitted together by our condition."

Elsie looked around the room wondering if she was hearing correctly. Mother sounded sad to hear that Anna had found a way to beat the fear. Yes, Anna was ignorant. Yes, she was a religious nut. But she was an ignorant, religious nut who had stumbled upon some way to get the brain to self-correct. So if she had to sit through the deluded rantings of a religious fanatic to find out how to duplicate whatever Anna had done, so be it.

In a sense, she understood Mother's disappointment in hearing of Anna's accidental discovery. Anna would attribute the self-correcting actions of her brain to the supernatural power of her Jesus—which, of course, she did—and use this as an occasion to further persecute the family.

But there was one more thing about Mother's response that was quite unsettling. It wasn't a new revelation of her mother's heart. Yet hearing it now, after discussing Anna's escape from fear, it reinforced the fact that Mother had done more than accept her bondage. She had learned to be comfortable in it, and had gone one step farther and now resented the idea of life without fear.

She didn't want Anna to be free. And if she didn't want Anna to be free, she didn't want her to be free. She hoped it wouldn't come to this. But deep down inside, she was afraid that her quest for freedom would inevitably require her to choose freedom from fear or acceptance from her family. Somehow she knew it could only be one or the other.

"I hope there's more than fear that knits us together, Mother," said Elsie.

"Don't turn your back on your family, Elsie. Don't go the way of that sister of yours."

Click.

Elsie heard it just as she knew her mother intended her to hear it. It was an ultimatum. She pulled the phone from her ear. Her first response was fear. She knew her mother's capacity for unforgiveness. And Nicole would follow Mother unquestioningly. She didn't want to lose her family. Her second response was anger. "I am not living like that. If someone like Anna can do it, I can do it."

*****

Elsie shook her head and brought the car to a slow stop. She glanced in every direction, hardly believing what she was doing. Granny wasn't giving up too much on the phone, and if she pressed her further, she'd only tell Mother. This was the only way.

"Amanda, we're going to play a game, okay? We're going to try to sneak past Grandma's house and go see Granny without anyone seeing us."

Amanda's eyes brightened. "Like hide and seek?"

"Sort of like that, baby. Can we do it? Do you think we can sneak past Grandma's house?" asked Elsie.

Amanda looked out the car window on her right and over the first wooden fence, through the woods and over the fence closest to the house. She looked at the long road that led to the parking area on the side of Grandma's house. "We can't do it. Grandma will see us."

"We can do it, Amanda," said Elsie. "See," she pointed, "if we go through the woods and all the way around the parking lot, we can come up from near the lake."

Elsie and Amanda both wore pants and long-sleeved shirts. But once Elsie stooped and stepped through the space in the fence, she helped Amanda over and carried her through the woods. No sense in gambling with poison ivy or, God forbid, snakes.

Elsie's eyes bounced back and forth from the uneven ground before her to the house. Blinds were open and curtains were pulled back. Mother had not yet developed a penchant for the dark. Elsie thought of that dismal possibility as she checked her footing. *I will not become Granny or Mother,* Elsie told herself.

Finally, Elsie and Amanda reached their exit point at the edge of the woods, about fifty yards from Granny's cottage. Elsie put Amanda down and got on one knee. "Okay, Amanda, this is it. We're almost there. Can we do it?"

"Yes. We can do it," she whispered.

"Okay, you have to be really quiet." She took her by the hand. "Let's go."

They ran to the back of Granny's cottage. Elsie thought about calling Granny. She dismissed it. Granny may call Mother. Of course, Granny may call Mother anyway in response to a surprise knock on the door. They made their way to the front door.

Elsie looked nervously at Mother's deck and back windows. She knocked at Granny's door. Suddenly, she wondered, *What if Mother's here with Granny? Ohhh...*

Thanks to Gary, Granny had gone hi-tech. She looked at the large screen of her thirteen-inch *MacBook Air*. She didn't know the difference in a Mac and a PC. She didn't know the difference in an operating system and an application. Who was *Google*? Was *Explorer* a spaceship? But she knew that she recognized the people she saw on the screen. It was Elsie and Amanda.

Of course, she took an insurance look out the window and another out the peephole. Deadbolt knobs turned. A chain slid. The door's nob turned, and Granny's face looked out the crack.

"Gran—ny!" shrieked Amanda.

"Ssshhh," said Elsie, looking towards Mother's house.

"Come in. Come in. Come in," Granny hurried them.

Elsie pushed Amanda through. Granny closed and secured the fort.

"I didn't know you were coming," said Granny. "Judith didn't tell me."

Amanda looked at Mommy with twinkling eyes.

"It was really spur of the moment, Granny."

It took nearly half an hour for Elsie to steer the conversation to this point. "Granny, it was the worse argument me and Anna have ever had. She seems to be an expert in pushing my buttons." Elsie mentioned nothing about her hitting Anna.

"Anna's an expert button pusher, period. Probably certified by the government," Granny joked.

"Sometimes her speech is so nonsensical that I can hardly follow her," said Elsie.

Granny's head nodded up and down in agreement as Elsie spoke.

"For instance, when we were fighting, she said something about you that..." Elsie blew out a breath of exasperation. "Oh, it's so ridiculous I'm not even going to bother you with it."

Silence.

Granny wasn't biting.

"Sometimes Anna can say things so outlandish that—"

"What did she say?" asked Granny.

Elsie looked at Granny apologetically. "Amanda, why don't you go play with the baby dolls you always play with when you come over here so Granny and I can talk. Okay, sweetie?" She waited for Amanda to get lost in the dolls and then began to talk in a low voice. "You know she believes in demons. She believes we all belong to the devil. Our family I mean. She believes our family belongs to the devil. She told me this. She gave me the exact time, day, and year we all came under the devil's power. She calls it a generational curse."

"Your mother says we're all cursed, too."

"Not like this, Granny. Mother doesn't say we're cursed by the devil. She doesn't believe in a devil. She just calls our condition a curse because…well, she doesn't believe it's demons."

"What she say about me? You said she said something about me?" asked Granny.

"Well, she didn't specifically say you, Granny. I had to deduce from her date that she was implicating you. Now that I think about it, I guess she could've been referring to your mother."

"Elsie, whatever you are trying to say, say it, child. You're exhausting me."

"Anna said she is no longer cursed. Her fears are gone. She says they left when some women at a Bible study she attends cast demons of fear out of her. She said that before the demons left her body, they spoke through her."

Granny perked up. "Spoke through her? Demons? You mean like you and I are talking right here and now?"

"Yes."

"Well, that's about the craziest thing that girl has said. And there is a very long list of crazy things she's said. Is there no way to get her away from those people? She wasn't always like this. I don't understand what can make an educated person go crazy like that?" Granny's eyes blinked quickly in thought.

"One of the things the demons said is they were given some kind of ownership of the girls on your side of the family at 10:53 a.m. on a Tuesday morning in 1917." Elsie's next words were interrupted and stopped by Granny's expression. Her face looked as though it had just received a low-level surge of electricity.

Granny's face lowered slowly before lifting again.

"Granny?" said Elsie.

"No one...knows that," Granny spoke slowly. "No one."

"No one knows what, Granny?"

"No one knows." Granny shook her head. "I never told anyone about what Momma told me."

Elsie looked intently at Granny, hungry for her to fill in the blanks. Something had obviously happened on that date. Then she recoiled at the thought that she had gotten this date from Anna. Granny's voice rescued her from her musings—but not for long.

"Momma told me that something bad happened to her on that day. It was easy to remember because it was the day after New Year's Day. She heard her parents talking about her father having to go off to the war. She says she got so scared that Papa was going to be killed that she fainted. She said when she awakened, something was standing over her. Some kind of monster. It said, 'You are mine.'"

Elsie watched Granny's eyes grow in fear.

"She said the monster jumped inside of her body. How does a little girl forget a story like that?" Granny looked at Elsie questioningly. "Now how do you suppose Anna found out about this? I—have—never—told anyone—about what Momma told me. I have too much respect for Momma to do that."

Elsie felt as though someone had snatched the rug from under her feet, causing her to fall hard on the back of her head. She was senseless. *How would Anna know of this? How could Anna's talking demons pick a date out of thin air with such significance? This can't be true. We're missing something,"* she thought. "I don't know," Elsie answered tentatively. "How could she have guessed

10:53 a.m.? Was it 10:53 a.m.?" She sounded like she hoped the time was wrong.

Granny was surprised that such an intelligent woman could ask such a dumb question. "Elsie, what difference does it make whether she said 10:53 a.m. or 10:53 p.m. or 5:30 or 12:30? She said Tuesday, didn't she?"

Elsie didn't want to answer. She needed time to figure this out rationally. "Yes."

"She said 1917, didn't she?"

Reluctantly, Elsie said, "Yes."

"Maybe this bunch of kooks she's fallen into are into some kind of psychic something or another," said Granny. "Reading minds. Who knows what they're into? Somebody told her about Momma."

Elsie sat up with renewed hope. Now this was a possibility. Psychic phenomenon. Extra sensory perception. She had read articles and stories here and there about this stuff. It was as hocus pocus as Anna's Bible and her demons. But even though ESP was unscientific now, it didn't mean it wouldn't be scientific tomorrow.

The microscope hadn't invented germs; it discovered them. It made them discoverable, seeable. Could there not be a day when some scientist would discover a way to prove that the brain had a way of manipulating energy outside of its own body? Elsie thought of microwaves, gravity, magnetic fields, radio and television signals, and how they affected things that came into contact with them.

She thought of the human body and how it generated electricity. She thought of how the body was comprised of atoms, and how those atoms were comprised of protons, neutrons, and electrons. She thought of how every action of the body was because an electronic signal was properly relayed from one part to another. It wasn't farfetched to contemplate that there could be something out there that enabled the manipulation of the body's electricity in such a way that it allowed a connection among brains. Would that not in fact resemble ESP?

Wait a minute. Wait a minute. Oh, my God! Listen to yourself, Elsie. You are becoming Anna. You are letting Anna drive you crazy.

"Granny, I'm sorry for bringing up Anna. There's a reason she's not welcome here," she whispered. "I don't need to sit her in your living room through conversation. It was wonderful seeing you, Granny." She turned to Amanda, who was looking intently at a three-foot doll and giving her instructions on brushing her teeth. She was about to call her.

"Did she say anything else?" asked Granny. "Any other dates?"

Elsie looked at Granny and felt like a bank robber whose masked just slipped off at the teller's window.

"I see that she did," said Granny. "What is it?"

It had honestly slipped Elsie's mind, but now that Granny reminded her, she didn't want to offer anything that may add the slightest credence to her sister's story. Even if it would later be proven to be something other than what her sister purported it to be.

She could lie. That way she could guarantee that Anna's interview with the devil would sound as foolish as it was. But why lie? There was no need, really. Anna had given her a date with a preposterous narrative. Yes, let's let Granny hear it all.

"Actually, she did, Granny. I had forgotten about it."

Granny looked sober. "Let's hear it."

"Remember, this is Anna we're talking about, Granny." Granny said nothing. "She said another demon bragged that he took her music on June 25th, 1966." Elsie added to emphasize how ridiculous this was by saying, "She wasn't even born yet."

Granny clutched her chest and gasped. Her face lost its color. She looked one way, then the other, as though she were looking for a place to run and hide.

"Granny!" Elsie yelled, but not loud enough for Amanda to hear.

"Get me some water," pleaded Granny. "I need some water."

Elsie hurried with the water.

Granny took a couple of big gulps. She handed the glass to Elsie and doubled over into her lap and cried heavily. Elsie didn't know anything else to do but hug her grandmother. Anna, had done it again.

"Is Granny crying?" Amanda asked.

Elsie smiled dutifully at Amanda as she rubbed Granny's back. "Granny's okay, baby. Go on and finish teaching Sarah how to cook lasagna."

After a long time of Granny crying into her lap, she raised up halfway. Her elbows rested on her legs as she spoke. "It was Saturday night. I was supposed to sing at a church the next morning. I had a beautiful voice, and I played piano and guitar. I guess you could've called me a hippie back then. I got saved in the Jesus Movement."

Saved in the Jesus Movement? Elsie could've lost consciousness right then. Granny was even more of an atheist than her and Mother. What did she mean, saved in the Jesus Movement?

Granny continued. "I was upstairs playing the guitar and singing worship songs to the Lord."

Worship songs…to the Lord? thought Elsie.

"It was just me. Nobody else was there. I thought I heard something like breaking glass downstairs. I stopped and listened, but didn't hear anything, so I kept playing and singing. I stopped playing and turned on the cassette player so I could keep the worship going. I got into the shower. I thought I heard someone singing with the cassette. Someone was.

"I wrapped a towel around me and went into the bedroom. An inebriated man in nothing but his shorts was on my bed. He had the longest knife I had ever seen in my life. He motioned me to sit on the bed. I did." Granny paused and swallowed with much difficulty. "He made me sing songs with him. Worship songs. Then he saw the guitar. Elsie, he made me play and sing worship songs. When he got tired of me playing," Granny looked at Elsie with eyes that could get no sadder, "he raped me. He made me sing songs about Jesus while he raped me."

Elsie's mouth dropped open in horror. Granny's confession had run over her like a truck. She instinctively looked at Amanda, contemplating the evil of the world. Painfully, she looked again into Granny's now dead eyes. "I'm sorry, Granny." This was all she could think to say.

"There is no God, Elsie. The God I loved didn't love me. Do you know why? It's because you have to exist to love someone. For there to be a God who loves us, there has to first be a God. And there is no way the God I loved would have allowed such a thing."

Elsie's lips trembled in sympathy for Granny, but hatred for God.

"Elsie, there is no God, but there is a devil, and I met him on June 25th in 1966. The man who broke into my home and raped me is the devil who stole my music."

Elsie left with a heavy heart and a new understanding of Granny's fear of music. Of course, Granny feared music. Every time she heard it, her brain linked it with a brutal and terrifying sexual assault. And in a way Elsie couldn't deeply understand—since she had never believed in God—she figured that Granny's brain linked music and singing with heartrending abandonment by God, and with a moral upheaval that left her philosophically bankrupt. But even more immediately traumatic was it put Granny back in her bedroom with a drunk rapist.

But what about her and Mother and Nicole? Maybe Mother knew about this, but Nicole didn't, and neither did she. So she was certain that she and Nicole weren't influenced by the story to take on its fears. What about genetics? Maybe the fear was physically passed down to them. *Wait,* she thought. *And lie dormant until exactly our thirty-sixth birthdays? And what about Mother? If the trauma caused something to happen genetically in Granny, why is it also in Mother? She was born before the trauma occurred.*

Elsie was befuddled at the Mother question, but she was angry at the elephant in the room. "Oh, Anna!" she said, lightly pounding the steering wheel as she prepared to make her and Amanda's clean getaway. *How did you find out about Granny's rape? Demons didn't tell you. So how did you find out?*

Chapter 12

Fear of Failure knew the meeting wouldn't be good. How could any meeting three stories below ground in a room known more for its murder of demons than its so-called conversations be anything but bad? But he had a stellar record; so he didn't think it would be terminally bad.

The two large demons posted outside the door did nothing to increase his confidence. One rapped on the door before opening it wide and looking disdainfully at Fear of Failure. Fear of Failure stepped into the door's entrance. He looked inside and doubted that he would live beyond this meeting.

Terror sat on a large chair that resembled a throne. It was on a raised platform. Fear of Failure looked up into his menacing eyes. To the right of Terror, but not on the platform, a large demon with his hands clasped behind his back paced back and forth. He looked intently and ominously at Fear of Failure as he paced.

The demon who had opened the door landed a heavy fist to the back of Fear of Failure's head. Fear of Failure awakened on his knees before the little throne. His hands were tied together and tied to his bound ankles. He didn't look behind him. He didn't need to. He knew the two door demons were right behind him. Under different circumstances, Fear of Failure would've been complimented that a demon of Terror's stature had so obviously recognized his capacity for fierce combat.

"Fear of Failure, you have a marvelous record," said Terror. "You've destroyed many dreams. You've thwarted the enemy's plans a thousand times by getting his sons and daughters to follow the path of fear instead of faith." Terror's eyes widened and glared. "It is only because of your enviable record that you are being treated so kindly here today."

My head. Did that beast crush my skull? he groggily wondered. But he wasn't so groggy that he'd provoke an unnecessary beating. "I am grateful for your kindness, my lord."

"Good. This meeting's conclusion has not yet been determined," said Terror. "Fear of Failure, my friend, Unreal, has concerns. I also have concerns. His concerns are that something's going wrong with Elsie. Something that is complicating his arrival. Something that is keeping him from sitting on the throne of her mind.

"Now my concerns are linked to his concerns. Unreal is looking for a place to rest. Somewhere he can express himself." Terror's expression darkened. "I am not looking for anything as grand as this. I just want a promotion!" he shouted.

"I am a great power," growled Unreal at Fear of Failure. "A great power should not be reduced to hanging around a house like a broke wino hanging around a liquor store. Elsie is mine! I should be *in—side* of her...like Phobia is inside of her mother." Unreal unclasped his hands from behind his back and stopped pacing. He pointed a long-clawed finger at the bowed demon and stepped closer to him. "Your incompetence is threatening—"

"Unreal," Terror cautioned. This was his demon. If any beating would be done, it would be at his command.

Unreal lowered his finger, but not his glare. He commenced to a slow pace.

"Unreal tells me something unusual happened today." Terror's eyes narrowed. "Something at Granny's?"

Fear of Failure looked accusingly into Unreal's weird eyes.

"Who's your lord?" yelled Terror.

"You are," Fear of Failure answered submissively.

"Then—look—at—me!" Terror demanded. Terror glanced at the fear spirit who stood against the far right wall before glaring again at Fear of Failure. "Unreal tells me that he followed Elsie until she parked near her mother's home. He says he then followed her as she crept through the woods."

Fear of Failure waited for Terror to finish. But he didn't finish. He just glared at him. Was he waiting for him to say something? "Is this why I am here? Because Elsie went into the woods?" He had to mask his irritation.

"No, Fear of Failure. It's not because Elsie went into the woods," Terror answered derisively. "It's because of what she did when she came out of the woods."

The bound demon's eyes narrowed in thought. Why would they be so upset about Elsie running around in the woods? Sure, it was peculiar for her to drive way over there only to walk around in the woods with her child and then return home. But wasn't that the object? To drive her nuts?

"My lord, when she came out of the woods, she went directly home," said Fear of Failure.

"When she came out of the woods, you idiot," said Unreal, "she went to Granny's house."

"I was with her," snapped Fear of Failure. "All of us were with her. We know where she went. She went to the woods. She returned to her car. She went home." Fear of Failure knew he was being disrespectful to a demon who, if he lived past this meeting, would become his immediate boss. But what choice did he have?

Unreal stepped toward the insubordinate demon. "I saw her, too. As did *my* demons. My home arrived at the woods with her dog of a child. We saw the wretched heifer take off out of the woods towards Granny's. Halfway there she and the child disappeared. Now why do you think that happened?"

Fear of Failure's eyes went large with fright.

Terror interrupted the beginning of his panicky thoughts. "I checked with the strongholds in Judith and Granny. They both had already reported that for seventy-three minutes Granny was nowhere to be found." Terror's neck stretched forward. "How does a stronghold inside of Granny lose contact with her for seventy-three minutes?"

Fear of Failure's eyes got even larger. The unspoken implication was bursting everyone's ear drums.

"You assured me that no one was praying for Elsie. That all was well. That her husband was leaving her. Now Elsie disappears, and Granny somehow ditches her stronghold for seventy-three minutes!"

"My lord—" began Fear of Failure.

"Shut up! Now I also find that after you assured me everything was going well that her abominable Christ-loving sister has started praying for her. You assured me that her self-righteousness and impatience had nullified her as a threat. But a spirit of anger has reported otherwise."

Fear of Failure was astonished at this calamitous revelation.

"Oh, save it, Fear of Failure," spat Terror. "Your report included—you even underlined it—that Elsie slapped Anna." The angry demon's voice dropped and came through gritted teeth. "But it conveniently left out these hideous words spoken from the mouth of a traitor. 'Lord, she can run from me, but she can't run from You. Chase her down, Lord. Don't let my sister go to hell.'"

Unreal glared at Fear of Failure.

The bound demon couldn't see them, but the two demons behind him glared at him.

The fear spirit standing next to the wall glared at him.

Terror turned his glare from him and stared at the floor. How often did a position like Director of the Fear Academy come open? He saw it slipping through his claws. He looked up in a glare. "Chase—her—down—Lord. Don't let my sister go to hell. Barely more than ten words, demon, and yet enough to attract the enemy's interference."

"My lord," pled Fear of Failure, "let me make this right. I'll recruit lying, seducing spirits to help me. Give me another chance. Oh, for the love of darkness, Terror! I am Fear of Failure! I have destroyed many."

Terror looked at the pleading demon with an upturned lip. He turned to Unreal. "Unreal? How should we conclude this case?"

Fear of Failure heard the demons behind him move closer. He looked at Unreal. "I am Fear of Failure. I will raise an army of lying spirits to help me. I will give you a home!"

Unreal deliberated the options. "Perhaps a good beating will suffice."

A good beating? What was a good beating? Fear of Failure gulped. It had to be better than a good death. He looked in dark hope at Terror.

"Perhaps," he said, as he looked sternly at the demon who could derail his promotion ambitions. "Perhaps not." He looked at him for several seconds. "Again, your stellar record has come to your rescue. "Beat him to within a breath of his life. I'm sure that he will not abuse my kindness again."

Immediately, the two guards began to savagely execute Terror's kindness on the bound demon.

Terror and Unreal walked around the beating and exited the room together.

"You will have your promotion," said Unreal.

"And you shall have your home," said Terror.

*****

Elsie looked guiltily around the Starbucks. She knew *Abuser* was written over her forehead. How had she allowed herself to get so angry as to strike another human being? And her own sister? It was inexplicable that she could behave this way. Elsie thought fearfully, *What else am I capable of?* The moment Elsie thought this, she overheard the loud voice of one of two men conversing at the next small table.

"John, that's just it. You're not as good as you think you are. That's why we need Jesus. The Bible says, 'The heart is deceitful above all things, and desperately wicked. Who can know it?' You did what you did not because you're basically good and had a bad moment. You did what you did because you're basically evil. Your heart is wicked beyond natural repair. John, you did what you are."

A Christian.

Elsie's nose instinctively turned up. One couldn't go anywhere without having to hear one of them trying to guilt someone into their religion. She got up and found another seat. She could still hear him. Who was he talking to? The guy was only two feet away from him. He was probably trying to evangelize them all on the sly. She got up and looked coldly in the not-too-subtle evangelist's direction before going out a door to sit at one of the outside tables.

"Well, hello Elsie," an old voice from behind creaked at her.

Elsie turned. It was that woman.

The old woman stood and went to Elsie's table and sat across from her. "What a coincidence. As large as Atlanta is I run into you in Inman Park and now in Roswell."

Elsie's face registered uncomfortable surprise. She did smile, however, before saying, "Yes. What a coincidence."

"Where's Amanda?"

Elsie was impressed that she remembered Amanda's name. She certainly couldn't remember this woman's name. "With my sister. She's spending a few days with her."

The old woman tapped Elsie's hand as she said, "While you sort out some things."

Elsie looked at her.

The old woman smiled. "What else could tear you away from that beautiful little girl? I saw how you looked at her."

Actually, there are a million other things besides sorting out some things, thought Elsie. "She wanted to spend some time with her cousins, and my sister wanted to spend some time with Amanda, so..."

"You look troubled."

"A make-up free face," offered Elsie.

"No. Not make-up. I've been all over the world. You have one of the most naturally beautiful faces I've ever seen." The woman looked into Elsie's eyes until Elsie remembered how she was overcome with fear the last time she spoke with this woman. The woman continued. "Looks more like you're wrestling with the fact that you're facing something you can't handle. Whatever it is, the Lord can help you. He's a very present help in the time of need."

Elsie studied this woman. First, the obnoxious Christian inside. Now this intrusive woman outside. Where would she have to go to get away from this rubbish? The roof? Probably one up there, too. "I don't mean to offend your beliefs, but I don't—"Elsie didn't want to get into this—"I'm a pretty resourceful woman." Elsie looked around for Anna. Where was she?

A pained look took over the woman's face. "Oh darling, you were going to say that you don't believe in God."

The spirit of anger erupted in a flame. This was the same demon who had attached himself to Elsie the night she slapped Anna. The demon's anger that evening had been purely opportunistic. You run across someone letting their anger rise, make it rise higher, hopefully to the *What have I done?* point. That point where the dupe let his anger cause him to do something really dumb.

Today, however, he inflamed himself for a strategic purpose. It was an old trick, but extremely effective. One that anger, pride, and religious demons used in concert all the time. Shut down the power of truth by inflaming yourself within the person hearing it. They'd get so caught up in anger that they'd be unable to think rationally. *Rule by emotion.* Worked nearly one hundred percent of the time.

And if the person was as prideful as Elsie…

This thought brought a smile of confidence to his face.

"I was going to say that, but I thought better of it." Elsie's face was tight as she spoke. "Some things are better left not said." Elsie pushed her chair back, preparing to leave.

"Some things are better left not believed," said the old woman. "Only a fool would believe there is no God."

Elsie stood and looked at this woman who had just called her a fool. Her words were harsh, but her tone and demeanor were not. Surprisingly, she didn't come across like the obnoxious loudmouth

Christian man inside. But she certainly did take liberties not given her. "Good af—"

"And, Elsie, only a fool who is afraid of the truth would run off as you are doing now. How long are you going to run? Where can you go to escape the truth? You can't outrun the curse."

The curse.

Elsie's jaw tightened in an odd look at the woman. "Why did you say that? What curse?"

The old woman's eyes and voice were kind. "What curse do you have?"

Elsie stiffened. "No. Why did you say that? Use that word? Curse? Why did you bring up a curse?" Elsie's eyes searched the parking lot for the answer.

"What you need is not in the parking lot, Elsie. There's no cure for the curse in the parking lot."

Elsie's hot eyes scanned the parking lot. She sat down and looked across the table at her mystery Christian interrogator. The woman had at least ten years on Granny. So she knew she wouldn't speak to her in the tone of voice her anger demanded. But old or not, she was tired of ignorant Christians harassing her. "Okay, you win. If we're going to talk about curses, and I assume my personal business as well, may I at least have your name?"

The woman smiled. "Of course, Elsie. Malak."

"Okay, Miss Malak, how's my sister, Anna?"

The old woman's face took its time forming a smile. "You're a keen woman, Elsie."

Elsie bobbed her head with a sly smile. "I knew it." She had asked Anna to meet her so she could apologize in person and Anna had turned it into another evangelism event. Elsie stood up and looked around the parking lot. She wanted Miss Evangelist to see that she wasn't as smart as she thought she was. *You're busted, Anna!* she thought triumphantly.

Elsie sat down and looked at Anna's partner. "Is Anna going to join us?"

"I don't know."

"Then why are we here? What's this about?" asked Elsie.

"You have questions. God has answers."

Oh, go ahead, Elsie. "And you're going to speak for God?"

"I'll do my best."

Elsie didn't know how much Anna had told this woman. She thought of where to begin her own interrogation. She looked again at this woman's advanced age. Was it possible? That would explain how Anna found out about the rape? "Do you know Granny?"

"Is this your grandmother?"

She didn't answer. "Yes. What do you know about Granny?"

"Anna has told me nothing about Granny," the old woman answered.

"Did Anna tell you about the family's curse?" Elsie's tone was almost flippant.

"You don't believe in curses."

"No. I don't. This is the twenty-first century. I believe in reality, not superstition." Elsie was doing fine with her anger. Actually, since pulling the curtain back on her sister's Starbuck's theater, the anger had been replaced with cynical amusement. Anna wasn't here, but her representative was. She'd be polite. But she'd let her have it.

"What kind of reality?" the old woman asked.

"The kind that passes the test of scientific investigation. Empirical evidence. The kind of evidence that is foreign to Christianity and its myths and ungrounded suppositions."

The old woman took a deep breath and looked at Elsie with a softness that Elsie felt. "Does your fear pass this test? Have you explained it to your satisfaction?"

The woman's words breached her calm. Setting her up to be witnessed to was one thing. Sharing embarrassing family secrets was something else. Was there no boundary Anna wouldn't cross?

"Don't be angry at Anna. She only wants you to experience the freedom she has found in Christ. Don't you want to be free?" the woman asked.

"You mean don't I want to be a Christian?" said Elsie.

"There is no other way to be free—truly free, except in Christ," said the woman. "Why do you resist your own salvation?"

Elsie's voice was hard. "Miss Malak, there is no God. No salvation. Therefore, no need for salvation."

The old woman's face still held a smile, but now it was mixed with a resoluteness that wasn't there before. "You despise Anna's belief in Christ. Yet Anna is free from the fear that is destroying your life. You ridicule her faith in God, but demons haven't stolen her music."

Elsie jerked slightly at this.

The old woman continued like a prosecuting attorney. "You mock her devotion to the Lord, but through the power of the Lord God Almighty she is now a CPA, and you with all of your answers to questions you do not understand have never recovered from dropping out of your residency. The Creator created you to know Him, to love Him, and to serve His people by mending their spines and brains, but your heart is full of pride, and your neck is stiff with rebellion. You would rather wallow in fear than walk in faith."

Elsie was shocked not only by what the woman said, and that she would speak so presumptuously, but that she spoke so forcefully. Her old body didn't seem capable of such a delivery. "That—was—cruel." Elsie's eyes watered with anger as she spoke. "You don't know what it's like to live with this—"

"Curse," the old woman interjected.

"Whatever it is! Call it whatever you want!" Elsie yelled, then lowered her voice, looking around at those who were looking at her yell at a woman who was presumably her grandmother. She struggled through emotion to speak, and to speak softly. "You don't know what it's like to live like this, with this fear. You don't know what it's like to pursue something nearly all your life and to get so close to it...." Elsie put her hand to her face and let the tears flow. There wasn't much she could do to stop them anyway. She pulled her hand away. "To get so close to it and drop out." Elsie's eyes were blank. "Just...drop...out. Because of a strange fear."

The old woman's eyes grew vibrant. She placed her hand atop one of Elsie's hands. "Elsie, what are you going to do about it?

Are you tired of living like this? Anna doesn't have this fear any more. She's free. Jesus set her free."

Elsie's eyes changed, also. They seemed as though they had just looked through a fog and focused on something previously hidden. "Were you there when my sister was healed? At the Bible study?"

"Yes. I was there."

"Is it true? Did voices come out of my sister?"

"Yes."

"You heard them?" asked Elsie.

"Yes. I heard them."

"You heard the voices speak of a claim they supposedly have on our family? And the dates? The dates the voices supposedly entered? And...Granny?" Elsie was talking to the old woman, but her eyes went blank again.

"I heard everything, Elsie. It's all true. Anna isn't making this up. Spirits of fear entered your family line in 1917. Your great grandmother was only six years old when it happened. Little children don't have the same defenses as adults. You went to medical school. You know that children's immune systems aren't the same as adults. It's the same in the spiritual dimension. The Bible shows vivid examples of children attacked by demons. If it can happen in the Bible, isn't it reasonable to assume it can happen outside of the Bible?

"When Lily overheard her parents talk about him going off to war, she got scared. She got really scared, Elsie. That's when it happened. Fear saw an open door and entered her."

Elsie looked sharply into the old woman's eyes. "My great grandmother's name wasn't Lily. It was Lucille."

The old woman looked dismayed. "What difference does it make, Elsie? God has given you enough evidence to choose life."

"I don't know what happened to Anna at the Bible study that triggered the action that caused her brain to self-correct the fear, but I'm going to find out. I'm going to find out, and I'm going to replicate it, Miss Malak. And I'm going to do this without becoming a Christian."

The old woman let out a long, tired sigh. She pushed herself from the table and stood up. A tear rolled down a cheek. "I can't give you more, but I can share this with you. Your brain is your own worst enemy. If you used it as much as you think you're using it, you would serve the Lord. You're being dishonest with yourself because you don't want to admit you're wrong." The old woman's eyes went resolute again. "The Lord puts before you now blessing and cursing. What do you choose? Heaven and hell awaits your answer."

Elsie's answer was immediate, crisp, and equally as resolute as the old woman's theater. "I'm going my own way."

The old woman looked around in every direction. She'd stop and fix her eyes in the direction of something as though beholding a car wreck. Her head would then snap in another direction to intently watch another non-event. She then looked into the sky and did the same thing, focusing on something before whipping around to look at another…what? Cloud?

Elsie watched this odd behavior. It wasn't the first time she'd seen something like this. Anna was always seeing and hearing things that weren't there.

"They're coming for you," said the old woman as she walked past Elsie.

Elsie looked out into the parking lot for Anna. "Who's coming for me?"

"Those whom you have called," said the old woman.

Chapter 13

Elsie didn't bother to watch Anna's brash, old co-conspirator as she walked away. The important thing was not what car she got into, but that she was walking away. *Away* being the key word.

Elsie may have no longer been in the neurosurgery residency program, but she was still brilliant. She focused that brilliant mind on the facts and her course of action as she now sat alone.

Fact. A strange fear had all but destroyed her and the females in her extended family.

Fact. She and the family had futilely tried everything medical and psychological to stop the fear.

Fact. The fear was getting worse in her.

Fact. The fear had left Anna.

Fact. Anna attributed her freedom to having so-called demons of fear cast out of her.

Fact. Anna disclosed dates about Granny and Granny's parents that were coincidentally significant.

The next fact was the only one that until now caused her to get angry.

Fact. Amanda's seven-day-a-week nightmares coincidentally stopped immediately after she went through her casting out demons routine with her.

Fact. Unless Anna was lying, Chrissie's nightmares had stopped after another of Anna's exorcisms.

It was the next three facts that muddied the waters and complicated Elsie's course of action.

Fact. There was no God.

Fact. There were no demons.

Fact. The Bible was the figment of someone's creative, manipulative imagination and filled with religious bigotry, silly superstitions, ridiculous miracles, and unscientific statements.

Reconciling Anna's freedom—Elsie reluctantly included Amanda and Chrissie in this line of reasoning—with Anna's worldview and demons was the problem. *Too bad there's not some authoritative, universal Go To life manual to answer these kinds of questions,* thought Elsie. *I'll just have to figure this out myself.*

Elsie didn't like her plan, but it was the only one that made sense. Sci-fi or not, there was no time to waste.

*****

They came from every direction. Some emerged from the ground around the coffee shop. Some simply appeared in the near horizon and walked menacingly toward their prey. Others shrieked as they descended from the sky. They had all heard the call of her rebellion.

From a distance, a distance imposed upon the self-proclaimed great demon, Unreal watched impatiently. How long would he have to loiter? He was no bum. He stood with his hands on his thick waist and watched Fear of Failure directing his forces. He watched him limp and hold his side as he walked with a bent over posture. The beating on Fear of Failure had left its evidence.

"How long before my home is ready?" bellowed Unreal.

"It won't be long now, my lord," answered the hurting demon. "Elsie is preparing to help us."

*****

Elsie saw the sudden shadow and felt the bird land on her left shoulder at the same time she heard its terrible shriek directly in her ear. She ducked, jumping up and slashing at the dark bird with her hand. Her table went flying and landed near another table and almost onto the lady's dog.

The large dog jumped up and ran against its leash, pulling the table it was tied to. A drink toppled onto the owner's lap. She jumped up partly because of the iced coffee that now iced her dress and thighs and partly because of the woman who had jumped up and was now flailing away at something only she could see.

Elsie stopped slashing at the bird. The bird that was there, but not there. It was a bird, wasn't it? Of course, it was. She hadn't seen it clearly. But she definitely felt it and heard it. Where had it gone? She looked around at several people who looked at her as though she were crazy. One lady physically turned her curious child's gaze away from her. That one cut her deeply. She had done that herself when Amanda's eyes locked on a homeless man who was having an animated conversation with himself. Now people were looking at her as though she were that man.

She quickly walked away and found her car. She stepped inside and closed the door and burst into tears over the steering wheel. "What's happening to me?" she cried.

"You're going crazy," said Fear of Insanity, who was seated next to her. "What else could it be?"

Elsie shook her head. "No. No. I'm not going crazy. I'll find a way. The answer is within me."

"The only thing that's within you, Elsie, is fear, and it's going to get worse. It's going to get so bad that Daniel's going to leave you and take Amanda." This was Fear of Abandonment.

Elsie shook her head more vigorously at this cruel thought. "Daniel wouldn't leave me. He loves me."

"He thinks that Amanda will get your fear by being around you. He has to leave you to protect Amanda. Makes sense, doesn't it?" Fear of Abandonment was relentless.

Elsie started the car. "I'm not crazy!" she shouted at the thoughts.

"Where is she going?" yelled Unreal from fifty feet away.

Fear of Failure's back was killing him. He bent over and yelled, "From bad to worse, my lord."

*****

The house never seemed as big as it did this moment. Maybe it was because of the persistent thoughts that said Daniel would take Amanda and leave her alone. Or maybe it was because she was already alone. Not physically. Something far worse. She was psychologically alone.

She knew only four people in the world who understood and knew the remote and harsh psychological island on which she lived. Granny. Mother. Nicole. Anna. Thinking of each name only made the island worse.

Fact.

Her mind switched back to its fact-finding mode.

Fact. Anna was the only one of the four who was not an atheist.

Elsie's lips turned up at the absurd implication and dropped the thought entirely. She went to the kitchen, got a bottle of water, and said, "Let's get this show on the road."

Fear of Failure echoed the command to his team. "You heard the lady. Let's get this show on the road."

Elsie spent hours on the Internet reading articles about parapsychology. Most of what she read confirmed what she knew to be true. Parapsychology was considered a pseudoscience for good reasons. The most basic of which was there was virtually no scientific evidence to support what amounted to suppositions and anecdotes. Better known as guesses and stories.

Another good reason for discounting this field as pseudoscience—and attaching *science* to the pseudo was a huge and undeserved and misleading compliment—was its undertones of accepting as fact the existence of a spiritual dimension.

She would of necessity navigate around that foolishness to explore other aspects that may contain a thread of something useful. Something that would help her understand how a novel method—something similar to Anna's practices—could manipulate the brain's energy in such a way that it produced the self-correcting effect that happened for Anna.

Elsie skipped the articles on reincarnation and séances and crystal balls and mediums. No research necessary. Anything she needed to know about this, she could find by looking at the movie *Ghost* again. But she didn't skip articles on telekinesis, mental telepathy, clairvoyance, and automatic writing.

She also surprised herself when she concluded, even if tentatively, that things she had scoffed at, things like dreams and near death experiences (NDEs) may provide her research some practical value. There was also something called astral projection.

Elsie made herself take off her skeptic's hat and put on her research hat. It was important for her to not allow her biases to impede her ability to examine these practices and see through a scientist's eyes whether or not there was something there that could possibly cause the brain to self-correct itself.

To help her research, Elsie hypothesized possible links between the psychic phenomenon practices and the human body's electrical energy. The basic premise was the scientific fact that every physical object was made of atoms.

Telekinesis was the act of influencing a physical system with nothing but mind power. What if the brain's atoms could be made to influence the atoms of other objects? Would that not physically affect that object?

Mental telepathy was the ability to mentally see an object with nothing but the mind. What if there are sending and receiving mechanisms of the brain outside of the five senses? A system that works like television? Would that not allow a person to send or receive messages with mind power alone?

Clairvoyance was the ability to know things without receiving the information through the five senses, especially of future events. *What if the brain's extrasensory ability somehow captured stray currents of energy, like a telephone receiver picking up a stray conversation? And what if it somehow had a way of picking up future transmissions now? Would that not allow a person to know present and future things without the use of the five senses?*

On and on Elsie went with these reasonings. Her brilliance and determination to not believe Anna's Christian worldview brought her to a new level of creativity.

At first glance, astral projection seemed preposterous. Then Elsie let her mind contemplate the possibilities. Astral projection was purportedly the ability to travel outside of one's physical body. The assumption, of course, was that there was such a thing as a non-physical body. A so-called astral body.

As Elsie fully expected, there wasn't a shred of evidence of any such astral body or astral projection. But this was not the time for being satisfied at snickering at the ignorance of the gullible. Her situation required her to contemplate possibilities. To connect dubious dots that may help her replicate Anna's self-correcting action in the brain without sacrificing her mind to Christian bigotry and nonsense.

So what if astral projection was really nothing more (although scientifically fantastic) than the brain projecting its energy? What about the theory that human cells have the capacity to hold memories? If this were true, could the brain's ability to project its energy join with its telepathic and clairvoyant abilities to create astral projection?

Elsie looked at the large computer screen and let out a heavy breath of relief. She hadn't expected to find science at the circus, and she had not. But she had found more than clowns and elephant droppings. She had found actionable possibilities. Something that had taken her off of defense and had put her on offense. She pushed the rolling desk chair away from the desk and closer to the demons looking over her shoulders and smiled.

They smiled, too.

*****

The demon standing behind Elsie, and the one wearing the widest smile, was of the seduction class. He specialized in creating some of the most powerful and nearly impregnable strongholds. These were strongholds of false beliefs and false doctrines.

His job here today was not merely to assist Fear of Failure secure a home for Unreal. It was to use this as an occasion to instruct less experienced seduction demons. The Academy of Seduction had sent over five apprentices.

Smooth was several inches taller than the average demon in his class. This was due to his evil accomplishments. Something referred to in the dark kingdom as growth in evil.

There were other much larger seduction spirits. Those who had graduated from deceiving sole individuals through stand-alone deceptions to deceiving multitudes through deceptions that were protected by layers of supporting lies. These varied deceptions were organized into doctrines. The most powerful of which included truths twisted or slanted to support the lies.

Smooth had never achieved this kind of success, but his resume was enviable, and his swagger and confidence matched it. He looked at Fear of Failure, who was standing behind the seduction spirits with divided attention, trading glances with him and Unreal across the street.

"What is this that we are witnessing?" He was only asking rhetorically. Thus, he cut off the demon who had begun to answer. "It is nothing new," he said in a deep, alluring whisper. "It is not a deep, dark secret. Rather, it is a routine spiritual law that you will learn to depend upon to gain increasing mastery over your targets."

"He's so smooth," said one demon to another.

"I could listen to him forever," said another.

"What is it, you ask?" said Smooth. "The enemy's own cursed book shows us how it works." The fact that the demons broke out into hush murmurings over this statement was proof of their inexperience, and he assumed their famished resumes. "Listen to me. This will take you far."

The apprentice demons looked intently at their instructor.

"Human nature is capable of believing anything," he said. "Don't lose time worrying about opposing facts. Instead, find out what lie your target desires to believe, then provide your facts."

Questions were on the faces of the student demons.

"*Your* facts," said Smooth. "If you are successful at finding out what lie your target desires to believe, you can supply them with lies to support their lie. You see this in human nature all the time. A woman is courted by a man. She clearly sees signs that he is not good for her." He smiled. "Does she stop seeing him? No. She adjusts what she sees by what she wants to see."

"She deceives herself?" asked a demon.

"Yes. She deceives herself," Smooth answered. "But it gets better. At some point in this dark process, if the target persists in willful ignorance, they can cross the line into divine discipline or even judgment from the enemy."

"What is taking so long?" yelled Unreal.

Smooth rolled his eyes. "Nothing like a bullhorn in a library," he said quietly to his adoring crowd.

They snickered with bouncing shoulders, snatching furtive glances at the homeless demon.

"You don't want to be like him," said Smooth. "He has a big mouth. It's why he's homeless now. Successful seducing spirits don't shout; they whisper."

"Hey," said one of the apprentices, "maybe we ought to make a sign for him that says *I will shout for a house.*"

"Didn't they make a detergent about him? *Shout?* How'd that commercial go? Shout it out?" said a demon.

"And we know it works," said another. "He shouted, and he's out."

More laughter and bouncing shoulders.

"Okay," said Smooth in his whispery voice, "enough about old wiggly eyes over there. Let's get back on topic. The sons and daughters of Adam can see what is *not* there, and they can *not* see what is clearly there. Eve believed our lord, Satan, even though she had no rational reason for doing so—and she hadn't even fallen yet. So think, if a perfect human can deceive herself, what are the possibilities of getting imperfect humans to deceive themselves?"

"Hey," said the demon with the Shout joke, "that's what happened to us, isn't it? We believed lord Satan's lie that we could make God resign. Look what happened to us."

Smooth, the apprentice demons, and Fear of Failure looked stonily at the talkative demon.

"What? I didn't mean—"

"You talk...too much," said Smooth in a slow, angry whisper. "Successful seducing spirits are masters of their mouths. We know what to say and what not to say. We know when to speak and when to shut up." His peering gaze emphasized those last words.

But the hapless demon didn't shut up. He looked around at the seven angry faces and offered feebly, "It's the truth. Look at us."

"What is your name, spirit?" Smooth demanded.

"Loquacious. My name's Loquacious."

Smooth was shocked. Then he was angry. Had the academy's entrance criteria dropped this low? How in the darkness did a loquacious spirit get into seduction school? "No wonder you can't control your mouth. Take your jokes and get out of here. I'll see to it that you're dismissed from the academy."

They all watched the talkative demon walk away mumbling something under his bad breath. After a minute of glaring at the banished demon, a demon asked, "You said there are places in the cursed book that talk about sons and daughters of Adam crossing a line of deception."

Smooth turned slowly from the direction of the big-mouthed demon. "The best example is the time of the final antichrist. It's recorded in 2 Thessalonians 2. When he comes, God will send the world a strong delusion so they can believe the lie."

"God?" said a few of the demons.

"All of you better learn the Scriptures. What kind of seducing spirits are you going to be if you don't know the Scriptures?" His voice was sharp with the aftermath of being reminded of his own stupidity. "Don't you know that our lord used the Scriptures against Christ when He was on that fast?"

The apprentices were silent at their chastening, with lowered heads and eyes deliberately not looking at their teacher. Smooth saw the effect of his words and behavior and felt ashamed. Not for making the apprentices feel bad, but because he prided himself on always being in control of himself.

Smooth spoke in a recovered voice, whispery and inviting. "The antichrist is the lie spoken of in Thessalonians. God orchestrates the introduction of the antichrist into the world and his rise to power because the sons and daughters of Adam reject truth. When you persistently reject truth, God gives you over to your lie."

One of the apprentices saw this as an opportunity to look good to the teacher. "That wretched apostle, Paul, said something similar in Romans 1."

Smooth was obviously impressed by the demon's knowledge. "Go on."

"He said that God gave people over to a darkened mind because they rejected what they knew to be true."

Smooth smiled and nodded at the demon. He looked at the others. "I would love to be surprised by more."

"In First Kings 22, God gave permission to a lying spirit to deceive King Ahab after he had repeatedly rejected Him," said a demon.

"It's not Kings. It's Second Chronicles 18," another demon corrected.

"It is Kings. I know what I'm talking about," the demon maintained.

"And I know what I'm talking about," the demon said with glaring eyes. "It's Chronicles."

Smooth smiled with renewed hope that this crew had potential. "It's both," he said. "It's in Kings and Chronicles." He bobbed his head. "Excellent. Excellent." He turned to Elsie. "Elsie does *not* want the Bible to be true. She despises the idea that she is a sinner in need of a savior. And she hates the idea of eternal punishment."

"That's why she's an atheist?" asked a demon.

"She's an atheist because she's full of pride." Smooth smiled approvingly. "Takes a lot of pride to declare that there's no God."

"Lot of stupidity, too," said another demon.

"Yes. That, too," Smooth agreed.

"But if she's an atheist, why is she turning to witchcraft?" asked a demon.

"She doesn't know it's witchcraft," said Smooth. "But even if she did, she'd still go there."

"How? How can an atheist reconcile looking for answers in witchcraft?"

"Aaahh, the capstone of this little lesson." Smooth got behind Elsie and massaged her neck and shoulders.

The demons were shocked that he could touch her.

"Come." Smooth beckoned with his head. "You can all touch her. She's given us permission."

The demons swarmed on such a delicious opportunity.

"My future destroyers, Elsie doesn't have a problem reconciling facts and lies because she has already made up her mind. She's going to witchcraft because she thinks it will support her lie that there is no God, and that there's a way out of her mess without Him."

"What's going on over there!" yelled Unreal. "When will she be ready? I've been waiting long enough! I'm no bum! I shouldn't be on the streets like this! Give me my house!"

Smooth rolled his eyes and kept massaging Elsie. "He is so dumb and ghetto. Does he naively think that witchcraft spirits won't rush in and claim ownership of Elsie at the first opportunity?"

Chapter 14

From a neurosurgery residency at Johns Hopkins to parapsychology and psychic phenomenon? One day studying the intricacies of the human brain and nervous system, and the next day trying to read thoughts and bend spoons with her mind. How the mighty had fallen!

Elsie was disgusted with herself. She was disgusted and most of all ashamed. Deep in her heart, she knew she was travelling down her version of the yellow brick road, off to see the wizard of Oz. The one glaring problem, she knew, was that no matter how adventuresome the journey, she wouldn't find the wizard. How could she? There was no wizard. The most she could hope to find at the end of such a ridiculous road was a strait jacket for her dubious efforts.

Day one of the psychic phenomenon journey, and as to be reluctantly expected, nothing. It was like throwing rocks into a pond and failing to generate one ripple. Elsie felt a sense of foreboding rising. Something had to happen, and it had to happen soon.

Something was about to happen.

*****

Two things had already begun to happen.

First, Elsie's inquiry into what she thought to be psychic phenomenon caused the darkness that was already over her home to thicken.

Second, when her finger pushed the enter button on her computer to pull up the first article on psychic phenomenon, the sound of a trumpet blew, notifying witchcraft spirits in the area that a son or daughter of Adam was trying to open the door to make contact with them.

Since witchcraft spirits were so powerful and their effects upon those they invaded so devastating, God had placed special restrictions upon their access to humans. The door separating them from sons and daughters of Adam could only be opened from the inside.

Elsie's hand pushed down on the door's handle.

*****

Elsie sat Indian style in front of the coffee table in the family room. She put the teaspoon on the table and rested her hands on her lap. She looked questioningly at the spoon. Now what? She closed her eyes and focused on bending the spoon with her brain's energy.

Elsie's three-minute timer went off. She opened her eyes and looked at the spoon. No change. She went through several more three-minute attempts. Same results. She knew her impatience was premature. What scientist had ever expected a major scientific breakthrough on the first day?

Nonetheless, an hour later Elsie's impatience had mixed with the growing acknowledgement that this was absolutely ridiculous. How had she gone from Johns Hopkins to this—this Anna-like behavior?

Elsie's self-recriminations were interrupted by a sound in the kitchen. There was no one there, but her. Daniel was at work. Amanda was still at Nicole's. She turned her head to the side and was about to shake off the sound when she heard it again. It sounded like something crinkling. Then a sound like something running across the kitchen floor—a tiny animal.

Elsie stood. *A rodent?* The thought was repulsive, but she wasn't afraid. She was much larger than any rodent. She'd kill it if she saw it. If she didn't see it, she'd get the exterminator out there today. She had Amanda to think about.

Elsie entered the kitchen with a large, closed umbrella in hand. Something was about to be speared. She looked on the floor at the balled up paper bag. "Now how'd that get there?" she said aloud. She stooped to pick it up.

Little feet ran across the floor behind her.

Elsie dropped the ball of paper and gripped the umbrella as though preparing for a pole vault. She ran to the big window that opened onto the deck. That's where the pattering of feet ended. One hand slowly pulled back the vertical blinds. The other prepared for the thrust.

"Come on," she said, coaxing the trespasser to its doom.

There was nothing there.

Little feet running on the other side of the large island.

Elsie ran to the sound.

Nothing.

"Where are you?" she demanded, as she searched the paths of the lower cabinets. From the corner of her left eye, she saw it running toward her. It took Elsie one violent overhand thrust with her two-handed, pole vault grip. The umbrella speared the moving target dead center.

There was no squealing or jerking or blood coming from the rodent.

There was no squealing or jerking or blood because paper balls didn't squeal, jerk, or bleed no matter what you did to them. Elsie had speared and killed a rolling wad of paper.

Now the question was, what had caused the paper ball to roll toward her? The other question was, since she had obviously not been chasing a paper ball, where was the rodent? She looked everywhere in the kitchen, but didn't find it. Where could it be? She remembered the strange bird attack at Starbucks. She looked on the counter at the dead ball of paper that had been last seen on the floor. That something odd was going on was an understatement. But exactly what was going on?

Elsie stood straight and looked around the large kitchen. Her hand rested on the handle of the umbrella as its point touched the floor, awaiting its next assignment. Now she wasn't sure what she had heard. Was this like the bird? But she had not only heard the bird. She had seen it and felt it land on her shoulder.

Elsie walked slowly toward the family room. Her eyes full of questions, and behind the questions, fears. Should she continue with the spoon experiment? Should she take a little rest and continue later? No. It had only been an hour. She needed to get back on track. She resumed her sitting position before the table.

The spoon. Where had she put it?

Elsie looked around the carpet next to the table. It wasn't there. She looked under the sofa. Not there. She searched the entire room, but it wasn't there. Now she knew she had left that spoon on the table; so where was it?

Little feet ran back and forth on the long foyer's hardwood floors. They took a right and were again in the kitchen. But this time, the rodent was running around as though it was being chased. She could clearly hear it running, sliding across the floor, and bumping into things.

Elsie charged into the kitchen with her weapon ready. This time she wouldn't spear a wad of paper. This rodent was good as dead!

Her eyes searched the kitchen as though she were in Iraq searching for an Isis ambush. The ambush was real. She walked past the deathly still attacker. Its tail was up and flush against its furry body as its big, black, oval-shaped eyes focused on her. It saw its landing site on her back. Its hind legs and long tail prepared for its assault.

Elsie felt something land on her back. She screamed, frantically wiggling her shoulders and reaching over one of them to snatch the thing off of her. She couldn't reach it, and it wouldn't let go. She felt its claws through her shirt. She twirled in a circle, looking behind her. She could see it, but not reach it. She tried to knock it off with the umbrella. It didn't work. Still screaming, and now cursing, Elsie threw down the umbrella and grabbed a pot and swung hard over her shoulder. She hit whatever it was and felt it drop to the floor. She turned to see her attacker.

On the floor facing her was a squirrel with a spoon in his mouth. He had it gripped in the middle. There was a three second *Are you kidding me?* moment before the pot came down toward the squirrel. There was a two and a half second internal alarm in the squirrel that told him it was time to move. The half-second difference saved his life.

CLANG!

The spoon-carrying squirrel ran around the kitchen as its pursuer slammed wherever it had just been.

On the counter. *CLANG!*

On the stove. *CLANG!*

On the table. *CLANG!*

Still on the table, to the right. *CLANG!*

Still on the table, to the left. *CLANG!*

Back and forth. From one end of the table to the right. Elsie smashed left and right, each time barely missing him. She backed up from the table and looked at the squirrel. It was a rodent. She was a former Johns Hopkins neurosurgery resident. She couldn't win the speed game. She'd have to outsmart him.

The squirrel looked at Elsie and stepped forward. It was like he was daring her. And had it not been preposterous, she would have sworn under oath that the rodent smiled a challenge at her.

Elsie gripped the pot's handle hard. She wore her own challenging grin. The plan was set. She had been smacking at this thing wherever it *was*. He'd then promptly hop in the opposite direction. She thought of this thing jumping on Amanda. It helped her resolve. Instead of hitting at where it *was*, she'd hit at where it was *going*.

She swung hard at where the rodent was going. *CLANG!*

The squirrel didn't move an inch. Spoon in mouth, he looked up at his attacker.

Squirrel or no squirrel, that thing had smiled. Elsie imagined it saying, "Is that the best you got?" She forgot it was simply a squirrel and let off five quick whacks at the table before chasing it onto the floor and back onto the counters, furiously whacking at it and getting only close enough to it to feel that the thing was toying with her. It jumped off the counter and ran into a corner.

"I've got you now," she said.

"You've got what now?"

Elsie looked up. "Daniel," she said, surprised to see him.

"You've got what?" His eyes were soft with tenderness, but his voice was tentative with fear. What did his wife have in the kitchen that he couldn't see?

"Get the umbrella," she said, pointing to it, but looking back in the area where the squirrel had suddenly disappeared. "It's a squirrel."

Daniel's movements were slow. His expression struggled to show his support. He picked up the umbrella. "Where is it?" he asked, his heart trying to manhandle his tear ducts. He fought them off. He had to be strong for the family.

Elsie looked everywhere for the squirrel she knew was there. Daniel looked everywhere for the squirrel he knew was not there. It was not there. He came up with a face-saving idea.

"Here. Let me open the door." He slid open the door to the deck. "Let's give that thing a way out. We don't want to have to chase it all around the house. We'd never catch it." He smiled softly at her. "I figured what's the use of living so close to the hospital if I can't sleep here a few hours before a long surgery. I'm going to go to the restroom and then catch a few winks. Okay?"

Elsie was devastated. She didn't want her husband to think she was going crazy. Her expression was nowhere in the neighborhood of a smile, but she tried through her brokenness. "Okay," was all she could say.

Elsie knew Daniel had opened the door to give her a way out. Always so kind. For her own sanity, she'd take that way out. She walked slowly to the family room and sat on the sofa to think.

The spoon. There it lay. As though it had been there all the time.

Elsie knew that it was even beyond her in this present state of mind to seriously contemplate whether a squirrel that she had heard in the kitchen had somehow doubled back and taken the spoon, tussled with her in the kitchen, then had beat her back into the family room to return the spoon.

Elsie grabbed her head and doubled over. Through her tears, she said over and over, "Am I going crazy?"

Her phone rang. It was Nicole's ring tone. She picked it up to read the text.

> Mommy, this is Amanda. Auntie took us to the park. We saw birds and squirrels. I prayed that Granny's bad squirrels would leave her. Don't let bad squirrels in our house. I love you.

A second text came immediately after the first.

> This is Nicole. Sorry about the prayer thing. Kids are kids. Granny's bad squirrels???

Elsie put the phone down and tried to hide herself in the sofa's fluffy cushions. What was going on?

Demons sat on the left and right of her to explain. Fear of Abandonment was one of them.

Chapter 15

Elsie was back in the family room sitting on the floor the moment Daniel left for the hospital. She knew now that it was only a matter of time before her condition forced him to do something drastic. She didn't know what drastic was, but she wasn't waiting around to find out.

She had had enough of that spoon. This time she'd experiment with something presumably easier. Slowly…slowly…slowly…she inhaled a deep breath, held it for a moment, and slowly exhaled. Over and over she did this as she focused on the picture of Nicole.

"Come. Come. Come," said Elsie, calling for the process to work.

But she was unknowingly calling for more than a process.

*****

"What does she want?" asked one of the apprentice seduction demons.

Smooth answered with a whispery, "She wants to read Nicole's mind."

"But she can't do that without witchcraft. Right?" asked another apprentice. "We're not calling in a witchcraft spirit, are we? He'll try to take over everything."

Smooth looked approvingly at the demon. He emitted a low, gurgling laugh. "I see we've run into the same witchcraft spirits.

No. Let's take care of this ourselves. We have to move quickly. I'm sure witchcraft demons have already heard her call." The demons watched Smooth as his different expressions revealed his evil calculations. He smiled and pointed to two of his students as he said, "Go to Nicole and fill her mind with Elsie. Elsie. Elsie. Elsie. Get her to call Elsie."

"But she's trying to read her mind," said a demon. "She's not trying to get a phone call."

Smooth smiled mischievously. "Oh, but that is exactly what she desires. And you're going to give her that desire."

The demon's mouth gaped in admiration.

"Go on," urged Smooth. He felt good and it could be heard in his voice and seen in the twinkle in his eyes. "Our dear Elsie is begging for deeper deception."

*****

Elsie jumped when she heard Nicole's ring tone. She stared at the phone with eyes wide enough to fall out of their sockets. "It worked," she said in a gasp. "Hel...lo."

"Hey, Elsie, I really don't know why I called," said Nicole. "I just suddenly started getting a bunch of strong thoughts about you. Nothing in particular. Just...thoughts."

Elsie and Nicole spoke for a couple of minutes before Elsie cut the call short. She needed to get off the phone and back to her experiments. She had tapped into something.

What about this astral projection stuff?

*****

"Ugh," she recognized the next ring tone. That was one she certainly hadn't summoned. Her first thought was to ignore it. She didn't need any interference, especially now that she was apparently making progress. Her next thought, however, prevailed. Now that the call had come, she wouldn't be able to stop thinking about that little charade Anna put on at Starbucks. "Anna," she declared into the phone.

The name came across to Anna like she should be ashamed of it. Her chest was immediately aflame with anger. She deliberately took her time before answering. *Help me, Lord. I don't want to blow up at my sister,* Anna pled with the Lord. She ignored the thought that was like a desperate prisoner trying to break out of prison. *You have some kind of nerve, you arrogant atheist fool! First, you slap me. Then you stand me up!*

Instead Anna said, "Hello, Elsie. I missed you at Starbucks. I was hoping we'd get a chance to talk face to face. I guess something came up. Life happens."

"Who was your friend?" Elsie asked with attitude.

Oh, of course, I forgive you for hitting me. The cynical thought had asked no permission to impose itself. "What friend? What are you talking about, Elsie?"

"Anna, I don't have time for this crap," said Elsie. "I am in the middle of something important. The old woman. You know who I'm talking about."

Be not be overcome with evil, but overcome evil with good, Anna coached herself. "What old woman, Elsie?" Anna's voice carried the strain of her resisting saying something else.

Elsie's eyes were hard. They bounced around the room as she contemplated hanging up on her. "The old woman who you put up to evangelizing me at Starbucks. The same old woman who you put up to evangelizing me a few weeks ago in Inman Park. You told her I'd be there."

"Elsie, I haven't the faintest idea what you're talking about. You're talking like a crazy woman." Anna regretted using that word the moment she heard it. She knew the next thing she'd hear would be *Click!* She had to talk fast. "I called because someone at the Bible study got a word for you. She said she saw you going into the dark den of a hungry lion. Elsie, I don't know what you're doing, but whatever it is—"

Click.

Elsie went deeper into the den.

*****

Fear of Failure looked across the street at Unreal and joined the barely hidden smirks of the seduction spirits.

"What is this?" Unreal bellowed angrily.

Witchcraft spirits were marching in the horizon toward them.

So I won't be working for you after all, thought Fear of Failure. He had no problem working for witchcraft spirits. They were exceedingly controlling, but they'd give him more respect than would Unreal. "They must have heard her call for them. I'm sure you'll still get your home." Fear of Failure shared sneering smiles with the seduction spirits when he said, "You'll just have to share your throne." Then in a voice too low for Unreal to hear, "If there's anything left to share."

One of the apprentice demons mimicked the boisterous demon as he went berserk. "I'm no bum. Hee, hee, hee. I'm a great power. Hee, hee, hee. This home is mine. I worked hard for it. I have a claim on it."

What the apprentice demon would never be able to mock was the phobia demon's determination to sit on the throne of Elsie's mind.

*****

The effect was immediate.

Elsie didn't feel a pulling sensation. Nor did she experience a leaving of some sort. She was simply *out.* Outside of her body. A few feet above it. She looked at her vacated body not knowing what to think. She had the sense that any question or conclusion would start or end with a faulty premise. *What is this?* was the only thought that made sense.

Elsie looked down at her hands first, then the other parts of her body. Body? Two bodies? There was a physical body on the floor. That was her; the real Elsie. But then there was this... Elsie the scientist looked for a more appropriate term. There was this projection of energy that mirrored her physical body. She was searching for dots to connect when she felt the urge to travel.

Elsie left the family room and went into what had to have been another dimension. This time there was a sense of traveling. Fast traveling. Something she knew was beyond the capacity of physical matter. But she was in the form of pure energy, was she not? Was she traveling at the speed of light? Or maybe even faster—the speed of thought! Superluminal travel! How fast was that? Theoretically, there was no limit.

She suddenly stopped. She was in deep space. Galaxies, interstellar dust, planetoids, asteroids, solar flares were in every direction, as far as she could perceive. It was beautiful. This is where it had all begun. The atheist in her had something philosophically that was akin to an orgasm. What she saw next increased its intensity.

She saw something happen that could be described as an explosion, but only if it could be magnified by the order of infinity. It was an explosion of such power and beauty that it filled the universe. It was a shame that the best minds had settled to call it simply *The Big Bang.*

She watched in awe as the universe expanded. Her mouth stayed open as she watched it cool until subatomic particles formed. She held her heart as she witnessed gravity's effect on primordial elements as it formed stars and planets and galaxies. But when she suddenly stood before a world made obvious by the dinosaurs she beheld to be tens of millions of years old, she gasped.

Her energy was taken to a prehistoric jungle where she beheld in fascination what any scientist of evolution would've given a lung to see. She saw prehistoric humans evolve right before her amazed eyes. From treetop monkeys to modern homo sapiens.

"I knew it," she said. It came out as a whisper, but her mind was screaming, *Eureka!*

Elsie didn't know how her projected energy could cry, but it did. She let the profuse tears roll freely. Each tear carried away from her the weight of religion. The weight of Christianity and Islam and

Hinduism and Buddhism and Judaism and every other religious dogma and superstition created by men. God was a myth. If there were a such thing as God, it was science. As contradictory as it sounded, she thanked the god of science that she was an atheist.

In a moment, Elsie's projected energy was reunited with her brain. She relaxed in the comfy sofa, basking in her new light and unaware of her new darkness.

And unaware of new torment which was now crossing the street.

*****

Seduction didn't yelp and jump up and down as his apprentices were doing, but his smile was large and smug. "And *that* is how you do it," he said.

The apprentices continued celebrating with whoops and high fives.

"Did you see how easy that was?" said one. "I thought it would be more difficult."

"It's always easy when you give 'em what they want," said Smooth, relishing his role as wise teacher.

"But," an excited demon struggled for words, "monkeys? From created in the image of God to...monkeys?"

"It is ridiculous." Smooth examined his nails. "But atheists love that monkey stuff. Come on. Let's go on to the next project. There are some backslidden Christians who want to believe that they don't have to stop sinning because the grace of God covers them. That ought to be fun."

One of the apprentices twisted his face every way imaginable trying to figure that one out. "Why, that's even dumber than this monkey business," he said.

Smooth nodded. "Yeah. That's about the dumbest I've seen. Let's give 'em what they want."

Unreal ran across the street and started walking when he got to the lawn. He looked over his shoulder at the fast approaching witchcraft spirits.

Too late, you vultures! Unreal bumped Fear of Failure out of his way. He did the same with a couple of apprentice demons. "I told you, I'm no bum."

Unreal pushed against her chest until he was buried inside. He beat the witchcraft spirits by only seconds.

Chapter 16

Elsie's hand slapped hard against her chest. She held it there, staring unbelievingly at the back of her hand. What she was thinking was absolutely ridiculous. But she knew what she felt. Something had entered her.

Laughter. Deep within her soul. Layered echoes of evil laughter rising...rising...rising. A laugh rose high above the others.

Elsie jumped up, still holding her chest, but now also her belly. There had been no transition from the euphoria of having her atheistic beliefs validated to the confused state of terror she was in now. Everything had changed with the suddenness and destruction of a stray bullet hitting a vital organ. What had just happened to her?

Thoughts of Anna and Amanda and the old woman crossed her mind. This meant nothing to her. Anna's Bible study came to mind. That was equally nonsensical.

Elsie moved from behind the coffee table as though it may have been aiding the enemy—whoever the enemy was. And there was an enemy. It was inside of her. This thought alone was enough to chase her out of there.

She ran from the family room with no destination in mind except to get out of there. *There*. Where *it* had entered her. The hallway. The dining room. The kitchen. The office. Bathrooms, bedrooms, and now sitting on the floor inside of the laundry room. There was no refuge. No peace. No quiet from the hideous, and now mocking, laughter. There was no escape from it because it was inside of her.

"Daniel," she moaned. "Daniel, help me."

But even as the pitiful words left her mouth, she knew she would never tell him. She couldn't. First, a phantom squirrel. Then tormenting laughter inside of her. She had told herself earlier that he would never leave her. But as good a man as he was, he was only a man. She'd already broken his heart, humiliated him, and turned his life upside down by dropping out of her residency. How much more could the poor man stand? She'd have to keep this to herself—if possible.

Unreal had finally received his home. He knew the best way to keep it—besides fighting off those scavenging witchcraft spirits—was to control Elsie through subtle manipulations. To mask his thoughts with her thoughts. To bury himself so deeply into her personality that she'd never consider that her growing problems—he'd make sure of that they grew!—were the work of an invader. Stealth. Secrecy. He needed to be quiet. Just...be...quiet.

But Smooth was right in his assessment of Unreal. He was ghetto.

"Elsie!" he yelled. "Elsie! My name is Unreal, and I'm your new master!"

*****

Anna looked at her phone until the tone stopped. *What does she want?* she thought. Her phone started ringing again.

And when you stand praying, if you have anything against anyone, forgive him, that your Father in heaven may also forgive your trespasses. But if you do not forgive, neither will your Father in heaven forgive your trespasses.

Anna let out a tired breath. She knew this was the Holy Spirit correcting her attitude. "This seventy times seven is wearing me out, Lord." She punched the pad and hesitated, not knowing what to say. Or rather, knowing what to say and not wanting to say it.

"Hello, Elsie." She shook her head at herself for the edge in her greeting.

"Anna, I need to talk."

*****

"What?" Terror screamed at the courier. "Where's Fear of Failure? Where's Unreal? Isn't he there?"

"Yes, my lord."

"Isn't she full of witchcraft spirits now?"

"She has three," said the courier.

"Three? There should be more." Terror waved off the courier spirit's attempt at an explanation. "Three witchcraft spirits ought to be enough anyway." He slammed his fist down on the desk and let out a long string of curse words. "How can she be at her weakest point ever and we find ourselves in this position? Go to Communications. Tell them to get some demons over there right now." Terror looked at the courier spirit with burning eyes. "There had better be a bad ending to that conversation. And I don't mean for us. Do you understand?"

The demon's large eyeballs bounced around in wonderment. It sounded like Terror would also hold him responsible for what happened between Anna and Elsie. "Yes, my lord. Uhhh, I yuh…"

"If I get bad news, you get bad news. Does that answer your question?" said Terror.

Unfortunately, it did. "Yes, my lord." The courier went to several departments and embellished Terror's threats to include anyone who could help save his own skin.

*****

"What do you want to talk about, Elsie?" said Anna.

"Miss Malak."

"Who's Miss Malak?"

"The…old…woman," answered Elsie impatiently. She needed help. She didn't have time to waste. She'd do whatever Anna asked her to do. No matter how stupid. This thing inside of her was now talking.

"Who…is…the…old…woman?" Anna was surprised at how quickly she felt anger, and at how quickly it had come out of her mouth.

"She's lying to you," a demon said to Elsie. "How can a Christian lie like that?"

"She thinks you're stupid," said another.

Elsie's concern about the thing inside of her was greater than whether or not Anna thought she was stupid. She ignored the thought and said, "The woman who you sent to meet me. She said something was coming to get me."

"There she goes again—accusing you of something. You're sick of her and your family treating you like this." The demons gathered around Anna had been briefed of the hot buttons. They watched to see how she took their prodding.

"Elsie, I stopped what I was doing to go meet you because I thought you wanted to talk. You could've had the decency—"

"Forget the old woman," Elsie said forcefully. "Just forget her. Okay?"

"She's yelling at you again," said one of the demons. "You're not a dog!"

"Don't you yell at me, Elsie," said Anna through her sanctified, clenched teeth. "I am not a dog." She was tired of her sister letting the devil use her mouth.

Ignore her. Just ignore her mouth, Elsie. You can do it, she thought. "Anna, do you really believe you can make demons leave people?"

"How many times do you have to say the same thing?" said a demon. "She never listens to you. Why is she asking you this again? You remember the last time she asked you questions like this? It was right before she slapped you. What do you think she's up to this time? I wouldn't put it past her to record this conversation and give it to your mother."

"How many times are you going to reject the Lord?" Each word came out of Anna's mouth louder than the one before it. She seemed on the verge of hysteria. "I've labored in love over the whole reprobate lot of you."

"Reprobate?" a demon asked Elsie. "Did she just call you reprobate? Reprobate means worthless. Worth—less. Worthless! Now that she's a CPA, you're worthless?"

Elsie ignored the demon's words. But she couldn't ignore the voice of the thing that was yelling in her mind this very moment. "God—! Will you just listen to me for once?" she screamed.

"That arrogant, pompous atheist. She took the Lord's name in vain. She took the Lord's name in vain. It's not enough that she answers your love by slapping you in the face," said the demon. "Now she takes the Lord's name in vain. What does the Scripture say? Shake the dust off your feet, Anna. You're just casting pearls to a swine."

Sister or not, Anna was not going to let this sinner dishonor the name of the Lord without saying something. "You—took—God's—name—in—vain. I am through with you." The sentence rolled off Anna's tongue.

"She's through with you?" asked a demon? "You call this idiot for help and *she's through with you*? Why did you ever think you could go to this arrogant ignoramus for help? Elsie, you have to help yourself."

Elsie was terrified and alone. Tears rolled out her eyes. "Anna," she said in a low, broken voice, "if there were a God, He'd be nothing like you."

Click.

The demons' celebration lasted all of half a second. Elsie had been thwarted, but only temporarily. Unreal's big mouth had scared the daughter of Adam so badly that she had been willing to go to Anna for help. Thanks to Unreal, she was now unpredictable.

*****

Fear of Failure was jittery. It could have been because Terror called an emergency meeting, and that meeting was in the same basement room where he had been beaten. But the prospect that this meeting would end with him again writhing on the floor in a broken, bloody mess was unlikely. This was a strategy session, not a beat-down session.

Terror peered at each demon individually and long enough that every demon was forced to eventually meet his fiery gaze. "Look around you," he said. "Take a good look."

The demons did so.

"Look...and...remember. For some of you may not ever see one another again," he said. "In fact, it is altogether possible that none of you will see anything again except the thick darkness of the Dark Prison." Terror sat back on his chair. "Good. I see that I now have your attention. You've been summoned to this meeting because I don't like what's happening with Elsie. I'm not going to ask how a good atheist was brought so low as to seek help from a follower of Christ.

"Unreal. He has an exceedingly big mouth. Opening that fat trap of his is how he got kicked out of his last house. But that's the past. We can't undo the past. But I do expect you to orchestrate the future. And so that my conscience will be clear should I have any or all of you put in the Dark Prison, we're going to go over some basics." Terror slammed his fist on the desk and screamed, "And you better look interested in what I am saying!" He paused. "I was summoned to the castle—"

There were murmurs.

"Quiet!" ordered Terror. His eyes rolled left to right, looking at the silenced demons. "Obviously I would not have been summoned to the castle had the matter not been of extreme importance. But my curiosity was answered when I found that our dear Elsie has been chosen by the enemy to...to..." He almost could not bring himself to say it. "She's been chosen to...."

The demon audience leaned forward.

"If we can't keep her bound with fear," Terror pushed the words from his mouth, "she's going to find a cure for Alzheimer's."

A demon standing in the middle of the others swayed with dizziness and glazed eyes before falling on the floor.

"What is this?" yelled Terror, lurching forward and leaning his powerful hands on his desk. "Get him up!"

A demon stood over the laid out spirit and slapped him several times as though he were trying to remove his face with each slap. "Get up! Get up! Get up!"

Another demon tried to help the process by kicking him twice in the ribs.

Terror watched in silent fury as they snatched the now conscious demon to his feet. "Well at least you understand the seriousness of this matter." Terror sat down. "Obviously, we can't let this happen. Fear," he said thoughtfully. "Fear. We've got to keep her full of fear." He looked at Fear of Failure. "We could've lost Elsie to that loose cannon of a sister of hers." He waited for effect to ask his next question. "Is anyone here familiar with how we lost Anna?"

No one answered one way or the other.

"There are varying reports," Terror answered his own question. "But most of them are unreliable. Filed by demons looking to cover their own butts. Here's what we know for sure. Two years ago Anna was just as much a slave as Elsie. Then she ran across a Lester Sumrall video."

Gasps filled the room.

Someone's murmur was louder than he had planned. "He was a dagger."

"Yes, he was a dagger," said Terror, "and thank the darkness he's dead. Thank the darkness there's only a handful of daggers and thorns to torment us. But our problem isn't daggers and thorns. It's Elsie's wanderings. Unreal scared her so bad she was ready to ask Anna to cast the demons out of her." He bounced his finger in the air. "She would've done it, too. As flaky as she is, she would've done it. We can thank the darkness for her temper." Terror shook his head at the near calamity. "Had she thought more about her sister's need than her own offense, there's a good possibility we'd all now be in the Dark Prison."

Terror slammed his fist on the desk again. "But I have no intention of going to the Dark Prison, or any other prison! Listen—

deliverance ministry." He said the words as though they tasted awful in his mouth. "The power that God has given His followers to cast us out of people. That is what makes even a flake like Anna dangerous. Look what she did to those two mutts, Amanda and Chrissie. She would've done the same to Elsie. We were lucky that time. We won't be the next time."

Everyone looked at Fear of Failure to ask the question they were afraid to ask. He tightened his lips in defiance of their prodding.

"What do you think, Fear of Failure?" asked Terror. "You and your crew have been with her a long time. What's her next move?"

The startled demon swallowed hard and mentally cursed the demons around him. "Uhh, my lord, she's quite stubborn and resourceful. She's a fighter. She doesn't like to give up."

"So what's her next move?" Terror's tone was impatient.

"She's going to find someone else to cast us out." His voice trailed off, expecting a strong rebuke.

Terror seemed to relax at this. He stretched out his thick arms and rolled his fingers on the desk. His face twisted into what may have been a grotesque smile. "You are exactly right. And what are we going to do about this?"

"Stop her," said Fear of Failure.

"You are predictably wrong."

"Wrong?"

"Wrong." Terror looked around the room. "If we can't keep Elsie from finding someone to cast us out, we must find the *right* someone to cast us out."

"I do not understand, my lord," said Fear of Failure.

"That is why I am sitting behind this desk, and you are standing before it."

Someone behind Fear of Failure snickered, but he dared not turn around to see who it was.

"Jesus said, 'If I cast out demons by the finger of God, know that the kingdom of God has come upon you.' What would happen if this explosive truth ever got out? If it ever became mainstream in the church? That they could demonstrate our defeat to the world through this wretched ministry God has given His followers?" Terror waited for an answer.

"We'd be exposed," said Fear of Failure. "We'd be crushed. Publicly."

"Exactly! We have absolutely no chance of winning a confrontation between a follower of Christ who uses His name in faith to cast us out."

"So then why aren't we going to stop her?" Fear of Failure humbly asked.

"Oh, but we are going to stop her—just not the way you think." Now there was something on Terror's face that resembled a smile. "We are going to stop her by sending her to the kind of deliverance ministry that helps us as much as it hurts us. By the time they finish with her, she'll have a new demon. A spirit of fear of deliverance ministry."

Fear of Failure interrupted the chuckling of the demons beside and behind him with a question that he had to ask. "Isn't this playing with fire? What if this backfires? What if she's really set free?"

The chuckling stopped. Flashes of the Dark Prison replaced the humor.

Terror wasn't angry. The demon had simply acknowledged the obvious. Trying to handle deliverance ministry was like playing catch with a live grenade. The chances of it blowing up in their faces were real. They could only hope for the best. "We'll just have to find the right deliverance minister, now won't we?"

Chapter 17

Fear of Failure, Fear of Abandonment, Fear of Music, and a host of other fear demons looked disbelieving at one another, then at the other group of demons across from them inside of Elsie.

"This is the plan?" Pride asked derisively. "This is the plan? Lead our house to a deliverance service at Apostolic Lighthouse of Deliverance International?"

"Maybe we ought to start giving blood to the Red Cross, too," said Anger.

"Hey, isn't that Apostle Mattie's church?" asked Fear of the Dark. He hadn't been able to manifest himself yet, but he knew his time would come.

"He's no apostle," said Pride. "He's a clown."

"Yeah, he's about as much of an apostle as I am King David," said a demon.

"But he's a dangerous clown," said Worship of Intellect. "There are a lot of homeless demons in Atlanta because of that clown. Don't let the circus environment and goofiness fool you. He and that wild bunch of his are a legitimate threat—even if they do put on a good show."

This had a sobering, silencing effect on the demons.

A different pride spirit broke the silence. "I will not be cast out of my home by a man wearing a red suit."

That was the lightness they needed. They laughed, although now a bit nervously because of Worship of Intellect's brooding.

Their nervousness increased the closer Elsie got to the church's door.

*****

Elsie was like most Atlanta suburbanites who lived outside the perimeter of Interstate 285. Atlanta proper was a place you heard about on the local news—the news was usually bad. Or it was a place to drive through on Interstates 75 or 85, or preferably around on Interstate 285. It was not a place a woman went alone at night to visit a strange church.

That the church was strange was without dispute. Its website provided all the proof necessary to qualify as strange. But what was stranger than dropping out of a Johns Hopkins residency? What was stranger than her growing fears? What was stranger than her sisters and mother and grandmother? What was stranger than the bird at Starbucks? What was stranger than the squirrel in her kitchen? And what was stranger than the laughing and loud voice she had heard inside of her earlier?

Strange had become her world. Elsie knew she could no longer ignore this unnerving fact. She'd have to use all her courage and resourcefulness to navigate the dangerous rapids of Crazy River to get her mind and life back.

So here she was. In Atlanta. Alone. At eight o'clock at night. Looking for someone to cast demons out of her. She'd call the condition anything if that's what it took to get rid of it.

At first, Elsie thought she may have punched the wrong address into her phone. She sat in the parking lot of a strip mall whose owner was saving quite a bit of money on not keeping up the place. There was no church building anywhere. Neither were any of the strip mall's businesses open. Yet there were many cars in the lot.

From the safety of her locked car, Elsie watched a woman with two small children exit her car and walk toward the long, unkempt building. When the woman neared a door, she saw a sign above it: Apostolic Lighthouse of Deliverance International.

She thought it odd that a church with international in its name should be so presumably small and located in a rundown strip mall. She took a long, safety-laced scan in every direction and exited the car into the dark parking lot.

Inside of Elsie, it was like the scene from *Saving Private Ryan,* where young World War II soldiers sat helpless in their amphibious assault vehicles in preparation for storming a beach where the well-entrenched Nazis were waiting with machine guns to blast them out of the water. Not one demon uttered a word. Even Unreal's lips were tight. Their nervous eyes did the talking for them.

Worship of Intellect looked at Pride trembling and thought, *What? No more jokes about the clown in the red suit?* Pride's fearful eyes locked with Worship of Intellect's eyes. He tried to inject some bravado into them, but the courage syringe was empty. This drew a sarcastic smirk from Worship of Intellect.

Elsie could hear loud music, really...loud...music. *Music! Oh, my God!* she screamed within. She remembered the...whatever they or it was that threatened her in her basement on her birthday. Her chest bounced with panicked beats from her heart. She looked for safety in the parking lot over her shoulder.

"Hi!" The enthusiastic greeting sounded like a quarterback calling for the center to hike the ball.

Elsie's head snapped back. She looked into the shiny face of a very dark black man with a huge smile and exceptionally white teeth. Her answer wasn't immediate. The greeting had caught her right before her sprint back to the car.

"You deed not come dees far just to go home." The man spoke with a heavy African accent.

Elsie managed a nervous smile and looked over his shoulder. There were probably seventy or eighty people stuffed inside. After her fifth or sixth breath, she noticed with surprise that the music wasn't bothering her. *Maybe I'm not like Mother. Maybe it only hits when I do it,* she thought...hopefully.

The man was right, Elsie agreed. She took tentative steps inside. She'd sit as close to the door as possible just in case she was wrong about the music.

"Deeliverance ees eene dee front of dee church and eene dee back of dee church," the man said with that huge smile. He held out his arm warmly toward the row Elsie was looking at.

"Thank you," she said, and took a seat on the second to the last row on the end near the aisle. Sitting while everyone else was up and singing made her feel like she was drawing attention to herself; so she stood up. But standing didn't change the fact that she was the only white person in the place. So like it or not, she had brought her own spotlight.

Finally, the singing was over and she could sit. The seating was tiered on elevated platforms, from the front to the back, each level rising only a few inches higher than the one below. But it was enough to allow Elsie a clear view of everything that happened up front.

And there was a lot going on up front.

A short, black man with African features paced back and forth across the floor. He wore a bright red three-piece suit with wide lapels. Elsie noted that the pants were too short and too tight. Her eyes widened at his mish-mashed socks, one white and one dark, which were clearly visible since his pants were too short. Her eyes landed next on the huge pink bow tie he wore.

There was a drum set and drummer to the right of him, and a man to the left of him sitting at the keyboards. They resembled owls as their necks stretched as they watched the preacher.

The preacher put the handheld microphone to his lips and looked into the audience with tightened eyes. He walked slowly, taking one long, gliding step after the other. His red, patent leather shoes fighting for attention.

"I eat devils!" he yelled into the microphone. "I eat demons! I eat Beelzebub! I eat Leviathan!"

People jumped up all around Elsie screaming and shouting and waving their hands. It was like being back at a university football game after a Bulldog touchdown. Only this wasn't a football game arena with screaming fans celebrating a touchdown. It was a building in the middle of the night in Atlanta filled with people who were screaming encouragement and adulation to a peculiarly dressed man who had just declared that he ate devils and demons.

The lady seated next to Elsie jumped up and screamed, "Eat hem, Apostle! Eat hem! Eat hem! Eat hem!"

Elsie readied her feet. The church's website had prepared her that she may have to make a quick getaway. She had worn flats for just this moment.

The red-suited preacher suddenly looked in her direction as though a spotlight had just dropped onto her. "Eene dee mighty name of Jesus, you will go nowhere! You will go nowhere until you have seen dee glory of God!" The preacher's neck stretched to his right as he looked toward her.

Elsie looked into his eyes and was sure he was looking directly at her. Then it dawned on her again that she was white. Of course, he had noticed her in the crowd. How could he not notice her? And what did he mean by ordering her to not leave? He couldn't make her stay.

Elsie looked back at the black-suited men standing at the two doors. She remembered Jim Jones and the hundreds of people who died with him. She remembered David Koresh and his compound of blind followers. Then the preacher said something that didn't help her nerves any.

He pointed his finger in Elsie's direction and said, "Eeef you try to leave before God moves, I will eat you like I eat devils."

Elsie was sure her heart had stopped.

The preacher opened his mouth wide and snapped his teeth together a few times and broke out into laughter. "I am playing weeth you. I don't eat people. Only demon. Only dee—mons!" he yelled.

"Eat the devil, Apostle Mattie! Eat hem!" yelled the lady next to her.

"I will eat him," the preacher answered. "But first I must tell you why I wear a red suit."

Elsie shook her head. *What?* she thought in amazement. *Why you wear a red suit?*

Each word rose and fell with punctuated enthusiasm. "I wear a red suit because of the blood of Jesus Christ. I wear a white sock because of dee purity of Jesus Christ. I wear a purple sock—"

A purple sock, thought Elsie.

"—because of the royalty of Jesus Christ," he continued. "Now why does dee man of God where a pink bowtie?" He chopped in the air as he spoke. "I wear a pink bowtie because it eese breast cancer awareness month. I want the devil to know that I am aware that he is behind cancer, and that eefe his cancer demon is stupid enough to come in here, I will eat him up the way they eat people up on *The Walking Dead*."

The pride demon in Elsie who had tried unsuccessfully earlier to look brave took another stab at it. "He talks a big game."

The demon's untimely words drew a lot of ungrateful and scolding eyes. "If I can keep my big mouth shut, why can't you?" said Unreal through clenched teeth.

"Because this fool has us sitting in here with chattering teeth like he's the apostle Paul." The narrow faced demon looked at his unappreciative audience with a grimace of his own. "He eats cancer. Yeah, right. I eat dee-mons!" he mocked.

Unreal's thick fist landed in the middle of Pride's face, pushing his nose so deep into his face that it would've taken the FBI to find it. Pride opened his mouth wide to give the explosion of pain a release. Unreal snatched him by the throat with a large, suffocating hand, and threw him onto his back. He covered his mouth and looked into the demon's watery eyes.

"I've walked through dry places too long…walked around like a bum. I'm not a bum. I—will—kill you," Unreal looked up at the other demons to make sure he was communicating, "and anyone else who tries to put me back on the street." He lowered his face to the demon's face. "I'm going to let you go, and you're going to let this fool talk about eating demons or cancer…or shrimp fried rice, for all I care. But you are not going to put me back on the street. Do you understand?"

Pride was losing consciousness.

Unreal squeezed his neck just before the bone began crushing.

Pride found a way to nod his head.

Unreal let go and sat his thick, muscled body down.

The preacher continued his challenge. "I have salt and pepper and a bottle of catsup for eeny cancer demon here today. Stage four cancer, are you here?"

Unreal looked at Pride.

Worship of Intellect cracked a smile when Pride looked at Unreal and dropped his eyes.

"How many people here have been healed of cancer eene dees meeneestry? Raise your hands. Up! Up! Up!" said the preacher.

Elsie looked around in disbelief at the five hands.

The woman next to her had her hand in the air. She turned to Elsie. "I had cancer here." The woman grabbed her large breast. "The doctor wanted to take my breast, but I went to the man of God, and he ate the cancer demon in the name of Jesus."

Elsie tried to produce a polite smile, but could only squint her eyes and look toward the cancer eating preacher in the red suit and pink bowtie.

"Ees cancer eene dees place tonight?" the preacher asked.

A woman to the far right of Elsie and lower to the floor raised her hand.

"What?" the preacher screamed. "A demon of cancer was stupid enough to come to dee church of Jesus Christ? Come, seestah," he hurried her by curling his fingers, "bring that cancer demon to dee Lord."

"Thank you, Jesus!" said the woman as she came.

The preacher looked at the audience. "Dees ees how you come to dee Lord. No shame! Are you ashamed, seestah?"

"No, Apostle," she waved her hands over her head, "I'm not ashamed."

"Cancer has come in dees place tonight?"

"Yes, Apostle."

"Where eese the cancer?" he asked.

"It's in my breast."

The preacher looked at the woman's chest. "Where eese that devil? Is he there?" He pointed at the lady's left breast so closely that it looked to Elsie that he may have actually poked it.

The woman put her hand to an eye and sniffled loudly as she shook her head.

The preacher yelled as he pointed his finger, "Eeef eat ees not dees one, eat ees dat one!"

Elsie was sure this time that the preacher had poked her breast, not once, but twice. *A preacher had actually poked a lady's breast in front of everyone—twice.* The only thing that kept Elsie from leaving that moment was a morbid curiosity of what he might do next. It was sick, but she had to stay.

"George," said the preacher to a man on the front row, "bring my salt and pepper and catsup." The man brought the seasoning and catsup. "Ees these your woman?" the preacher said to the man who had been standing next to the woman.

"Yes, Apostle."

"Come! Come! Come!" said the preacher.

The man hurried down and stood next to the woman.

"Ees dees your wife?"

"No, Apostle. We're getting married," the man answered.

The apostle looked around the audience as he bounced his finger in the air. He turned to the man and bounced his finger at him. "Are you a fornicator?" He spoke loud enough for everyone to hear.

The man's eyes bulged. "No, Apostle. I'm not a fornicator."

The preacher turned his head sideways and stuck his finger out halfway. "Have you touched dees?" He was pointing at the woman's breasts.

The man's teeth chattered.

"He touched both of them, Apostle!" the woman blurted out. "I told him I did not want him to do this thing. I told him it was dirty and unholy."

The chattering moved from the man's teeth to his whole body. He was a tall man, but he seemed to be shrinking by the moment.

"Ees dees filthy thing true?" demanded the apostle.

"Yes, Apostle." The man's voice was low with shame.

"Then you are a for—nee—ca—tor! Come here!"

The man stepped forward.

The apostle switched hands with the microphone. "Bend your face down here."

The man did so.

SLAP!

The powerful blow rocked the man to the side.

"Come back here," said the apostle. "You touched two breasts, you get two slaps. Put your face right here."

The man did so.

The apostle switched hands with the microphone.

SLAP!

"Now get on your knees and cry out to the holy God for forgiveness. You are filthy." The apostle's words were harsh, but now they sounded to be coming from a brokenhearted father rather than a cruel disciplinarian. "God says he will kill you if you touch her breasts again before you get married."

"Thank you, Apostle," the man whimpered.

The apostle stood in front of the woman. "When he touched your breasts, what did you do? Deed you speet on him?"

"No, Apostle." Her voice was low.

"I said, deed you speet on heem!"

The woman broke. "No, Apostle, I deed not speet on heem."

"Deed you smack heem, like I smack heem tonight?"

"No, Apostle, I deed not smack heem like you smack heem tonight."

"You should have speet in hees face and smack heem!" The preacher looked to his left. "First Lady," he called.

A woman with a colorful, flowing dress and a matching hat stood. She wore a stern expression and had a body that was a good argument for a professional female football league. She walked with purpose toward her husband, looking at the fornicator as though she wanted to tackle him. Her glaring eyes left the man and settled on the woman. "Your body ees dee temple of dee Holy Ghost. Eat eese not for forneecation. Come here," she said.

The weeping woman stepped forward and stuck out her face.

SLAP!

She pulled back, put her hand to her stinging face, and cried into her hand. The first lady waited for her to put her face back out there.

SLAP!

"You are een seestah Benson home group. Are you not?" First Lady asked.

The woman sniffled, "Yes, First Lady."

First Lady looked out over the audience like an eagle searching for a meal. She saw the rabbit slouching behind someone in one of the middle rows. "Seestah Benson! You are a leader een this church. Come before the Lord," she ordered.

The lady rose slowly at first, stunned at the sudden turn of events, then hurried in obedience to First Lady. She stood before her in a beautifully elaborate and colorful dress with an equally impressive head wrap.

First Lady stood before her with a mixture of fire and tears in her eyes. "How deed these happen? Do you remember what happened to Israel when Achan hid the clothes and money he stole? How the whole nation was cursed because of heem? How could you let a sheep under your care stray like these? Come here," she ordered.

The woman stepped forward.

SLAP!

She rubbed her face and prepared for the other.

SLAP!

The lady went to her knees with her hands to her face. She prayed to God through her tears.

First Lady looked at the audience. "Every home group leader een these chuch, stand up."

Several people stood.

"You are leaders over God's flock. You are overseers. God holds the apostle responsible for your souls, and the apostle holds me responsible for the seestahs in the chuch. And I hold you responsible for helping me watch over the seestahs in the chuch.

Seestahs, we fast Monday, Tuesday, and Wednesday for holiness. This will not happen again. Amen?"

The sisters agreed all over the church with their own "Amen."

First Lady pulled Sister Benson up and hugged her. "I forgive you and God forgives you." First Lady looked at the sinning sister. "Abena forgives you, too, for not watching over her soul properly. Now go to your seat. The man of God must eat a cancer."

"God ees holy!" screamed the apostle. "We come to a holy God with holy hands." He looked at the man who had sinned with his hands. "Go sit down, brother. You will stand next to theese seestah in prayer once you are married."

Elsie heard the woman's comment about eating cancer. With all of the breast poking and face slapping going on, she had forgotten there was a preacher down there whose diet was cancer. She shook her head. *This must be a movie set,* she thought, only half joking. Yet she found herself inching forward in her seat like everyone else.

"The devil eese stupid," said the preacher, "but sometimes he eese not so stupid. He may be gone with his luggage already."

There was laughter from the audience.

The preacher poked at the lady's right breast. "Theese eese where he attacked you?"

"Yes, Apostle."

The preacher went to the podium and put down his microphone. He got the salt and pepper and catsup. Elsie scooted to the edge of her seat.

"First Lady," he called. "This must be decently and in order," he said for the audience. His wife returned and stood by him. "Steek out your chest."

Elsie's mouth was open as wide as it could get. *Stick out your chest? What is he going to do?* she thought. She watched with a mixture of horror and sick humor as this man sprinkled salt and pepper on the lady's breasts area as though they were scrambled eggs. He took the catsup, removed the cap, and dumped catsup on the dress over both breasts. Elsie let out an involuntary gasp.

"Eat hem, Apostle!" yelled the lady next to Elsie. Then several others joined her weird encouragement.

Elsie's mind raced to the only logical place this absolutely ridiculous event could be taking them. He was going to start biting this lady's breasts in front of the whole church. Elsie's mouth cranked open even wider. She trembled at what the preacher was about to do. There was no way she could watch such a predatory violation of gullible trust. But there was also no way she could not watch it.

The apostle looked at the audience. "What does dee Scripture say? 'They shall lay hands on dee seek and they shall recover.' In a flash, he turned on the woman like he was a gunfighter. Both hands landed on a breast. He squeezed hard and said, "In dee name of Jesus Christ, come out of theese woman of God. Cancer, I eat you NOW!" The apostle snatched his hands away from her breasts. "Wait...wait...wait...wait...there! There it is! Eat hem, Holy Ghost!"

Elsie's answer was an unequivocal no. She wasn't waiting for anything else. She had seen enough. She lifted a few inches from her seat and the woman screamed.

"Aaaaahhhh, Apostle, I feel it. Fire! Fire! It's burning right here!" She grabbed both breasts.

Elsie looked at the woman and froze, elevated from her seat. She slowly sat back down.

She wasn't the only shocked onlooker. The demons inside of her were more shocked at what they saw than she was at what she saw.

*****

"That's Gruesome. I know him," said a demon. "I worked with him and—" The demon's mouth was open, but the rest of his sentence had become unnecessary. For the other demon he was going to name was thrown out right behind Gruesome. The other demon was Curse.

"That's Curse," said Unreal.

Pride was still afraid to speak. He looked silently in shock as Gruesome and Curse landed hard on the ground in the parking lot and tumbled a few times before coming to a rolling stop. He watched again as an angel threw several pieces of their luggage out after them.

"There's your clown, Pride," said Worship of Intellect. "You have to use your head with matters like this. God doesn't use people because they're perfect or because they know everything. He uses them because they're available and because they believe His word. You've got to learn to look past the red suits. That's what He does."

Unreal looked at Pride, saying nothing, but communicating emphatically.

"Maybe this is a good time for us to leave," said the pride demon.

"It is a good time for us to leave," said Unreal. "But if we try to make her leave, it may draw attention to ourselves. We'll have to be quiet and sit through this until she decides to go. Control your natures. Whatever you do, do not manifest."

*****

Elsie found herself witnessing one bizarre event after another. Each was grounds enough to sprint to the parking lot. But each was also strange enough and strong enough to hold her captive to the next certain lunacy.

Next up was a woman seeking prayer. For the life of her, Elsie couldn't figure out why the preacher had to make a public spectacle of everyone who came up for prayer.

"I have prayed for this woman before," he said. "Her mind eese messed up. Give me the oil."

Oil? thought Elsie. *Salt, pepper, catsup, and now oil? What is this nut going to do now?*

The preacher took a small, glass container of oil and poured all of it on top of her head. It dripped down the front and sides of her face. He then dug his hands into her hair and proceeded to do what only could be described as massaging it. His hands momentarily dropped from her head. Her short, red hair was a mess. It sat atop her head giving her the appearance of a traumatized rooster. The woman tried to fix her hair.

"Don't worry about your hair. You are retarded, seestah! What do you want from God? A nice hairdo or you want to stop being retarded?" said the preacher.

She looked at him with a strange, glazed look.

That is horrible! Why would he humiliate this poor woman like this? Elsie's anger grew stronger than her curiosity. She stood halfway up when she heard him ask her, "Eees the feelthy person who molested you here?" Elsie sat down like she was a meteor hitting the earth.

The woman looked toward the section she had come from.

"Eees the feelthy devil over there?" the apostle demanded with eyes burning in that direction.

"No," she said.

"Are you sure the nasty person who made you crazy is not here? Eees eat your father? Your mother? Eees eat a cousin or uncle?" The apostle looked at the congregation. "Cousins and uncles do a lot of molesting."

"No," answered the woman.

The apostle looked suspiciously in the area the woman had been sitting. He placed his hands on her head again. "You dumb, slow devil, come out of her."

She hit the floor. "I won't come out of her. You can't make me come out," a man's voice boomed out of her. She then slithered like a snake with her arms pasted to her sides. She moved so fast that the preacher had to run after her.

That's when Elsie ran for the car. "This is my first and last deliverance service."

*****

Terror sat behind his desk and looked at the courier spirit with hard eyes.

"Mission accomplished, my Lord. Your plan worked perfectly. We don't have to worry about Elsie going to any more deliverance services."

Chapter 18

Elsie stepped out into the darkness of the parking lot and took several hurried, nearly running, steps before becoming aware of her surroundings. It was now after ten o'clock, and if this area looked unsafe when she arrived, it was worse now.

There were still many cars parked in the lot closest to the deliverance church. That was good. There was a white utility van parked next to her car on the driver's side. A van that wasn't there when she arrived. That was bad.

Elsie slowed her steps and surveyed the area. She stopped within twenty feet of her car and the van. Something didn't feel right. She approached her car from the passenger side, entering quickly, and slamming and locking the door. She crawled over the stick and was driving off before her behind hit the leather seat.

She looked in her rearview mirror at the van as she drove away. It remained motionless. Elsie refused to interpret her rapidly beating heart as misplaced fear or foolishness. She got to the edge of the parking lot and prepared to turn onto the street. A last look over her left shoulder. Her neck stretched as she searched for the van. It wasn't there. Rapid breaths joined her rapid heartbeats.

Elsie turned vigorously onto the street. Her fear set the speed limit. It almost caused her to ignore the red light in front of her, but she stopped. A few long moments passed. She looked to the left at a vehicle that pulled up beside her. It was a white utility van. It looked just like the one that had been in the parking lot! The passenger window came down. A white man with a hairy face hung his tattooed arm out and motioned to the back of her car. He seemed to be saying something about her tire.

Elsie looked at him and looked at the light. She looked back at him and went through the light. The van immediately crossed the intersection and got behind her car. She looked at the light in her rearview mirror. It was green. Maybe they weren't following her. She thought of turning down one of the narrow side streets. If the van turned, she was being followed.

Elsie waited until she was at the corner before making a hard right into the neighborhood of tiny houses and cars on both sides of the street that tightened the narrow street. A vehicle's lights turned the corner behind her. Adrenaline pushed Elsie's gas pedal. She went faster than she'd ever dare to go on a residential street. The lights kept up with her.

My phone! Elsie fumbled frantically through her purse, trying to keep her eyes on the narrow street. Her hand located the phone. She pulled it out and looked down at it. That quick moment of inattention was all it took.

A driver's side car door opened on the right side of the narrow street. Elsie took it off. She jumped and the phone went out of her hand and onto the floor on the passenger side. She looked wide-eyed into the mirror at someone standing in the street and pointing at her. Elsie was horrified at what she had done, but she couldn't stop. Another glance showed that her pursuers had stopped at the scene of the crime.

Elsie pushed the thought out of her mind that they had stopped to help. No. They had stopped because they couldn't get around the person, and presumably the door on the street. She found the safety of the interstate and entered. The moment she did, a deluge of tears came out.

It wasn't just that someone had just tried to— Elsie wiped her face with one hand. Who knew what they were planning to do to her? *If I hadn't entered my car on the passenger side, they would have kidnapped me.* The horror of this thought opened the deluge again. She wiped her eyes as fast as the tears came out. She didn't want to be weak, but she found herself crying, "They would've raped and killed me."

But the white van wasn't the source of every tear. She stared numbly at the fast-approaching white lines before her. She had ventured into the heart of the city alone at night to attend (of all things!) a so-called deliverance service.

A deliverance service!

And what had she gotten for jumping into Anna's Pentecostal snake pit? She had witnessed the most bizarre and nearly criminal religious service imaginable. A preacher who poked and grabbed women's breasts as part of the service. A preacher who called people retarded. A woman who slithered on the floor like a snake.

Elsie couldn't go on to the next thought. How did she do that? I saw her move like a snake. Her arms were at her sides. There is no way someone can move like that—and that fast. And what about that voice? A man's voice. What did it say? "I won't come out. You can't make me come out."

A thought did make her move on.

I'm a criminal. I tore off someone's door and kept going. Elsie's eyes nervously scanned for police cars. I—am—a criminal. What am I going to do?

Elsie drove and thought and cried and drove and thought and cried. Nothing seemed to make sense. She had never felt like this before. Even when she had dropped out of her residency, she didn't feel like this. The fear had slammed her so hard into the ground that her imprint was in it. But as devastating as that had been, and still was, she had never been as confused as she was now.

For the fear had not dropped out of nowhere. Her family *did* have a problem with irrational, life-changing fear. So when it came, it came not as a true surprise, but as a crushing disappointment.

What she felt now was something akin to being in a blender. She was so mixed up that, philosophically speaking, she didn't know whether she was going or coming, whether she was heading north or south.

She had tapped into her brain's energy and had somehow traveled into the past and saw the big bang. But tonight she had also heard a male voice come out of a woman who was effortlessly slithering on the floor so fast that the preacher had to run to keep up with her. And besides this, there was the laughter and the voice inside of her. She hadn't heard it in hours, but she knew it was there.

How was she to reconcile what she had experienced? Was each experience simply different branches of the same tree? Or were they contradictions? Was one proving the illegitimacy of the other? If so, which was to be discarded?

By the time Elsie parked the car in her garage and watched the garage door close, she knew exactly what she was going to do to find the truth.

*****

Elsie looked at the door that led to the basement. "I am not afraid of you," she said to whatever the condition was that was trying to drive her insane. It didn't make sense to talk to a condition, but speaking to it out loud made her feel better.

She put her hand on the knob and turned it slowly. She flipped the light switch and looked down the stairs, trying desperately to not let her memory of her birthday keep her from going down there. She couldn't be like Nicole and Mother and Granny. She couldn't accommodate the fear. She had to face it and fight.

Elsie's first few steps were tentative. The rest were determined. She turned the right corner and said in a low, angry voice, "Tonight. I'm going to find out tonight."

She looked around the room. She knew that trying this wouldn't necessarily connect all the dots, no matter how it turned out. But at the speed at which she was deteriorating, she had to do something. She couldn't become Mother. *At this rate, I'll be the worst of the bunch in just days. I have to do something now!*

Elsie looked at the guitar on the floor. For some reason, Daniel had left it there. She wondered why he had done that. Then she concluded that he either forgot, or he had deliberately left it there to give her the opportunity to pick it up. She knew how his mind worked. And she knew that he knew she'd want to be the one to pick it up.

She stared at it for a long time before taking three quick strides to it and lifting it with a yell as though she were a weightlifter. And the guitar in her hand was like a weight, but not a physical weight. Instant torment dropped over her like a heavy blanket, causing her to stumble with a sick stomach and a dizzy head. She fought through it, and with deliberate slowness put the guitar on its stand. Refusing the compulsion to jump back, she looked at the guitar, which was looking back at her like a cobra about to strike, and said, "I'm going to play you again."

You will never play an instrument again. You will never sing again.

Elsie heard the thought within her as clearly as if someone were in the room with her. "Screw you," she said, and turned and went to the sofa and sat down.

Elsie recalled her conversations with Anna. She recalled what she witnessed at the deliverance church. She may not have understood how everything related to the other, but if she was going to deal with this scientifically, she'd have to acknowledge every fact, no matter how distasteful that fact may be. And it was a fact that there was something peculiar about the name of Jesus. This was the common denominator between Anna's and Amanda's and Chrissie's freedom from fear, and what she had seen with the snake woman at the church.

Elsie pushed the cynical thoughts of hocus pocus from her mind. Facts were facts. "In the name of," she began, then stopped. She ran upstairs and found some cooking oil and got a towel and returned to the basement. She draped the towel across her neck and shoulders. Science or not, she shook her head at what she was about to do with the oil. She poured about half a cup on her head and pressed her fingers against her forehead. "In the name of Jesus Christ, I command you to leave!"

*****

Unreal's head whipped around in every direction. "Who said that?" he demanded.

"I don't know," said Fear of Failure. "But whoever said it has no authority to use the name." He turned to the others. "You recognize the voice."

No one recognized the voice.

Out of the darkness, three angry witchcraft spirits burst into the midst of the other demons. Their eyes flamed with anger. "Who was that?" they demanded. "Who challenged us?"

The command cut through the darkness again.

"Is this Elsie?" one of the witchcraft demons asked in a rage.

"The slave commands its master?" said another witchcraft spirit.

Unreal's anger erupted in a flame when it became clear that his home had illegally ordered him to leave. He had been made homeless before by authorized users of the name. But never had he been so insulted as to be ordered about by a slave of darkness. He exploded in a roar.

Elsie had entered the dark den of demonic lions and had slapped each one in the face.

*****

Elsie was on to something. She knew she was. She could feel it.

Then she heard it.

Deep within her soul came a roar like an angry beast. Then a chorus of roars. Elsie wasn't afraid. Instead, she was encouraged. The name was working. The roars were getting closer to the surface. It was making the condition leave. She smiled. She didn't know the scientific significance of how using the name of a dead

Jew whom Christians had turned into a god could cause her brain to self-correct, but she'd enjoy its power now and try to understand it later.

"That's right! Come out in Jesus name!" she yelled with joyful tears streaming down her face.

The roaring was so loud now that it sounded like the beasts were standing in the room before her. Elsie's eyes opened and her heart almost stopped from fear. The room was dark with monsters too horrible to imagine. Elsie's feet pushed frantically into the carpet in a vain attempt to bury herself between the sofa's cushions.

"How dare you use the name of Jesus!" said one of the beasts. He tore into Elsie with slashing claws.

She screamed and tried to fight him off. Now the others were on her. Somehow the pain enabled her to jump up and run towards the stairs. A demon grabbed her by the back of the neck and shoulder and threw her hard into the sofa. She landed face first into the cushions. Blows struck her from every direction and in every place. Her face jerked to the left and right with slaps until she fell on her belly to the floor.

Unreal screamed a hideous scream with his chin pointed toward the ceiling. His scream finished, he glared at his home. "Look at me!"

Elsie turned her face sideways.

"Why are you using the name?" Unreal demanded. "Who told you you could use the name?"

My God, what have I done? thought Elsie. *What have I done?* She watched the monster move closer. "I didn't know...."

Unreal dropped to a knee and got in Elsie's face. Smelling his breath was like being interrogated by an angry garbage can. "You didn't know that I'm not a bum? You didn't know that you are my house? You didn't know that you belong to me?"

"She called us! She belongs to us!" This was a witchcraft spirit.

Elsie was petrified on the floor. Her eyes knew what they saw. Her ears knew what they heard. Her body was aching from their blows. But her brain was fighting it all. Monsters in the basement arguing with one another about which monster she belonged to? This was *not* happening.

One of them interrupted her thoughts and grabbed a handful of her hair and started dragging her. She grabbed hold of its arm with both hands to keep it from pulling out her hair. The monster slung her towards the guitar.

"Look at it, slave," he growled. "You will never play it again!" The monster was behind her with what she figured was a knee in her back. She felt her head jerk up. She was only inches from the guitar. "Say it, slave! Say it! I will never play it again!"

Terror-filled tears rolled out of Elsie's eyes in two rivers. She was either going crazy, had gone crazy, or she was really in a room filled with monsters.

"Say it!" yelled the monster.

"No! I won't say it! I won't say it!" Elsie felt as though there were two of her. One was scared to death and would've promised anything to get rid of these creatures. The other was just as scared of the monsters, but more scared to live like her mother and grandmother than to let this creature take her music.

The creature pulled Elsie's head until she felt like her throat would pop from the tension. "You can't stop us, Elsie. You have no power. No authority."

Suddenly she was free—not from the creatures. Just that creature. The thing that had her had been snatched off and thrown across the room by one of three monsters that appeared to be working together.

Two of them faced the monster that was snatched off of her. One of the two said to the monster, "She belongs to us! She called us!"

The other grabbed both her ankles with only one large hand and dragged her up the stairs. "You called us," he said repeatedly as Elsie's back bounced painfully on the stairs. He pulled her into the office and pointed at the computer and chair. "Here!" Then he pulled her into the family room and pointed at the floor between the coffee table and sofa. "Here! You called us here! We have a legal right to be here. You have no right to make us leave."

Elsie's feet were in the air. Her back was on the ground. She looked up into the hideous, hate-filled face of whatever this thing was. *I can't take any more,* she said to herself. "Let—me—go!" she screamed.

Her feet dropped to the floor.

*****

Amanda's eyes popped open. This was a bad dream, but it wasn't like the bad dreams she used to have when monsters chased her. This time they were chasing Mommy. She sat up in bed and looked around. She got on her knees beside the bed.

"God, please don't let the monsters get Mommy. Amen." She got back into bed and went almost immediately to sleep.

*****

Elsie remained on the floor nearly an hour after the thing dropped her feet and disappeared. Why move? One place was just as good as any other to be terrified and confused. But there was another reason she didn't move from this room. There were no monsters in this room, and there was no sane reason to go into a room where one might be.

Finally, she got off the floor and laid on the sofa. Smiling was out of the question, and feeling hopeful would've been a stretch. But she had ended this... *episode* by telling it to stop.

It wasn't enough for hope, but it was enough for something. She just needed to find what that something was.

Chapter 19

Elsie's eyes formed tight, still sleepy slits, then sprung open with bad expectations. She shot to an alarmed sitting position on the sofa from where she had fallen asleep the night before. For a split second, there was the hope that she had suffered a terribly realistic nightmare. But the split second's hope turned into reality's despair when she attempted to rise to her feet. She was sore all over, especially her back.

Elsie pushed herself up and stood. She knew where she was physically—*I'm at home...in the family room*—but where was her mind? It was in some dimension of sci-fi and horror. She didn't move from her spot. Her questions keeping her still.

She bent from side to side and to the front and back. She felt like she had been beaten. Horror struck her like lightning, frying the circuitry of her sanity and sense of safety.

"Oh!" she gasped. What she knew was real was really...*real.* She had been attacked by... Elsie reached without looking for the sofa. She dropped numbly onto it and stared at a spot on the table before her.

Monsters.

Hearing voices inside of her head could be attributed to many things. Mental illness being one of them. Seeing monsters in the basement could be attributed to many things. Mental illness being one of them. Hearing and seeing monsters in the basement and being beaten by them could be attributed to only one thing.

Monsters.

What were they? Where had she picked them up?

Elsie knew that the more she understood about these creatures, the better off she'd be. At least that's what she hoped. She began by their appearance. Big. Dark. Terrifyingly ugly. Vicious. Evil. Intelligent.

Intelligent.

She pondered. Many animals were intelligent. But how many animals spoke English? The monsters talked. She thought of hallucinations. Anything could talk in a hallucination. She pressed her lower back and winced. Hallucinations didn't drag people up the stairs. These were real talking monsters. This brought up another darkly fascinating issue.

It was what they talked about. The creatures argued with one another, and challenged and reasoned with one another about why she was the property of one and not the other. They were possessive. Over her.

Slave.

They had referred to her as slave. They said she had called them. The one who dragged her up the stairs talked about having a legal right to her. He had dragged her to the office and the family room. And in both places he had said it was there that she had called them. As far as he was concerned, this gave him the legal right—

Elsie slammed the brakes. She went into reverse and backed up and stopped at her weird conversation with Anna, which was still weird, but now for different reasons. *Legal right.* That's what Anna said her demon said about their family. That he had a legal right to them.

Elsie recalled Granny corroborating the date that Anna's demon had given the women at the Bible study as his legal receipt of ownership of her family line. She didn't know what this similar language meant, but it was a connecting dot. She continued her analysis.

These creatures hadn't looked at her as a predator eyes a meal. This wasn't lion and antelope stuff. These things looked at her with hatred. Deep, personal hatred, as though they had a history. But what kind of history did she have with other dimension monsters? With no dot in view for a possible connection, she moved on.

The next thought was like lighting a match in a dark cave. She could now see her hand, but that was about it.

The monsters hated her, yes. But that's not why they were enraged. They were enraged because she had used the name of Jesus. This didn't make a bit of sense. What was it about that name that would enrage monsters from another dimension? Obviously, there was more to this than the literal name *Jesus*. It was just a name. So what was it?

Did the name represent something? Was there a numerical significance that...that what? She followed this line of reasoning anyway. Jesus had five letters. Did the number five mean something? That was probably too simplistic. Maybe each letter represented something that...

Elsie cursed in frustration. She knew she was ignorantly groping in the dark. She willed herself to think scientifically. *What if the name of Jesus has some kind of inherent power and authority?*

It would take more than the discipline of science to not scoff at this. The thought was beyond ridiculous. Elsie knew she had just crossed over to superstition. *Has it come to this?* she chided herself. *Oh, the power of desperation. It's like I'm drowning and I'm grasping at a broomstick to stay afloat.*

Elsie thought about her being beaten by monsters and gave herself permission to think ridiculous thoughts. Sometimes great discoveries came as a result of someone thinking a ridiculous thought. She quieted her biases and pushed forward.

Now, the truth was that the monsters recognized the name of Jesus. That first one had behaved as though she had done something immoral by using the name. He had said, "How dare you use the name of Jesus!" she thought. The other had said, "Who told you you could use the name?"

The monsters questioned her as though she had no right to the name. Elsie pondered. She had not gotten the idea that no one could use the name. It came across like *she* couldn't use the name.

And that was another thing. They called it "the name," as though it was known, as though it was understood to be in a class all its own.

For the sake of scientific inquiry, this line of reasoning had to be contemplated, but it was troubling. It wasn't merely its superstition premise. Back to her drowning analogy, now she was not only grasping at something that couldn't possibly keep her from going under. She was being carried out into deeper waters by the remote—and thoroughly repugnant—possibility that she would discover something about this name that would challenge her worldview of atheism.

Now that she thought about it, it would be foolish to summarily dismiss a superstition that had through the ages deceived hundreds of millions of people. And some of whom who were otherwise intelligent, and some even brilliant.

However, as a caveat, she took courage in the fact that whatever she found out about this name, she would eventually be able explain within the context of science and her atheistic beliefs.

Elsie sucked in a startled breath, clutching her chest and looking toward the kitchen from where the noise came. She sat frozen for a few moments. She looked toward the hall. She could run outdoors. Another clinking sound in the kitchen. Her wide eyes landed in that direction. No. She wouldn't run. This was her house. Besides, if she ran outside, how long would she remain outside?

Elsie walked with feather steps toward the kitchen.

Was it the squirrel?

Was it a monster?

Please be the squirrel, thought Elsie.

She looked inside and saw nothing. Something popped up from behind the island.

"AAAAAAAAaaaaaaaaahhhhhhh!" screamed Elsie and hit the floor, falling on her backside. She pushed herself backward with a thousand pumps of her feet against the floor.

"Elsie," he said.

Elsie turned around and raced away on her hands and knees, screaming. "AAAAAAAAaaaaahhh! Leave me alone!"

Daniel hopped after his fleeing wife. "Elsie! Elsie! It's just me. Daniel." His crawling wife turned a corner. "Elsie!" He caught up with her and had to grab and roll and wrestle with her on the floor before she stopped trying to get away. His arms wrapped around her from behind, pinning her arms to her sides. "It's me, Elsie. It's me," he whispered.

Elsie tried to speak, but she couldn't get the words past her frantic breaths.

"It's okay, Elsie. I'm here." Daniel held her for several minutes, then helped her up. He looked at her and his mouth opened like a draw bridge. "What happened to you?"

Elsie looked up at Daniel. "What? What do you mean?" She spoke with a slight trembling of the lips and a heavier trembling of the body.

Daniel rubbed her shoulders and arms. "You're scared to death. What's wrong with you? What happened to your face? Where'd the bruises come from?" He looked at her arms. They were bruised. His fingers touched lightly on a bruise. He slowly pulled his hand back with a troubled thought.

Elsie looked at Daniel's hand until it hung by his side. She looked into his eyes, eyes that seemed to be processing new, terrible information. His face turned hard. She saw him change from her Daniel to her husband. Her protector. Something dropped over him. Something angry. Something violent. She had never seen this before.

"Tell me what happened." His voice quivered in low anger and brokenness.

She reached up with one hand and touched his cheek. "No. No. Nothing like that. Nothing..." she shook her head, trying desperately to pull something out of her mind to give him.

Something that would answer his questions without making him think she was crazy. "I fell down the basement stairs."

Daniel tenderly touched her shoulder and turned her to face him. "Tell me what happened. You don't have anything to be ashamed of." His voice was filled with compassion and support.

Elsie looked at him with a pained smile and took his hand and put it to her face. She knew he still thought she may have been assaulted by a man. That he would respond this way made her fall in love with him all over again. But this understanding of his was for a physical assault by a man. Not a physical assault by monsters from another dimension.

"I fell down the basement stairs. I hadn't gone down there since…well, since my birthday." She offered another pained smile. "You know how I am. I wanted to face my fears. I wanted to prove to myself that I'm not my mother and that I'm not Granny."

Daniel looked at her without blinking.

Elsie swallowed and looked at him with what she hoped were confident, triumphant eyes. "I'm not. I'm not Mother. I'm not Granny. I played. I sang."

Daniel's penetrating, unblinking eyes almost made her tell him the truth and beg him to never stop believing in her, to never leave her.

He looked at the sticky mess in her hair, her swollen face, and bruised arms. His fingertips lightly coursed one of her arms. He wouldn't make her lie again by asking her why she had reacted with such fear. Didn't he already know the answer to that? He offered her his own pained smile. "Okay, Elsie. I'm going to finish cooking breakfast. Coffee's probably ready."

Tears pushed against Elsie's fake smile. She hummed acknowledgement. She followed him to the kitchen. He poured a cup of coffee and fixed it the way she liked it. He gave it to her without looking at her eyes. She knew that he knew she was lying. And she knew that her lies were killing him. But even Daniel wouldn't understand monsters.

You've got cancer, said Fear of Cancer.

This strong thought made her lower her coffee cup to the table with a trembling hand.

*****

Elsie knew that Daniel's sudden need to go to the hospital was probably because of her brain and not someone else's. She watched through the blinds as he drove away, and was saddened when he didn't look back at her and give that last smiling glance. She knew that was too much to expect, but she wanted and needed it, nonetheless.

This brief visit with her had been just enough time for her to further confirm his fears that she was Mother and Granny. And it had been just enough time to break his heart again with obvious lies.

Alone again.

But was she alone? Would she ever be truly alone?

You have cancer, said the demon.

Elsie took her thoughts to the kitchen. Coffee couldn't help her problems, but Daniel had made it for her. He was gone, but the evidence of his love for her was still there—in a coffee mug. She looked at the picture and writing on its side. A man caught in an affair with a female coffee bean, and the man saying to a woman, "Don't ask me if I love her."

She smiled. *Only in New Orleans,* she thought, remembering their trip there last fall. That hadn't been that long ago. She would've never thought that only months later, she'd be holding on to a mug in the place of her husband and trying to decide whether it was better to have a severe mental illness or to have monsters.

Elsie contemplated the prospect of Daniel making a preemptive move and having her committed for psychiatric evaluation. She knew this was an extreme move that he would only do if he thought she was a danger to herself or someone else. She thought about her behavior when he popped up from behind the island. *That was bizarre, but not enough that he'd have me committed,* she surmised. Her eyes moved thoughtfully from the mug to the bruises on her arms.

"Ohhh, boy," she said, and blew out a defeated breath. "Bruises. Now *that's* enough." *Something else to worry about,* she thought.

You have breast cancer, said the demon. *It's going to kill you.*

She shook her head. "Daniel…no," she pleaded with him in his absence. "Drugs and locking me up in a psyche ward won't get rid of—"she stopped herself from taking ownership of them by saying *my* monsters—"the monsters. They have a right." Elsie broke a little. "Some kind of a legal right."

She sipped the coffee. Nothing worse than lukewarm coffee. She set the mug down. How much time did she have before Daniel either said they needed to talk about *doing* something about her condition, or before she looked up one day to find a police officer at the front door to escort her to a mental health facility for evaluation? Would Daniel do this based on what happened today?

She hopped up and went and got her laptop. She went online and searched the Official Code of Georgia. She knew people, even spouses, couldn't simply have someone committed involuntarily to a mental health facility without due process. She needed to know exactly what that due process was.

Elsie had thought Daniel needed to get a couple of medical affidavits to start the process. She was surprised to find that that was only one option. The other was that he could have her committed to an emergency receiving facility with only a certification from a specified medical professional. He satisfied this criterion himself. And he certainly had friends who did, also.

If he did this, there were review and rebuttal processes that could get her out of there. She could file for a petition for a psychiatric evaluation. They'd have to give her a hearing within ten to fifteen days, and she could use an attorney. If the hearing was favorable, she could be home within five days.

The bad news was that if the hearing didn't go well, she could be held involuntarily for up to six months—even a year if they felt she needed to stay longer.

Elsie pushed the computer away from her and weighed the possibilities. In the sad event that Daniel took this path, there was no reason why she wouldn't be released—at the most, within two to three weeks.

Two to three weeks confined to a mental health facility.

Remember that commercial about the roach motel? said the spirit of fear. *Roaches check in, but they don't check out. That's you, Elsie. Daniel's going to check your butt into the crazy house, and we'll see you next year this time.*

Elsie thought of a *Black Flag* insecticide commercial she hadn't seen in decades. *Roaches check in, but they don't check out.* This was ridiculous. The worst case scenario was one year, not forever. Yet, a forced one-year stint in a mental health facility was devastating to ponder. *That will not happen,* she told herself vigorously.

She pulled the computer back. Why would they keep her that long? She went to OCGA § 37-3-1(9.1) She skimmed the law. "…presents a substantial risk of imminent harm…manifested by recent overt acts or recent expressed threats of violence…unable to care for that person's own physical health and safety as to create an imminently life-endangering crisis…"

Elsie's first thought was that this certainly didn't describe her. Then she made herself think a more morbid thought. This was now. What about tomorrow? What would happen if Daniel had her committed for evaluation and those monsters went berserk? She'd be locked up until some chief medical officer and his board decided that she was no longer mentally ill. If the monsters never went away, and if they manifested frequently, she'd never get out.

Elsie's soul twisted. A tear appeared and rolled from her eye as if from a towel being wrung out of its last drop of water. "Daniel, please don't," she begged in a frightened whisper. "I'll get better. I'll find a way to beat this. I won't let them control me. I promise you."

The demon spoke louder, and this time not alone. He had a gang of five helping him. A spirit of infirmity. Two spirits of death. A spirit of torment. And a spirit of cancer—he'd enter once the fear of cancer was accepted as a reality. "You have cancer! It is in your breast, and it is killing you!"

"I promise, Daniel," Elsie whispered with borrowed conviction, "I'm not my mother. I'm not Granny. I can beat this."

A thought entered her mind of a movie star who had revealed her battle with breast cancer. Elsie pressed her fingers into a breast and felt a flash of fear. She pressed again, wondering if all was well.

Chapter 20

Elsie sat with her arms crossed, looking at the Georgia Code on the computer screen as though she were staring down the phony smile of a greasy haired used car salesman who was presenting her with his last best offer.

As much as it hurt to contemplate Daniel forcing her into a mental health facility, she did understand. Everything pointed to severe mental illness. The family history. Her residency dropout. Her increasingly bizarre behavior. No known medical cause. From his perspective, what else could it be but severe mental illness? And if she now told him, Oh, and I now see monsters... Well, that wasn't going to happen.

And there was something else that wasn't going to happen. Not if she could help it—and she could. Elsie wasn't going to be locked up. She'd make sure of that. She'd have to take her own preemptive steps.

The first step was to go shopping.

*****

Elsie went from store to store and had the same feeling in each place that she was being followed. At her second store, she was sure of it. The parking lot was filled and a steady stream of people were coming and going, but she felt unsure about going out there alone. She could've handled her purchase herself, but she asked for assistance. Her eyes searched in every direction for—

She didn't know what she was looking for. All she knew was that she could literally feel in her flesh that she was being watched and followed.

"Thank you," she said to the diminutive guy who had helped her.

She sat down and smiled at the thought that she probably outweighed him by ten pounds. She stopped smiling when her eyes looked through the passenger window and fell upon a white van. It was close enough to look eerily familiar to the van that had chased her. Yet it was far away enough for her to not be sure. But she could see that at least two men were in it.

Elsie eyed the van and turned the ignition. It looked as though they were looking at her. She was tired of this. She looked around to make sure she wouldn't run over anyone. Her foot pressed hard on the gas pedal. The tires squealed as she made the quick, sharp right, and rolled decisively toward the van.

The van rolled out of its spot at an unnatural speed, took a quick right, and dashed away—at least that's how Elsie interpreted it. It was already a foregone conclusion in her mind that she was not going to let this van get away. A slow walking woman with a stroller and another child, and a car backing out of a spot, changed those plans.

Elsie watched the van turn a corner and disappear out of her sight. She slammed both hands on the steering and let out three quick curse words. Once the anger over losing the van lessened, fear replaced it.

What if that was the same van that followed me from the church? That means they know where I live. They're after me! Elsie thought about telling Daniel. She had to tell Daniel. She stopped. I can't tell Daniel. He'll think my fear is turning into paranoia.

There was only one thing Elsie could do.

She adjusted her beliefs and went to another store. She left that store with the faint sound of a chorus of evil laughter in her head, with a more bellicose laugh rising above the rest.

*****

Shopping done, Elsie returned home and sat in the enclosed garage. She just needed a moment before going inside. She wondered at the irony of how she felt. She should've felt more empowered. Instead, she felt weakened, compromised. Whoever those men were in the van, they were the ones calling the shots. Her fear of them was calling the shots.

Elsie closed her eyes and leaned against the headrest. She was tired. Her mind was tired. Her soul was tired. The tears that now rolled down her cheeks were tired. How long could she go on like this? The family fear curse. Monsters. The white van. The threat of being locked up. Elsie wouldn't voice it, nor would she allow herself to consciously think it. But she couldn't stop the ground from shaking beneath her. Life was crashing atop her, and she felt the full weight of its debris pinning her helplessly.

Helpless.

Elsie's eyes opened in defiance of the thought. Her face hardened in resolve. She gathered the stuff she purchased, angrily snatching one piece after another. She had never been weak a day in her life, and she wouldn't start now. She positioned and covered the purchased items and prepared herself mentally for whatever may come next.

Next was not far away.

*****

Elsie knew she was going to the basement. She had to. It was the easiest and most immediate way for her to gauge whether she was getting better. Not that she had any reason to think she may be getting better. She didn't. Instead, she had growing evidence that she was getting worse fast. And that was all the more reason she had to go to the basement. For the moment she stopped fighting, she'd become Mother and Granny.

But the fight would have to wait a few moments while Elsie sat and allowed herself to smile. There wasn't much to smile about these days. But if her pouring cooking oil over her hair didn't qualify, what did? *That was a mess getting that out!* She thought of the breast-poking, breast-grabbing, red-suit preacher. That earned more than a smile. That got a laugh.

Elsie's laughter faded as thoughts of the slithering woman jarred her mind. The woman had said, "I won't come out of her. You can't make me leave." *An odd way to refer to yourself.*

She thought of all of those people claiming to have been healed of cancer. There were four or five of them. Had they all been deceived? The woman next to her at the church had claimed to be healed of breast cancer. This wasn't a televangelist. It was just a spontaneous, private testimony from someone sitting next to her. *Why would she lie to me?* thought Elsie.

Elsie let her mind rest from its questionings. After a minute or so, she headed for the door to the basement. She put her hand on the knob only minutes after Anna texted this message to the women's Bible study group: *Pray for my sister Elsie. Atheist. Very proud. Ask God to humble her so she can receive the truth. No matter what it takes. She's like Pharoah.*

Elsie wanted her steps down the basement stairs to match the defiance she felt in her heart upstairs. They didn't. They were slow, each foot landing on the bottom step as though it had no business being there and was just waiting for the slightest pretext to run back to the safety of the floor above.

She landed at the stairs' bottom and looked at the guitar. That's where she needed to go. Only several feet separated her from the instrument, but it might as well have been several miles. She looked at it as though it was both a beloved friend and a lethal enemy and was unsure of its intent toward her. Each step toward it was no less sure than the one before.

Finally, she was within an arm's reach. *Touch it. Pick it up. Music is your gift. You can't let them take it,* Elsie told herself. She looked at it until her still body betrayed her with trembling just as her eyes had betrayed her with tears.

Fear of Music grew angrier the closer she got to his instrument. He looked at her trembling hand with glaring eyes for the slightest forward movement. *What are you doing, Slave? This is my instrument! Do—not—touch—my—instrument!*

The thought was loud in her mind. She jerked her hand back farther than she had put it before her. She kept moving it until her hand was behind her back, as though she was hiding it.

Fear of Music's skin pulled back from a low-growling, narrow mouth filled with sharp teeth. He watched as her hand came out of hiding and again reached for his instrument. The goat's trembling fingers were almost on the neck of his guitar.

Elsie's will defiantly pushed her fearful hand forward. She put her hand on the guitar and gripped it tightly, waiting for the assault. The monsters had only beat her when she had used the name of Jesus against them. Would that remain the only trigger for a beating, or would her fighting for her music cause another one?

She looked around. The room was still.

She listened. Her mind was quiet.

She waited for the attack. It didn't come.

Elsie slowly lifted the guitar from the stand. She walked with light steps toward the sofa. She stood before it, let out a breath, and slowly turned around. She sat down.

All hell broke loose.

The dread that fell upon Elsie immediately snatched away her mental and physical equilibrium. She fell off the sofa and spiraled downward, tumbling and twirling violently, hundreds, maybe thousands of feet before she slammed onto the floor. Her motionless body was immovable. Her eyes fluttered open and shut. They opened again, and the room's walls moved in and out like an accordion. The ceiling went up and down until her brain gave the command to throw up, which she did.

Elsie had no concept of time as this blender of dread overcame her with fear and tried to shake her innards out of her body. She lifted her face off the carpet with the greatest effort, only for it to slam down again.

The noise.

The noise was booming and piercing. It felt like it was literally cutting through her body. She had to stop the noise or it would kill her. Intuitively, she knew what would stop the noise. The guitar had fallen across her back. She had to get away from it. But she couldn't. She had no strength. Fear had sucked the life from her muscles. Elsie moved anyway, dragging herself inch by inch until the offending weapon was no longer touching her body.

A half hour later Elsie recovered enough to escape to the bottom of the stairs. Her depleted body took another ten minutes to make it up the stairs, and after another two hours of bitter crying on the floor near the top door leading to the basement, she fell asleep.

She awakened to a more dangerous and different kind of threat.

*****

Elsie lifted herself and walked through the house in the residue of a stupor of disorientation. Physically, she felt more depleted than after she had run the Yakima River Canyon Marathon. She couldn't explain how touching a guitar and crawling up a flight of stairs had left her in such a weakened condition, but it had. What had these monsters done to her?

Elsie let her thousand-pound body sink into the sofa. She looked at the ceiling and got no answers. Her eyes closed. Perhaps the darkness would give her light. It didn't. Tears came out the corners of her eyes carrying white flags. The monsters were too strong for her. She was like Nicole and Mother and Granny. They had taken her music. She would never play another instrument. She'd never sing again.

After a few moments of bearing the weight of this silent confession, Elsie blinked hard and snatched the white flags of surrender, snapped them, and threw them to the ground. She wouldn't be going back down to that basement any time soon. But she would be back. There was a way to beat these things. She would find that way. *I am not my Mother! I will find a way!* she screamed inside.

Elsie slept for hours and woke up all at once, alert and refreshed. She turned her head and looked at the open blinds as though instructed to do so. Her long legs swung around. She lifted herself and went to the window.

A white van was backed into and parked in her driveway!

A chill shot through Elsie's body. Her paralysis lasted only a moment. She snatched herself from the window and stood beside it. She dropped to a crouch, then to her hands and knees and crawled to the other side of the window. She jumped up and ran to the door. It was locked. She ran upstairs to the bedroom. Her mind slipped for a moment. *Where did I put it?*

Elsie ran to her deep walk-in closet and pulled down the case. She had put it up there thinking she'd have time to decide where to permanently hide it. She opened the case and pulled out the gun.

The guy at the gun store had made the mistake of offering to show her the "female" guns. Presumably, Elsie figured, this meant a smaller caliber with less kick. He even had pink handguns. Her silent, hard stare served its purpose and he quickly transitioned to a more business-like tone and another set of guns. Her answers were crisp and no-nonsense.

"Yes, I understand the difference in a revolver and a semi-automatic." "Yes, I understand what you've explained about single-action, double-action, and double-action-only revolvers." "No, I want a double-action-only, .38 Special, and a box of hollow-point bullets."

Elsie wasn't a stranger to guns, and she wasn't afraid of them. She just didn't believe in them. But after seeing the white van in the parking lot of the sporting goods store, she found that she believed even less in her being kidnapped, raped, and murdered. She loaded six bullets into her new partner and exited the closet. Now, it seemed that a semi-automatic and a fifteen-round magazine wasn't a bad idea. But she'd make do with her revolver. She only had six bullets, but she had no intentions of missing her targets.

Elsie neared the bedroom door and thought unbelievably, *I haven't called 911.* She let out a curse when she realized her phone was downstairs. She'd use the land line. She lifted it to her ear and looked hard at the door. The phone was dead.

She heard the front door close. This surprised her. Why would someone break into a home and not close the door quietly? Daniel? It was Daniel! She started to call out his name and stopped. She crept to a room across the hall and looked out the window. The van was still there, but Daniel's car wasn't, and she hadn't heard the garage door open.

Her stalkers were in the house!

Elsie remembered seeing two of them. Six bullets, two intruders. What should she do? Wait for them to come after her? Go after them?

"Ellll-seee, we know you're in here...some—where."

The man's brazen voice called out for her in a sing-song, mocking tone, as though this was a game.

"We're not going to hurt you, Elsie," another voice said. "Not if you come out. Now if you make this hard on us, we're gonna have to make this hard on you."

A hundred thoughts fought for Elsie's attention. Two finally emerged victorious. *You know your house better than they do.* The other was, *Be strong, Elsie. Go get them.*

Elsie stuck her head out the door and pulled it back quickly, just like she had seen the cops do on TV. Nothing. She could clearly hear them downstairs. Why were they being so loud? Their confidence tried to convince her that she couldn't win. Why were they being so brazen? What did they know that she didn't know?

"We missed you the other night, Elsie. Coulda had a real nice time—the three of us," said the first man Elsie had heard.

Elsie crept to the top of the stairs. She put her left hand under the gun hand, which she held close to her chest, and pointed the gun's barrel upward and away from her face. It would be better to sneak quickly down the stairs rather than slowly. Slow would just give them more time to discover her.

Elsie hurried down the stairs without making the slightest noise. Sounds to the right of her. She jumped out and saw both of them. *Both of them! Good!* She didn't say, "Stop!" Or, "Put your hands up!" or anything like that. Her finger pulled the trigger a moment after the one closest to her caught a glimpse of her and said, "Watch out!"

The two intruders scattered as hollow point bullets exploded in quick succession. Elsie jumped back to the other side of the stairs. Her loud, rapid breaths were like pistons shooting in and out of her mouth too fast to distinguish one from the other. Her heart's thumping seemed out of control. Elsie struggled to not past out.

Be quiet, Elsie. Be quiet, she told herself, but she couldn't. Her body was acting on its own. Her trigger finger had acted on its own, betraying her plan to take well-executed, deliberate shots at their torsos. Instead, when she saw them, something grabbed her arms and finger and aimed and shot at the fast moving men until there was nothing but clicking sounds coming from the gun.

Elsie's mind didn't tell her to run upstairs for more bullets. Just as it had not told her to carry more bullets with her down the stairs. But it was telling her something now. It was telling her there was no way she had missed. The men had surprised her with their quickness, but she had gotten off a few nice, clean, unobstructed shots. Maybe neither of them was hit more than once, but she was sure both had been hit at least once.

Elsie looked at her empty gun barrel. She made herself breathe slowly. "If you're not already dead, you're going to be—if you don't leave now." Her voice was strong. She waited a few moments. "If I have to go around that corner, both of you are going to die."

One of the men responded immediately, and in a voice that was stronger than it should've been coming from a man who had been shot. "And if you don't come around this corner, we're going to kill Daniel when he comes home. Then we're going to go to your loving sister's house and kill her and Amanda and anyone else we find there. How about that, Elsie?"

The man's words froze her in place.

"El—sie, I know you heard me, darlin. What's it gonna be? How much you love ya family?"

The other man joined her torture. "You emptied your gun, Elsie. You're not fast enough to get back upstairs and reload before we catch you. If it comes to that...well, my friend here said you got a family to think about. All you have to do is stop the tough girl act and wave the white flag. It's not that hard, Elsie."

Elsie's mind exploded into a thousand thoughts that bounced and slammed into one another like they were popcorn kernels battling for space, not one of them showing her a way out. Her hope sank like a collapsed lung. It was hard for her to breathe. A tingling hand went slowly to her chest. She couldn't think of a way out.

What were they going to do to her? Well, that was a needless question to ask, now wasn't it? But would they kill her? That was out of her hands. Her concern now was for her family. She had to save them. The gun dropped from her hand onto the floor.

Elsie walked slowly around the corner and looked at two men, one standing, one sitting, both big, neither bleeding.

"Here." The sitting man threw something to her feet.

Elsie looked down. Handcuffs.

"Put 'em on," said the other man.

She picked them up and snapped one on and was about to snap on the other.

"Behind your back," said the sitting man.

Chapter 21

Daniel looked questioningly in the garage from his car as the door was still lifting. He parked the car, lowered the door, and entered the house through the kitchen. He called Elsie's name and got no response.

The basement, he thought.

He went downstairs. Elsie had been down there; the guitar had been moved. It was on the floor by the sofa. He looked at the guitar knowing it had a story to tell. He left it on the floor for his wife's next attempt to play it and went up the stairs two at a time.

He stood outside the basement door wondering where she could be at this hour. He pulled his phone out and called her number. In a second, he heard her phone ringing. He followed the ring into the family room. There it was on the table. He picked it up and checked her text messages. He checked her recent sent and received calls.

"Elsie, where are you?" he said, remembering the squirrel, and how she acted when she saw him in the kitchen earlier that morning. Then there were the bruises on her arms, her swollen face, the sticky stuff in her hair. She wasn't in her right mind. *Why did I leave her here alone?* he asked himself angrily. *I never should've left her.*

He hurried up the dark stairs. He wasn't expecting her to be there, but he needed to physically check everywhere in the house before he started making phone calls and before he called the police.

He didn't find Elsie, but he did find something in her closet on the floor that heightened his fears and made his mouth go dry. An open gun case and an opened box of bullets next to it. He picked the box up. What was she doing with a gun? His eyes widened. "Oh, my God!" he said, expecting the worse. "No. No. No. Oh, God, no. Please, no," he begged with watering eyes. He knew he was going to find her body somewhere. "Nooooooooooooooooo," he moaned as though a spear was in his gut.

Daniel ran through the house screaming Elsie's name and looking everywhere. He ran downstairs and checked every room. She wasn't there. He walked into the kitchen and started punching numbers.

None of her family had seen her. Another name popped into mind. He brushed his anger aside. He had to find his wife. "Hello, Anna, this is Daniel. I'm sorry for calling so late. I came home and Elsie's not here. Have you seen or talked to her today?"

Anna looked at the time. "What? It's almost midnight. She didn't tell you where she was going?"

Daniel kept himself from starting his response with GD and ending it with, "Would I be calling you if she had told me where she was going?" Instead, he pushed the anger down and said, "No, she didn't tell me."

"What about where she works? Maybe they called her."

Daniel's heart lifted. Elsie was a contract RN and had rarely accepted night work, but maybe...just maybe. His heart sank again. Why would she take a loaded gun to work? *Why do you have a gun, period!*

"Daniel—"

"Anna, if you hear from her—"

"Daniel, you sound worried," said Anna. "Can I pray for you?" She began an immediate prayer.

Daniel listened with an impatience that could've strangled Anna.

"Lord Jesus, I ask you to protect my sister wherever she is. And show Daniel you're real by causing her to call him. Please comfort his heart while he waits for the call. And thank you for giving my sister such a good man to take care—"

Daniel's phone beeped. He looked at it with wide eyes. *Huh? Are you kidding me? Can't be.*

"Anna—"

"Elsie, isn't it?" said Anna. "God is real, Daniel. Don't forget who made her call. We didn't come from monkeys. We have a creator. Good night."

Daniel was too relieved to spend more than a moment thinking how presumptuous she was to take credit for Elsie calling. "Thank you, Anna. Sorry to call so late. Good night."

"God bless both of you, Daniel," said Anna.

"Elsie, is that you?" he asked.

"Daniel, I can't talk long. They don't know I'm on the phone," Elsie whispered.

"Who doesn't know you're on the phone?"

"I don't know who they are. Two men. They followed me and broke in the house. They told me if I didn't leave with them, they'd kill you and Amanda. They took me away in a white van. I had to go, Daniel."

Daniel listened to the hushed whisperings with new horror. The situation had gone from suicide to mass murder to kidnap in a matter of a couple of minutes. "Where are you? Do you know where you are?" he asked. "I'll call the police. I'll come get you."

"There are two of them, Daniel," she warned.

"Where are you?" he asked again. "I need to know where you are."

"I don't know. Somewhere in the mountains."

"Somewhere in the mountains?" Daniel thought about what showed up on his phone. "Are you near a window? Can you see anything?"

"Yes," she whispered. I can't see it now. It's too dark now. But earlier I saw water. Lots of water. Like a big lake."

Daniel dropped his head into his hand, his mind bouncing back and forth between fear and despair. He was hoping for despair. "Did you see a boat docked near where the men have you?"

Elsie thought. "Yes. A pontoon. A red pontoon."

A heavy-breath cry came up and out of Daniel in light waves. "Okay, Elsie. That'll help us find you." An alarm went off inside of him. "Elsie, what did you do with the gun? Have you used the gun?"

"I tried to shoot them. When they broke in the house. I tried to shoot them near the kitchen. Daniel, they're coming."

The phone went dead.

Daniel wished he could fall to the floor and cry like a baby. He wished he could cry until he died. Until his body matched the death he felt inside. But he didn't have time for grief. He had to rescue Elsie. He turned and stopped, looking at the wall. What was this? It was a mess. A chunk—no, two chunks of backsplash was missing. It looked as though—*Oh, God! Bullet holes!* Daniel looked around and wondered how he had missed this mess. Elsie had shot the place full of holes!

Daniel pushed 91 into his phone and stopped. There had been a lot of negative publicity about cops shooting down people. Cops had a tough and dangerous job, and he had the utmost respect for them. But some of the videos he had seen showed either good cops making bad decisions, or bad cops being bad. He canceled the call. If Elsie waved that gun at a cop, she'd be shot dead. He'd do this alone.

Daniel rushed to the car and headed for Lake Lanier.

*****

An hour and a half later Daniel pulled into their Lake Lanier home. The only vehicle he saw was Elsie's. He pushed the garage door opener. No cars. He hadn't expected to see any other cars, but he had to make sure. Elsie sounded so convincing.

Remembering the gun, Daniel stuck only his head in the door. "Elsie," he called. No answer. He turned on the light and stepped in, looking around, ready to duck and run for cover. "Elsie, it's Daniel."

Elsie's eyes widened. Was it really Daniel? She heard the voice again. It *was* Daniel. He was here! The men? Where were they? *Oh, Daniel, be careful. They've got guns.*

"Elsie."

Daniel was getting closer.

The men must have left. It was safe for her to call out to him. "In here, Daniel. Hurry!"

Daniel opened the bedroom door.

Elsie was on the bed lying on her back with her hands behind her waist. She looked up smiling behind tears. "I knew you'd come for me. Untie my legs. We can leave before they come back."

Daniel looked at her legs. There was nothing to untie. He moved slowly to her feet and began to untie her.

She hopped up and turned her back to him. "How do we get these handcuffs off?"

Daniel squeezed both her shoulders and tenderly lowered his nose to the back of her head and inhaled with closed eyes. "I'll get them off." He moved his hands on and around her wrists. "They're off."

Elsie felt them come off and heard them fall to the floor.

She turned quickly around. "We have to go!"

Two big, loving, male hands gripped her face. Hands that had earlier wondered whether they'd ever feel her alive again. He held her face upward for his lips to meet hers. They did.

She tried to talk.

His kisses smothered her words.

"But the men," she was finally able to protest.

Daniel looked at his beautiful Elsie. He didn't know if she'd ever be normal again. But he knew he'd do whatever it took to get her the help she needed—even if it hurt him. Right now, however, her husband who hadn't had her in what seemed ages needed a prescription only her body she could fill.

He looked into her eyes and began with the buttons on her blouse. His voice was low and full of desire. "Don't worry about the other men. I've taken care of them. There's only one man you need to think about right now, and that man is me."

Elsie's world, even if it was now a cruel mixture of fact and fantasy, real and Unreal, was not without a long denied hunger for her husband. She closed her eyes and focused on what he was lovingly, then impatiently, then roughly doing to her. It was beautifully satisfying, but not enough to entirely muffle the evil laughter in the back of her mind and the monster's voice that repeated over and over, "You are mine."

*****

Unreal looked at Terror. "You are impressed."

Terror had always had a deep respect for Unreal's phobic abilities. That is why he tolerated the demon's big mouth and uncouth ways. But this was remarkable. He had delivered. Elsie was now in Unreal's world. He didn't have to worry about her ruining his plans to become director of Fear Academy. "More than you can imagine."

"And the fun's just begun," said Unreal.

Chapter 22

Elsie lay on her side with her tearful eyes wide open. They'd been open for over two hours. Daniel was asleep, next to her on his side and pressed against her back. His arm was draped across her with a hand that though sleeping still had a light, sensuous grip on her. Oh, that she could lie there forever and never get up. Never having to rise from her husband's loving embrace to face the hell her life had become. Never having to turn over and look into his sad eyes to see that her actions had emphatically declared to them both that she was already worse than Nicole, Mother, and Granny.

Elsie's mind floated mockingly, accusingly to episodes in her life where she had beat the odds. Where she had won when she should have lost. Where she had nothing but her will to sustain her until she could find a way to turn the impossible into the possible.

She wasn't supposed to be able to be so heavily involved in extracurricular activities in high school and college and get straight A's and perfect SAT and MCAT scores. She did.

She wasn't supposed to win a marathon with so little training. There was no way to beat the three-year-in-a-row winner. She did.

On and on they came. One unlikely achievement after the other.

Strong Elsie.

Elsie the indomitable.

The woman who refuses to lose.

Even Wonder Woman.

Then another set of thoughts, rogue thoughts, alien thoughts jumping the border fence of the Elsie legend, rushed her in mass. There was no way to stop them all. They trampled her legend, and when the dust settled, she knew that the legend had always been a myth. There were some things even she couldn't do.

Wonder Woman's not severely mentally ill; I am. I'm not Wonder Woman, thought Elsie. *I'm just a woman. A woman who doesn't know what's real and what's unreal. A woman who has no idea how to stop her life from spiraling out of control. A woman who is scared. I'm scared.*

The tears continued to roll down Elsie's face, and for the first time in her life she allowed tears to give her relief. For the first time in her life, she wasn't angry at herself for crying. It was an odd, liberating feeling allowing herself to feel weakness and not fight it.

A thought seemed to follow every other tear.

What disease do I have? Is it going to get worse? Better? Is the disease creating the monsters? Or are the monsters really monsters? How could a hallucination beat me and drag me up the stairs? Was I really beaten? Was I really dragged up the stairs? If not, where did the bruises come from?

An old question came around the bend like a long-distance runner deliberately pacing himself slower before turning on the burners and beating everyone across the finish line. *What about Anna and her freedom from fear?*

"Sweetheart, are you awake?" Daniel asked softly.

Sweetheart, Elsie said to herself. Her condition had stressed Daniel so much that his spoken terms of endearment had become rare. She didn't answer. She wanted to hear it again.

"Sweetheart," he said.

"Yes, Daniel, I'm awake."

"You know where we are?" he asked.

"We're at the lake house."

"You know how we got here?"

Elsie knew that Daniel could have asked this as, "Do you know that you're severely mentally ill?" She appreciated that he didn't. "Yes. I drove myself here."

There was a long silence.

"There are bullet holes in the kitchen," he said softly.

Elsie wished there was a way she'd never have to look into Daniel's hurt eyes to discuss her illness or how she had failed him and Amanda. He was a good man and deserved so much more than she had given.

She turned over on her back and looked up at him. He deserved this much. "I shot at intruders who weren't there. I'm a danger to myself and others." Elsie looked through his tender eyes and controlled expression and saw his heart rupture with grief. "Daniel, it's okay. You're only a man. You have a right to feel pain and disappointment. You have a right to be confused and heartbroken."

He rubbed the side of her face ever so lightly. "You're the strongest person I've ever met." His eyes dropped and looked again into her eyes. "I'm sorry."

"For what, Daniel? You've done nothing wrong."

"I'm sorry for not loving you more. For not supporting you better. For being selfish. For leaving you alone when you needed me the most. For not being a better husband."

Elsie lifted herself to one elbow and shook her head. "You're wrong. You've been everything you say you haven't been. I couldn't ask for a better husband. What's happened to me is not your fault. This is all me, Daniel. It's a family illness. Something I should not have allowed you to marry into."

"You didn't know, Elsie. How could you have seen this coming? No one could've seen this coming."

Elsie looked at Daniel and said with quivering lips, "I'm scared. I don't know what to do. I don't know what's going to happen to me."

He had never seen her afraid before. He had never heard her say she didn't know what to do. She always knew what to do. Even when she dropped out of residency, she never considered it final.

It was the reason why she became a registered nurse. She'd only accept a handful of work days a month, but this was her way of maintaining a formal connection with a hospital. Her way of saying, "I will return."

"And Daniel...I know that you're scared, too. It's okay. It's okay for us to be scared."

"I'll be strong for us, Elsie."

She gripped his arm. "No, I don't need you to be strong. I need you to be weak." Her new freedom to cry without resisting was expressing itself. "I need you to let it out. I need you to hurt with me. To cry with me."

"Elsie...."

"I'm never going to finish my residency, Daniel. I'm never going to sing or play an instrument again. I can't beat this fear. Please, cry with me." Sobs drove her head into his chest.

He hugged her into himself and momentarily fought the emotion that pushed up from his chest into his throat. In a moment, his masculine resistance gave way to his human weakness and he burst into sobs, his own tears dropping onto his wife's hair and face.

Deep in Elsie's fearful heart, she heard the resilient question on its victory lap, *What about Anna and her freedom from fear?*

*****

Daniel and Elsie had agreed at the lake house that she would voluntarily admit herself to Peachview Pines, a mental health facility run by one of his golfing buddies and his wife. She had asked him to promise her that he wouldn't do anything to make her stay longer than two weeks. He answered her request with a teary-eyed, "I love you."

Elsie didn't press Daniel for a firm commitment because she didn't want to make him lie. She was seeing intruders that weren't there, and even shooting at them. She was a danger to herself and others. If he truly loved her and Amanda, he had to do everything within his power to help her and protect their child—

even if it meant locking her up. He did, however, follow up his vague answer with the news that he had invited the psychiatrist couple to have dinner with them at their home. Tonight.

Daniel's stated reason was so that Elsie could meet with and talk to them in a nonprofessional, non-clinical environment before being admitted. Elsie's perceived reason was so they could observe and evaluate her in her home environment. Plus, they could see for themselves how she shot up the place.

The other reason, Elsie knew—and understood and even appreciated—was that even now Daniel was fighting himself on what remedial path to take. The professional opinions of two psychiatrists would help.

Several hours later Daniel, Elsie, and Drs. Jeremy and Inez Smith sat in the dining room eating dinner. Elsie had earlier furtively noticed Daniel showing bullet holes to each of them when he was sure she wasn't watching. She also noticed Jeremy taking inconspicuous pictures of the bullet holes with his phone camera on her way to the restroom that she had no present need of using.

Jeremy and Inez were personable, good conversationalists, and apparently devoted to the betterment of their patients. They were also quite good at initiating and orchestrating evaluative conversations without appearing to do so.

What a team you two are, Emily observed. *We haven't had one official doctor-patient discussion and already you have enough to start Daniel's tough love.* She studied everything about these two and found herself accurately anticipating their masked communications to one another. A look, a smile, a raised eyebrow. Watching them, Elsie felt like an amateur codebreaker.

After one such intercepted communication, Elsie anticipated Inez's need to use the restroom. "Oop, let me quickly take care of the restroom for anyone who may need it." She left the room and the professionals began to whisper.

Elsie took care of the restroom and answered a hunch and looked out the family room window onto the street. A marked police cruiser was parked on their side of the street about fifty feet away. It was between their house and the Burkinson's. Now why would he park there and not in front of the Burkinson's? She could see two officers in the car. "You're not there for the Burkinson's, are you?" she said aloud.

Elsie returned to the dining room and smiled at Rachel. "It's ready. It's right around here and down this hall."

Inez followed her, and Elsie returned to the dining room. Elsie knew the clock was ticking when Inez returned to the room and gave her husband and Daniel the look. "Please excuse me. Now it's my turn to go to the restroom."

Elsie went to the restroom and retrieved her phone from behind the stand-up picture frame and ran like a cat up the stairs and into the large washroom to get one of her pre-emptive purchases she made the day before. She'd listen to the recording on her phone before using it. She had downloaded the recording app for just this kind of situation. She pushed the button.

Nothing. For some reason the app didn't work.

The three witchcraft spirits that Elsie had picked up laughed at her and at the other demons inside of her, especially Unreal. "You didn't see that coming, did you? We're witchcraft."

Swoosh! Klunk!

Swoosh! Klunk!

Swoosh! Klunk!

Three large witchcraft demons lay sprawled in awkward positions on top one another. It happened too fast to qualify as a surprise. Their demonic competitors would let them know what happened once they awakened. But, first, they had to be still enough so they could be around to taunt the witchcraft spirits later.

The large mercy angel stared intensely into Unreal's wavy eyes. Unreal didn't move. The mercy angel moved his eyes from one demon to the other looking for the slightest movement, anything that resembled aggression. Their rebellious natures wouldn't let them totally follow the path of safety without an inner struggle, but they all managed.

The phone recording came on. Elsie's mouth dropped open as she listened.

"Run, Elsie!" said the mercy angel without taking his eyes off the demons. "Run to the safety of the Lord!"

Elsie felt a surge of adrenaline. She grabbed the box and ran to the room. She tore the box open and pulled out the fire escape ladder. She dropped to her knees and snatched the gloves under the bed and jammed her hands into them. She opened the window, hooked the ladder, and climbed out and down, jumping to the ground when she was within six feet of it. She sprinted to the part of the eight-foot tall wood fence where she had hammered two blocks of wood, one higher than the other, to help her get over with minimum effort, and most of all, quickly.

Once over, Elsie immediately got on a knee and pulled the flashlight out of the plastic pouch she had positioned. She turned it on and let it lead her to the small tarp that covered the bicycle she had bought at the sporting goods store. She looked back at the house, then in every direction to make sure no one else was in the woods. It was their property, but that didn't mean no one was back there.

Satisfied that she was the only one in the woods, she took off her shoes, pants, and blouse. She pulled out the biking outfit, sneakers, wig, and helmet. In under a minute, she was a new person. She stuffed the clothes they'd be looking for into her backpack and put it on her back. She took a last look at her house and rolled the bike through the woods and onto the street.

*****

The doorbell rang and Daniel let the male and female police officers in the house. "She's in the restroom," he said, feeling like the one who betrayed Jesus.

They waited for a while, listening to the bathroom fan. Finally, Daniel knocked on the door. "Elsie." She didn't answer. He looked at the officers. "Elsie." He knocked when she didn't answer. He turned the knob. It was locked. The male police stepped forward and Daniel put up a palm. He reached above the door's ledge and pulled down a thin piece of metal and stuck it in the hole of the door's knob. He opened the door and stated the obvious. "She's not here."

"Elsie," Daniel called out, going from room to room. He got to their bedroom and looked at the open window and something hooked to its ledge. He moved closer and saw the box, then the ladder. He cursed. "Elsie, what are you doing?"

*****

The cops put out an All Points Bulletin for a tall, white, blonde female on foot, dressed in tan pants and a white blouse. The police who were there with Daniel scurried out the door and drove around the neighborhood. Elsie was nowhere to be found. The only woman they saw outdoors was a Caucasian female on a bike with long black hair under a helmet, and wearing skin-tight, colorful bicycle garb. The woman waved at the cops as she pedaled past their oncoming car.

Elsie rode hard and fast. One thought was in her mind: *What about Anna and her freedom from fear?*

*****

"What's going on? What's going on? What's going on?" screamed Unreal. "Why didn't we know about this? Where'd that mercy angel come from? What attracted him to her? She doesn't even believe in the Creator! She believes in monkeys! They're not putting me out, I tell you! I'm no bum! I will not leave my house!"

"That freak angel told her to run to the safety of the Lord." This was Pride, who had gotten a burst of courage since the mercy angel's departure.

Worship of Intellect smirked at Pride. "You could've called him a freak when he was here."

Pride answered with a squinched nose and an upturned cheek.

Unreal flinched. "He did, didn't he? What do you think he meant by that?"

"It…could only…mean one thing, Unreal," said one of the witchcraft spirits who had been knocked out and was now sitting on his butt, speaking in a groggy slur, and wondering why he was sitting and why the other witchcraft spirits were laid out. "The enemy's…going…to try…to take that atheist…from us."

*****

Terror glared at every demon in his office and rested his burning eyes on Unreal, his friend. Only he wasn't looking at him as a friend. He was looking at him as though there was only a fraction of a second separating him from leaping across his desk and tearing into the phobic powerhouse.

"Unreal!" Terror screamed, and slammed his heavy fist on his desk five times, screaming a curse word each time his fist hit it. "You said you had everything under control! How could you let this happen?"

Terror's sudden and public outburst caught Unreal by surprise. He understood the pressure Terror was under, but that didn't stop his own anger from rising for being treated like this in front of his subordinates. He looked at Terror with a hard look. "I'm no bum."

Terror stood up straighter and taller. "So—you—say. If you're no bum, tell me how a proud atheist with no prayer support is now taking orders from an angel."

Unreal was under pressure, too. He wasn't trying to get a promotion like Terror. He was trying to keep from getting the boot again. His words were mixed with angry grit. "It wasn't just any angel."

"What kind of angel was it?" yelled Terror.

"It was a mercy angel," Unreal answered.

Terror's large head involuntarily backed up a few inches. "Ugh," he grunted.

"Yes, ugh," mimicked Unreal. "A mercy angel. He came out of nowhere and knocked all hell out of the witchcraft demons before we even knew he was there. He then did that macho stare down thing they always do."

"What did you do? Did you try to stop him? You had him outnumbered," Terror pressed.

"Listen to yourself," Unreal yelled. "Did we try to stop him? We don't have an answer for the mercy of God and these freak mercy angels of his. You know that. Would it have been better for us to jump him so the rest of his big head cannibal friends could pop out of nowhere and bite our heads off? Where would that leave you and your directorship?"

Unreal's insubordination appeared to have calmed the dark power. The big mouth demon was right. Terror sat down. "A mercy angel," he mused.

"Yes, Terror, he was just...*there*," said a demon. "It doesn't make sense. She's an atheist. She doesn't deserve mercy."

This statement earned the unbelieving stares of Terror, Unreal, Fear of Failure, and the others. "Now if she deserved mercy, it wouldn't be mercy, now would it?" said Terror.

The demon's expression showed that he didn't understand.

"Who are you? What is your name? I don't recognize you," said Terror. "Is he one of yours, Fear of Failure?"

"Absolutely not," came the quick answer. Fear of Failure stepped away from him. "I don't know who this idiot is."

"Who are you, demon?" demanded Terror.

"I'm hemorrhoids."

Terror didn't try to stop the laughter in the room.

"He's a pain in the butt," said one of the laughing demons.

Terror shook his head in disgust. "Lord Satan, has it come to this? No wonder we're always playing catch-up. Hemorrhoids? Why are you here?"

The demon shrugged. "I don't know. The door was open. I saw a crack and slipped in with the spirits of infirmity. You want me to leave?"

Terror looked at the hapless demon in disbelief. "Yes. Please...leave."

The spirit walked gingerly out the room.

"Hey, looks like he's got hemorrhoids," a demon whispered to another.

"Enough of that pain in the butt!" said Terror. "Elsie. I'm assigning an observer spirit. He reports directly to me. Give him whatever he needs. Do not interfere with his work. Do you understand? I am *not* getting any more surprises." He looked at Unreal and the rest of the demons he had summoned. "What are you going to do about Elsie running to the safety of the Lord?"

Unreal spoke for them all. "We're going to stop her."

Chapter 23

Elsie's plans had one simple objective: don't get locked up. So far, so good. She'd keep it that way. Daniel and the police would check all the obvious places first. Family and friends. None of these would be getting a call or visit any time soon from her.

Elsie thought about her disguise. It was good enough for a dark-haired woman on a bike to fool passing cops in a car who were looking for a walking blond. It probably wouldn't be good enough to fool hotel staff who were able to compare a good photo with a woman standing a few feet away from them in the light. No local hotels or motels.

Elsie pedaled realizing that her plan to get away had been brilliant, but her plan for what to do afterwards was maybe not so brilliant. Actually, now that she had given the posse the slip, there was no plan except to keep pedaling.

She thought of something. As far as they knew, she was walking. So they'd only check the local hotels and motels. If she rode far enough away, she'd probably be safe. Probably safe was better than not safe, so she hit the Silver Comet trail. She had about an hour before sunset.

This was a sixty-one mile paved trail that used to be a rail line. It ran from Smyrna, Georgia to the Georgia-Alabama border. Some parts of it were secluded, surrounded by trees and bushes or rock formations, and some parts were long strait shots with nothing on either side but homes or fields of grass. The trail had a reputation for being safe. However, a woman had been murdered on the trail in 2009. Another had been brutally beaten in 2004, and there had been a few incidents of robberies. So she wasn't taking her safety for granted. She no longer had the gun, but she had purchased something that would help.

Elsie pedaled another ten minutes and entered the trail. In her top left shirt pocket was her *helper*. She mentally turned into Elsie the woman who beat the three-year-in-a-row marathon winner and pedaled like there was no tomorrow. The trail was safe, but it would be getting dark soon, and she wasn't volunteering to be the trail's exception to its safety record.

She whizzed down the trail, passing a walker here and there. There weren't many people out in the late afternoon. *Probably too close to sunset,* she thought. She sped down a long straight path and was getting near to a bend where there were dense trees on both sides. She'd have to slow down.

*****

Unreal and the other demons looked at their man around the bend. He was a sexual offender parolee who had gone to prison for kidnapping and raping a woman. He had served ten years of his mandatory twenty-five year sentence before convincing the parole board that he had learned his lesson and was no longer a threat to society.

Harold was no longer a threat to society, as far he knew. He certainly had no intentions of hurting anyone like that again. But Harold hadn't planned to hurt that other lady either. It wasn't something he had planned. It just happened.

As usual, that day over ten years ago, he had gorged himself on beer and porn videos before falling asleep. An hour later he awakened with a desire to go walk in the park. When he saw the woman jogging, she was just a woman jogging. Then he snatched her. When the police asked him why he did it, he told the truth. He said, "I don't know. Something just came over me."

This would mark Harold's tenth day out of prison. Earlier, he had downed some beers while watching porn when he got a sudden, strong urge to go walk on the Silver Comet trail. He didn't know why he took his knife.

Harold circled the bend in the path and went into the bushes to take a leak. That's when he saw the biker with long black hair flapping in the wind. Girl's hair. And girl's legs. He waited.

*****

Elsie got closer to the bend in the path. She couldn't see anyone behind or in front of her. As she rolled toward the bend, it was like rolling into a growing bad feeling. The feeling got worse with every revolution of the spinning tires.

Stop, Elsie. Walk the bike around the bend. The angel's voice was low, but made almost inaudible by the noise of her pride, self-will, and rebellion.

Elsie felt something wasn't right. She stood on the bike's pedals and pushed harder on them. She was going to punch it through so fast that whatever was around that corner would see only a whiz go by.

Harold had a big, long stick in his hands waiting for the fast approaching girl's hair and girl's legs—especially the legs. One swing and she'd be knocked off the bike. A couple of blows to the head with the stick and she'd be knocked out cold, or almost knocked out, which would be even better. He'd drag her and her bike into the bushes and do his thing. He may not even have to kill this one if he hit her right the first time.

The mercy angel had permission to speak only once. He watched her with a heavy heart.

Elsie braked hard about forty feet from the bend. The tires skidded to a stop. This was odd, but she looked at the overpass and the bend in the path and felt that something was waiting for her just around the corner. Something bad or something good. She didn't know how to interpret this fuzzy feeling. It seemed to have something to do with learning to trust in something other than herself. Something other than what she could figure out.

"Okay," she said to herself. "A new way. The old way hasn't helped very much." She said this with the foreboding thought in the back of her mind that sooner or later they would catch up with her, and she'd be locked up. Once locked up, those monsters would keep her there forever.

When Elsie said "Okay," a light from heaven streaked to the mercy angel with further instructions. The angel went around the bend where Harold was waiting.

Elsie got off the bike and walked warily toward the bend and overpass. She was twenty feet away when she heard three loud sneezes coming from the bushes to the right, just around the bend. She reached into the backpack and pulled out her helper. She held it in her right hand and rested that hand on the seat as she pushed the bike, guiding it with her left hand.

Now she heard sneezing and coughing coming from the bushes on the right. She focused her attention there, but made quick glances to the left also, just in case the person on the right was trying to distract her for someone on the left.

She stopped when a man emerged from the bushes with a stick in his hand and wiping his mouth with the sleeve of his arm. The man had an up-to-no-good look about him. And it wasn't just that he was scraggly and unshaven. It wasn't even the way he held the stick, or the fact that he came out of the bushes. It was his eyes. They looked dull with evil.

"You okay?" said Elsie, continuing to walk, and continuing to be aware of her left side as well. She noted that his dull eyes brightened as they lingered on her legs.

"Yeah," he said, moving closer. "Bad cough."

Elsie wondered what kind of running shape this guy was in. She walked with the bike as far away from her body as possible.

"You think you can give me a lift for a mile?" His feet kept moving toward her.

"Not built for two," she said and kept walking.

He sped up. "You got the time?" The powerful stick bounced by his leg in his underhand grip.

Elsie stopped and looked dead in his eyes. "You want the time?"

The man was within a quick charge of her. He looked to the left and right and said, "Yeah."

"It's time to stop jumping out of bushes," she said, just before he turned his face back to her and said, "Yeah."

It was at that last turn of his head that Elsie lifted her hand and introduced Harold to her helper. It was a can of bear spray. Not to be confused with pepper spray designed for protection against humans. Bear spray was created powerfully enough and specifically to stop a charging several-hundred-pound bear by setting his eyes and lungs on fire.

Since the sight of a charging bear was enough to throw anyone's aim off, bear spray canisters were designed to be forgiving to the person using it. The minimum distance recommended to spray the brand Elsie had was thirty-two feet. At that range, the canister would produce a thick plume of chemicals the bear couldn't escape.

This guy was well within that range. So Elsie closed her mouth and covered her eyes the moment she blasted him in the face. With her eyes barely open beneath her hand, she followed his screams with several more seconds of misty, chemical hell. Then she ran with her bike beside her for several feet before hopping on and riding off.

Harold spent the next half-hour on his knees blind, coughing, and throwing up.

Elsie spent the next half-hour thinking about how different the outcome would have been had she not listened to that still, small voice inside of her. The peculiar thing about the voice—it was more like a thought or a knowing—was that even though it came from deep within her, she knew it didn't originate with her.

This was more than a passing curiosity. Listening to this, whatever it was, saved her life. *I need to know what this thing is,* she thought. *And I need to find out why the name worked for Anna, but it only got me a beating from monsters.*

*****

Elsie rolled up to the hotel lobby in Smyrna near the Cumberland Mall. Daniel and the cops would not be looking for a walking person to check in to a hotel so many miles away. She looked at the big television screens as she waited in line. News. She watched for a few seconds, then turned away. She looked toward the back of the large lobby and noticed see-through containers of cookies and bowls of fruit.

She had been too nervous to eat much at dinner, and she had ridden her bike over thirty miles. Not to mention the near assault. An apple would take off the edge. She rolled her bike deep into the lobby, put the kickstand on, and got an apple and a cookie. Hey, she'd just taken out a bad guy with bear spray. She deserved a cookie. She also deserved a rest.

She'd sit just to relax for a minute before getting back in line. She bit the cookie and almost choked on it when she saw herself on television. And it wasn't just the real her. It was the made-up her. The disguised her.

Apparently some kid saw her coming out of the woods of someone's private property and filmed her with his phone camera. Now she was sitting in a lobby full of televisions and full of people listening to a reporter describe how she was suffering from hallucinations and was wanted by the police for questioning in a hit and run.

The warm chocolate chip cookie sat lodged at the back of Elsie's mouth. She was afraid that swallowing would draw attention to herself. Attention that she already had, if people looking at her, then looking at the television, then looking back at her, then looking back at the television meant anything.

Elsie scanned the lobby for any uniformed police officers. Seeing none, she calmly stood up and rolled her bike toward the front doors. She was ready to sprint at the slightest provocation.

She saw a plump woman looking at her and walking toward the front desk at an uncomfortable pace. When the lady pointed at Elsie, Elsie trotted to the door with her bike, exited, and disappeared into the night.

She had only been running over an hour, and already she was mentally exhausted. You couldn't let your guard down for a moment. How did crooks do it? Then she remembered: she was a crook! Every cop around was looking for both Elsies. The blonde walker, and the black-hair bike rider.

Elsie thought about riding down Cobb Parkway/Hwy 41. It was a main street with lots of people. Which was the reason she knew she couldn't do it. She had to take back roads. Residential roads. But roads to where? She had nowhere to go. She felt things closing in on her. "I've got to keep riding," she said.

Elsie was now cold. She chided herself. *All my planning. Hanging ladders, bicycle, bear spray, no coat. Another proof that I'm not Wonder Woman. May as well put old Elsie's clothes on over these. They know who I am anyway.*

She put the pants and blouse on and looked around the area for a safe place to gather her thoughts and figure out her next move. She turned off of Spring Street onto a residential street and pedaled slowly. No need for speed when you didn't know where you were going. She saw a small park. The park was dark, but there was a large tree almost in the center of the grass. She could lie the bike down flat and sit against the unlit tree. No one would see her unless they were looking for her. And if that were the case, she'd see them before they saw her.

Elsie sat and leaned against the tree and immediately burst into tears.

Why are you crying, Atheist?

"It's just me. I'm all alone. I'm going crazy, and they want to lock me up."

Have you no monkeys to help you?

Elsie lifted her head from between her legs, which she was hugging, and tried to stop crying long enough to say, "What? Monkeys?"

*****

Unreal grabbed his chest and doubled over with deep, painful coughs that wouldn't stop. Fear of Failure was on one knee, choking, and looking up at the pride spirits, who seemed to be putting on a show with their choking. *Even now the fools want to be seen,* thought Fear of Failure. Everyone was suddenly choking and vomiting. Out of the darkness, the three witchcraft spirits fell to their hands and knees, coughing up awful liquids that moved like a live worm soup on the ground. One by one each coughing, retching demon crawled out of Elsie.

"What was that?" asked a demon.

"Someone's talking to her," said Worship of Intellect. "They want a private conversation."

"Someone? Someone?" yelled Unreal. "We know who someone is! It's Him. It's Him, and this is illegal! He has no right to her! She doesn't want Him! This is no way to put me on the street!"

"He does have a right to her! He has a right to everything and everybody!"

Every demon turned at hearing this voice.

Terror stood there with his hands on his hips.

Once Unreal got over his surprise at seeing Terror, his nature took over. "He flailed his arms in protest. "But she doesn't want Him! She's an atheist! She doesn't believe in Him!"

Terror took three steps forward that put him only inches from a demon it seemed he no longer considered a friend. "It doesn't make a difference what she wants, He wants her. It doesn't make a difference that she's an atheist. He exists. It doesn't' make a difference what she believes. He cannot deny himself. Look at me—all of you. This is now out of our hands."

A pang of fear shot through Unreal. "What do you mean out of our hands?"

"Mercy angels are everywhere." Terror waved his hand in disgust. "Getting reports from every direction. It's up to the woman now."

"Up to the woman?" Unreal asked the question as though this was Terror's decision.

Terror turned on Unreal in a flash. "That's the very reason why you've made a career of getting your wide butt kicked out of homes, Unreal! Use that big crooked head of yours for something other than cracking open walnuts. It's always up to the woman or the man or the child. We—have—never been able to keep anyone out of heaven who wanted to go. Like it or not, we're not God. He is," he said with a finger pointed upward.

Unreal studied his friend's face. "You're not getting the directorship, are you?" His voice was sympathetic.

Terror turned away. "They selected Frightful, Horrible's friend."

"I knew it!" yelled Unreal, flailing his arm. "They were going to do that anyway. This isn't right! You're good demon. You've wrecked more lives in your sleep than that pin head Frightful has done in a thousand years."

"And your house, my friend," said Terror. He put a sympathetic hand on Unreal's shoulder. "You may have to put your walking shoes on again. I fear these mercy angels will make a bum of you."

Unreal's wavy eyes waved a lot. "I don't want to walk the streets again. It's dry out there. And it takes me such a long time to find a suitable home." He looked up at Terror. "I'll not go down without a fight."

Terror looked at the demons. "None of us are going down without a fight. Remember, this woman has a calling to find a cure for Alzheimer's disease. Trust me. It would be better to be eaten by mercy angels than to face Lord Satan for losing this woman."

Despondency settled upon the demons. They understood Terror clearly. This had turned into a suicide mission.

*****

What are you going to do, Elsie?

"I don't know."

What are you going to do, Elsie?

"I don't know!" she screamed, then looked around to see if anyone heard her talking to herself. Her mind was so messed up that voices inside of her were now more of a nuisance than a surprise. She guessed that was a sure sign of going or being crazy.

You are Elsie the strong. Elsie the brilliant. What is the strong, brilliant Elsie going to do?

"I'm not strong! I'm not brilliant! I thought I was, but I'm not. I'm not. I'm weak…and I don't know anything. And I'm all alone. I'm going to lose my family. I'm going to lose my freedom. I'm going to lose my mind."

Elsie's anguish of soul overwhelmed her and toppled her onto her side. She lay in a fetal position, releasing great, irresistible sobs into the stillness of the dark park. The great covering of the tree didn't block heaven's view of the sobbing daughter of Adam.

Elsie, go to Kennesaw Mountain. I will contend with you there.

This wasn't one of the tormenting, heckling voices. This voice was softer, calmer, but authoritative. Authoritative, but not bossy and domineering like the other voices. "Kennesaw Mountain? Who are you?" Elsie waited for an answer from a voice she was only half sure she heard. But she had heard it. She knew she heard it. Didn't she?

Kennesaw Mountain? she thought, shaking her head. *That's ten or twelve miles north on bicycle. After riding thirty plus miles south earlier? Why Kennesaw Mountain? And why am I even thinking about following the directions of a voice that I'm not even sure I heard?*

Elsie thought about the Silver Comet trail and the man with the stick. The voice had told her to stop the bike and walk it around the bend. She had wanted to speed up and zip by any danger. It didn't make sense at the time, but the voice had been right. Had she gone her own way and sped up, the man's stick would've knocked her silly. She no doubt would've awakened in the bushes, beaten and raped—if she had been so lucky to wake up at all.

Obeying the voice had saved her life once. Could it happen again? Could this voice show her how to get her mind back? And what did the voice mean by, I will contend with you there?

It wants to contend with me? As in argue? thought Elsie. *Why would this thing want to argue with me?*

Elsie licked her lips with a purpose. She mounted the bike and took off on Spring Road to get to Kennesaw Mountain for answers.

Chapter 24

Elsie would have enjoyed the bike ride had it been under different circumstances. It had been quite a while since she biked anything close to forty miles. But this wasn't different circumstances. She was literally riding for her life. And now here she was rolling in the darkness with her bike's light doing little more than proving it was really dark.

Elsie grimaced at the holes in her getaway plan. "Elsie," she said aloud, "if there's ever a next getaway done on a bicycle, you may want to remember to purchase batteries for the light."

She got off the bike and slowly walked it as she thought. Kennesaw Mountain was called Kennesaw *Mountain* for good reason. It was a mountain and it was large. It rose over eighteen hundred feet and was nearly three thousand acres of national park. And it was closed. So just what was she supposed to do?

Of course, closed didn't mean inaccessible. She didn't need to go through the main gate, and she wasn't driving. Plus, she was sure the voice didn't mean for her to go *into* the park. Elsie looked to her left at one of the grass fields of the park property from Stilesboro Road. She cut across the two-lane highway, turned down Kennesaw Mountain Drive, and rode the bike deep enough into the dark grass field that no passing cop would see her and kindly offer to take her to jail.

Elsie put the bike on its side and sat. It had gotten colder, and the blouse on top of the bike top did help—a little. Funny, the wig helped out, too. At least her head was warm. She leaned back on both hands and looked up at the clear, star-filled sky. Everything seemed so tranquil up there. She knew that it wasn't, though.

Probably one day scientists would discover a planet capable of sustaining life, and maybe even find one with life. But as far as anyone presently knew, not a one of those beautiful lights could sustain life.

The phrase *beautiful, but dead* came to mind.

Elsie thought on this as she gazed at the lights. Billions, even trillions of stars and planets, all of them beautiful from a distance, and all of them dead and deadly. Deadly atmospheres. Deadly energy. Deadly weather. Deadly earthquakes. Deadly scarcity. Beautiful, but dead. Beautiful, but deadly. Alive from a distance; dead and deadly up close.

"Beautiful Elsie," she whispered. "You belong up there." Elsie lowered her head and thought about where she was and what she was doing. Her eyes watered. "The police want to put me in jail. My husband wants to put in a mental health facility. I'm cold and sitting in a field late at night"—it hurt to say the next words— "waiting for a voice to talk to me." She thought about the absurdity of her predicament. "I'm waiting in a field for *a voice* to tell me how to get rid of the voices and monsters that are driving me crazy. Oh, God! What is wrong with me?"

You have no God, strong Elsie. Have you no monkeys to help you?

Elsie instinctively looked around frantically at the sound of the voice. She saw no one. Of course, she saw no one. She was the only one out there. Her and a voice. A voice that could speak so lightly that she barely noticed it even as a thought. Or it could speak so emphatically—like just now—that it sounded like it came from inside and outside of her.

"Why do you mock me?" she said.

Because you are strong and need no one. You have all the answers.

Elsie felt her hope slipping away at the voice's taunts. "Why do—I came here because you told me to come. I came for answers. Why are you doing this to me? Are you a monster?" Elsie's head dropped when she answered her own question. "First, the lake house. Now here. I'm following monsters."

Elsie thought it was impossible for her to cry harder and more desperately than she had done the past couple of days. She was wrong. She was sure that her wailing would attract any park rangers in the area. But she was incapable of keeping her bitterness and hopelessness from piercing the field's quiet with cries of death. She fell to her side and cried. She rolled over onto her back and cried. She made it to her feet and fell to her knees and looked up to the night sky and screamed, "Why are you doing this to me? Why are you tormenting me?"

Who are you talking to, strong Elsie?

"I'm talking to you!" Elsie screamed, punctuating her frustration with a curse. "And why the hell do you keep calling me strong? Why? Why?" she screamed.

"Who are you talking to?"

The voice was right there in front of her.

Elsie snapped her face from the sky and looked into the face of a person who had seemingly popped out of nowhere. Her knees buckled in fear and she fell backward, looking up at the person. She stretched her neck forward trying to make herself believe what she was seeing. "You. What the—?"

"Hell is more than a word, Elsie. It's a terrible place of everlasting punishment." A few seconds of silence passed. "Be still and know that I am God. You can hear God when you're still," said the old woman. "It's a Scripture. Who were you talking to? Who were you contending with?"

The old woman's use of that word demanded Elsie's attention. "Contending?"

"Yes," said the old woman. "It sounded like you were arguing with someone. Contending."

Elsie was stuck to her fallen position as she thought of the voice. *Go to Kennesaw Mountain. I will contend with you there.* "Who are you? I saw you at the restaurant. Then Starbucks. Now here. Now *here!*" Elsie yelled.

"You look like you are coming apart at the seams," said the old woman. "Why would such a strong woman fall apart like this? I remember vividly when I saw you last, you stated emphatically that you were 'a pretty resourceful woman.' Did I quote you correctly?"

Elsie said nothing. She wanted answers, but they wouldn't come from this woman. She needed to hear from that voice again.

The old woman's eyes narrowed. "Then I didn't misquote you. Good. I don't want to put words in your mouth. Oh, Elsie," she continued, "have your resources in which you've trusted so much proven adequate?"

"I—want—to know—" Elsie dropped it. What difference did it make what she was doing out here?

"You could file for bankruptcy, Elsie?"

"What?"

"Why don't you stand up? There's no need for you stay down there."

Elsie stood up and looked at the much shorter old woman. "What are you talking about *bankruptcy*?"

"Hmm." The old woman turned toward the mountain. "You said you had resources for life. But it is obvious that life has demanded something of you which your resources can't satisfy." She turned to Elsie. "Since your resources are inadequate, you need to file bankruptcy. You need to go to the judge to reorganize."

Elsie was incredulous. What had become of her life? Now not only was she waiting around in a dark field at night for a voice—which it turned out could be a monster!—to tell her how to get rid of the other voices in her head, she was being lectured to in riddles by an old woman who periodically and mysteriously popped up in her life for just this reason.

Elsie looked at the woman and went through a few expressions trying to figure out how she just happened to be here with her in a dark field in Kennesaw. The first two times—yeah. Definitely Anna. But this? She didn't even know she was going to be here. How could this woman have known?

The old woman started walking in the general direction of the mountain.

"Where are you going?" asked Elsie. It seemed to make no sense to ask her where she was going. What difference did it make? But then the whole evening made no sense. Her life made no sense. So she asked.

Without looking back, the old woman answered, "Abraham climbed God's mountain and met God. Moses climbed God's mountain and met God. I'm going to climb God's mountain."

That was an odd answer. But nearly everything this woman said was odd. "The mountain is closed," said Elsie.

"The mountain belongs to God. It's open," replied the old woman.

Elsie watched the woman walk away. She had a slight, inexplicable inclination to go with her, but she needed to stay in the field and wait for the voice. If she was following a monster's voice, thinking it was a new, helpful voice, better to find out sooner rather than later.

"Are you going to climb God's mountain, Elsie?"

"I have to stay here."

The old woman's steps carried her more quickly than Elsie expected them to. "Come climb God's mountain with me, strong Elsie."

Elsie's now large eyes burned into the figure that was getting smaller with each second she stared in indecision. *Strong Elsie.* "Why'd you call me that? Why'd you call me strong Elsie?"

The old woman sped up.

Elsie marveled at the unlikely robustness of the old woman. "Why did you call me strong Elsie?" When the old woman failed to answer, Elsie made the decision. She picked the bike up and started toward the old woman.

"Leave the bike, strong Elsie," she said without turning around.

Elsie dropped it and ran after the irksome, old riddler.

*****

The old woman's quick, long strides baffled Elsie as she sped up her trot to catch up. Just as she did, the old woman's pace matched that of a woman of advanced age. Elsie looked at her quizzically, but left it alone. There were more important things to be concerned about.

"Why did you call me strong Elsie?"

"Because you are."

"No." Elsie's voice was loud with frustration. "Why did you choose *that* word?"

The old woman stopped and looked intently into Elsie's eyes. "Who were you contending with back there? You were looking into the sky and yelling at someone. You were demanding answers. You were making accusations. Of whom? You don't believe in God. You told me so. I said, 'Only a fool would believe there is no God.' You said, 'Miss Malak, there is no God.'"

The old woman smiled at Elsie the way a brilliant professor might smile at a cocky, challenging student. "Elsie the brilliant. Elsie the atheist. Since you know of a certainty that there is no God, who were you contending with?"

Elsie was not only surprised by the rebuff. She was surprised by the distance the old woman suddenly put between them with her sprint walk. Elsie caught up with a trot. Surprisingly, the old woman's pace quickened. Elsie felt like she was in a speed walking race. "Miss Malak."

She didn't answer.

"Miss Malak," Elsie said again.

The old woman didn't answer and didn't slow down.

Elsie put her hand on her shoulder. "Okay," she gave in.

The old woman stopped and looked up into Elsie's eyes with that intent gaze. "You were crying bitterly and talking to someone in the sky. Since there is no God, who were you talking to?"

Elsie gripped her head and ran her hands down her face with a deep breath that was ready to cry again. "I have some issues I'm dealing with, and I was just trying to work through them. That's why I'm out here."

The old woman looked at her with a wrinkly half-smile that didn't look convinced. "Strong Elsie. Working out her issues."

"Yes," Elsie offered.

The old woman took off in that sudden accelerated speed walk again.

"Miss Malak," Elsie called from a standstill.

No answer, but another acceleration of old legs chomping over grass in the dark.

"What do you want?" she called to the diminishing figure. "Will you please stop and talk to me?"

The old woman kept up her pace.

Elsie's eyes narrowed in anger. "I am *not* going to chase you. I told you that I needed to stay here in the field."

The old woman's fast legs carried her deeper into the darkness.

Elsie cursed and took off after her. She caught up with her. "What do you want?" she threw the words out there.

The lady stopped. "Why do you want to talk to an old woman? You are strong, Elsie. You have things under control. Go back and fight your monsters by screaming at the stars." The old legs took off again.

Monsters?

This time Elsie didn't let those old legs escape into the darkness. She sprinted to the old woman and firmly grabbed her shoulder. Perhaps too firm to be appropriate.

The old woman stopped and looked at Elsie's hand on her shoulder. "Will you strike me as you did your sister?"

Elsie pulled her hand back as though she had just been caught stealing. "How'd you know that?" she stammered.

"All things are naked and open to the eyes of Him to whom we must give account," said the old woman.

"Anna, she told you." It made sense now. "You and Anna, you're together. Aren't you?"

"Anna is with us, but not as you suppose."

"I knew it." Elsie thought of Starbucks. "She told you about that incident."

"Incident? By incident you mean following your rebellion and hatred of God and those who are good by responding to her love with a slap to the face. You drew blood from a holy one."

"She did tell you," said Elsie.

The old woman looked toward the mountain and back at Elsie. "A man whose own works were evil, rose up and killed his own brother because that brother's works were acceptable to God and his own were not. He hid the body and went on his way thinking that God did not see the deed." The old woman moved closer to Elsie. "The righteous man's blood called out from the ground and testified against the evil brother. Anna's blood has testified against you." The woman paused. "But the holy one has prayed for you. Now let me alone and go back and scream at the stars. I must climb the mountain of God."

The old woman took off again.

This time Elsie didn't run after her. Confusion kept her still in a whirling mass of questions. Fears. Residencies. Music. Red suits. Anna. White vans. Intruders. Handcuffs. Guns. Bad voices. Good voices. Monsters. Psych wards. Amanda. Chrissie. Nightmares. No more nightmares. Granny. The bird at Starbucks. Wanted by the cops. Self-correcting brain. Floating in space. The Big Bang. The name. Beaten for trying to use the name. The man with the stick. *Go to Kennesaw Mountain. I will contend with you there.* This old woman.

The old woman was gone. She had disappeared into the darkness as Elsie pondered. She needed to wait for the voice that told her to come to the mountain. She looked back at the field from where she and the old woman walked. There was nothing special about that spot. The voice said go to Kennesaw Mountain, not go to the field near the mountain. If she followed the woman to the mountain, she could try to get answers from her while she waited for the voice.

Elsie sprinted into the darkness.

*****

Elsie stopped at a four-foot fence. She looked to the left and right. No old woman. The fence was made of long pieces of horizontal wood beams with enough room for a person to step through them. The old woman's surprising spryness convinced her that she probably had no problem getting through the fence.

"Miss Malak," she called, looking over the fence and into the darkness.

"What do you want, strong Elsie?"

Elsie stepped through the fence and looked into the darkness. The voice sounded like it came from several places in the woods. She walked, then trotted closer to the beginning of the trees, and stopped. She looked into the thick darkness. "Miss Malak, where are you? I can't see you."

"Where are you looking?" responded the voice.

"I'm looking into the darkness."

"You cannot see anything in the darkness, strong Elsie. Try looking at the light," said the voice.

"I don't see it," said Elsie.

"Strong Elsie, if you look at the darkness, you will only see darkness. To see the light, you must look up."

Elsie looked up and saw a light deeper in the woods and high in the trees. *What is that?* she wondered.

"Do you see it, strong Elsie? Do you see the light?" asked the voice.

"Yes, I see it."

"Keep your eyes on the light and follow my word, and you will be able to find me even in the thick darkness," the voice instructed.

"I'm coming in," yelled Elsie. The adventure of the moment helped her forget, if just for a little while, the problems that led her to these dark woods. She progressed deeper into the darkness. "I don't see the light any more, Miss Malak. I can't follow the light."

"Sometimes the light is right before you. Sometimes it's obscured. If you can't see the light, follow my word. I'll keep speaking to you, strong Elsie. If you follow my word, it will lead back to the light. Do you see the light yet?"

"Not yet," said Elsie. She stopped and looked behind her.

"Press toward the mark, strong Elsie," the voice came from everywhere. "Looking behind you won't get you any closer to me."

"You see me?"

"I have always seen you."

"Keep talking," said Elsie.

"Then keep listening, and keep obeying," said the voice. "If I speak and you don't listen, you won't find what you are looking for."

Elsie intermittently followed the voice and the light deep into the woods until the mysterious light suddenly vanished. It wasn't obscured, it was gone. She saw it when it disappeared just above her in the trees.

"The light's gone, Miss Malak. Where are you?"

The voice didn't answer.

"Miss Malak, can you hear me?" Elsie yelled.

No answer.

Boom!

Elsie flinched and looked around in the darkness. "What was that?" she said to herself.

Drops of water began falling all around her. Then it seemed like someone removed the thick canopy of leaves above and ushered a torrential downpour upon her spot. *Where'd the storm come from?* she wondered. A frigid wind blew through the woods and cut through her clothes. She grabbed her arms and took tentative steps toward the tree she had seen when the light was still there.

"Miss Malak!" Elsie yelled. "Miss Malak!"

"Elsie, can you hear me?" the voice echoed in the darkness.

"Yes! Yes! I'm over here!"

"I know where you are, strong Elsie. Who were you contending with in the field?"

What? Contending? "We need to get out of here!" said Elsie.

"You are an atheist, Elsie, and you are strong. Why were you screaming at the sky?"

"I told you. I came here to think. I've got some problems I'm dealing with."

"So now your issues are problems."

Elsie grimaced angrily in the dark. She was wet and cold and stuck in the dark, and this old woman wanted to use this as an occasion to lecture her about God. "Yes! They're problems! Can we talk about this after we get out of the rain?"

Elsie heard another boom in the sky, but this time it came after the boom that hit a tree not too far from her. *Lightning!* She instinctively dropped to a stoop and pushed into the tree's trunk. Lightning was as unforgiving as it was indiscriminant. Her frightened glance upwards revealed flashes of light popping the tops of trees that preceded trailing booms in the sky.

Alone, shivering, cold, wet, and lost in the dark woods of Kennesaw Mountain, Elsie realized in growing fear that there was a real possibility that a lightning strike might alleviate her concerns of being locked up and losing her mind.

The crackling sounds of trees being struck by lightning all around her challenged the saying that lightning doesn't strike the same place twice. If that was true, why was it striking in a circle around her? She was certain she heard trees falling nearby after being struck by lightning. Her eyes widened in the darkness and followed her ears. A tree was falling. She heard the sounds of branches snapping as the tree got closer to the ground.

As the tree got closer to her!

Elsie couldn't see, but she could hear. And what she heard was her about to be crushed by a falling tree. Better to be knocked out by running into a standing tree than to be crushed by a falling tree. She took off running.

She heard the tree hit the area she had run from. She heard this a moment after she felt no ground under her feet. The multitude of thoughts that flash through a human mind in a moment when it realizes it's about to die stopped almost as soon as they began. For it was only a moment before the ground that disappeared from under Elsie's running feet was found.

It was her right side that found it first. Then it was both legs, her butt, then her back and head as she flipped and rolled down the hill. One by one every part of her body emphatically discovered the missing ground. She rolled to an aching stop a few seconds later with her eyes closed.

"Elsie. Elsie," the voice called. "Wake up."

Elsie's eyes fluttered, then opened. Looking down at her in the darkness was a blurred vision of the old woman. Elsie tried once to move and couldn't. For some reason, she didn't panic. She looked at the woman without trying again to move.

"The sons and daughters of Adam are strong...until their strength fails them. They know everything...until their knowledge proves terminal. They deny God's existence...until their own existence is threatened."

Elsie's eyes closed. They opened again. Her body was sucked dry of strength. There was only enough to turn her head and let gravity pull her face to the side as she lay on her back. Through her fog, she saw the tiny, swirling fire. It must've been something from the lightning.

The tiny, swirling fire grew to a large, swirling fire. Elsie watched it rise like a small tornado and descend on top of her. Words and sentences of fire floated within the swirling flame like orderly debris. But the words and sentences scrolled before her only after she heard them everywhere, but especially from deep within.

> *Who is this who darkens counsel by words without knowledge? Now prepare yourself like a strong woman; I will question you, and you shall answer Me. Where were you when I laid the foundations of the earth? Tell Me if you have understanding. Who determined its measurements? Surely you know!*

Question after question after question thundered in Elsie's consciousness before corresponding sentences scrolled before her. There were so many that she could never naturally remember them. Yet they seemed burned into her being as everlasting indictments of her ignorance, arrogance, and presumption. Then the majestic voice boomed final questions.

Shall the one who contends with the Almighty correct Him? Would you condemn Me that you may be justified?

Finally, the whirlwind was gone.

Elsie tried to move and found that her body was responsive again, although hurting. She remembered. Lightning. Running through the darkness. Going over an embankment and tumbling down the side of the mountain.

"How are you?" the old woman asked.

Elsie turned. "You." She sat up on her backside. It wasn't raining.

"Elsie, it's late at night. You have a husband and daughter. You should be home with your family. Why are you here and not at home?"

Elsie's face was in the old woman's direction, but her mind was in the whirlwind of fire. Her distant expression was Elsie's only answer.

"Your issues—the problems you spoke of. They're too much, aren't they? Even for strong Elsie. You're here running from your problems. And you weren't screaming at the sky, were you?" asked the old woman.

Elsie looked at the old woman. There seemed to be a dull light that emanated from her, allowing Elsie to see her. She didn't bother wondering about this light. It was just another odd something she didn't understand. "I'm not strong."

"Why are you here?"

Elsie told her almost everything. The family fears. Her residency dropout. Her music. The voices. The monsters. The intruders. Running from Daniel and the police.

"And that led you here?" asked the old woman.

"A voice told me to come here."

"What did the voice tell you to do once you got here?"

"Nothing. It didn't tell me to do anything. It just said it would contend with me."

"Are you sure that's all the voice told you to do—just come here? Nothing else?"

Elsie's eyes dropped in thought. She shook her head. "No. It just said to come here."

"The voice did not tell you to run to the safety of the Lord?"

Elsie's head snapped up. She hadn't remembered this until now. The voice had said this. But it was foolish, so she let the thought die a moment after it came to mind. "Yes, it did tell me to run to the safety of the Lord. How did you know this?"

"This is not as mysterious as it appears, Elsie," she answered.

Elsie waited for an explanation to prove this.

"There is no safety other than in the Lord. No matter where you run, the only safety you will ever find is in the Lord."

Elsie listened to this explanation. It was logical within a Christian context, but there was more to this coincidence than met the eye. She looked at the dull glow of the old woman and got off her behind to one knee. She rested an elbow on the knee she leaned on and thought about the whirlwind. There was much more to this old woman than she was letting on.

The old woman looked into Elsie's eyes that were gazing into her own. Her wrinkles didn't reveal the smile that lurked underneath. "The man with the stick would've raped and killed you."

Elsie hadn't told the old woman about the man with the stick. Her gazing eyes narrowed suspiciously, knowingly.

The old woman saw the intent just behind the gaze. She turned her back to Elsie and said, "I have to leave you now, strong Elsie. I have to climb God's mountain."

Elsie's battered but strong thigh catapulted her toward the old woman's back. In one long leap, she flew through the air saying, "No you don't!" She landed close enough to grab the back of the woman's coat and drag her roughly to the ground.

Chapter 25

Elsie's five-foot-nine, one-hundred and thirty-five pound frame, though battered and bruised from the fall down the steep hill, was still fit, toned, and muscled from running and strength training. She figured she had at least a twenty-five or thirty pound advantage over the old woman, and was no less than forty-five years younger. That's why she was shocked as she struggled to hold on to her.

The old woman had fallen to her back. Elsie was on the woman's side with her head under the right arm, and Elsie's own right arm was over the woman's chest and shoulder, locking hands and pinning her as though this were a refereed wrestling match. But the old woman's body was like flexible, hardened rubber that wouldn't stop moving. Elsie struggled to keep her grip.

"Miss Malak, I'm sorry for doing—whoa!"

Elsie's legs swung high over her and landed on the ground as a sudden burst from the woman slung her to the other side. Now the woman was on top, and Elsie was on the bottom, but her strong grip was still intact. This was irrelevant. For the woman got on both knees with Elsie hanging on her, knees dangling in the air and trying to pull her back down. The woman slowly, but irresistibly stood to her feet. Elsie let her legs touch the ground, but she wouldn't let go.

The old woman stood there with Elsie locked hard around her upper body. "Elsie, what are you doing?"

Elsie took a deep, needed breath. "Who are you? What are you?"

"El—see. Elsie, let me go."

The old voice wasn't fooling Elsie. "Who are you! Are you the voice? Are you a monster?"

"You are the monster, Elsie," the old woman squeezed the words out through Elsie's vice grip. "All those who love death hate me."

"What are you talking about?" demanded Elsie.

"Those who regard worthless idols forsake their own mercy," came the answer.

"Stop talking to me in riddles! Who are you?"

"I have to climb God's mountain, strong Elsie. You must go the way of your god; I must go the way of my God."

"I'm not letting you go until I get some answers. I mean it, Miss Malak. I know you're not who you say you are." Elsie wondered how she'd stop this woman if she continued to resist. "And how are you doing this? How are you fighting me?"

"I'm not fighting you, strong Elsie. You are fighting me. You have always fought me."

"Stop it!" screamed Elsie. "Stop your riddles and talk to me." Elsie's eyes widened in surprised alarm. She felt the old woman's hand grabbing the inside of her thigh. Then she felt a powerful hand lifting her off the ground. Elsie had to move quickly. She wrapped her leg behind the woman and torqued her body, tripping the old woman to the ground. They lay side by side, tussling in the dark for supremacy.

Elsie rolled behind the woman and got her arm under the woman's throat, while wrapping her legs around the woman's waist. She wasn't trying to choke her, but the woman wouldn't stop pulling forward. So Elsie found herself choking an old woman in the dark.

"Hearing, you hear and do not understand. Seeing, you see and do not perceive," the old woman's words came out of a throat being closed by Elsie's desperate arm."

"Stop fighting me, Miss Malak. I don't want to hurt you. Just answer my questions, and I'll let you go."

"For your heart has grown dull," the woman grunted. "Your ears are hard of hearing. Your eyes you have closed, lest you see with your eyes and hear with your ears and turn and understand and be healed."

"Miss Malak," Elsie took several heavy breaths, grateful to be in a position to rest and catch her breath, "please stop fighting me."

The woman stopped pulling against Elsie. They lay there saying nothing.

"Are you the voice?" Elsie broke the silence.

"Who were you screaming at in the sky?"

Elsie looked to the left and right in frustration, shaking her head. "I don't believe in God, Miss Malak." She immediately thought of the whirlwind.

"Then why scream at Him? Why demand answers from someone who doesn't exist? Why would an atheist do this? And I will not accept I don't know."

Elsie's voice revealed her resignation. "Because I'm desperate, Miss Malak. I don't know what's happened to my life. I know there's no God, but...."

"But you demanded answers of Him anyway."

"Yes."

"And has this God who doesn't exist answered you," asked the old woman. When Elsie didn't answer, the woman said, "Then He has answered you."

"No," said Elsie. "I saw something...but I've been seeing lots of things. I don't know what's real and what's not."

"Am I real?"

"Honestly, I don't know."

"Elsie, we're lying here on the ground. You're wrapped around me like a snake. How can you not know if I'm real?"

"I thought the intruders were real, and they weren't."

"What about the monsters?" asked the woman.

"Yes. I think so. They beat me, and I have the bruises. So, yes, they're real."

"And your fears? They are real?"

"Yes."

"Professing to be wise, they became fools," said the woman.

Elsie frowned at the riddle.

"Why do you not believe Africa exists?" said the woman.

The nonsensical question out of nowhere earned another shaking of the head from Elsie. "Miss Malak, I just want to ask you some questions. Please, can we just speak plainly?"

""Why do you not believe Africa exists?" the question was repeated.

"I believe Africa exists! Okay?" Elsie snapped.

"But you have never been there. You believe Africa exists, and you have never been there," the woman pressed. "Your pride and worship of intellect tell you that you are better than Anna because she believes in God—a God you say she can't see. A God you say doesn't exist. But a God you scream at when you are desperate for help."

"Miss Malak, this is ridiculous. Africa is a continent. It's real."

"Elsie, you believe Africa is real because of the testimony of others...because of what you've read...because of maps you've seen...because of television."

"I can go to Africa, Miss Malak! This isn't a superstition! It doesn't require blind faith! I can purchase a ticket and go to Africa." Elsie hoped she'd be able to get around the woman's foolishness and get some straight answers. She was prepared to hold onto this woman all night if necessary.

"But you haven't been to Africa, Elsie. Until you go to Africa and see it for yourself, you're just believing in circumstantial evidence."

"You win, Miss Malak. I'm guilty of believing in the existence of a continent I haven't personally visited."

"You believe in many things because of circumstantial evidence. You and all of society live your life based on decisions made with nothing more than circumstantial evidence. Anna believes in God because of overwhelming circumstantial evidence."

So that's where this is going? thought Elsie.

"The heavens declare His glory," said the old woman. "The divine attributes of the Almighty are all around you. The only reason you don't see them is because you don't want to see them."

"Miss Malak, that is a stretch going from believing in the existence of Africa to the existence of an invisible God. Please— can I just ask you some questions? I think you may be able to help me. Please, Miss Malak, I have to get well before they find me."

"Elsie, it is simple. You are right. You can prove the existence of Africa by going to Africa. But you can't get there without interrupting your life, purchasing a ticket, and flying several hours. It costs you time, effort, and even discomfort, Elsie. Why is it acceptable to you that the attainment of the things of this world should require such effort, but the Almighty should be as easily grasped and as easily flicked away as a blade of grass?"

The old woman looked at Elsie's big wedding ring stone. "You understand and accept what makes a diamond valuable, but reject the Almighty for these very reasons. You are as I said in the beginning. You are a fool. Now, I must leave you with your god."

Elsie gritted her teeth and prepared to squeeze.

The old woman placed her hand on top of the arm Elsie had planted under her neck and pulled. Elsie strained to hold it, but to no avail. Her arm lifted as though she wasn't resisting at all. The woman did the same with the other hand. Elsie's arms were wide as the woman held them. In one quick move, the woman spun and was on top of Elsie.

"Elsie, unwrap your legs."

"I'm not going to let you go. I can't, Miss Malak."

"Elsie, you have your god. Leave me alone. I must go."

Elsie looked up and tightened her legs around the woman's waist. She tried to wiggle her hands free, but the woman's grip was like iron. And she held her without the slightest difficulty. "I can't let you go, Miss Malak. I know you know how to help me.

You have to tell me how to get rid of these fears and these monsters."

"You are too strong and smart for my help. I must go to the weak and ignorant."

"No!" Elsie's legs tightened.

The old woman took Elsie's outstretched arms and put both of them in one of her hands, pinning them together and to the ground.

Elsie looked wide-eyed at the woman's free arm and realized that this old woman had pinned both her hands with one hand. "Who are you?" she screamed.

"Let me go, Elsie."

"No! They're going to lock me up! I'm going to lose my family!"

The old woman reached her free hand in back of her and touched Elsie's leg.

Elsie grimaced, shaking her head, screaming, "No!" Finally, the pain was too great. Her legs dropped to the ground.

In a flash, the old woman was several feet away and climbing up the side of the hill that Elsie had rolled down. In another flash, Elsie was tackling her from behind. They fell and tussled again. This time the old woman got the best of her. She sat on Elsie's chest with both of her hands pinned to the ground above her head.

"You are the voice," said Elsie.

"Why do you bother me, Elsie? We have nothing in common."

"I need help."

"What kind of help?"

"The fears. The monsters. How do I get rid of them?" Elsie was crying.

The old woman looked down at her with gentle eyes. "Why are you crying, Atheist? Have you no monkeys to help you?"

The tears in Elsie's eyes stood still at this. Where had she heard this before? "The park!" she yelled. "Under the tree when I was crying! You're the voice! You're the voice! You told me to come here, Miss Malak!"

"Elsie, listen to me."

Elsie waited expectantly.

"I can't help you. You are too strong and smart for me to help you. Now, let me alone. You must live in the world you have created. I will see you at the resurrection of the unrighteous." The old woman let go of Elsie and slowly pulled her hands back. "I'm going to go now."

Elsie made no move to stop her.

The woman got off of Elsie's stomach and stood up. She took several steps and looked back at Elsie with an expression of disappointment.

Elsie was on her knees. Nothing was as it seemed. Questions and answers, problems and solutions, they all seemed to be one and the same. And now the voice and this old woman. She couldn't explain it, but she was certain that this woman and the voice were one. The voice had saved her life and told her to come here. But now that she was here, this woman the voice said she couldn't help her.

Elsie looked at the image get darker up the hill's slope. This woman was the voice. She thought again about what the voice said. *Go to Kennesaw Mountain. I will contend with you there.*

"I will contend with you there," Elsie muttered as she watched the woman slowly climb away.

The old woman heard the sound behind her, but didn't turn around. The disappointment left her face.

Elsie grabbed the woman around the waist and yanked her backwards, holding on as they tumbled and rolled to the bottom. This time Elsie jumped on top of the woman's stomach and pinned her hands above her head.

"You're the voice. You saved me from being raped and murdered. I was the same person then that I am now. You didn't bring me this far to leave me. You want something from me. Tell me—what do you want? Whatever you want, I'll do it." Elsie panted heavily, waiting for something that would give her back her life.

"You're too—"

"Too strong. Too smart. I know. How do I fix it? How do I stop being my own worst enemy?"

"Elsie, I'm an old woman, and you're sitting on my stomach. Let me up."

Elsie looked down at her and tightened the grips on her wrists. Her head shook slowly. "No, Miss Malak, I can't let you go. I don't know what or who you are, but you are not an old woman."

They looked at one another in the dark.

After a few moments, the old woman said, "There was a Gentile woman with a desperate problem. Her daughter was grievously ill—attacked by a demon. No one but God could help her."

"Demon?" Elsie was surprised that the woman would use this language. "You mean monster?"

"I mean demon, Elsie." The old woman gave Elsie a few moments. "The Gentile woman sought help of the Lord, but He refused her."

A chill gripped Elsie's heart. "He said no?"

"For a while, He did—yes. But He eventually gave her her heart's desire."

Elsie knew there were more parts missing than revealed in this story, but she brightened with desperate hope at hearing how a woman with a hopeless situation was helped. She also recognized that the old woman said this help came from God. For the sake of expediency, she muzzled her objections. Every minute that passed brought her closer to the locked door of a psych ward. There simply wasn't time to waste quibbling over terms.

"What made God change His mind?" she asked.

"She did."

"A woman made God change His mind?"

The old woman's face grew tender under its bountiful wrinkles. "That's what it looked like to her. That's what it looks like to those who read the story. The deeper truth, Elsie, is that God's desire to help this woman was greater than her desire to be helped."

"Then why'd He say no? Why not help her as soon as she asked for help?"

"God resists the proud, but gives grace to the humble," the woman answered. "He answers prayers perfectly and at the best possible time."

"What does this mean?"

"It means strong, brilliant Elsie questions God's ways and timing because she thinks it could be better done another way." The woman looked intently into Elsie's eyes. "Where were you when I laid the foundations of the earth?" She saw that Elsie recalled these words. "God asked another person that question who questioned His ways as you do. But that person had a good heart. A humble heart. He was not like you. So God could talk to him."

Elsie was offended, but again, time was running out. She needed answers. "Not like me? What have I done? Did I do something—something that...I don't know, that caused this stuff to happen?"

"The Gentile woman God helped. She had persistent faith. She refused to be denied. Her faith prevailed upon God, and so she was helped."

The woman was totally ignoring her last question. *Okay, we'll deal with this one,* thought Elsie. "So God wants to help us, but we have to go through this process of groveling and humiliation before He'll do anything." She tried to mask her cynicism at this thought, but it came out sounding the way she felt.

"It is a process of humiliation for you, Elsie, because you're strong and full of pride. You don't need anyone. But now you do, don't you?"

"Yes, but Miss Malak, I'm willing to change. I can do it. I'll do whatever you say. Anything to get rid of these fears and these horrible monsters."

"Even believe in God?" The old woman was making a statement, as well as asking a question.

Elsie hesitated. "Yes."

"And Jesus? You'd accept Him as God and Lord of all?"

Elsie hesitated longer. "Yes. If it will get rid of the fears and monsters."

The old woman's arms pushed up quickly and irresistibly against Elsie's grip on her wrists. She turned both of her hands around Elsie's wrists and instantly Elsie was the one being held.

Only she was being held by two iron clamps encased in old flesh. The woman's torso rose and she pulled Elsie's twisted arms to the left of her without any resistance. Elsie's body followed her arms.

The woman stood up and looked at a surprised Elsie and clapped her hands. "What a wonderful day this is for the Almighty. Elsie the strong, Elsie the brilliant, Elsie the atheist, has agreed to acknowledge that Jesus is Lord if this will make the fears and monsters go away."

Elsie hopped to her feet. Her only hope was slipping away. "I don't understand!" she pressed. "What do you want? I said I'd acknowledge your god."

The old woman looked at Elsie with finality in her eyes. Elsie saw it and could've died right that moment. She could try fighting this…woman…person…being…whatever she or it was. But she couldn't stop her from leaving. Not really. They both knew that the wrestling matches had been fixed. That woman could walk away whenever she wanted to.

Elsie dropped to her knees and grabbed the woman's ankles and put her face to the ground. "I'm sorry, Miss Malak. I am proud. I've always been proud. I don't know how to not be proud. I don't know how to not be strong. It's all I know." She looked up with desperate tears rolling down her face, tears that were trying to save her life. "And, yes, Miss Malak, I'm an atheist. I don't believe in God."

Elsie took both of the old woman's hands and held them to save her life. "The fears are so tormenting…so debilitating, and the monsters are so horrible that I'd probably do anything to get rid of them." Elsie guided the woman's hands to her wet face and buried her face into them and continued to cry. "But I am honest when I say that were the fears and monsters to disappear forever from my life this moment, I'd be left with questions that I know cannot be answered by atheism. Something is out there. Someone is out there. I just don't know what or who. I'm so confused I don't even know where to begin to find the answers."

The old woman tenderly lifted the crying woman's face. "Elsie."

Elsie looked up with the attitude of a little child. She was ready for whatever this being told her. "Yes?"

"You are still strong…still brilliant…still proud."

Elsie's eyes registered her fear. She shook her head. "No. No. I'm not—"

The old woman put her fingers across the panicked woman's lips. "Sshhhhh, daughter of Adam. You are still strong and brilliant and proud. But you are no longer too strong and brilliant and proud for me to help you."

Finally!

Elsie's eyes danced with hope. "Then you're going to help me?"

"I will continue what I began before the foundation of the world."

Elsie's eyes crinkled at this odd saying. She didn't know what it meant, or from what source the woman was quoting. "Who said that?" she asked.

The old woman smiled. "The Lord whom you will come to know and love and serve."

Elsie thought of the depth of these words. *Knowing, loving, serving.* If there was something or someone out there that she would fall in love with so much that she'd be compelled to serve him, then she wanted to know what or who this thing or person was. "Who is this Lord you speak of? I want it. I want this life."

"Elsie, you remember when you tried to make the monsters leave you?"

She nodded. "Yes. I used the name to get rid of them."

"And you were beat severely for this."

"Yes."

"Go to your sister, Anna. She will explain all to you and give you freedom found in the words of eternal life."

Elsie felt something inside of her leap with excitement. "Eternal life?"

The old woman rubbed Elsie's face. "Oh, precious, precious Elsie. This is why you are here. It is why we are here—all of us." The old woman made a gesturing sweep of her hand as though she was pointing to many others. "Anna's prayers."

"Anna?"

"And Amanda and Chrissie. They've asked mercy of the Judge of all the earth on your behalf. It is why Satan was not able to kill you on the Silver Comet trail."

"They're all praying for me?" The puzzle's pieces started coming together quickly. *Christianity? Jesus Christ? Oh—my— God!*

"Stand," said the old woman.

Elsie bounced off her knees. She stood before the woman awaiting instructions. Whatever they were, she would do.

"What is your name?"

Elsie didn't know what the woman was asking. She gave a look of bafflement and shook her head. "Elsie," she said, as though it may be the wrong name.

The old woman looked at her with a large grin. "Elsie. EL see. Do you know what EL means?"

"No. Please tell me."

"You are hungry now for truth. EL means God. See God, Elsie. Whenever you hear your name being called, they are saying see God."

Tears joined Elsie's smile. *EL-Sie.*

The old woman took her by the hand and turned toward the hill. "You remember I told you that Abraham and Moses climbed God's mountain and met with God? We must climb God's mountain. Are you ready?"

The question seemed too fantastic to ask, but Elsie did, hoping with all her heart that the old woman would astound her once more. "I can see God?"

"If you climb His mountain—yes. It is why He created you."

Yes!" The answer came out of her mouth like it was shot out of a cannon. "I want to see Him!"

"Then come." The old woman took her by the wrist and started up the hill.

Elsie knew the old woman was something other than an old woman. But her physical capabilities and her appearance were in such contrast that Elsie couldn't stop glancing at her. She climbed the steep hill as though it were flat terrain. And when Elsie found a part difficult, the woman pulled her up with such strength that they never broke a stride. The *old woman* did this.

There was something else peculiar about the hike up this hill and subsequent trails and hills toward the summit. The old woman's mysterious dull glow progressively became a more mysterious bright glow. Light actually emanated from her so strongly that they could see at least ten feet around them.

"You're glowing," Elsie said at one time.

"The day will come when you will shine like the brightness of the firmament. You will shine like the stars forever and ever. Never again to be beautiful but dead, EL-Sie."

Elsie was stunned by the old woman's invasion of her thoughts, and slowed momentarily to wonder and comment about this. But the old woman moved like she was on a schedule, holding tightly to her wrist, pulling her up the steep path.

Ten yards from reaching the summit, the old woman's glow disappeared entirely. Elsie could no longer see her. But even more odd was that the absence of her light created a darkness that seemed unnatural. Elsie literally could not see anything. This startled her, but the woman's strong grip around her wrist removed her fear. She knew that no matter how dark it was, or how dark it became, she would be okay if the old woman kept holding her.

The old woman came off the side of the steep incline first. She pulled Elsie up behind her. When she did, Elsie stepped out of the thick darkness. Elsie looked up at the man who held her wrist and gasped. She felt her strength leave every part of her body, and she fell to the ground in a terrified, satisfied heap, unable to move, but fully able to think.

The voice. It's You. My creator. Jesus. Elsie felt a hand touch her on the shoulder.

"Stand, EL-Sie." The Man's voice sent waves of peace through Elsie's soul.

Elsie felt strength returning to her body through the bottom of her feet, the tips of her fingers, and the top of her head. She knew instinctively that the Lord was not there to hurt her. And more importantly and equally fascinating was she felt deep love coming from Him. He knew her. He loved her. He wanted to serve her.

Yet there was still something about Him and being face to face with Him that was terrifying. For the first time in Elsie's life, she understood what sin was. It was lawlessness. It was rebellion against His rule. She understood something else also that could've killed her of fright were it not for the kindness she felt coming from Him.

What she understood was that she was not only guilty of committing sin. She was sin. She was everything He was not. A natural enemy. And there was nothing she could do in her own power to change this.

Elsie got to her hands and knees and tried to rise, but fell upon her face in brokenness and tears. A torrent of cries and wails escaped her mouth as she writhed on the ground in the agony of the knowledge that she had lived a life of rebellion against her Creator and Judge.

The Lord and His host let the daughter of Adam feel and express the weight of her sins against heaven and earth. Once the Lord was satisfied that the truth had done a good work, He said, "Rise, El-Sie."

Elsie's heavy crying didn't stop, but she stood almost immediately in response to her Creator and Judge. She dared not lift her head.

"Look at Me, El-Sie."

The tenderness of the Lord's invitation provided her the courage she needed to look Him in His face. But it didn't take away the crushing weight of shame that threatened to drive her back onto the ground beneath His feet.

"Go to your sister, Anna. Do all she tells you, and you shall live. And when you have entered life and freedom, remember your family—as I remembered you."

Words could not express what Elsie felt. They couldn't express what she wanted to say. What she needed to say! "Yes, Lord," she said just above a whisper. It was all the volume shame would allow.

Then the Creator did something that broke Elsie's heart so thoroughly, it would never recover. He stepped forward and cupped her face and kissed her on the forehead. "Go, El-Sie, to those who have labored for your soul."

She watched the Lord walk away. Suddenly, a light shone from heaven onto Him, and He ascended in its light. Elsie watched in silent awe and with a wide mouth. Her hand pressed hard against her heart.

"Why do you stand there gazing up into heaven?"

Elsie turned to the voice.

A tall man stood before her in a flowing white robe. He had a dull glow. "This same Jesus, who was taken up from you into heaven, will so come in like manner as you saw Him go into heaven. But you go and do those things which were commanded of you. For the time is short."

She watched this man turn and walk into the darkness of the trees until he and his light were gone. It hadn't come to Elsie's mind until it was too late that she was now left alone under a dark sky, surrounded by a thick forest of trees.

The just shall walk by faith, she heard in her heart.

Elsie started walking. She walked into the thick darkness and once there, she felt someone take hold of her wrist.

Chapter 26

Anna looked at the phone and blinked. *Lord, please help me to be kind to my sister. Please—I always blow it,* she pleaded. "Elsie?"

"Yeah, it's me, Anna. Do you think we could get together and pray? I need help, and I need it fast. Has anyone been by looking for me? Has the police contacted you?"

"The police? Why would they be contacting me?"

"Some things have happened, Anna—strange things."

Elsie's request finally caught up with Anna's brain. "Elsie, did you just say you want to get together to pray?"

"I know, Anna. I know how this must sound, but...." *I have to get free of these things before they find me,* thought Elsie.

Anna glanced around at the traffic and tried not to let this unbelievable development cause her to hit another car. "But what?" Anna heard Elsie burst out crying in the background. She had tried to muffle her cries, but they were too loud to hide. "But what? What happened?"

Elsie caught the last of Anna's question as she put the phone to her ear. Her voice was halted between words, struggling mightily to get out. "I...saw...Him. Je...sus...The Lord, Anna. I don't...know why, but..." Elsie doubled over in sobs that wouldn't let her continue.

Anna made sense of enough of the jumbled words that she knew it was park now or hit someone. She turned off the street and hit the entrance hard to a Wal-Mart parking lot like she was a cop in hot pursuit. She came to an abrupt halt in a corner by some bushes. She punctuated each word as though Elsie had just told her she won a hundred million dollar lottery. "What—did—you—say?"

Elsie tried to answer, but emotion would only let her cry.

"Elsie, are you okay?"

Elsie shook her head. "I saw Him," she blurted between sobs. "Jesus...I saw Him."

Anna's eyes teared. The greatness of what Elsie said caused her head to shake in disbelief of its impossibility. But Anna's heart wasn't shaking in disbelief. It was dancing and leaping and shouting, "Hallelujah!"

"Elsie...Elsie," now Anna was struggling, "are...are you saying...you saw the Lord?"

"Yesssssss," the exuberant one word answer lasted five seconds until Elsie's tears resumed control.

Anna looked around the parking lot several times, wiping the stream of tears from her eyes. It had to be true. Nothing else could bring Elsie to this point. Tears of gratitude replaced the tears she had wiped away. Then her own desire to see the Lord flooded her heart, and she filled the car with her own loud sobs.

Elsie stopped crying before Anna did. "Anna?"

A few sobbing moments passed. "I'm here."

"Daniel is trying to have me put into a psych ward."

"What?" Anna asked in shock. "Why in the world—?"

"And the police are after me for that and for a hit and run."

"A hit and run? Elsie, you ran over someone—and kept going?"

"Yes. I mean no. It was a car door. It was a narrow street, and the guy opened the door when someone was chasing me. I took it off, Anna. I couldn't stop."

"Someone was *chasing* you? In a car?"

"No. A van. Two guys in a van. But the guys and the van weren't really—" Elsie stopped. If she told her too much right now, Anna may see why Daniel was trying to get her locked up. "It's a lot to digest, Anna. Please, come and get me. Don't tell anyone you've talked to me. You're the only one who can help. The Lord told me to call you. He said you would explain everything to me and give me the words of eternal life."

Anna smiled through her tears. She never thought getting hit by a truck could feel so good. "Tell me where you are. I'm already in the car. I'll be right there!"

*****

Anna sipped her caramel macchiota while she studied Elsie's face—it was soft. Her last Starbucks meeting with Elsie never happened. Now she knew why. "What did you say her name was?" asked Anna.

"Miss Malak."

Anna's head dropped, mouth wide open, as she looked at her sister. "Elsie, our pastor has been teaching a series on angels. Malak means angel. Oh, my Gaaawd! That's why she—he knew all of those things about you. It was an angel." Anna looked at Elsie with a look of astonishment as she shook her head and said, "You saw an angel, Elsie. An angel!" Her feet rapped a hundred times on the floor in excitement.

"I saw more than an angel, Anna."

Anna's smile froze. More than an angel? What was more than an angel? She looked around the coffee store and scooted her chair up as close as it could get to the table without rupturing something inside her belly. "What did you see?" she asked in a whisper.

"I told you on the phone. I saw the Lord. I saw Jesus." Elsie's eyes had the look of a miner who had purchased an abandoned mine for a dollar and had just discovered a billion dollars worth of gold in its caves.

Anna's own eyes widened as she saw the joy in Elsie's eyes. She pushed harder against the table. "You don't mean an angel. You mean the Lord Himself. I thought that's what you meant when you called me, but then I thought you meant you saw an angel." Her tears started up again. "You saw *Jesus*."

Elsie filled Anna in on everything that happened. "Here," she gave her some napkins to wipe her eyes. "Then when we got to the top of the mountain and stepped into the light, the angel was no longer holding my wrist. Jesus was holding my wrist."

Anna gasped and stared at Elsie. The gasp didn't do the trick. She had to get up. She did. She walked slowly toward a door, crying softly and shaking her head in awe. She turned back and walked past Elsie and circled the big coffee shelves in the middle of the floor. When she got to the other side where Elsie couldn't see her, Elsie heard, "Glo—ry to God! Thank You, Lord!"

Anna came around the bend and looked at Elsie. "I'm sorry. I'm sorry. I don't mean to make a scene. I'm just so happy for you."

Elsie stood up and hugged her sister. Both sisters cried and held one another's heads in their hands. "Don't apologize for making a scene, Anna. I thought there was no God." Elsie shook Anna's face. "But you prayed for me, and God showed Himself to me. I wasn't afraid to say there was no God. I'm not going to be afraid to say there is a God. I intend to make a scene."

Anna smiled widely and cried, "Yes."

Elsie's face kept its joy, but it was now tinted with seriousness. "He said you would explain everything to me and give me words of eternal life."

"Sit down!" Anna pushed down on Elsie's shoulders. "Elsie, the monsters are demons. They work for Satan. The reason you couldn't make them leave is because you aren't authorized to use the name of Jesus. You have to be saved to use His name."

"How do I get saved?"

Anna looked into her sister's face and had to convince herself she wasn't in that fantasy world Elsie told her about. How many times had she argued with her sister about salvation and the things of God and—nothing. Just nothing. Now her sister the atheist, the ex-atheist, was practically begging her to explain salvation to her. And according to Elsie, Jesus said it was because of her prayers for her.

Anna's eyes and smile were soft. "Oh, Elsie, all you have to do is agree with God and serve God."

"I want to serve Him, Anna." Elsie's words were eager. "What must I agree with? I believe whatever He says. I'll do whatever He wants. I don't care if it costs me everything. I don't want anything but Him. Tell me."

"That's it! That's it, Elsie! You said it. You repent. You turn from your life, and you take His life. He becomes your life."

"That's what I want, Anna. I'm not fighting Him any longer. And I'll never deny Him again." Elsie smiled at Anna. "Will you stop crying long enough to tell your sister how to get eternal life?"

Anna laughed and cried. "Yes. Oh," she exhaled and wiped her eyes. "You need to confess that you're a sinner—"

"I'm a sinner," Elsie interrupted. "A proud, arrogant sinner." She waited for further instructions.

Anna cried some more and wiped her eyes. She held Elsie's hands. "You need to ask God to forgive you of a life of sin. And you must believe that God sent Jesus into the earth to live and die for you, Elsie—to save you from your sins. You need to believe that God raised Him from the dead, and that He's coming back again. And you need to love and serve Him with your whole heart. That's what He wants of you."

Elsie squeezed Anna's hands until Anna had to say something for her to loosen her grip. "I'm just so excited, Anna. I want it. I want it all." Elsie didn't drop her head and pray. She lifted her face and hands toward the heavens above the ceiling. "Lord Jesus, I'm sorry for denying you and going my own way. But never again. I'm Yours now. I know You're alive. Please save me. Please take away my sins. Please give me eternal life. I know that You died and rose from the grave." She paused. "May I have eternal life now?"

Anna looked at her sister with her hands lifted in Starbucks and unashamedly asking God to forgive her. When Elsie opened her eyes and lowered her hands, Anna said, "I seem to remember a certain somebody calling me a Jesus freak."

Elsie's smile was mixed with determination. "And now another certain somebody is a Jesus freak."

"What's wrong?" Anna asked when she saw the grimace replace Elsie's smile.

"Noooooooooo, we won't leave!" Elsie screamed. "She belongs to us!"

*****

Once Anna recovered from the shock of hearing demons scream out of her sister, she quickly marched her nauseated sister from Starbucks and into her car. She looked across at her and toughened her expression. No demon was going to do her sister like this. Uh uh. Not after all that prayer.

Anna put her right hand on her sister's forehead. "Come out of Elsie! Do it now in the name of Jesus!"

Elsie's head turned slowly to Anna. Anna looked into Elsie's eyes and saw nothing but blackness. No white. No blue. Just two evil balls of wavy blackness. A low, deep voice came out of her mouth with the speed of thick, slow-moving molasses from a bottle. It seemed to take forever. "Get your hand off of my house or I will kill you in this car."

A lot of things rushed through Anna's mind. Then those black balls of wavy evil narrowed. She snatched her hand down and leaned against the car door, looking at Elsie and wondering what to do next. Sure, she had cast demons out of Chrissie and Amanda. But that was different. They were children; sweet little girls. No black eyeballs. No man's voice. No threats of murder.

Elsie's head turned slowly back to the front and lowered, eyes open in a wicked gaze.

Anna was more confused than afraid, but she was sitting in the car with a black-eyed demon that had threatened to kill her. So she wasn't eager to enroll in a crash course on advanced deliverance ministry under these circumstances. She pulled out her phone.

"Sheila, listen, this is Anna. I have got myself in a demonic mess here. Elsie is with me in the car. She is saved. Yes, that's what I said. Jesus appeared to her. Listen, I will talk to you about that later. Right now, I need some help. She is full of demons, and they are screaming and threatening to kill me. Her eyes are black. What am I supposed to do with this? This is not the same as casting demons out of little girls who don't even know what's going on."

Anna listened unimpressed by Sheila's pep talk without taking her eyes off of Elsie. "Uh huh. Uh huh. Uh huh." She leaned forward and looked at the thick white spit drooling from Elsie's mouth. She looked at the black eyeballs. "Not doing it, Sheila. What's Plan B?"

*****

Forty-five minutes later, Anna and Elsie sat in the living room of Sheila Maddox, a mother of four home-schooled children, who as part of Plan B, were ushered off down the street to a friend of Sheila's who also home-schooled, but definitely did not do demons.

A year ago Sheila also did not do demons. A year ago she was like her friend Rachel, who had unexpectedly dropped by, and who was sitting next to her. A good Christian who loved Jesus and believed some of the Bible. At least enough to get saved and live right. But totally ignorant of demons and any manifestation of God beyond forgiveness of sins.

Sheila loved Rachel like the blood sister she never had. They had met at a Florida State University student Bible study a decade ago. Sheila was a nice, tongues-talking Church of God Christian, and Rachel was a full-blown, take-no-prisoners, Southern Baptist, anti-charismatic Christian, but they became instant friends anyway.

Over the years, their against-the-odds friendship deepened. They could talk about anything, and they did—anything but the power of God. That was the deal. Neither would try to talk the other into or out of a belief.

The Plan B squad was Sheila, Anna, and Miriam, a former alcoholic with big, wild eyes and big, wild hair, who was now as strung out on Jesus as she ever was addicted to alcohol. She was also addicted to setting people free.

Miriam looked at Elsie with a hungry look. She was hungry to cast out another demon. It had been nearly two weeks since the last one. For her, the more ruckus, the better. She rubbed her hands together. "Hi, Elsie."

Elsie looked at the woman, feeling like a rotisserie chicken being eyeballed by a starving witch. This was going to be interesting. "Hello."

"Miriam," said Sheila, "don't start until we return. I need to talk to Rachel."

Still rubbing her hands and looking at Elsie, she said with glinting eyes full of plans, "We'll try not to."

Sheila tapped Rachel on the thigh. They both rose and went into the kitchen.

"What's up?" asked Rachel.

Sheila started to speak, then stopped. She sniffed, looked at Rachel with a frown, and put her nose to her neck. "That smells an awful lot like the perfume you swore was abhorrent and was going to be accidently lost."

One of Rachel's eyebrows lifted above her mischievous smile. "That was before Glen showed me last night," she paused and shifted her head downward and looked up for extra naughtiness, "and this morning how *much* he likes it. I'm going to purchase a half-gallon of it on the way home. I'm going to take a bath in the stuff."

Sheila shook her head. "You are one frisky realtor."

"You'll get no objection from me. Now what's up?"

"What's up is we're getting ready to pray for the lady named Elsie."

"Okay. I don't have to be anywhere until three. I could use a little prayer."

"Uhhh, this is not going to be a little prayer. It's going to be a big prayer."

Rachel gave her an "*And?*" look.

"Okaaay, actually, it's going to get a little weird," Sheila warned.

"I know you pray in tongues, Sheila. If you promise to not tell my Sunday school class, I promise to not slit my wrists. Deal?" Rachel looked at her with big eyes. "I promise."

"Elsie is here because she's having problems with demons, Rachel. She just got saved this morning, and the demons don't want to let her go. They're talking through her. Me and Miriam and Anna are going to cast these things out of her."

Rachel tugged with both hands at the edges of her short, brown suede blazer. She pushed the tip of her tongue through her straight, white teeth the way she always did when she heard something crazy. She knew she did this—Sheila told her she did—but cute habits were better managed than stopped.

"Yeah," said a smiling Sheila, "so you may wanna sit this one out, my wonderful, starched Baptist sister."

"Nope. I'm staying," Rachel answered matter-of-factly. "I want to see for myself what snake handlers do behind closed doors, my wonderful, weird charismatic sister."

Sheila looked at her mouthy friend. "So, you think I'm weird."

Rachel returned the grin. "So, you think I'm starched."

Sheila nodded with a smile that she knew Rachel didn't understand. "Ever read one of those warning signs in a parking lot of a restaurant about leaving stuff in the car?"

"The ones that say they're not responsible for my losses if something is taken? Yeah, I've seen 'em."

"Uh huh," said Sheila. "Well, remember that in case you lose something."

Rachel lifted her eyebrows and stuck out her neck for an explanation.

"I was under the impression we were going to pray sometime today," Miriam yelled from the living room.

"They're calling for your weird, charismatic sister," Sheila said to Rachel.

"Let's go," said Rachel.

Chapter 27

Elsie read the looks on the women's faces. She knew this Sheila woman was one of the people who had been praying for her. Anna told her this much. But now there was a tentativeness about them. A football team in a huddle where no one seemed willing to call a play—even the lady with the wild eyes and wild hair.

"I've been a proud atheist most of my life. I was certain there was no God, but He appeared to me and told me to do whatever my sister, Anna, tells me to do. I asked God to forgive me for my foolish rebellion." Elsie's eyes went from one lady to the other. "But I've got demons. I thought they were monsters, but they're demons. They've stolen nearly everything from me. Now they're trying to drive me crazy." She ended her words looking at Sheila. "What do I do?"

"We'll get those things out of you, Elsie." Sheila said this with a calm smile. "You've come to the right place."

Rachel sat with her knees touching one another and her hands resting on her legs. She sat up a little. *Demons? Monsters?*

Elsie formed the beginnings of a smile. Sheila was warm and unpretentious, but confident, like a nice boxer on a twenty-fight win streak. She knew she was in good hands with this unassuming woman. The good feeling she got from this lady made room for a light moment. "I think so. There's just one problem."

"What's that, Elsie?" asked Sheila.

"You're wearing a Florida Gators sweatshirt," she said. "Tell me you're not going to pray for me wearing that thing."

"Does it make you uncomfortable?" Sheila asked, not understanding. "I'll change it if it will make you feel better."

Elsie cracked a rival's grin. "I'm a Bulldog."

Sheila laughed and rose and made a sympathetic face before going toward her with extended arms and hugging her. "Ohhhh, you poor thing. You're a Georgia Bulldog. That explains it. No wonder you've got demons." Sheila rubbed Elsie's back as she hugged her. "You're living in sin and denial. I've got another Gators shirt I can let you wear while we pray. It'll make the demons come out easier." Sheila pulled back and looked into Elsie's smiling face and added, "And while we're at it, we may want to get rid of that Bulldog demon, too."

"If that's what it takes," Elsie said, shaking her head in dejection, wearing a defeated smile.

"Uhhh, I don't think so," said Anna defiantly, a Bulldog herself. "You don't have to wallow in the swamp to get delivered Elsie."

Rachel was a rabid Gator, but she didn't add anything. She was content to appreciate the fun bantering and normalcy. Nothing weird yet, except the mention of monsters and demons. She was eager for them to start praying for Elsie.

"Okay, but I offered," said Sheila. "Elsie, what I need you to do is change seats and sit here." She pointed to a kitchen chair that Miriam brought into the room. "This is the prayer chair."

Elsie sat and rested her hands on her laps with a look of expectancy. She looked at Anna. "Well, Anna, you got me."

"Jesus got you, Elsie," Anna replied with moist eyes, working to keep them from streaming.

"You ready, Elsie?" asked Sheila.

Elsie thought of all she had been through, and of the ticking clock. She had to get rid of these things before Daniel and the cops caught up to her. "More than ready—desperate."

"That's good," said Sheila. "Deliverance ministry is for the desperate. People who come with strings attached usually don't get anything. At least not permanently."

"No strings. No hidden motives. I just want to serve Jesus Christ with my whole heart, and I can't do that living in fear, or with these things living inside of me," she said.

The others were standing around Elsie's chair; Rachel was still seated. She inched forward and opened her mouth and closed it.

"Rachel? You wanted to say something?" said Sheila.

"Uh, yeah…" Her voice trailed. She didn't want to come off wrong. She was the sole non-charismatic, and she had invited herself to their prayer meeting.

"It's okay, Rachel. Has the Lord given you something?" said Sheila.

Has the Lord given me something? That thought bounced around her mind. That was one of the things about Sheila. She talked like she had a hotline to heaven. "No. I'm not saying that," said Rachel. "I was just wondering—you're a Christian, right? So how can you have a demon living inside of you? God and Satan can't live in the same place. Right?" she added as non-confrontationally as she could.

Anna and Miriam looked at Sheila. Elsie looked at Rachel—wondering.

Rachel took the momentary pause as a sign she was interrupting. "We can talk later, Sheila. You go on."

"No. That's a good question, Rachel. It comes up a lot in my classes at church. There's a lot of good material out there—books and You Tube videos. Derek Prince, Dr. Charles Kraft, Bill Subritzky, Frank Hammond. Prince does a good job with that question." Sheila smiled inside. Rachel had asked; she was only answering. "I recommend Prince's book, *They Shall Expel Demons.*

"But the short answer is Christians often object to the concept of demons being cast out of Christians on those grounds—that God and Satan can't both be inside of a Christian at the same time. There's a book I have where the guy deals with that pretty good." She looked around the room. It was on a table. She picked it up and flipped pages. "Here. He lists some places in the Bible where God and Satan were in the same place.

"Let's see… He quotes Isaiah 14 and Ezekiel 28, talking about Satan getting kicked out of heaven. He asks the question, 'But have you ever considered how odd it appears that Satan was ever in heaven?'"

"I never thought of that," said Anna. "That's something."

"Good point, right?" said Sheila. "If God and Satan can't be in the same place at the same time, how was Satan in heaven to be kicked out? Then he mentions Satan being in the Garden of Eden where Adam and Eve were—and they were perfect. So you don't have to be in sin for Satan to show his butt. Uhhh, he shows that in Job 1 Satan showed up at a meeting of God and His holy angels. How'd he do that if he can't do that?" She found another place in the book. "Ooo! Here's a good one. Remember when Jesus was in the wilderness on His forty-day fast? The Bible says Satan went to Him and tempted Him. We know this happened at least three times. Jesus was God and Satan had no problem approaching Him."

Sheila saw Rachel's squinted eyes drop in thought. She closed the book. "What about this? Anna, we brought this up when you were delivered. If God and Satan can't be in the same place at the same time, either God doesn't exist, or Satan doesn't exist. Because the Bible says God is everywhere. Remember Psalm 139? Rachel, you know that Psalm. How many times did Richard teach from it back in college? 'If I ascend into heaven, You are there. If I make my bed in hell, behold You are there.' There is no place that Satan can go that God is not already there."

Rachel sat back with a thoughtful expression. Sheila knew that mind of hers was dissecting and analyzing, looking for the weaknesses in her arguments. Finally, Rachel pushed back all the way into the cushion of the sofa, apparently without an immediate objection.

"Does that answer the question, Rachel?" Sheila asked, hopeful that God was doing a work, and now recognizing that Rachel being here was no accident. God had set her up!

"What book was that you used?"

"Deliverance from Demons and Diseases," she answered, giving the author's name, too.

"Rachel," said Elsie, "I have never read the Bible a day in my life; so I can't comment on what's in there. The only Scriptures I've come in contact with are those that Anna has shared with me, and those used in atheist books to prove there is no God. So I'm no expert on the Bible. But I can tell you what has happened to me."

Rachel's eyes sparkled with interest.

"All my life I've been told that I'm brilliant and beautiful and there's nothing I can't do. I came to believe all of this at a very early age, and I did everything within my power to prove it all true. I guess I found the knack, because I set my goals high and reached or exceeded *all of them.* I guess I got so full of myself that there was no place for a sovereign God in my world. By the time I graduated from high school, I was a vocal, diehard atheist.

"When I got to college, it was perfect for someone like me who didn't believe in God. I went from bad to worse. I read all of Richard Dawkins's books. All of Christopher Hitchens's books. Actually carried around his book, *God is Not Great.* Underlined it everywhere. But God in His mercy made my self-made world crumble around me. Anna will bear witness to what I'm saying. And I'm sure she's shared a lot with the prayer group here." Elsie looked at each of the women, her eyes locking onto theirs. "Thank you for praying for me." She looked at Anna. "Thank you for not giving up on me."

Anna kissed her on the top of her head. "I can never give up on you, Elsie."

Elsie reached up and grasped her arm. "Thank you."

Rachel found a sneaky tear coursing down her face. She flicked it away with a finger and waited for more.

"My family, our family, has a problem with debilitating, irrational fear," Elsie continued. "It hits the women. It got our granny, our mother, our sister Nicole. It had Anna until she was set free in this prayer group. It even attacked our little girls." Elsie's eyes began to show the brokenness of her heart. She wiped at the tears.

"I told myself it would not get me. That I was stronger than the fear. In my pride I said the others got the fear because they were weak. Then something happened that devastated me."

Anna knew what was coming next. She cried for Elsie.

"I bet you've never met a nurse who got a perfect score on the MCAT and who graduated from Johns Hopkins University medical school at the top of her class." Elsie wiped a tear. "Guess what—you're looking at her. I was two years from completing my residency in neurosurgery when," she fought to continue, taking a few open-mouthed breaths, "when the fear hit. The great Elsie dropped out of residency.

"Little by little the fear started encroaching on other areas of my life. I told myself that it wasn't happening—that I was strong, and I would find a way to beat it. All this time my husband has been stellar. I don't deserve him. He doesn't deserve what I've put him through." Elsie stared at the floor and saw the demise of her dashed dreams and teetering marriage. She saw Amanda. She looked up.

"Rachel, Anna tried to help me and I was too proud and stubborn to listen. Then Jesus sent an angel to talk to me. I wouldn't listen. He warned me they were coming for me, but I wouldn't listen."

"Who was coming for you?" Rachel asked, in a tone that masked her interest. Weird or not, she was captivated by the power of the love these two sisters had for one another, and by the characters in her story: Jesus, angels, monsters, demons.

"I was told, 'Those whom you have called.' I didn't know the angel meant demons."

Rachel leaned forward. "He said you *called* demons? What did he mean by that?"

Sheila snuck a look at Miriam. Miriam knew what this meant. She turned to the side and started praying hard under her breath for Rachel.

"When I first thought about it, I thought the angel was referring to my rebellion and willful ignorance. But now I see it was speaking of more. After the angel appeared to me, I went on the Internet and researched parapsychology."

Miriam stopped praying in tongues. "*Para* psychology? What in the world is *para* psychology?"

Elsie said, "Telekinesis, clairvoyance, mental telepathy, astral projection—"

Miriam's wide, wild eyes got wider and wilder. Even her hair seemed to get spookier. "You did *what?* Astral projection? Oh Lord!" She made a beeline out of the room. "She's been floating all over the place. This is going to be a mess. I'm going to get some towels."

"And get a bucket, Miriam," said Sheila. "Looks like we've got some witchcraft demons to deal with."

Chapter 28

Anna's eyes bulged at this information. Her mouth dropped open as she tried to figure this out. "Elsie, I'm not getting this. When did you go from an atheist who didn't believe in the supernatural to witchcraft? That's a—"she shook her head and let out an audible breath—"I mean you didn't take baby steps here. You skipped right over the Grand Canyon. When you'd do this?"

"Just a couple of days ago," she answered. "Right after I left your house. I figured you'd done something that caused your brain to self-correct the fear." Elsie looked at a room full of expressions that said no one knew what she was talking about. "I couldn't accept that you were healed by Jesus. He didn't exist. So I looked at it scientifically."

"For the life of me, I don't know why people just don't go straight to God," said Miriam. "What is scientific about messing with demons?"

"Nothing." Elsie shook her head. "I was desperate. Desperate to not believe God. So I came up with this theory that Anna had unwittingly done something that caused her brain to fix itself of the fear. That's why I tried those things. Believe me, I had no idea I was messing with demons."

"That her brain fixed itself, huh?" Miriam shook her head and exhaled. "Well, I've beat up on you enough. Let's get these things out of you."

"Please," said Elsie. "It's time. I want to be like Anna. I want to be free."

"Well, darling, you're going to be. Right, Sheila?" said Miriam.

Sheila smiled her answer. "Okay, Elsie, since you're new at this—"she looked at Rachel—"you, too, Rach, I'm going to explain some things. We're going to pray and turn this over to the Holy Spirit. We're going to set the rules and let Satan know what his boundaries are. And we're going to claim protection from any retaliation.

"We're going to take turns leading. Me or Anna or Miriam will speak directly to the demons," Sheila smiled at Anna's look of surprise, "the others will be praying in English or in tongues."

"You said 'boundaries,'" said Elsie.

"That means we tell the devil what to do," said Miriam. "He likes to show his butt, and since you went messing around with witchcraft demons, there's probably no way around seeing it. But we can put a limit on it. Witchcraft or not, we're not gonna let him run things. That's what we mean."

Elsie smiled a nervous smile. "That's nice to know. I've seen his butt. It ain't pretty."

Miriam smiled. Anna's sister had done something really stupid and dangerous, but she liked her. She was alright. "No, it's not," she said.

"Now, Elsie, these things are going to fight back. That's okay." She looked at Elsie's eyes. "Really, it is. Trust me." Elsie did. "Their power is darkness and deception. Any time they're forced into the open, it's a good thing—well, if you know what to do with them." Sheila smiled reassuringly. "We know what to do with them, sweetie."

Elsie knew she was in good hands, but the beatings she had gotten from the demons were fresh in her mind, and the bruises were fresh on her body. She couldn't stop the growing fear she had.

"Now what I want you to do while we pray, Elsie, is to just sit and relax. Don't pray out loud. Okay? This is your time. Just relax. We'll do the work. You do the receiving. You may hear something or feel something odd when we're praying. If you do, just stop us and let us know what's going on. That helps us to flow with God, okay?"

"Okay," said Elsie. Her fear was growing more intense.

"They may threaten you or say something stupid. Don't you worry about it none," said Miriam.

"That's right," added Sheila. "They have very few options when they're dealing with someone who's skilled in deliverance ministry. They can try to hide. They can try to intimidate you so you will cut the session short and ask us to stop."

"But that's not gonna happen," said wild eyes.

"No. That's not going to happen," said Elsie, pressing past the fear she could literally feel crawling under her skin.

"Didn't think so," said Sheila. "Or they can fight. We're not going to let them hide. You don't scare easily. And they can't win the fight. So, you see, there's not a lot they can do."

"How will we know when they're gone?" asked Elsie.

Sheila looked at Anna.

They had to wait while Anna used both hands to wipe her wet face. She spoke with a voice straining under the weight of tears of joy. "You'll know, Elsie. When they left me," she wiped her face, "I heard a lot of screaming inside of me. Then I felt them being pulled out of my head." Anna exhaled a sudden burst of emotion as she thought of her own deliverance. "And they were gone. I was free."

Now Elsie was crying. She looked up at her wonderful sister and opened her mouth—and roared like a lion."

*****

Unreal roared again.

A crowd of evil spirits looked at him. Each set of eyes shouting, "What are you doing?"

"I'm not a bum!" Unreal answered the crowd. "It took me a long time to get this house. You think I'm going to let these misfits take it from me?"

The massive crowd of demons who stared unbelievingly at Unreal seemed to be on the verge of forgetting protocol and attacking the great phobic spirit. Immediate survival was more important than protocol.

Teeth and fangs and claws readied for action.

They surrounded him.

Behind the circle of demons and out of the darkness rushed three witchcraft spirits. They snatched and elbowed and pushed demons out of their way. "Get out of the way! Move! Move it, I said!"

The three witchcraft demons stood before Unreal with glaring red eyes. They hurled questions, accusations, and insults at him so fast he could never hope to answer them all. He didn't try. He simply stood there with his claws bared and ready to fight to the death.

"You idiot! What are you doing?"

"Are you trying to get us all kicked out?"

"This is why you're always on the street, you retard!"

"Everything is always about you, isn't it, you egomaniac!"

"If you get us kicked out, we'll rip you to shreds!"

On and on went the witchcraft spirits.

"Quiet! All of you!" This was another voice out of the darkness. A dark figure emerged. It was Terror. He had several guards with him just in case. He and his guards walked down the open line of demons. They stopped and surrounded Unreal and the witchcraft spirits. "Move away."

"This idiot is going to cost us our home and you your new job," answered a witchcraft spirit, unaware that the job was already lost.

Terror's guards pulled their weapons. The circle widened around them.

"I will not ask you again," said Terror.

They looked into one another's eyes for a long few seconds. The spirit backed down and they all three went back into the darkness, bumping and pushing demons out of the way as they went.

Unreal looked at Terror like he would thank him properly for this later. Terror's face hardened even more. He stepped closer and whispered in his ear. "You have a big mouth, Unreal. It would have been right to let them separate your empty head from your body." Terror backed away and spoke to the crowd. "Stick together. Hold the line. We cannot lose Elsie. Too much is at stake. Thanks to Unreal, they know you're here. So you can't hide. And you know Elsie. The winch doesn't know how to give up. The most you can do is try your best to outlast them. I'll try to get you rein—" His words were interrupted.

"And in the name of Jesus Christ, we refuse to let you get any outside help!" said Sheila.

Every demon looked at Terror.

"Did you hear that?" said Unreal. "No reinforcements."

Terror looked at him with a seething anger. Anger due to Unreal's big mouth. "Of course, I heard it. Why wouldn't I hear it? You heard it, didn't you?" Terror looked at the crowd of demons. He knew they were unnerved and needed encouragement. "If you stick together—" He was interrupted again.

"Lord Jesus, we ask that you confuse the enemy the way you confused the armies of the aliens when they came against Israel in the Old Testament," prayed Miriam.

The anxious crowd of demons looking at Terror looked more anxious. "What now?" asked one. "They're trying to confuse."

Terror looked at the demons. He lost his train of thought. He looked at Unreal. Unreal looked at him wondering about the goofy look on his face.

"I gotta go," said Terror. He left mumbling something under his breath as his guards followed behind, trying hard to remember why they were there.

Unreal and the other demons were dumbfounded by Terror's behavior. He saw something fall to the floor. None of Terror's guards bothered to pick it up. He did. It was a scroll. He opened it and smiled. *This is why you came, my friend,* he thought. He remembered a Scripture from the cursed book. *He who covers his sins will not prosper, but whoever confesses and forsakes them will have mercy.*

Unreal knew there was no way proud Elsie would ever come that clean. She wasn't going anywhere, and neither was he and his fear spirits.

*****

Rachel jumped at Unreal's roaring.

Anna didn't jump, but she did stiffen. "It's going to be alright, Elsie," she said.

"Why is she laughing?" asked Rachel.

"That's not Elsie," said Sheila.

"Oh," was all Rachel answered.

"Still want to stay?" Sheila asked.

Rachel nodded with wide eyes.

"I'll kill her before I let you cast me out. I'm nobody's bum."

Sheila and Miriam looked at one another.

Elsie had a slight noticeable tremble. Her eyes stared straight ahead with a dead look, like a life-like mannequin. A tear came out the corner of one of them.

Sheila said, "Anna, take your sister's hand."

Anna sat on a chair on one side of Elsie; Sheila was on the other side. Miriam walked the floor behind her, praying in tongues and every now and then giving her own commands of faith in a low voice, but not interfering with Sheila's leadership.

Anna took Elsie's hand. "I'm here, Elsie."

Sheila had the other hand in both of hers. She looked into Elsie's dead eyes. "In Jesus' name I forbid you to hide. I forbid you to fight back. I forbid you to hurt Elsie. You're not killing anyone. Now in Jesus name, come out of her." Her voice was soft, and were it not for the intensity of her expression, she could have been placing an order in a nice restaurant.

"I don't have to come out."

"I said come out," said Sheila.

"And I said no."

This back and forth went on for a couple of minutes until finally there was no response whatsoever from whatever was defying Sheila. "Okay," said Sheila in her soft voice as she shook her head. She lifted her other hand without taking her eyes off of Elsie's face. "Come, Holy Spirit. Come and fill this place. We can do nothing without You, but we can do all things through You. Please manifest Your presence here. All things are made manifest in Your light."

*****

The demons inside of Elsie heard the prayer and exchanged nervous looks. This wasn't going well at all. This warrior had called in the Holy Spirit. Now anything was liable to happen! Something had to be done quickly.

"Hey, look!" a demon squealed as he looked up, down, and all around. "That bat is taking our darkness. How are we going to win without darkness? It won't be long now."

The demon would soon discover that he was as prophetic as he was observant.

Unreal looked around at the thick darkness that was becoming less thick by the moment. His big head whipped around. "Fear of Failure, get the other fear spirits and follow me." He held up the scroll. "We have a dark place. Come!' He turned and walked briskly toward an area of darkness that remained unbothered.

The whole troop of demons followed. He turned and looked at the other spirits following him and the fear spirits. "I said fear spirits! If you're not a spirit of fear, get lost!"

"What about us?" said a pride spirit.

"Yeah, what about us?" said Worship of Intellect. "This isn't a good idea. It's not rational."

Now there was a rowdy chorus of demons shouting, "What about us?"

Unreal looked at them with an upturned lip. "What about you? I don't need you. You're on your own." He took his scroll and entered the remaining darkness with his supporting cast.

Unreal was disgusted to find that the darkness he thought was exclusively his and his fear demons was already crowded with witchcraft spirits and their buddies.

"There goes the neighborhood," a witchcraft spirit taunted when Unreal entered the darkness.

"Oh, whatever," responded Unreal.

"The demons we have to work with to stay off the streets," another witchcraft demon derisively added.

"Come out!"

Every demon heard the piercing command. Those in the darkness pushed backward as far as they could go. Those left in the light had a quick and decisive discussion.

"Somebody's gotta go, and it sure as darkness won't be me."

This demon was big enough to back up his statement. But not every demon was this fortunate. They looked at a demon that stood at the very edge of the darkness, half in and half out.

"Wait a minute," he said, snatching his arm away from a demon who grabbed it. "I'm with Unreal. I'm a spirit of fear."

*****

"I said come out," Sheila repeated softly.

The exposed demons gathered in a corner of the room. They peered at the thick door and at the light that was visible at the bottom.

"I hear something," said Elsie.

"What do you hear?" asked Sheila.

"Arguing." Elsie's eyes were closed. "And I see demons grabbing a demon. They got him, and they're standing by the door—waiting."

"Waiting for what?"

"Waiting for you to tell him to leave. Please make him leave," said Elsie.

"I can make him leave, Elsie," said Sheila, "but the more we know about what's hurting you, the more effective you'll be at not opening the door to him again. Okay?"

"Okay."

"Do you know what kind of spirit this is?" asked Sheila.

"No. He just looks like a dark figure. He's not very big," said Elsie.

"Okay, Elsie, use your authority. You're in the family now; so you can use Jesus's name. Order him to reveal himself to you."

Almost immediately Elsie whispered, "Cancer."

Anna gasped. "Cancer?"

"No, not cancer. Fear of cancer," said Elsie. "I started getting thoughts that I had cancer. At first I ignored it, but the thoughts got stronger and more persistent, and I got scared."

Sheila wasted no time. "Fear of Cancer, come out."

"Wait! Wait! Wait!" the demon begged his comrades. "For the love of darkness, don't do this!"

The door opened and they tossed out the sacrifice.

Elsie coughed deeply one time. She put her hand to her ear and started crying. "It left," she said.

Rachel found herself standing. "You felt something leave?"

Elsie's reply was soft and filled with joyous tears. "Yes!"

Rachel's hand went to her chest. This was weird stuff, but something about it was real. She slowly lowered and sat herself down, wondering, wondering hard.

Sheila turned it over to Miriam. She was quite a bit more animated and loud than Sheila, but she cleaned house of almost every demon that was left exposed in the light.

Miriam looked at Anna. "Your turn."

"What?" she answered.

"She's your sister, isn't she? Your turn. This is the easy part. The hard part was you loving her and praying her into the kingdom." Miriam looked at Anna with a smile. "You deserve this, Anna. It's a good thing you've done for your sister. Now go on and finish it."

Chapter 29

Elsie's eyes were closed tight. The skin across the backs of her hands was stretched to its limit as she gripped the hands of Anna and Sheila even tighter. Waves of debilitating fear rolled back and forth through her like an angry ocean crashing against rocks, regrouping, and crashing again and again.

If this were all there was going on inside of her, she could have gritted her teeth and suffered through it in silence. That's what she wanted to do—suffer in silence. Not giving these things the satisfaction of knowing they were hurting her. But she felt the fear literally crawling just beneath her skin in every part of her body.

She heard demons laughing at her. Her lips tightened in defiance. This proved futile, however. Elsie was strong, but she was also human. She willed herself to keep her mouth close. She wouldn't scream. Why should she? She wasn't afraid. The Lord hadn't brought her this far to leave her. When all was said and done, she'd be free. Just as free as Anna!

But all wasn't said and done. This thing was crawling in every part of her body. *It was inside of her!* It was almost unbearable. Elsie felt her lips opening. It was like fear had stuck a crowbar into her mouth and was prying it open.

It wasn't the fact that Elsie screamed that startled Sheila and Miriam. That happened a lot in deliverance sessions. It was how long the loud wail of agony lasted. She must have screamed for at least two full minutes without taking a breath. When the last of the piercing wail escaped Elsie's spit covered lips, her head dropped to her chest in supernatural exhaustion.

Anna wiped Elsie's mouth with a tissue and looked at Sheila for guidance.

"What is the Holy Spirit telling you to do?" Sheila asked.

Anna's lip dropped in thought. What did you do after something like this? "Ummm..." She waited for Sheila or Miriam to answer her "Ummm" with directions. None came. "Uhhh, Lord, please comfort and encourage my sister." She dabbed at Elsie's nostrils with tissue and looked at Sheila.

"You're doing fine. There's no formula for this, Anna, except listening to God, loving who you're praying for, and taking authority over Satan in Jesus's name and telling him to leave. Don't complicate it."

"I'm no bum."

Anna looked at Elsie and looked back at Sheila, then looked at Elsie again. "Elsie, no, no, of course not. You're not a bum. You're a child of God now."

"I don't think that's Elsie," said a suspicious-looking Miriam.

Anna questioned with her eyes.

"I think that thing in her is saying he's not a bum," said Miriam.

"Show him that he is a bum, Anna," said Sheila calmly.

"Elsie," Anna put her fingers under Elsie's chin to lift her face. She lifted it, but Elsie's eyes were closed. "Open your eyes." She didn't. "Open your eyes, Elsie." She didn't. Anna looked at Sheila.

"It helps sometimes for them to have their eyes open, but God's not limited to open eyes. That thing can hear you without her eyes being open. Cast it out."

Anna looked at Elsie, but she spoke beyond what she saw. "In Jesus name, come out of her, you bum! Come out now!"

"I'm no bum! You can't make me go anywhere! I'm too strong."

"I said come out of my sister!" Anna yelled.

"I don't have to. You have no right to make me leave."

"I have the name of Jesus, and that's all the right I need! Come out!"

Antichrist spoke up. "There is no authority in the name of that dead, two-bit Jew. You are trusting in a myth. There's no spinach in the can, Popeye."

"So you like cartoons?" said Anna, her spirit receiving a burst from heaven. "Let's see how you like angels." She closed her eyes to pray.

"Keep your eyes open when you're ministering deliverance, Anna," said Miriam, startling Anna. "The Bible says to watch and pray. And I can't think of a better time to obey that Scripture than when you're tangling with a cocky demon. Right, Sheila?"

"That's right, Miriam," she said. "Not a good idea to enter battle with your eyes closed unless you're sure your partner's got you covered. Someone needs to be watching."

"Okay," said Anna. "Lord, we ask you to send your mighty angels to make this demon obey us. My sister has been through so much. Please help her now."

*****

Antichrist's black eyes looked confidently through his tight eyelids. Elsie had treacherously betrayed them and turned her back on her faith in God's nonexistence. But this didn't mean she was totally free of his influence. She had turned her back on the obvious darkness. The big lies that God didn't exist, and that Jesus wasn't God.

But every big lie was supported by lots of little lies, and that's where Antichrist may still have her. Sure, she now knew the truth that Jesus Christ was risen from the dead and that He was God. But were there other areas in her life where she welcomed his influence? Any area at all where her behavior showed that God wasn't welcome in it. Such an area would be an antichrist sphere of influence. And even a little area would give him the protection he needed.

All I need is a little leaven, he thought. *Give me something to work with.* He looked down at the bottom of the big, thick door that separated him and the others from any external threat. Light was visible through the opening at the door's bottom.

Antichrist backed up as close as he could to the edge of the darkness. The sharp point of a fear demon's sword poked him in the back, reminding him that the space was taken. He cast a quick glance to those hiding in the darkness and growled. He looked with extreme unease at the two areas under the door that suddenly grew immensely brighter than the other light.

"Show me some love, Elsie," he said. "All I need is a little something to work with."

On the other side of the mammoth door, a large warrior angel lifted his powerful leg and slammed the bottom of his boot against the door. The force ripped bolts and hinges out of the walls. Antichrist and the others watched the big door slide across the floor to the right.

"I am here for Antichrist—and anyone who tries to help him."

Antichrist looked at the angel. The heavenly warrior's thick hands gripped two long swords. *Anyone who tries to help?* He knew none of the cowards hiding in the darkness would have a sudden change of heart and come to his rescue.

The demon pulled his own weapons. "I have a right to—"

SWISH! SWISH!

Only one sword was used. A forehand across the neck. A backhand slicing through the torso. Antichrist's head dropped to the floor and rolled left. His torso fell forward. His legs and butt sat down behind the torso.

The angel looked into the darkness. "I will be back—with others." He backed away and out of the doorless entry.

"Did you hear that?" said a terrified fear demon.

Unreal backhanded the demon with the closed fist that clutched his scroll. "We're not going anywhere! I've got this!" he yelled, flashing the document in his hand.

*****

Elsie wrapped her arms around her belly and doubled over into a long, low growl. It was nowhere as long as the scream, but it sounded like a deep pain. To Elsie, it felt like a deep pain. Like her innards were being squeezed.

Then she felt the tearing of claws inside of her head. But it wasn't a slash here or there. It was more like the slashings of a threatened thing fighting for its life. Like a cornered cat fighting a large dog. Little claws fueled by terror and desperation, swinging furiously at its larger and more powerful attacker in the hopes of not becoming a meal.

Elsie sat up and let out a long breath. Her eyes were tired, but the fight was still in them. "Well, that one didn't want to go."

"They never do," said Miriam. "Freeloaders."

"Do you know what kind of spirit it was?" asked Anna.

"An evil spirit," said Elsie. A slight smile formed on her fatigue-framed face.

Anna joined her sister's smile. "You're doing great, Elsie."

"Thanks, coach." Elsie closed her eyes and took three deep breaths. "It wasn't just one. It was a lot of them. Unbelief, pride, lies, hatred of God, atheism, anger—there were so many." A look of worry replaced her smile. "Fear is still there, Anna." She placed a strong grip on Anna's forearm. "I still have the fear."

"Don't you worry, Elsie. We're going to get 'em," said Miriam.

"Did it take this long for you, Anna?" asked Elsie.

"No. But I wasn't as stubborn as you," she answered with a smile.

"And she also didn't throw a party and invite every witchcraft demon in town," said Miriam.

Something like a tired smile reappeared on Elsie's face. "Yeah, well, Anna never could throw a good party." She looked at Anna. "Come on. Let's finish this."

Anna looked at her sister's beautiful face. Could this really be happening? Were they really casting demons out of Elsie? And was Elsie really telling her to hurry it up? *Oh, thank You, Jesus! I love You so much!*

Two hours later Elsie was on her back looking up at eight eyeballs and trying to make sense of what they were saying. She felt as though she had been pushed off a ten-foot ledge onto the concrete over and over again. But the pain was beautiful. For every witchcraft and occult demon had been kicked out or destroyed.

Elsie pushed the words up from her hurting chest and out her hurting head and hurting mouth. "Can we go after fear now? It's time."

"It is time, Elsie," said Anna.

An hour later, Elsie was still on her back and still full of fear. She was trying as hard as she could to not lose faith, but no matter what Anna and Sheila and Miriam did or said, the things inside of her responded with laughter and taunts. They declared so confidently that they weren't leaving that Elsie was finding it hard to think otherwise.

"What do we do?" She looked up at Sheila with eyes that didn't conceal her anxiety.

Sheila was her knees beside her. She rubbed her forehead and face. "You saw the Lord, remember?"

Elsie's chest and belly rose and lowered with her rapid breaths. Sheila's face was calm; her voice reassuring. This helped. "Yes, I saw Him."

Sheila smiled at her. "Remember that, sweetie."

Elsie clutched at her words. "I will."

"Just lie here and rest for a few minutes, Elsie," said Sheila. "Anna, you're doing fine. Just rest with her for a few. I'm going to call my friend and ask her to keep the kids down there until we get finished here. I don't think it'll be much longer."

"You think so?" asked Elsie.

"Yeah. Don't worry about these demons. They're acting like this because they've got a temporary legal right. God will tell us what they've got. We'll get them," said Sheila.

Elsie's head popped up as she lay on her back. "Legal right. Remember, Anna? Legal right. Could that be it? Do we need to deal with the curse?"

Sheila and Miriam looked at one another wondering how they could have forgotten something so basic. Miriam looked at Elsie and chuckled. "Once we get you taken care of, I'm gonna have you cast the demon of forgetfulness out of me and Sheila."

Sheila put up her index finger and smiled. "Hold up." She texted a message to her friend about her children. "Okay, let's get back to it."

The ladies took authority over everything they could think of. They came against the generational curse. They made sure Elsie didn't have any unforgiveness in her heart. They had her to again renounce witchcraft and atheism. They helped her search her heart for anything that could possibly stand in the way of God's power.

I'm never leaving you, you nut case, said Unreal inside of her. *When I finish with you, you won't know the difference between day and night. You won't know what's real and what's me. You'll be so crazy, you won't know you're crazy.*

Elsie looked at the women with eyes that now carried the fullness of her fears. "Why won't they leave me? Jesus appeared to me, Anna. Why won't they leave?" Her troubled voice matched her eyes.

Rachel gasped and grabbed her chest, staring straight ahead at a picture only she could see. Everyone, including Elsie, looked at her. Elsie sat up on the floor. Rachel's mouth went wide before she took on a hard grimace and fell to her knees with deep sobs that rocked her whole body.

Miriam rushed to her and bent down and hugged the shaking woman. "It's okay, darling, we're here. God's doing something. Don't be afraid. Just let him have his way."

Rachel cried for half an hour before coming to a near stop and starting up again just as strong as when she first began. In another half hour, she could fight the crying just enough to get out three words: "I'm sorry, God."

The women watched her for another ten minutes say, "I'm sorry, God." Each time Miriam said, "It's okay. God forgives you," Rachel countered between sobs, "But you don't understand."

By now everyone was gathered around Rachel. She sat on the edge of the sofa and held a tissue-filled hand to her crying face. She listened to everyone trying to make her feel better. Her face lifted with a brightness and calm that was sudden and unscheduled. "I'm free," she said softly. "It's gone. The deep pain in my heart and the wall between me and Jesus is gone."

Sheila was baffled. She had known Rachel for fourteen years and she had never seen or heard anything in her friend that resembled what she described. She wasn't into the things of the Spirit, but she loved God, regularly read her Bible, witnessed, and lived right. What was this deep pain? And why did she feel there was a wall between her and the Lord?

Sheila stroked her friend's hair. "Whatever is bothering—"

"I killed my baby, Sheila. I went to bed with Danny right after Bible study one night. I got pregnant and had an abortion." Rachel's words put a muzzle on everyone's mouth.

Everyone but one.

*****

Unreal's roar filled the darkness, but didn't reach Elsie's mouth. The demons around him moved away, giving him all the room he needed to throw his fit. Flailing arms with half-spins, kicking at the air, cussing and spitting—a demonic tornado in search of new ways to release his anger.

"Where'd she come from? Who is she? Why is she here? She talks too much! She talks entirely—too—much!" Unreal stopped his wild spinning and looked around. He was standing in the light! "Uh oh," he said, before jumping back into the darkness.

Every demon turned with anxious eyes toward the doorway. "You hear that?" tremored one.

"Sounds like someone's coming," said another.

Unreal's face hardened. "A lot of someones."

*****

Rachel's words were slow and halting. Her voice sounded like it was carrying the strain and pain of a broken heart as she spoke. But what they heard was not what she felt. What the women heard were sounds of something that once was there, but now was gone. Like the thunder of a fighter jet heard only after the jet itself is long gone.

"I didn't plan—we didn't plan to commit fornication. We were blindsided by passion. I didn't even know all of that was going on between us until it was too late. We should've never been alone together." She paused. "Then my sin caught up with me. I panicked and got an abortion." Rachel looked at Sheila. "Ken wonders why I get so depressed every June. My baby was due in June. That's the birth month. I've lived with the memory of this sin all these years."

Sheila let her mind go back. Some odd things now made sense. There were times that Rachel got really depressed. Now that she thought about it, maybe it was once a year for weeks at a time. And there were times when she seemed sad when the subject of pregnancy and infants came up. And there did seem to be always some reason for her to not attend baby showers.

Sheila spoke. "I'm not trying to make light of this at all—you know that. You were a Christian, Rachel. Didn't you confess this to God a long time ago?"

The smile on Rachel's face and the brutality of her answer seemed at odds. "Not as murder."

A thoughtful silence commanded the room.

"My sin was so great that I never allowed myself to think about it for long. Whenever something happened that made it impossible for me to pretend it never happened, I tried to cover its sinfulness by admitting to myself that I *stopped* the pregnancy. Or that I *terminated* or *ended* the pregnancy. I never called it what it is. I never called it murder.

"When you and the others were casting those things out of Elsie, you explained to her how she couldn't hide any sin. That if she did, Satan would have a legal right to stay. I saw that I had deceived myself into thinking I repented when I really did not. It looked like I did, but in reality I was covering my sins by calling something as horrible as killing my child a terminated or ended pregnancy."

Rachel wiped both eyes and looked at each woman. "I've already said this, but I want to say it one more time before I leave. This is for the devil's benefit because this is the last day he'll ever be able to use it against me. I committed a sexual sin and consequently got pregnant. I tried to cover my sin by murdering my child. I tried to cover the murder by calling it something clinical and sterile and pushing it to the back of my mind.

"But today I've acknowledged my sin and have asked God to forgive me. What I did was horrible and unfixable. I don't deserve to be forgiven. But God has forgiven me, and I'm going to go with that—all the way. I'm not living in shame and condemnation one more day."

Rachel stood.

"You're leaving?" asked Elsie.

Rachel smiled with a depth of joy that Sheila didn't recall ever seeing. "I think it's obvious now that my coming here was no accident. God was behind this whole thing. I need to go home and talk to Ken. Please pray that God covers the discussion. It happened before we were married, but I should've told him."

The ladies held hands and prayed for Rachel and Ken. When they finished, Sheila and Miriam walked her to the door.

Rachel hugged Miriam first. She got to Sheila and took both of her hands and looked at her with tears ready to roll. "I love you, Sheila. I truly don't know how much longer I could've gone on like that."

"And I love you, Rachel—starch and all."

Rachel's eyes emptied. "About that starch," she smiled and sniffled, "After what I've seen and experienced, I don't think that's going to work anymore."

Sheila laughed her tears out. "I didn't think so."

"You know," said Rachel, "there are probably millions of women in the church who need what God gave me today."

"That's right. There are," said Miriam, hair wilder from combat, eyes wide with excitement. "You hear the call?"

Rachel looked at Miriam, then Sheila. "I hear it. Count me in."

The moment the door closed behind Rachel, a piercing scream came from the living room.

*****

Unreal was stunned at the turn of events. He could almost feel the shiver of walking the streets in the cold like a bum. Or dabbing his brow with a handkerchief as he walked aimlessly on hot days. And the laughter. The laughter of fools making fun of him behind his back for being kicked out again. Against his wishes, he found his mind taking him to thoughts of whether he'd give up his suitcase for a large backpack.

I'd look like less of a bum if I wore a nice backpack, he thought.

The demons sharing the stronghold stared at their volatile leader, wondering what he was thinking. No doubt he was formulating a battle plan against the inevitable assault of angels.

But I can carry more in a suitcase. And some bums do carry backpacks now, Unreal pondered. *Lost my coat, hat, and gloves at the last house I lost. Going to have to replace—*

Unreal shook himself. "Wait a minute! I'm no bum! I'm not going anywhere!" He looked at his demons. He thrust his hand in the air. "As long as we have this document, we don't have to go—"

Elsie's prayer interrupted him. "I'm sorry, Lord, for killing my baby. It was murder. Please forgive me. I don't want anything to stand in the way of our relationship. Now please fill me with Your Holy Spirit."

Unreal looked like a demonic version of the statue of liberty. Frozen in place, with his hand stretched out, clutching the piece of paper that was his insurance policy. He couldn't believe his ears.

POOF!

Unreal yelled in pain and jerked his flaming hand out of the air and buried the fire in his robe.

A demon sprinted out of the crowd of demons and out of the doorway before Unreal or anyone knew what had happened. Two more seconds, two more escaped demons. Unreal ran toward the doorway and turned with his sword loosely in his scorched hand to face his deserting demons.

"The next one who tries to—"

Another demon, a small one, sprinted out of the darkness. He broke out into a zig zag the closer he got to Unreal. Unreal tried to keep his eyes on the speedy demon. He lifted his sword. "I'm going to slice your little dark—"

Another demon sprinted to the left of Unreal and the other demon. Unreal took his eyes off the first demon for a fraction of a second to look at the other demon. That fraction of a second was all the first demon needed. He slid past Unreal and through the doorway like he was sliding into third base. *Safe!* Unreal saw that he lost that one and turned to stop the other. The other zipped past him right when he turned to see where he was.

Unreal ran to the doorway and stood directly in front of it. "Which one of you cowards want to try it now?"

The sound of approaching boots landing heavily on the ground took everyone's attention off of Unreal. The demons shared a moment of hopelessness before turning their attention back to their suicidal, if not stupid, leader.

"Are you happy now?" a voice shot out of the darkness.

"We've got our own General Custer," another voice said.

"Who said that?" shouted Unreal. But he didn't wait for an answer. The boots were too close to stand one more second in the light. He ran for his life toward the darkness as his renegade demons ran past him toward the door. There wasn't time for him to deal with this desertion. So he crouched in the dark, watching and waiting for the angels.

The phobic demon watched every demon toss his weapons in a large pile and get on their knees with their hands atop their heads. The sight was disgusting—and loaded with possibility. He went as deep into the darkness as he could without losing sight of what was going on.

Total darkness. Total silence.

Maybe...just maybe.

The angels poured forth in overwhelming force. There was no way they were ever going to win a face-to-face battle with these killers. He watched the angels walk up and down the line of his cowards, looking, probing. He watched three times as a certain angel, probably the leader of this pack of wolves, yank up a demon by his hair and thrust a blade into his chest. So much for the God of love.

"You will leave this daughter of God," said the angel with the dagger dripping with demon blood. "Stand to your feet. Any sudden moves and you will be destroyed."

The demons stood with their heads bowed.

"One line separated by ten feet," said the angel. "You will know you are too close to one another if a sword or dagger enters your rebellious body. Now move!"

One by one the demons marched out under the scrutiny of large angelic warriors who appeared to need only the slightest excuse to slice and dice demons. A demon carrying something on his back got close to the front. Several angels closed in around him. They looked at the next few demons in line. All of them were carrying or pushing something.

"Stop the line!" an angel commanded. He pointed. "You!"

The demon told himself to not pass out. "Yes, servant of the Lord Most High, true and holy."

The angel was unimpressed. "What is that on your back?"

The demon looked behind and gulped. "A guitar."

The angel looked more intently at the demon. "I know it is a guitar. What is it doing on your back? Take it off." The angel looked at the other demons with their equipment. He pointed at them in turn. "You, put down the mic stand. You two, push that piano back over there. You, do the same with the keyboards. You, put the xylophone over there with the rest of the instruments."

Unreal knew they were vastly outnumbered, but how could those demons allow this angel to take their spoils without so much as a whimper? Was there not one real demon among those cowards? Not one who would fight to the death?

"Unreal!"

It was the bloodthirsty angel calling his name! Unreal's teeth went into earthquake mode, chattering so loudly he was sure those in the light heard him.

The angel watched Unreal's sword slide out of the darkness and across the floor. Next came his dagger. Next came Unreal. He had a suitcase in his hand. He walked to the end of the line, put the suitcase down, got on his knees, and put his hands atop his big head.

The angel peered at the phobic demon with holy anger. He gripped his dagger and walked with hard steps to Unreal. He got on one knee. "Lift up your head, demon."

Unreal swallowed and lifted his head.

The angel looked into Unreal's wavy eyes without blinking. Unreal couldn't hide his fear, but neither could he hide his contempt. The angel lifted his dagger and put its tip to Unreal's throat. "Anna has escaped. Chrissie has escaped. Amanda has escaped. Elsie has escaped. But you will not escape."

There was a quick thrust in and upward.

Unreal knew the dagger was now in his thick neck and head because he felt the angel's large hand under his chin—and because he couldn't breathe.

The angel yanked the dagger out.

Unreal put a hand to his neck and the other on his suitcase and used it to lift himself to his feet. He picked the suitcase up and staggered three steps before taking a slow fall forward, his wavy eyes finally settled. As his face got closer to crashing to the floor, he thought, *I'm no bum.*

It was almost over.

Chapter 30

Anna and Elsie sat in the car in Sheila's driveway. Sheila had walked them to the car and was saying goodbye again. This was the third goodbye. So many wonderful things had happened that no one wanted the day to end.

Sheila stepped back from Anna's side of the car and bent down. She looked across to Elsie and said with tears, "Isn't God good, Elsie? Isn't He good?"

That's all it took. Elsie and Anna went back to a level seven of ten on the crying scale.

Sheila straitened up and closed her eyes and exhaled. "That's enough. I'm not saying anything else. You'll never get out of here if I do. You girls better get out of here before I ask you to stay for dinner."

Anna looked up and grinned with tears and gratitude that seeped into Sheila's bones. "Thank you, Sheila. Thank you for letting God use you. Thank you for giving me back my sister."

Sheila bent down again. This time hugging Anna through the open window. "Oh, sweetie, serving God is our reasonable service." She pecked her on the cheek. "Now go. I know Daniel must be worried stiff about Elsie."

Elsie was crying too heavily to speak. So she simply bent her head down so Sheila could see her and shook her head.

"Bye-bye, sweetie," said Sheila.

Anna backed out of the driveway and onto the street. She and Elsie waved at Sheila, who had been waving at them the whole time Anna was backing the car out. Sheila watched the car until it reached the corner and turned out of view. She didn't see Anna pull over because she was crying too strongly to drive.

When Anna's and Elsie's crying finally became manageable, Elsie asked, "Will you take me somewhere before I go home?"

*****

Anna turned into one of the parking spaces at Kennesaw Mountain.

Elsie looked forward onto the grass field and went into a zone. She looked at Anna. "This won't take long."

She got out of the car and walked several steps before returning to the car. "I need the bike," she told Anna before getting it off the back rack.

Anna watched her walk it deep into the field and put it on its side before getting on her knees and lifting her hands high above her. This, of course, caused another eruption of tears in the car. Anna was still crying twenty minutes later when Elsie returned.

Elsie got in the car and closed the door. Her attention went immediately to the spot she had just left in the field. Her eyes went to the heavens above the field. She smiled and looked at Anna. "Are you ever going to stop crying?"

Anna looked at her and rested her hand over her mouth. She shook her head. "No."

"I guess I was pretty bad, huh?"

Anna shook her head with a crying smile. "Deplorable."

Elsie kissed her wet cheek. "I'm ready to go home."

*****

Anna rolled onto Elsie's driveway. She and Elsie got out of the car. Elsie looked in the garage window. Daniel's car wasn't there. Elsie got an idea. But first she had to take care of something.

They went inside.

"You still like bon fires?" asked Elsie.

Anna gave a cautious, "Yeesss."

"Good. We're going to have one. Follow me." Elsie's eyes were vibrant.

Anna followed her throughout the large house and watched in amazement as she gathered pictures, newspaper articles, MCAT scores, certificates, ribbons, trophies, and plaques.

"Here," she handed Elsie a trophy, "you carry that."

Anna's mouth fell open. "This is your marathon trophy. You're not getting rid of this?"

Elsie looked at her with determination. "Yes. I am. My heart wasn't right when I trained for that race. It wasn't right when I crossed the finish line. It wasn't right when I shook hands with the runner-up. It wasn't right when I brought the trophy home. I was full of pride, and pride is what almost destroyed me. It's what kept me from God all these years." Her face hardened. "I'm burning it."

Anna drew back. "Okay. You don't have to sock me in the nose again."

Elsie's face turned soft. "I'm so sorry for that. I really am. I wish I could live that night over. Never again, Anna. I owe you my life."

"I forgive you, Elsie."

Elsie smiled, wiped her eyes, and let out an emotional breath. "Looks like I'm going to spend the rest of my life crying. Come on. There's some more trash I've got to get rid of."

In a little while they stood in the back yard with a pile of stuff that represented Elsie's accomplishments. Elsie walked over to it and squirted a bunch of lighter fluid. She looked at Anna. "Wait!"

Elsie took off and came back with the parapsychology articles she had printed off. She also had an armload of books. She dumped this stuff in the pile and said, "There's more. I'm going to need your help."

It took the sisters two trips to carry the pillow cases filled with books. They dumped the books on the pile.

Anna huffed. "That's a lot of books."

Elsie huffed. "That's a lot of lies."

Anna held up her left arm and pinched it.

"Satisfied?" Elsie smiled. "No dream. It's real."

Those words. They hit her. This was real, and she knew it was real. She wasn't confused. She wasn't deceived. She knew what was real and what was unreal. She wasn't spending the rest of her life locked up or on drugs or fighting monsters. She dropped to her knees and lifted her hands. Her mouth moved in silent trembling, but it was her heart that did the talking.

Her heart emptied of its spontaneous praise, Elsie stood and asked, "Is there anything in the Bible about getting rid of old things and going forward? Something that talks about giving up the accomplishments of this world to gain Christ?"

Anna's face went from a slow, dim glow to a bright, sun-filled smile. "Are you kidding me? Yeah. That's what the whole Bible is about, Kiddo." She pulled out her phone and found Philippians 3:8. "Here."

Elsie read it to herself and a tear rolled down her face. "This is good. It's exactly what's in my heart. She looked at the pile and lifted a hand to heaven and read. "'What is more, I consider everything a loss because of the surpassing worth of knowing Christ Jesus my Lord, for whose sake I have lost all things. I consider them garbage that I may gain Christ.' Garbage, Lord. That's what the world is without You."

"Oh, Elsie, what has happened to you?" asked Anna.

"I saw the Lord," she answered. She squirted a lot more lighter fluid on the pile. "Would you like the honor?" she asked, holding out a book of matches.

"This honor is yours, Elsie."

Elsie's hand didn't drop. "You prayed me in, Anna. I would be crazy the rest of my life if it weren't for you."

"We'll both light it."

Elsie and Anna tossed match after match on the pile. They watched for several tear-filled minutes until Elsie turned to Anna with a mischievous grin. "I have another idea."

*****

Elsie's idea required coordination, favor, and good luck—Anna reminded her that it wasn't luck they needed; it was providence. Elsie didn't object. If this was going to work, they would definitely need God.

At 8:15 p.m. Dr. Daniel Miller walked down the hallway on his way to one of the hospital's larger conference rooms. He was tired and looked forward to getting some rest—even a little rest—before getting back mentally into the grind of waiting for Elsie to contact him. She was in trouble. Hallucinating. This was bad. But somehow he found himself holding onto a hope that as bad as it looked, it was going to turn out well.

He wondered whether he had unwittingly caught his little girl's hope. She had told him that God was taking care of Mommy. And she had made him pray with her for Mommy. He didn't believe in God, but it wouldn't hurt anything to pray with his little girl. It's not like it was going to turn him into a Christian to pray one time.

Now he found himself crazily wondering, if not desperately hoping, if that thought he heard when he prayed with Amanda was just him, or— Couldn't be. He was just a desperate husband who had foolishly heard what he didn't hear because he needed to hear it. But his unbelief didn't stop him from thinking how welcome it would be if the thought had come from an almighty God of love. He pondered the thought.

Don't worry, Daniel. Trust Me. I will bring Elsie home.

For obvious reasons, it was an odd thought. What made it odder was Daniel calling himself by name. His musings stopped when he saw Diane AKA Dr. Stewart walking toward the conference room door from the opposite end of the hall.

"Welcome respite," she said with her permanent smile. "Even Superman appreciates birthday cake and punch."

"The sacrifices we make for our friends," he said. He opened the door and motioned her to go in first. "Whose birthday is it?"

"Why don't we go inside and find out?" She walked past him and into the room.

Daniel went inside. There were probably forty people. They'd never had that many people before for something like this.

Especially a last minute invitation. He looked around wondering. He went to a nurse. "Whose birthday is it?"

"I don't know. All I heard was cake and punch and I reported for duty."

"Okay. Thanks."

He asked a few more people and no one seemed to know whose birthday it was. He asked another doctor. She shook her head and said, "Daniel, I declare," and just walked away.

What was that about? he thought. Enough of this cloak and dagger stuff over whose cake he was going to eat. He walked to the table and looked at the writing on the large cake. He looked at it for several seconds, unable to hear or see anything else in the room but those words:

I'm Free!
Happy Birthday To You & Me
Elsie

Was this his Elsie? Could this be his Elsie?

Then he heard the guitar coming from the front. Familiar chords. Music she created. Something like a stream of warm, liquid hope rushed through his entire being. Both palms went heavily to the table. He leaned with his head down, supporting his desperate hopes, not wanting to look up and find that he had entered Elsie's world of delusions and unreality.

Then came the words. A song she had written about a fairy tale love that couldn't be killed. Words that bypassed his head and went straight to his heart. With a low grunt, he sucked in the breath that shot out of his belly. He could no longer look away. He lifted his head and turned left. There. In the front of the room. Standing tall. Elsie.

She was magnificent.

She wore clothing that was simple in appearance, but rich in meaning. Blue jeans, a sweatshirt, and short brown boots. What made these clothes significant was she had worn them the day she dropped out of residency and hadn't worn them since. There was no mistaking this.

The jeans still had a smidgeon of white paint on the left thigh she got while painting. The sweatshirt had *Johns Hopkins School of Medicine* on it. He sure hadn't seen that shirt since she dropped. And those boots—well, how could he mistake boots that had survived two World Wars, the Korean War, Vietnam, Afghanistan, and Iraq? There was such a thing as attire that was fashionably distressed. These were just distressed. Always had been. But they were beautiful on her feet.

Her short blond hair wrapped around her delicate ear like it had been trained in obedience school. She wasn't wearing make-up. She did that every so often, and when she did it was like beholding a Rembrandt painting without its frame. Nothing lost but an artificial and unnecessary border that once accented splendidly natural beauty.

Across her back and shoulder was the strap of her guitar. The same guitar that she had run from in terror as though it were a rattle snake. She held it with toned arms and picked its strings with the ease and skill of a master and joined it perfectly with the voice of an angel.

Daniel marveled at the sight. But his fascination deepened as he wondered at her glow. He had shared many wonderful moments with his wife, but he had *never ever ever* seen her glow like this. She seemed like someone who had found the tree of life and had filled her belly with its fruit.

Then he saw something that took him in a different direction of amazement. Anna was here. In the far left of the room. She was crying and looking at Elsie with a look of adoration times one hundred. And Elsie was now looking at her with the most tender expression. What in the world was going on? He didn't know what had brought about this incredible change, but—"

He looked at Anna and Elsie gushing over one another from a distance. Anna? Elsie? He lowered his head and raised it with an interesting and probable possibility. As unlikely as it would have seemed before this evening, it was obvious. Anna had something to do with his wife being up there doing something that she couldn't do before, and something that her sister, mother, and grandmother still couldn't do. She had something to do with that absolutely mesmerizing glow on his wife's face. She had something to do with the tears of joy that were flowing freely on his wife's face.

Daniel thought of Amanda. She wasn't here—but really she was. She was there on that stage, beautiful and singing and making music. His little girl would have a rich and satisfying life. The curse of fear no longer owned his wife, and he knew it now had no claim on his daughter. He turned away from the eyes that were alternately looking at him and Elsie. He put his hand to his forehead. There was nothing wrong with his forehead. There was something wrong with his eyes. They were emptying water.

Anna saw this and started toward him.

A lot happened in the few moments it took her to get there.

Anna touched his arm. "Daniel," she said.

He kept his hand to his forehead and looked down at her. "Elsie's a Christian now, isn't she?"

"Yes, Daniel, she is."

His head bobbed. "I know. I know she is. So is Amanda." He looked at her and let the tears fall from his eyes as he spoke. "You saved my little girl, and you saved my Elsie." He suppressed a breath that threatened to get out of control. "Elsie—she's free. God has taken away the fear."

"He's freed her from everything, Daniel. She has her mind back. But most of all, He has freed her from herself." Anna's grip on his shoulder tightened.

He looked at her, interpreting her eyes and squeezing fingers. "What about—?"

"Yes—I will—I do," he interjected.

Anna shook her head with a nervous smile. "Yes what? You will what?"

He looked at Elsie and her glow and her doing what only God could have made possible. He looked at Anna, a woman who he thought at one time was an irritating and embarrassing waste of a human being. "Yes, I want Jesus Christ. Yes, I will serve Him until the day I die. Yes, I do love Him for what He has done."

Anna looked up at Daniel with a heart bursting with joy, but a mouth that could say nothing, and legs that were becoming unreliable. "I—I—"

Now he squeezed her shoulder. He looked at her with the same tender love that Elsie had looked at her with earlier. "And I love you for not giving up on Elsie. I know it wasn't easy. She can be quite, shall we say, determined when she believes something. But you didn't give up. The only thing that stood between Elsie going insane and my little girl one day doing the same and me losing my family was you." He smiled at her in admiration. "You loved my Elsie enough to never stop praying. Thank you, Anna." He kissed her on the forehead.

"Oh Lord, I have to sit down," she said.

"Hey, God didn't happen to talk to the cops and fix that guy's car door that Elsie tore off when she was being chased by the boogie man, did He?" he asked.

"I don't think so."

"Then you're not through helping your sister," he said. "We'll work this one together. You handle the spiritual side and explain to God how I need my wife and how Amanda needs her mother. I'll handle the human side and explain to whoever I need to explain to that Elsie was sick. I think we've got enough medical, psychological, and psychiatric documentation to help our cause and half of Atlanta. Deal?"

"Deal."

They both looked at Elsie.

"What do you think her next wild idea is going to be?" asked Anna.

Daniel's eyes twinkled as he looked at his wife and answered. "Oh, I've got a pretty good idea."

Chapter 31

Daniel was right about his wife's next wild idea, but it was put on hold until it was certain she wasn't going to jail. Daniel was also right about the medical, psychological, and psychiatric documentation. There was lots of it. Enough to convince the judge that there were extenuating circumstances. But she did require Elsie to take care of the damages to the victim's car.

Elsie was antsy about the next phase of their lives; so she and Daniel left the courthouse and immediately and happily took care of that matter. The day's whirlwind of activity continued with her making a phone call and having another conversation with Dr. Winslow. He was delighted to hear the outcome and promised to get back to her in a couple of days. In a couple of days he did just that, and the meeting was set.

*****

Today Elsie walked everywhere slow. Extra slow. She looked around at the brick buildings as though she had never been there and was positively overwhelmed by what she saw. Like a first-time visitor to New York City whose head was on a swivel. The only thing missing was a camera hanging around her neck with a twelve-inch lens.

She sat on benches and under trees that brought back fond memories. She even dropped by Café Q in the MSE Library for a cup of coffee. It was better now than it was back then. She walked the grounds of the freshman quad, and the lower and upper quads and released praises to God with nearly every step. She went to Gilman Hall and stood before the Korean War and Vietnam War memorial and read the names with new appreciation—twelve eternal souls. They weren't descendants of monkeys. They were people created by God in His image for His pleasure and for His purposes. She wondered whether they were in heaven.

She stopped before the tall statue of Daniel Coit Gilman and looked up at him in his doctoral robe. She thought of his outstanding accomplishments and enduring legacies and thanked him for his contributions to her life. She thought of how drastically her life had changed in the year since she had become a follower of Christ. She looked at the first president's sculpted face and asked him, "What does it profit a man if he gains the whole world and loses his soul? Did you know the Lord? It's beautiful knowing and loving and serving Him."

Elsie's feet touched every part of the institution's grounds. The Glass Pavilion, the Ralph S. O'Conner Recreation Center, and the hut. She walked by the housing buildings. AMR, AMR II, Buildings A and B. When she got to Wolman, she stopped at the two glass and wood double doors and smiled, remembering a nice kiss Daniel had planted on her in front of them. She walked by McCoy and Bradford and UniOne and the other student housing buildings, wiping tears the whole time. Her tour down memory lane ended with her venturing away and walking up and down St. Paul Street.

The next day Elsie put on a pair of blue jeans that had a white smidgeon of paint on the left thigh, a Johns Hopkins University Medical School sweatshirt, and a pair of short brown boots that looked like they'd been through several wars. She dropped to her knees just before she opened the door to leave and prayed.

"Lord Jesus, thank you for making this possible. You got me in the first time. You got me in this time. There won't be a third time, Lord, because I know you now. I'm not alone any more. I'm not my own god any more. Whatever I do, I do through Christ now.

And I can do all things through Christ who strengthens me. Thank You, Lord Jesus."

She popped up and plopped back down. "Oh, and thank you again for saving Granny before she died. And thank you for saving Nicole and Momma. One more thing. Thank you for figuring out this long distance thing and working out the logistics for us and Amanda. Brilliant. Just absolutely brilliant. Has anyone ever told You that You're brilliant? If not, You heard it first from me. You—are—brilliant! Okay, let's go."

Elsie opened the door and hurried down the stairs—unafraid.

*****

Elsie wore a low-level smile as she exited the elevator and made her way to the hall that led to his office. He came out of his office holding and looking at a clipboard. She saw him before he saw her. Her smile grew larger with each step she took. By the time she was a few yards away, her face was wet with joy.

He flipped a paper and looked up. "Elsie!" said the department director, Dr. Winslow. He extended his hand and they shook. Then he shook his head. "That won't do. I trust you won't report me to HR." He hugged her, and she hugged back. He stepped back and said to her with a large smile, "Assistant resident, Elsie Miller, welcome back to the Johns Hopkins University neurosurgery residency program." His eyes were full of compassion and promise. "I know it's been a long, hard road, but good to have you back, Elsie."

She wiped her eyes. "Long…and hard, but the Lord has carried me every step of the way."

A Note from the Author
(Just in case you missed the note at the front of the book.)

Hello! If this is your first time reading one of my stories, I welcome you and thank you for choosing my book to read among the millions that are available. If you have read at least one of my stories and have returned for more, that says it all! I can't think of a greater compliment and vote of confidence than for someone to read one of my books and ask for more. ☺

May I ask you a favor?

Once you read the book, if you find that you enjoyed the story, would you mind going online to Amazon.com, iTunes, Kobo, Barnes and Noble, or wherever you purchased the book and writing a review? Many people determine from book reviews whether or not a story is worth their time. Your review (even a short one!) can help convince others to join the fun!

Let's Stay In Touch!

Readers who sign up for my mailing list receive and/or do the following:

- Receive advance news of stories I'm working on.
- Receive *free* portions of stories before they are published.
- Receive whatever wonderful written *freebie* I can come up with.
- Provide me with feedback on what they liked or disliked about a story.
- Share their ideas about what they'd like to see in future stories. (*Trial By Fire* was written in part because a fan of *Bones of Fire* strongly encouraged me to turn the book into a series!)

Join my newsletter at www.ericmhill.com/newsletter. Here's my contact info: ericmhillauthor@yahoo.com or Twitter.com/ericmhillatl.
God bless you!

Made in the USA
Columbia, SC
19 December 2022